Su...
the Arms of the
Sheikh

*Delectable, glamorous seductions and
seriously gorgeous desert males…*

**Three passionate, exotic romances from
three beloved Mills & Boon authors!**

*In March 2009 Mills & Boon bring
you two classic collections, each
featuring three favourite romances
by our bestselling authors...*

SURRENDER IN THE ARMS OF THE SHEIKH

Exposed: The Sheikh's Mistress
by Sharon Kendrick
Stolen by the Sheikh by Trish Morey
Fit for a Sheikh by Carol Grace

THE MILLIONAIRE'S VIRGIN

Virgin for Sale by Susan Stephens
The Rich Man's Virgin
by Lindsay Armstrong
The Bedroom Assignment
by Sophie Weston

Surrender in the Arms of the Sheikh

EXPOSED: THE SHEIKH'S MISTRESS
by
Sharon Kendrick

STOLEN BY THE SHEIKH
by
Trish Morey

FIT FOR A SHEIKH
by
Carol Grace

MILLS & BOON®
Pure reading pleasure™

Harlequin Mills & Boon Limited,
Eton House, 18-24 Paradise Road, Richmond, Surrey TW9 1SR

SURRENDER IN THE ARMS OF THE SHEIKH
© by Harlequin Enterprises II B.V./S.à.r.l 2009

*Exposed: The Sheikh's Mistress, Stolen by the Sheikh and Fit for
a Sheikh were first published in Great Britain by Harlequin Mills
& Boon Limited in separate, single volumes.*

Exposed: The Sheikh's Mistress © Sharon Kendrick 2005
Stolen by the Sheikh © Trish Morey 2005
Fit for a Sheikh © Carol Culver 2001

ISBN: 978 0 263 87126 5

05-0309

*Printed and bound in Spain
by Litografia Rosés S.A., Barcelona*

EXPOSED: THE SHEIKH'S MISTRESS

by

Sharon Kendrick

With special thanks to Paul McLaughlin,
editor of *Kroll's Report On Fraud* –
and a pretty mean writer himself!

Sharon Kendrick started story-telling at the age
of eleven and has never really stopped. She likes to
write fast-paced, feel-good romances with heroes
who are so sexy they'll make your toes curl!

Born in west London, she now lives in the beautiful
city of Winchester – where she can see the cathedral
from her window (but only if she stands on tip-toe).
She has two children, Celia and Patrick, and her
passions include music, books, cooking and eating –
and drifting off into wonderful daydreams while she
works out new plots!

**Don't miss Sharon Kendrick's exciting new
novel, *Constantine's Defiant Mistress*, available in
July 2009 from Mills & Boon® Modern™.**

CHAPTER ONE

IF ONLY there had been some kind of warning…storm clouds gathering on the horizon, perhaps, or a sudden chill wind which iced your skin. Like an omen. But the day was sunny and golden with not an omen in sight, and 'if only' were the two most useless words in the language—Sienna knew that more than anyone.

And even if she had known—what could she have done that would have made things different? Nothing. She was as powerless as a leaf torn from its branch by a cruel autumn wind.

Yet her mood was light as she slipped into the back entrance of the Brooke Hotel, via the garden. The ivy-covered walkway was her favourite way into the building, for when you stood in the secret courtyard it was difficult to believe that you were right in the centre of London—with the hubbub and bustle of the busy streets only a stone's throw away.

Here the sounds of the city were muted and soft-ened by the tall, waving branches of trees which acted as a haven for all kinds of birds. Bees buzzed drows-ily around the flowers and little ladybirds landed on your bare flesh and sometimes nipped it if you weren't looking. These days she was essentially a city

5

girl, but this place reminded her of a country child-hood which seemed another world away.

Sienna loved the Brooke. It was where she had fled to. Where she had been promoted. Where she had made the slightly scary decision to go freelance—but the hotel still provided the bulk of her work. As an events organiser, she organised weddings, birthday parties, book launches and bar mitzvahs—and her name was becoming well-known on the busy London social circuit. From fairly humble and untrained be-ginnings, she had certainly landed on her feet.

And if she ever stopped to think how she'd got here... Well, that was the whole point—she didn't ever think about it. Thinking never got you anywhere. It took you to all kinds of dark and disturbing places and in the end it changed precisely nothing. In life you just had to learn from your mistakes. To get through the bad times in the hope that there would be some good ones waiting round the corner. And there were. Of course there were.

Today, the dark onyx reception desk was massed with startling orange Bird of Paradise flowers mixed in with black irises and red lilies. It was a dramatic look, and not one favoured by shrinking violets—but then those kind of people didn't tend to stay here.

Money and power and a hungry desire for some-thing 'different' were the driving forces behind the screamingly influential clientele of the Brooke. Film-stars. Entrepreneurs. Royalty. Anyone who was anyone.

They all flocked to the converted eighteenth-century mansion where there was never an empty room. Where, as a client, you paid through the nose for luxury and discretion.

Sienna rode up in the penthouse elevator. She was meeting a Mr Altair, and before she met a client she always allowed herself a little daydream about just what kind of party they would want. A themed affair, perhaps? Like the time she had decked out a marquee to recreate a French circus—and had only just managed to persuade the trapeze artist not to flounce off in a huff because he hadn't had star billing!

Or the time she had crammed a ballroom with a thousand red roses for one of the most over-the-top engagement parties she had ever had a hand in.

Sienna smiled. Her job required that she had the organisational skills of an army general—combined with the smooth tongue of a career diplomat.

As the lift doors slid open, the door to the penthouse was opened by a tall, olive-skinned man. Some sixth sense should have told her then—but why would it? With his black eyes and the expensive suit which didn't *quite* disguise the gun in his breast pocket the man looked like any other foreign 'minder'. Which she supposed was the modern word for bodyguard—and she came across plenty of those in this line of work.

'Hello.' She smiled. 'My name is Sienna Baker and I have an appointment with Mr Altair.'

A flicker of something she couldn't quite put her

finger on passed over his impassive features, but he merely nodded and pushed the door to the apartment open. He stood by to let her pass but did not follow her inside, and as the door clicked shut behind her Sienna felt inexplicably apprehensive. As if she was closed in. Trapped. Though agoraphobia would be the last thing she should be suffering from in a room of these dimensions.

She looked around her, her senses swamped by the sudden crowding of different sensations which began to jostle for supremacy in her mind.

For a moment she was dazzled by the sheer impact of the light which spilled in from the enormous windows, and she screwed her eyes up in confusion as the faintest trace of a disturbingly familiar scent began to drift towards her. The exotic smell both tantalised her and began to make her stomach twist painfully, and she couldn't work out why.

And then she saw the man standing completely still with his back to her, silhouetted against the London skyline—tall and dark and lean and proud, as if he had been carved from some black and unforgiving rock—and Sienna felt the blood drain from her face as he moved, like a statue coming to life.

She sucked in a breath of disbelief as her eyes flickered over him, her mind screaming out its protest as she began to register every detail about him. The slick black hair with the faint wave to it. The broad shoulders and the long legs. The arrogant and autocratic stance. Oh, please, no. Please. No. But now the scent which pervaded the suite became more understandable—and wasn't smell supposed to be the most evocative of all the senses?

Did she whimper or make a sound? Was that why he had begun to turn around? And now the breath caught in her throat as she began to issue a silent and heartfelt prayer. She prayed like she hadn't done for a long, long time, since she had been begging some mysterious presence to take the pain away. If no one had been listening then, then let them be listening now.

Don't let it be him. Oh, please don't let it be him. But her heart plummeted like a stone as he turned to face her.

Hashim surveyed her with cold and glittering black eyes, acknowledging the heavy stab of desire in his loins with a grim kind of pleasure, remembering the splayed abandon of her legs the last time he had seen her, and the aching only increased.

He had long denied himself this moment because he had told himself that he could, but in the end desire had proved irresistible. Hashim despised the weakness which made him want her, yet he embraced it, too. And he intended to savour every moment of it. This woman who had deceived him would pay, and she would pay with her body!

He let the narrowed ebony gleam of his eyes linger on her figure, to see if time had marred its perfection, but it was as firm and as lushly slim as a prized young

Saluki—the silky-sleek hunting dogs much favoured by the tribes of his native land.

It was hard to pin down what made her quite so desirable—for hers was not a fashionable look. She was too petite and curvy for modern tastes, yet her body was to die for. And if you added to that the ingredients of innocence and sensuality…

Innocence!

Hashim's mouth hardened as he thought of what a sham appearances could be.

He let his gaze drift upwards, to her face. How white her skin was, he observed with impartial interest—and how contrasting the deep rose of her lips. Ah, those lips! One of the very first things he had noticed about her had been her natural pout, which some women spent thousands of dollars at plastic surgeons trying to recreate.

Now those same lips trembled under his scrutiny, and he longed to crush their petal softness beneath the hard, seeking warmth of his own. But that would have to wait…and the waiting would only increase his eventual pleasure.

'Sienna,' he murmured as the warm throb of blood beat between his legs.

The way he said it took her back to somewhere which was out of bounds, and her heart buckled with pain as she stared at the man she had once believed herself to be in love with.

He was both ugly and beautiful, his face unique—defined by hard contours and the ravages of warfare.

An exotic, foreign face. The cruel beak of a nose and harsh slash of his mouth only added to his allure, and those clever black eyes could make a woman feel as if he was slowly stripping her bare...

Seeing him again was a moment she had lived out in her mind over and over again—though not much lately, it was true. But wasn't it simply human nature to wonder how she would react if ever she saw him again? As time had passed she had convinced herself that the sobbing wreck of her early days had been replaced by a confident woman who would give him a cool smile and say, *Hashim! Well, long time no see!*

How wrong she had been. How very wrong and how very *stupid*. As if any woman could look at a man like that without wanting to melt into a helpless puddle of longing at his feet. But the longing was eclipsed by another emotion, and that was wariness...or was it *fear*? What the hell was he doing here?

'Hashim,' she whispered, like someone waking from a long dream. 'Is it really you?'

'It really is.' His hard eyes mocked her, enjoying her discomfiture in a way he had not enjoyed anything for a long time. 'You seem surprised, Sienna.'

'Surprise implies something pleasant,' she said shakily.

He arched heavy black brows in sardonic query. 'And this is not?'

'Of course it's not!' Nervously, she flicked her tongue over her lips to moisten them, and then wished she hadn't, for his black eyes were drawn to the movement as a snake to the charmer's pipe. 'I'm shocked—like anyone would be.'

'I disagree—a lot of women might be delighted to see a man who had once featured in their lives, but I guess it's different in your case.'

Her eyes pleaded with him to stop, but he did not, and his hard mouth twisted into a cruel imitation of a smile.

'I expect your past is always coming back to unsettle you in all kinds of ways—but you have only yourself to blame, my dear. If you didn't keep so many unsavoury secrets, then you might be able to sleep a little easier.' He allowed his eyes to linger on the exquisite swell of her breasts and the swift shaft of desire became blunted with the memory of betrayal. His mouth hardened. 'Though I can't imagine any man letting *you* sleep easy at night.' Except maybe him. The mad, duped fool who had protected her and respected her. Who had cherished her as if she had been a delicate and priceless piece of porcelain.

And then seen her crushed into smithereens before his eyes.

But he was a fool no more...that day had gone...never to return.

Sienna wanted to tell him not to stare at her that way, but she knew if she did that then he would do it all the more. He was not a man to be thwarted or dictated to, and in his hard black eyes was the glitter of danger. She swallowed, terrified to ask the question because of what the answer might be. Until she told herself that this was just some horrible, unfortunate coincidence—it had to be…

Or was it? Suddenly she wasn't so sure. Did anything ever happen completely by chance?

'What are you doing here, Hashim?'

He thought how easily his name came to her lips. How little she realised the honour accorded to her by being able to speak it so freely where most women would dip their eyes in deference! Even the sophisticated women in his life—and there had been many—had always been slightly in awe of his power and position. He stared at her, and the anticipation of what he was about to do made his blood sing with pleasure. 'You know very well why I am here,' he reprimanded silkily.

For a second her world was suspended in a moment of disbelief as she was frozen by the stark sensual intent in his eyes. And it was as if just that one sizzling look had begun something which her unresisting body was powerless to stop. She shook her head, trying to stop the stealthy and hated shiver of desire. 'No, I don't.'

'Shame on you, Sienna—is this how you always react when you are booked in to have a business meeting? You are being paid to organise a party for me—remember?'

His soft, mocking words made her throat close over with fear and she swallowed it down. There was no way she could have any kind of meeting with him—business or otherwise. He must know that!

'No!' she said, as calmly as she could. But as she shook her head the heavy weight of her piled-up hair wobbled, as if itching to cascade down her back. 'That's not what I meant, and you know it!' She looked around her with slight desperation, as if any minute now she would suddenly wake up and discover that the whole incident had been some ghastly nightmare. 'I'm supposed to be meeting a Mr Altair! Not you.'

He gave a cold smile. 'But "Mr Altair" *is* me, Sienna. Didn't you realise?' His smile grew even colder, even though the undulating movement of her hair made him ache to unpin it and set it free. Free to tumble onto the warm nakedness of his chest. And his belly…

'Altair is one of my many aliases,' he drawled. 'Surely I used it when I knew you?'

'No,' she whispered. 'No, you didn't.'

'Ah. So much changes with the passage of time, does it not, Sienna? What else has changed, I wonder?'

She felt like a woman who had woken up in an alien place, where all the rules of survival had changed, and she knew that she had to take control—not just of herself but of the situation, too. She was no longer a young girl, besotted and completely fixated by a man who was light-years away from her in terms of experience. The wrong man, she reminded herself painfully.

With an effort, she gave him a smile. A rueful, grown-up smile. 'Look, Hashim, I presume that now you've seen me you've changed your mind. We aren't going to be able to do this—you know we aren't.'

His eyes glittered with provocation. 'To what… precisely…do you refer? What aren't we going to be able to *do*, Sienna?'

She didn't rise to the sexual taunt. If she kept it on a business level then she might be safe—but if she allowed the discussion to stray into the personal or—even worse—the past, then she really was in danger.

'But what are you doing here?' she questioned, still with the last vague hope that things were not what they seemed. 'When you always stay at the Granchester?'

'Maybe I find that the memories there are too tainted,' he mocked. 'Or maybe I find that I just can't resist the attractions on offer here…' Once again he let his eyes linger with insolent hunger on the swell of her magnificent breasts. 'Your…reputation in the capital is growing, Sienna,' he added silkily.

She didn't suppose he was alluding to her backlog of satisfied clients. It was not a compliment at all, but a thinly veiled insult, implying…implying… Oh, she knew damn well what he was implying! Feeling as though her lungs had been scorched, she sucked in a breath to steady herself. 'But presumably you're not expecting me to work with you,' she said quietly.

He gave a heady, husky laugh of anticipation. 'For an employee you sure as hell make a lot of presumptions. It could get you into a lot of trouble if you're not careful.'

She had forgotten what a curious mixture he was, of the ancient and the modern, the forward-thinking and the ludicrously old-fashioned. He was one of the most intelligent men she had ever met—so why the hell was he deliberately misunderstanding her reservations? 'Oh, Hashim—don't be so...dense!'

'Dense?' He tilted his chin imperiously and his eyes narrowed into glittering ebony shards. 'You dare to address *me*—a *sheikh*—in such a way?'

In the past he had never pulled rank—but then he hadn't needed to. She hadn't cared about his position—hadn't even known about it to start with. And by the time she did it hadn't mattered. Or at least she'd thought it hadn't—but that was yet another indication of just how out of her depth she had been. Because of course it had.

It had mattered a lot.

CHAPTER TWO

SHE should never have met him, of course, for theirs were two such different paths in life—destined never to cross. But country girls sometimes went to live in big cities and became receptionists in super-smart hotels—the kind of places where you bumped into real-live sheikhs when you were on your way to work. Just like a fairy tale. And sometimes the fairy tale came true—but what it was easy to forget was that there was always a dark side to the story.

Sienna had gone to London for the usual reasons—and then some more. In the midst of crisis she had needed money and a solution. And after that... Well, after that she had needed to forget. And, as well as offering her anonymity, the big city had also offered her the opportunity to work her way up the ladder in the hotel industry—and to live rent-free in one of the most expensive parts of London. A perk which had made up for the long and unsociable hours.

The first time she had seen Hashim, Sienna had been on her way to the hotel for a late shift. It had been a beautiful day, and she'd been enjoying the sunshine.

She'd been wearing nothing out of the ordinary—a floaty kind of summer dress—but her hair had been

17

down and she'd walked with the unconscious vigour
of youth. In her daydream she'd barely noticed the
slight commotion of people milling around the dark-
windowed   limousine   of   the   world-renowned
Granchester Hotel.

And then she had seen the figure emerging from
the car. He'd been tall, with a natural autocratic poise,
dressed in a coolly pale suit which had made the dark
olive of his skin look so silken. It had gleamed soft
gold and contrasted with the hard ebony glitter of his
eyes.

For a split-second as they'd looked at one another
it had been like something out of one of the old-
fashioned films she'd always been a sucker for. As if
she had been waiting all her life to see just that man
looking at her in just that intent and interested way.
His eyes had narrowed as a bodyguard had shot an
arm out in front of her, bringing her to a halt.

'What do you think you're doing?' she had protested, and the man had smiled a hard kind of smile,
and then said something in a husky tongue which was
foreign to her.

'Let her pass,' he clipped out, as if he was trans-
lating the command for her benefit, and the bodyguard grunted and moved aside. Sienna inclined her
head.

'Thank you.' She walked off down the road, somehow aware that the black eyes watched her, burning
into her back, branding her with their strange exotic
power.

And then, a few weeks later, he came into the hotel and Sienna just froze.

He looked…she swallowed…he looked so vibrant…so *different*—as if someone had plucked a bright and very exotic bloom and placed it in a vase of white flowers. She could see people in the foyer giving him sly little glances, and others—women—giving not so shy ones. And his two bodyguards—ever-present in the background, solid as a brick wall and silently sending out messages to *keep away*.

Experience had made Sienna wary of men, and so her unexpected reaction to this one took her by surprise. When desire had never really touched you it was a bit earth-shattering when it did. 'Um, um…' She could feel her cheeks growing pink. How unprofessional! 'I mean, good morning, sir.'

Hashim's eyes narrowed with interest. It was the girl with the green eyes and the body! And what a body!

Carelessly, he flicked his hand to indicate that the bodyguards should remain where they were, and he moved forward to the desk himself, fully aware of the impact he was making as he stared down into her face. 'Hello again,' he said softly.

His accent was silky, rich and deep, and the tiny blush which had begun deepened to heat her cheeks. Her heart thumping in her chest as if it had just discovered how to beat, Sienna jabbed her finger at the booking diary. 'Can I…can I help you, sir?'

The side of him which had been indulged from the

cradle wanted to lower his head and whisper that, yes, she could spend the afternoon in bed with him—but her innocent blush meant that he had unconsciously moved her into a category of women with whom it was not acceptable to flirt outrageously.

'I am meeting one of your guests here for lunch,' he said instead.

'And the guest's name, sir?' she questioned, looking down at her booking list and wishing she could stop blushing.

He gave it, and saw her eyes widen—for the politician he was meeting was well known, and Hashim knew very well the potency of power and connections. He had lived with them all his life.

'He's waiting at the table, sir. I'll take you in to join him.'

She stood up to show him the way, and he enjoyed following her into the restaurant, so that he could watch her unobserved.

She was not tall, but he liked that—for he believed that a woman should look up to a man—and although her hips were narrow, her bottom was as curved as her breasts, and designed to be cupped by the warmth of a man's hand.

But it was her green eyes, shaped like almonds, and the pinkness of her cheeks and the rose pout of her lips which stayed in his mind. During lunch he gestured for one of his guards to approach, lowering his head to give an instruction in his native tongue, and the guard was dispatched to the reception desk to acquire her phone number.

But Sienna refused to give it. What a cheek—sending his henchman! And in a way it just confirmed her rather jaundiced view of men. She wished she could go on her break right then, but it wasn't for ages, and when he came out of the restaurant she was still sitting there.

She looked straight through him, as if he wasn't there—something which had never happened to him before. But he was too intrigued to be outraged, and some alien emotion directed his steps towards her.

'You wouldn't give me your phone number,' he mused.

'You didn't ask me.'

'And was that such an unforgivable sin?' he teased.

She turned her head away, unsure how to cope with him, this powerfully built and exotic man who was making her feel things she wasn't used to feeling.

'What is your name?' he asked, without warning, and she turned back to find herself imprisoned in the blazing ebony spotlight of his eyes.

'Sienna,' she whispered, as if he had sucked the word clean out of her, without her permission.

'Sienna,' he repeated softly, and nodded. 'So, are you going to have dinner with me, Sienna?'

Somewhere in the recess of her mind was the thought that staff *definitely* weren't supposed to fraternise with the guests—until she remembered that he wasn't actually a guest. And even further back was another thought—that she was rather good at getting out of her depth. 'I'm not sure.'

'Why not?' he questioned softly.

'Because I don't even know your name.'

'Ah! Did not one of your finest poets once ask: "What's in a name?"' His black eyes narrowed. 'My name is Sheikh Hashim Al Aswad.'

Sheikh? *Sheikh?* Something in his eyes made her stare at him, aghast. 'You're not really a sheikh, are you?'

'I'm afraid I am,' he replied gravely.

Sienna stared up at him. Now his dark looks and foreign air and the unmistakable aura of authority made sense. 'But what on earth would I wear?'

And he laughed. 'It doesn't matter,' he said truthfully. 'You are so young and so beautiful that you would look wonderful in anything.' Or nothing, of course.

That night he took her to a restaurant which overlooked the silver snake of the river which wound its way through the city. The stars outside seemed close enough to touch. And the evening felt magical enough for Sienna to feel that she could.

She had thought she might feel awkward and out of her depth, but instead she was so—*excited*, and determined to enjoy every second of it. Even the simple little cotton dress she chose seemed okay, because her thick dark hair reached almost to her waist, and she wore it loose and saw the narrow-eyed look of approval he gave and knew she'd got it just right.

It felt like an old-fashioned date was supposed to feel. Hashim ignored the fact that there were two armed bodyguards seated a few tables away, and more outside. This felt different, and he wasn't quite sure why. Because she seemed so transparently innocent?

'So tell me about yourself,' he instructed.

Sienna hesitated, wondering where to begin. Was this true lives or true confessions? She had once done something she didn't feel too great about—but that one-off act didn't define her as a person, surely? She'd probably never see him again after tonight—so why let him in on a secret which might ruin the evening?

She thought about what a man born to a sheikhdom would most like to hear. Well, she couldn't compete on a material front, that was for sure! She leaned forward and clasped her hands on the starched linen tablecloth, and tried to paint a picture of a very different life.

'I grew up in a little village. You know—a proper English village, with lambs gambolling around the meadows in the springtime and cherry blossom on the trees.'

'And in summer?'

'It rained!' She wriggled her shoulders. 'Well, actually, it didn't—it just seems to now, whenever I go back. But maybe that's because I'm an adult now. When I was little the sun always seemed to be shining and golden.' She stared into his face, thinking that she had never seen eyes quite so black. 'I suppose that most people's childhoods are like that. We view them through rose-tinted glasses.'

He thought not. Certainly his own had been nothing like that, but he would not describe it, nor compare the two. He would not have dreamed of expressing his own thoughts about growing up. Privacy was second nature to him and always had been—drilled into him from the very beginning. Instead, he picked up on the wisftfulness in her voice. 'If it was so idyllic, then why did you leave?'

Sienna fiddled with her napkin. 'Birds need to fly the nest.'

'Indeed they do.' His eyes narrowed. 'And is life outside the nest all you dreamed it would be?'

Sienna hesitated. It could be scary. It gave you opportunities, and they could be scarier still. 'Well, you gain freedom, of course—but you lose stability. I guess that's what life is like, though—gains and losses—hopefully it all balances out in the end.'

'You have a very wise head on such young shoulders,' he said gravely.

'You're making fun of me.'

'No.' He shook his head and gave a gentle smile. 'No, I am not. I find your attitude quite charming, if you must know. How old *are* you, by the way?'

Would he think her too young? *Too young for what, Sienna?* 'Nearly twenty.'

But he smiled. 'Only nearly?' he teased.

'Now you,' she said. 'What on earth do sheikhs *do*?'

His mouth twitched. She really *was* irresistible. 'Sometimes I ask myself the very same question. Mainly, they rule a country, and that involves much fighting and the quest for power—but they also oversee oil exports, which is why I am here.' *And they are surrounded by a wealth that most people couldn't begin to comprehend.* Especially not her.

Sienna crumbled a piece of unwanted bread. 'So where's home?'

For a moment he said nothing, and then gave an odd kind of smile. 'Qudamah is my home—but I come from a race of nomadic people.' His black eyes glittered. 'We do not settle easily.'

If she had been older she would have recognised that he was defining boundaries—but as it was his romantic words simply fired up her already overworking imagination.

Later, in the darkened limousine, his hard thigh brushed against hers and Sienna could hardly breathe. But there was no kiss, merely the request—no, the *demand* that he see her again.

It all happened so fast—Hashim's life slipped into a different timescale and he found himself experiencing something which was unknown to him: a tumult of feelings which he was too seasoned and too cynical to call love. Yet his ancestors had been poets and sages, as well as warriors, and he was prepared to acknowledge that somehow Sienna touched a part of him which had before gone neglected. It was as if her innocence and her beauty had begun a slow melt of something he had not known was frozen.

Maybe it was his heart.

She trembled when he kissed her, and he could feel the tension of both eagerness and fear when he took her in his arms. It seemed unbelievable—given her age and her liberal Western upbringing—but something told him that his instinct was correct.

One evening his eyes burned into her as he stared down into her flushed face. 'You are innocent of men?' he demanded.

'Yes,' she admitted in a low voice, wondering if that admission would drive him away from her. 'Yes, I am.'

'Innocent virgin,' he moaned as he kissed her. '*My* innocent virgin.'

Of course that changed everything. The knowledge of her purity filled him with delight, but there was also the certainty that he now bore a heavy responsibility towards her. For a man whose life had been burdened with responsibility, it was another he could have done without—and yet he found himself embracing it.

He saw her whenever he could, wondering if the frequency of their meetings would remove some of the magic, but the magic remained. He had spent his life avoiding any kind of commitment, yet now he saw that as a deficiency, not a blessing.

He took her to discreet restaurants and she showed

him the hidden, secret places of the city. She made him feel alive. Never before had sex been denied him, but this was a self-imposed restraint, and he discovered that doing without something you really wanted could be unbearably erotic.

And yet her innocence made her suitable. Eminently suitable. Of course many bridges must first be crossed, and the first of those would be to introduce her to his family. But without pressure on either side. On neutral territory.

'How would you like to accompany me to a wedding, sweet Sienna?' he asked her one afternoon, looping his arms around her waist.

Sienna looked up into his black eyes. 'Whose? Where? When?'

'My cousin's,' he murmured. 'In the South of France, next month. My mother and sisters will be there.' He glittered a smile at her. 'Will you come as my guest?'

Sienna knew that this was important. A statement. An indication that things were getting serious. She gave him a slow smile of delight. 'I'd love to,' she said simply.

Hashim spoke to one of his aides. 'Will you arrange it, please?'

'But, Your Highness, you are quite sure?'

Hashim frowned. He would not be dictated to! The history of his country was studded with examples of sheikhs who had taken commoners as wives...

But a couple of days later there was a rap on the

door when he was working in his study, and Hashim looked up to see the Arctic dark eyes of his equerry, who was carrying what looked like a glossy magazine between his fingers, as if it was contaminated.

'Yes, what is it, Abdul-Aziz?' he demanded imperiously. 'I am going out shortly.'

His equerry's face was grim. 'Before you do, Your Highness, there is something I must draw your attention to.'

For the umpteenth time, Sienna raked her hands back through her hair—fizzing over with a mixture of excitement and nerves.

Hashim was sending a car for her and they were having dinner at the Granchester Hotel, where he was staying.

She was still reeling from his invitation to the family wedding—so excited at the prospect of going public with him that she hadn't had time to worry about what she was going to say to his mother.

She would just be herself, without artifice or airs, for that was who Hashim liked her to be. She gave herself a little shiver of excitement as she walked up the imposing marble stairs of the Granchester Hotel.

But Hashim was not there to greet her, and neither were any of his staff. Not even the hatchet-faced Abdul-Aziz. Instead, she got a message delivered with a rather knowing look from the receptionist as she was directed up to his suite.

It isn't the way you think it is! Sienna wanted to

say to her. *Hashim has never treated me with anything but respect!* But as she rode up in the private lift which led to the penthouse she wondered why he had changed the pattern of their meetings.

Hashim opened the door himself, and Sienna was taken aback when she saw him—for she had never seen him dressed like this before. Tonight he looked exactly as she had imagined a sheikh *would* look.

Gone were the immaculate hand-made suits he usually favoured—which contrasted with his exotic looks and made him such a tantalising combination of East and West. Instead he was wearing a pair of filmy silk trousers in a deep claret colour, with a silky top in the same material. The rich hue made the most of his exotic colouring, and Sienna felt the roof of her mouth dry—for he was barefoot and the shirt was open, and through it she could see his olive hair-roughened chest, darkened with contours of muscle and sinew.

She had never been confronted quite so vividly by his overt masculinity before, and her heart gave a startled little leap as she found herself wondering if he was actually wearing any underwear at all.

But it was more than his state of undress which unsettled her—for his eyes looked *dangerous* tonight. Steely and brittle. Like jet. Something stopped her from hurling herself into his arms in the breathless way which always made him laugh—and she wasn't sure whether it was excitement or fear. But why on earth would she be frightened?

'You look beautiful tonight, Sienna,' he said deliberately.

Were nerves getting the better of her, or was there an odd undertone to his voice? 'Thank you. I—' But her words were lost beneath the hard, heady pressure of his mouth, for he had pulled her into his arms without warning and had begun to kiss her in a way which took her breath away. 'Hashim!' she gasped.

Her mouth opened up beneath his and it was enough to ignite all the fire and the fury which had been smouldering away inside him. He kissed her until she was melting and aching and moaning beneath his seasoned touch, and only then did he lift his head and glitter a hard, bright question down at her.

'Hashim…what?' he questioned huskily, moving his mouth to her throat to trace a featherlight kiss along its silken path.

It would be madness to protest that he had never kissed her like this before—not when she had spent hours wondering why.

'Oh-oh-oh!' She shuddered as he lightly drifted his hand over her breast.

A grim, silent smile of triumph curved his hard lips as his fingertips returned to whisper over their pert lushness. 'Oh, what, Sienna?' came the silken query. 'Is that good?'

'Oh! *Oh!*' she gasped. 'So good!'

A tiny pulse flickered in the centre of one tensed olive cheek. 'Tell me what it is you want,' he grated.

Instinct took over from reservation and sent the

words spilling out of their own accord. 'That,' she sighed, as his fingers brushed fleetingly against the aching mounds of her breasts. 'That's what I want!'

He cupped the magnificent swell in his hand and rubbed a slow and deliberate circle with his thumb. 'Like *this*, you mean?'

She nodded as pleasure constricted her throat into a tight, dry band.

'I can't hear you, Sienna,' he urged softly.

'Yes,' she moaned. 'Yes! Just like that. Oh, Hashim…'

How he had misjudged her! Oh, yes! He could feel her responsive body pressing close to his, and knew that if he put his hand up her skirt she would not stop him. How far would she let him go in public? Would she let him unzip himself and plunge right in? Probably.

'You want that I should make love to you by the lift?' he demanded hotly.

In some dim recess of her mind she was aware that he sounded almost…*harsh…disapproving…* But maybe that was because he had been holding back for so long. Didn't they say that men had difficulty controlling their sexual hunger? Sienna drew back and swallowed breathlessly, lifting the palm of her hand to touch his rugged face, but it looked oddly cold and forbidding. Obviously he was holding himself tightly in check and she must not make him wait any longer—he had played the gentleman to her heart's content. It was time.

'Let's go to bed,' she whispered daringly.

His mouth hardened. 'Yes,' agreed Hashim, in an odd kind of voice. 'Why don't we?'

Without warning he shut the door with an echoing slam, then picked her up and carried her towards a vast double bed which was covered with a lavish embroidered gold coverlet.

'Fit for a king!' Sienna murmured with delight, but there was no answering smile in his eyes as he put her down on it.

'Only a sheikh this time, I'm afraid,' he responded tonelessly. 'Are you disappointed?'

She wanted to ask him if something was wrong, but by then he had come to lie down beside her and her last reservations melted away.

'Now, then,' he said decisively, and began to unbutton her dress, a pure feral smile of hunger emphasising the deep lines around his mouth. 'Ah…' He sucked in a slow breath of pleasure as her breasts were revealed to him, spilling lushly pale from the pink lace which confined them. 'So firm. So tight. So taut. Like two rich, ripe fruits. Beautiful. So very, very beautiful. You have the most beautiful breasts that I have ever seen, Sienna. What a lucky man I am.'

Something in his words unsettled her—but any slight anxiety she experienced was allayed with the expert motion of his fingertips, and Sienna closed her eyes.

'Yes,' he murmured approvingly. 'Lie back and enjoy it.'

Oh, but he was so thoughtful. Beneath that steely exterior he cared for her own pleasure first and foremost. She felt him unclip her bra and give a shuddering sigh. Her eyelashes fluttered open and she surprised a look of almost…*reluctance*…on his face. But then he lowered his head towards her and she could feel the approaching warmth of his breath.

'Hashim…' She swallowed. She wasn't sure that he'd heard her. 'Hashim,' she said again, almost desperately this time, for more than anything she wanted him to kiss her, to whisper sweet words to accompany these erotic gestures.

'Shh,' he instructed silkily, for he knew from experience that conversation could break the mood and concentration. He knew what he wanted and he was going to allow nothing—*nothing*—to stop him from achieving it.

Sienna squirmed on the cold coverlet and the expert movement of his hands made her need for reassurance vanish. Her breasts had never felt like this before. As if they had swollen to twice their normal size and were prickling with excitement—the blood coursing through them so that the slightest touch sent shafts of pure pleasure spiralling through her. She squealed as his tongue licked against the sensitised flesh.

'You are very responsive for one so…*innocent*,' he observed against her puckered nipple.

Another shaft of pleasure so acute that it bordered

on pain shot through her, and she was aware of an empty, echoing longing, just crying out to be filled. 'A-am I?'

'Yes, you are. And now you will be more responsive still….'

Sienna's breath caught in her throat, for his hand was moving downwards now, inching towards the heated clamour—the very heart of where she most wanted to be touched—and Sienna silently prayed that he wouldn't stop.

'I won't,' he said roughly, and she realised that she must have spoken the words out loud.

'Hashim,' she whispered, letting her lips rest against the soft furnace of his skin. 'Hashim, I love you.'

For a moment he stilled, then shook his head very slightly, silencing her with his expert caress. He touched her molten and responsive heat with such delicate skill until she gasped in disbelief—like someone frantically seeking something only not quite sure what. Restlessly, her head moved from side to side as she stumbled towards a place of promise so beautiful that she was certain it could not really exist.

But it did. Oh, it did. She found it and fell into it, sobbing out her fulfilment, scarcely aware of Hashim pulling away from her. But, as reason and sanity began to seep back in, she realised that he was getting off the bed and moving away.

Over to the other side of the room and as far away from her as possible!

She blinked as she struggled to catch her breath. 'Hashim?' she croaked in confusion. 'Is anything wrong?'

'Wrong?' He paused before answering her question, sucking in a deep breath as he sought—successfully—to bring his desire under control, to be replaced with the slow simmer of rage. 'I think that we're through with playing games, don't you?'

Sienna sat up on the bed, aware that her clothing was in disarray, feeling somehow cheapened as she stared into the forbidding mask of his face. A Hashim she'd never seen before, and one she barely recognised. 'Why are you behaving like this?' she questioned in bewilderment. 'Don't you...don't you want to make love to me? Properly?'

'You think I would deign to contaminate myself by *entering* you?' he questioned insultingly. 'You who have fooled me!'

'I don't have a clue what you're talking about!' But some self-protective instinct made her begin to button her dress with trembling fingers.

'The sweet little virgin!' he ground out furiously. 'Like hell you are! Sweet little virgins don't take their clothes off and pose for pornographic photos!'

And then it all became horribly, horribly clear. That calendar. Those twelve photos. Oh, those wretched, wretched photos.

Sienna flinched and let out a shuddering sigh. 'You've seen them?'

Had there perhaps been some insane part of him

which had been hoping that it was all a mistake—that she had a secret identical sister waiting in the wings, perhaps? Because, if so, that futile thought was banished by the look of guilt on her face.

His hopes and dreams for what might have been now crumbled before his eyes like desert dust as he realised his mistake. He had believed her to be the woman he *wanted* her to be, not the woman she really was. He had been sucked in by her beauty and her air of innocence. Oh, what a fool he had been!

'Yes, I've seen them!' he grated, remembering that he had been about to introduce her to his family! That he had actually been entertaining thoughts of her as a future bride. Fool!

'Hashim—please—it isn't how it looks,' she said desperately.

She had agreed to do the calendar as a one-off to get her mother the operation she'd needed. Her mother had been crippled with pain and facing ruin, and the badly needed operation had been expensive. It had been an unconventional way to get the money, yes—but the only way which had been open to her at the time. And surely if Hashim realised how *desperate* she had felt. How *hopeless* her mother's predicament…

'Please, Hashim…I can explain—'

'What? How you came to be rubbing your breasts and simulating *orgasm*?' he cut in brutally, but despite his disgust he nevertheless felt the hard leap of desire. For even though their existence destroyed any future between them, he was not hypocritical enough to deny that they were magnificent photographs. 'You think that there is any acceptable explanation for *that*?' he snapped.

'It isn't—'

But his rage was such that he barely heard her. 'On the head of my camel you are a magnificent actress—I commend you for that! You have succeeded in fooling me. And you have lied to me,' he added bitterly, remembering the way she had told him that she was a virgin—and that she *loved* him.

'I did not lie to you! I just…' She looked at him and shrugged her shoulders helplessly. 'Couldn't think of the right time to tell you.'

'But there would never have been a right time! In my culture, such conduct from the consort to the Sheikh would be utterly repellent—surely you must have known that?'

Sienna stared at him. Of course she had. Was that another reason why she had buried it away? As if by doing that she could pretend it had never happened? So that she wouldn't have to face the repercussions of her actions? Could carry on living in her little fantasy world with Hashim—untouched by the past and untroubled by the future? But had she ever imagined that the outcome would be any different from this? That there would be some magical, fairy-tale solution despite what she'd done?

No. Hashim would never forgive her.

The reality of seeing the contempt in his black eyes

was almost too much to bear, and Sienna stood up and picked up her shoes, her hair falling down over her face, concealing her pain from him.

But she paused by the door, lifting her gaze to his, unable to suppress the tiny flicker of hope which stubbornly refused to die.

'Is that it, then, Hashim? Is it…over?'

'Over?' His mouth hardened, for he wanted to wound her. To hurt her as she had hurt him. To destroy her dreams as she had destroyed his. 'I think you forget yourself. Did you ever expect that it would be anything other than a very temporary diversion?' he questioned imperiously. 'For I am the Sheikh and you are but a commoner.' His made his final thrust. 'A true commoner.'

CHAPTER THREE

How painful the past could be.

But as the mists of memory cleared, and Sienna looked into Hashim's steely black eyes, the pain came flooding back as if the years in between had never happened.

She remembered the way she had stumbled from his suite that evening, the tears beginning to slip from beneath her eyelids. Somehow she had made it home and howled into her pillow like a wounded animal. She had never known that it was possible to cry that much. Or to hurt that much. To be revolted by the thought of food and want only to sleep—but sleep had never seemed to come, and when it had, it mocked her with images of the dark face she had grown to love so much.

For the first and only time in her life she had understood the meaning of the word heartbreak—and she never wanted to experience it again.

It had taken her countless months to put her life back on track, to rejoin the human race. But a lot had changed since then—and most importantly *she* had changed. She was no longer the innocent young girl who didn't have a clue about life or how to handle men.

Just keep telling yourself that, she thought, with

more than a hint of desperation as she met his glittering stare.

'You're remembering the last time we saw each other,' he observed, an odd kind of note in his voice.

Had her face given her away? Maybe he had read in it her vulnerability and her anguish. 'How could I not?' she questioned, trying to keep her voice from shaking. 'I only have to look at you and it all comes flooding back.'

He stared at her and his black eyes were as hard as jet. Did she imagine that it was any different for him? He felt the hard leap of desire. 'So it does,' he agreed softly.

'Maybe we should try a joint counselling session,' she suggested, trying to keep it light. 'You know—like people who want to stop smoking.'

How flippant she sounded, he thought—and how cynical. Were those traits that she had kept cleverly hidden from him? And why not? Had she not been a woman adept in the art of concealment? 'But maybe I'm not ready to stop,' he said deliberately.

Sienna felt an odd kind of lump in her throat, and something both seductive and yet infinitely threatening hovered unseen and unspoken in the air. Now her voice did tremble. 'And wh—what's that supposed to mean?'

'Well, at least for you it was a…how shall I put this?' A cruel kind of smile lifted the corners of his lips. 'A satisfying encounter.'

His implication was very plain and very insulting, but it wasn't even true—or at least not in the way that

mattered. Maybe in one sense it had been satisfying—
on a purely physical level, yes—but on an emotional
one it had been as barren as one of the deserts in his
homeland. Fulfilment without tenderness was never
satisfying for a woman, and it had left her empty—
as if he'd ripped out an essential part of her and carried it off with him. 'Is that how you would describe
it?' she questioned bleakly.

'Wouldn't you?' he mocked.

'Not really, no.' She looked into the cold black
eyes and knew that he would never understand in a
million years—nor even want to try. Why would he?
Sienna shook her head, hoping to drive away some
of the sadness. 'Anyway, what's the point in discussing it? Things have moved on.'

His face remained impassive, but inside he felt the
flicker of anger mixed into a potent cocktail with sexual hunger and anticipation. She had fooled him once,
but never again! Did she really think for a moment
that now that he had her in his sights he was about
to let her go? Did she not realise what he wanted?
That he had come here to achieve just this?

But, like the expert hunter he was, he knew that
there were many ways to play with your quarry. Had
she too regretted the abrupt end to that meeting?
Perhaps for her as well as for him there had been
bitter regrets that their lovemaking had not been complete?

'Yes, things have moved on,' he agreed. 'But they
seem to have brought us back to the same place. I am

here and you are here—so just what do you think we ought to do about it?'

He took a step closer to her. He was close enough now for her to study him properly, so that she could see how much he had changed—though none of the fundamentals had. He was still the most breathtakingly masculine man she had ever laid eyes on. As if he had stepped from another age and another time. His own particular scent drifted up her nostrils—a vital, spicy scent that spoke of raw virility and reached out to the most feminine side of her.

Briefly, Sienna closed her eyes in helpless recognition, and when she opened them again it was to see the warm ebony fire in his. She could feel herself drawn to him. Like a child who had been left outside in the cold for too long. He promised the certainty of warmth. Of comfort. And security.

She wasn't aware that he had moved again, but he must have done—please God it hadn't been her—because suddenly she was in his arms, her senses not giving her time to question her sanity as he bent his head to graze his lips across hers.

It was electric. Like fire. Ice. All extremes which could shock the system to its very core—that was Hashim's kiss. It awakened in her something which had lain dormant, sleeping since the last time she had been in his arms. Back then she had—in her naivety—imagined that all kisses would press the button to instant sensual combustion, but in the interim she had discovered how way off the mark she had been.

His expert lips were both hard and soft, seeking yet

commanding—and they tasted sweeter than the richest honey. Her own opened beneath them, to taste the warmth, to feel the seductive slide of his tongue into the moist interior of her mouth, and she gasped, buckled, so that his arms caught her against him, imprisoning her in an iron-hard grip which made her melt against him.

A great wave of longing swept through her. Physical—oh, yes—but something else besides. Something which was infinitely more powerful and far more dangerous. As if Hashim alone could fill some emotional space which seemed ever-constant inside her.

For countless seconds she felt the rush of blood and the clamour of response—the warm, primitive throb of blood as it centred and pooled at a place which made her ache. She felt one of his hands reach down to cup her buttock, and silently she begged him to move his fingers round, to delve into that secret place once more.

He seemed to read her thoughts—for he laughed as he moved his hand, teasingly drifting his fingers across her aching mound. She moaned in sweet response. He murmured something in a tongue which was foreign to her, but the mocking and triumphant tone of his words spilled over her heated senses like icy water and Sienna froze in disbelief.

What the hell was she doing?

With a wrenching effort she tore herself away, staring at him wide-eyed. Her breathing was ragged and her pulse was racing like a piston as she struggled to calm herself, smoothing down her dress frantically. Her face was on fire, and so, too—surely—was her heart. 'What the hell do you think you're doing?'

His smile was arrogant, though his eyes were cold. 'Exactly what you wanted me to do.'

'No!'

'Yes. You are hungry for me,' he taunted. 'I could do it to you right now and you would not stop me.'

Too angry and uncaring to think of the consequences, Sienna raised her hand as if to strike him, but he reacted instantly—quicker and more deadly than a cobra as he caught her wrist in his hand.

'You dare to strike the Sheikh?' he thundered.

'You dare to foist yourself on me?'

'Foist?' Giving a cruel laugh, he dropped her hand. He had demonstrated his superior speed and dexterity—she would not be fool enough to try that again. 'I can think of many different words to describe a woman grinding her hips against a man in silent plea to have him enter her—but foist is not one which springs to mind.'

She felt the flush of mortification. 'You…you…'

'Oh, spare me your empty insults, Sienna. They count for absolutely nothing when we both know that what I say is true. You want me,' he stated flatly.

'Don't flatter yourself!'

'Ah! Denial is such a powerful force, is it not?' he mused. 'Especially in women.'

As well as weaving subtle mazes with his clever words, was he telling the truth? Did she want him still? Maybe physically, yes. But emotionally—never!

'Just because you know which buttons to press, and all the ways to seduce a woman—'

'Now you are flattering *me*,' he interposed cruelly.

'It doesn't mean she necessarily *wants you*,' she stormed. 'It just means that her body is reacting as it has been conditioned to do by nature—there's a world of difference.'

'And do you turn on so easily for all men?'

'You're disgusting!'

'You have grown fiery,' he observed, noticing that she had chosen not to answer the question—though his arrogant pride would not allow him to believe that she would melt for another man in quite the way she did for him. 'Very fiery. Yes. I like that in a woman.'

'But I'm not looking for your approval. I have grown up, Hashim—I'm no longer the docile young girl who thought you were the greatest thing since sliced bread!'

It was both the right thing and the wrong thing to say, for while it burst the strangely seductive bubble of thwarted desire, it reminded him of her lying and cheating and duplicity.

'Yes, so docile,' he hissed like a rattlesnake. 'So young and so *innocent*! Like hell you were.'

She stared at the stark condemnation which was sparking from his eyes. He had judged her, and found her wanting. And, damn him, he was right—she *was* still wanting. Wanting him. 'Oh, Hashim, I was innocent in so many ways,' she said, her voice sad now. 'Why don't we forget the whole thing? Let me just walk out of this door right now and out of your life for ever.'

Was she mad? Did she not recognise his intent, nor realise that when he desired something it was always his for the taking? His mouth hardened. No, of course she hadn't recognised it—how could she when she had never seen it before? Her experience with him had been bizarre—and unique. Five years ago he had found himself bewitched by her and he had tempered his usual autocratic wishes—except that it had seemed to happen without any conscious effort on his part.

Now let her see the real Hashim! Who treated women as they liked to be treated! If you were cold and disdainful it seemed to make them want you more—never was a woman more giving in the bedroom than to a man who had treated her with contempt.

'I think you forget yourself,' he said icily. 'I have hired your services and therefore you will behave as such. You will show me respect and listen to my wishes.'

'*Respect?*' she echoed. 'Are you out of your mind?'

'Yes, respect,' he ground out. 'That is if you know the meaning of the word.'

Sienna blinked as a tremor of fear ran through her. Surely he didn't think…didn't think… She drew in a deep breath. Appeal to his sense of reason, she told herself. He is a powerful and successful man, and surely he will understand that it would be folly to extend this torturous interview for a second longer than necessary.

'Hashim,' she said quietly. 'You can't honestly expect me to organise a party for you.'

'Why not?'

'Because…because there's too much history between us!'

'Now you flatter *yourself*,' he bit back. 'A few shared outings does not qualify as history. Nor does the fact that you opened your legs for me.' He saw her face drain of all colour, but he pressed on ruthlessly. 'But it is your reputation that has excited my interest.' He paused deliberately. 'Your reputation is admirable, Sienna—at least in a purely professional sense. Your work is highly regarded and I want you to organise a party for me.'

'*Want* or demand?' she questioned.

'The interpretation is yours.'

'And if I refuse?' she questioned quietly.

'Don't go there,' he warned softly.

'I have nothing to lose by turning you down.' And everything to gain. Like her sanity.

'You don't think so? On what grounds? And could you cope with the consequences of your action?'

Sienna wrinkled her nose. 'Consequences?'

'Sure. I would inform the manager here of my extreme *displeasure* that you had reneged on an agreement. How would you explain it to him? Do tell, for it fascinates me.' The black eyes challenged her.

Appeal to him. Ask him nicely. And even though

the words threatened to choke her, she got them out. 'I'm hoping it won't come to that, Hashim.'

But he carried on as if she hadn't spoken. 'Would you explain that I'd once felt you climax beneath my fingers? I'm sure he'd be *very* interested to hear that—it might even turn him on—but do you think it qualifies you to refuse my request?'

'Don't be so disgusting!'

'That's twice you've used that word,' he mused. 'You think sexuality is disgusting? How you surprise me—since your own must have earned you a great deal.' Had she blown all the money? he wondered. And why in hell hadn't she capitalised more? Used that amazing body to make herself a small fortune? Become rich by exploiting her fabulous breasts, instead of fixing up other people's parties?

Sienna tried one last time. 'You are right—my reputation *is* good *and* well-established. So much so that I can afford to turn you down!'

'People will hear—for I will make sure of it. And they will wonder and ask you why. What will you say to them? Will you lie, Sienna? Stupid question—of course you will!'

She shook her head. 'I could say that we dated a couple of years ago—I could…pretend.' She stumbled on her ironic use of the word. 'Pretend that I would find it too painful to work for you.'

'And you will look foolish.'

'I can live with that.'

'You may not have the luxury of making that decision.' A look of determination hardened his eyes to jet. 'Either you work for me or your career is over. That much you can believe.'

There was a pause. 'This is *London*—in the twenty-first century,' she told him, her voice rising in disbelief. 'Not some desert kingdom where your word is law! You may be a rich and powerful man, but in the end you're just a client. Same as any other,' she finished defiantly.

Her spirit and resistance was making his hunger grow—did she not realise that either? 'You can stand there and attempt to argue with me all day, but it will make no difference in the end. For I mean what I say, Sienna—if you do not accept this commission, then I will ruin you.'

'*Ruin* me?' Her laugh was high, and slightly hysterical. 'Even if you could—' Something was beginning to tell her that his threat was not an idle one. 'Even if you could—why would you?'

'Because you are like a dark stain in my memory,' he breathed. 'An encounter I should never have had, but which I cannot close the book on until it has been brought to its rightful conclusion.'

The meaning of his words was beginning to sink in, but Sienna didn't quite believe it—didn't dare believe it. She could hear the deafening pound of her heartbeat. 'And what conclusion is that?'

There was a pause, and he captured her eyes in mocking taunt. 'You only have to say the word, Sienna, and we can have an action replay. We can put an end to the business we started five years ago.' Deliberately he stroked his palm down the muscular flank of his thigh and his eyes became narrowed, opaque. 'Like right now, if you like.'

His heartless words tore into her and Sienna recoiled from the blatant sexuality which shimmered from him like a halo. 'Are you suggesting…suggesting that I go to *bed* with you?'

'I'm not particularly fussy about the venue,' he drawled, and nodded his dark head in the direction of a sumptuous scarlet velvet *chaise-longue*. 'That might provide a stimulating setting, don't you think? Ever done it on one of those?'

The question made her feel cheap, but presumably that had been his intention. 'You have to be out of your mind,' she breathed.

'My mind has nothing to do with it,' he said silkily. 'So what do you say, Sienna—are going to risk all you've worked for going up in smoke, or are you going to do the sensible thing and accept the commission?'

Sensible? She suspected that jumping off a high cliff would have been more sensible, but Sienna cared desperately about the career she had worked so hard for. Her job relied almost entirely on word-of-mouth recommendations, and even if she fudged the real reasons for her reluctance to work for Hashim it would reflect badly on her. Very badly. People might start to think she had issues…that she was difficult to work with…

Did she have a choice?

No.

But if she was to be forced into a corner by his

autocratic will, then it was vital that she stopped behaving like a victim. Was she going to let him think that she was scared of him? Cowed by him? Unable to resist his sensual lure?

Never!

She nodded, drawing in a deep breath to give her courage. 'Very well. Since you give me little choice I will accept your commission. Satisfied?'

Hashim felt the stirring of excitement and anticipation. So he had won the first battle. A battle he had not been expecting—but when he stopped to think about it would instant capitulation have pleased him? No. Nothing in life felt so good as something which you had to fight for. 'Oh, no, Sienna—not at all satisfied. But I intend to be. Believe me when I tell you that.'

She could hear the sultry note of desire which had deepened his voice and decided to ignore it. Act professionally, she reminded herself.

'Right,' she said coolly. 'Let's talk business—'

'Alas!'

He cut her short with an imperious wave of his hand, though he didn't look or sound in the least bit regretful.

'It cannot be now,' he murmured. 'For I have another appointment.'

Sienna stared at him, knowing that he could have broken any darned appointment he wanted but was choosing not to.

'So I will meet with you tomorrow to discuss the

details of my…*requirements*. Over dinner, of course,'
he finished silkily.

She opened her mouth to say that she didn't do
dinner with clients—except that would not have been
true. Of course she did. She could not refuse him—
he knew it and she knew it. Never in her life had she
felt so helpless—like a fish with a great big hook in
its mouth, just about to be reeled in by a heartless
man who would like to gobble her up for breakfast.

'Very well. Dinner tomorrow it is. But you can
wipe that triumphant smile off your face right now,
Hashim—because the party is *all* you are getting and
I mean that. There's no *way* I'm going to sleep with
you!'

He said nothing, but gave a mocking smile, lifting
a thick brown envelope from the ornate table beside
the door and handing it to her. 'You may want to
look at this,' he said.

Something in his eyes told her that this was nothing
to do with the party, and her heart began to pound.
She realised the contents at the exact moment she
asked the question. 'What is it?'

'Oh, just an old calendar,' he drawled. 'You may
recognise it.'

CHAPTER FOUR

SIENNA took the envelope downstairs to an empty office, then pulled out the calendar and stared at it dully. She hadn't seen it for a long, long time, and she was scarcely able to recognise herself in the sexy and provocative poses. She guessed that by today's standards it was pretty tame—but even so, nothing could disguise the earthy sensuality of the pictures.

They had flown her out to the Caribbean and dressed her in a variety of clothes—well, that wasn't strictly true, for the garments had all been designed to reveal rather than conceal, and they had all left her breasts on show. But that had been the whole point.

A filmy kaftan soaked with water. The bottom half of a low-slung bikini. A glittery thong. Sienna closed her eyes, but was unable to block out the vivid, Technicolor images.

She remembered her initial feeling of panic when they had told her what they wanted her to do. It had taken two rum punches before she had been able to lie face down in the sand and smoulder at the camera for the first of the shots.

And Sienna would never forget the moment she'd seen a Polaroid of her pouting glossy self, with sand-sprinkled skin and messy hair, and dark, peeking nipples. How she had given a little gasp of disbelief and been slightly repulsed by the glinting approval in the eyes of the art director.

Even now she could squirm at how naïve she had been. And even now the photos still had the power to shock her. With trembling fingers she shoved the calendar into her briefcase and let herself out of the hotel, taking in great gulps of hot and sticky summer air.

She spent a restless night, and the following day there was a constant dull ache at her temples. When she walked through the hotel foyer dressed for dinner she felt as if she was going to her own execution.

'Cheer up!' said the night porter. 'It might never happen! Going somewhere special, are you?'

Serena gave a wan smile. 'I'm having dinner with one of the guests in the Rainbow Room.'

'Lucky you!'

Sienna gave a hollow laugh. 'Yes, lucky me!' she echoed wryly. 'Still, at least it's beautifully air-conditioned up there. The temperature outside is claustrophobic.'

'Tell me about it!' said the porter.

Overnight a heatwave seemed to have descended on the capital, with all the force and stifling nature of a heavy fire blanket dropped down to envelop the city. The streets outside the cool hotel had been curiously airless, and Sienna's throat felt as tight as if she were still out in them.

As she rode up in the lift she stared at herself in the tinted mirror. The cool linen dress she wore still looked fresh, and the apricot hue of the glass gave her face a healthy-looking glow which completely belied the way she was feeling inside. But she was not going to let that overwhelm her. And she was not going to let him intimidate her.

The nude photos were part of her past. She couldn't change that, and neither could she rewrite her brief and confusing relationship with Hashim. But she had learned along the way, and that was the whole point of experience—good *or* bad.

Those had been pivotal events in her life which had made her into the cool and confident professional she was today. The change hadn't been easy, or instant, and she was not going to throw it all away because Hashim wanted to exact some kind of erotic payback for what had happened all those years ago. Or rather, what had *not* happened.

He despised her—he had made that perfectly clear—even though his body still wanted her. And on some level she still wanted him, too. But she would not allow herself to be picked up and used like some kind of convenience—to be tossed away at the earliest opportunity. And she would not repeat the mistakes of yesterday.

If he said things to rile or provoke her she would not rise to them. They could not have a scene if she didn't react to him. If he attempted to taunt her then she would just give him a cool and glacial smile. She would remain brisk, crisp and polite—in short, she would be utterly professional, and he would be unable to find fault with her.

Surprisingly, he was already at the table. She was a little early, and had expected him to be late, but, no, there he was. Waiting. Making the rest of the room shrink into insignificance. At a shadowed corner table sat two of the ever-present bodyguards.

Sienna walked towards him, looking for some kind of acknowledgement—a nod of his dark head in greeting—but there was nothing. Just those black eyes trained on her like twin barrels of a hunter's gun.

His hard, lean body was completely still, but his stance was tense, the powerful limbs coiled like a lion before pouncing. He seemed completely oblivious to the covert glances of the other diners in the room. To the almost tangible air of excitement among the normally celebrity-jaded waiters.

Hashim watched her approach, helpless and yet furious with himself for being unable to suppress the instant leap of lust he felt, for he had trained himself to control his desires. To be master of his wants and needs—not servant to them. A man who could control his sexual hunger was all-powerful, for sex made men weak. And his control had never failed him. How else could he have so ruthlessly given Sienna pleasure and then denied himself the relief of his own body? And bitterly regretted it ever since!

Yet on one level she remained a mystery to him. He had known women more beautiful than her—so

what was the secret of her particular allure? The seductive sway of her hips? The too-big eyes which
looked like those of a startled deer? Or just the fact
that he had never had her when other men had? That
he had paid homage to her virginity only to have its
falseness revealed to him in the most humiliating way
of all.

He let his eyes rove over the breasts themselves—
so proud and magnificent and full. Yet she was hiding
her most marketable asset beneath that rather unre-
markable linen dress. His lips curled. How he hated
linen—surely the most unflattering material a woman
could wear, with its coarse feel and its tendency to
crumple. And surely it was a little late in the day for
such unwelcome modesty?

Yet the very *familiarity* of seeing her again was
taking him into the unknown realms of fantasy. The
past was a place he did not revisit. At least never
before now. His restless and nomadic nature saw no
point to it. For him there was not the comfort—nor
the danger—of long-standing friendships. His destiny
was to stand alone.

Then why are you breaking your own rules?
taunted a small voice in his head.

He did not rise to greet her when she got to the
table, and, interestingly, this small lack of courtesy
wounded her. Could he not just have pretended—
gone through the motions of normality?

'Hello, Hashim,' she said, as calmly as possible.

'Sienna.' Not a flicker of emotion crossed over the diamond-hard features. 'Please sit down.'

'Thank you.' She glanced up at the waiter, who pulled her chair out, and then there was nowhere else to look other than into the enigmatic black eyes. Their dark light swept over her, and she felt a moment of sheer physical weakness until she remembered her vow of earlier. Professionalism. 'So.' She flicked him a quick smile. 'Where shall we begin?'

'So quick to do business?' he murmured.

'One should always strive for professionalism,' she answered coolly.

'Ironically, that is what Abdul-Aziz always says.'

Sienna remembered the aide who had seemed to so dislike her. 'And is he here with you now?'

Hashim shook his head. Hot-headedly, he had blamed his aide for showing him the calendar, even though he had only been doing his job. But for a while the Sheikh had seen him as a bearer of bad tidings—and he was as superstitious as the next Qudamah man. So he had sent him home, and in a way the split had been necessary—for the older man had begun to see himself in a role which was not befitting a royal aide. He had begun to love the fatherless Hashim as a son. And Hashim had no need of extra love.

'Abdul-Aziz was posted back to Qudamah,' he said. 'He is married now, with a son of his own.'

'Married?'

'Yes.' And then, because this exchange seemed almost too *cosy*, too familiar, he allowed his eyes to drift over her face. 'Aren't you going to thank me for the calendar?' he questioned deliberately.

She had wondered when he would get around to mentioning it, and she had practised her response until she had it word-perfect. 'No, I'm not. And if you continue to talk about it then I will walk out of here right now.'

He gave a faint smile. 'Then I guess we'd better get the ordering out of the way.'

She glanced down at the menu, which was like a blur though she knew it backwards. 'I'd like the Dover Sole, please. Grilled, no sauce. With a side salad.'

'The choice of a woman on a diet,' he observed.

'Not at all. A woman who is careful about what she eats, that's all.'

'Careful?' His black eyes glittered. 'How very curious. Not a word I would have associated with you.'

She leaned forward. Big mistake—for now she was in full range of his subtle, spicy scent, and it crept over her like sensual fingers. She sat right back again. 'Why don't we clear something up before we go any further? You don't know me. Maybe you never did— but you certainly don't now. So you aren't qualified to make any judgments about me. Understand?'

The waiter reappeared as Hashim glittered her a look which said *Aren't I?* Sienna watched as he gave the order quickly, almost impatiently—like someone who had spent much of his life eating in expensive restaurants and was bored by them. She guessed he had.

And now take charge, she told herself. Behave like you would with any other new client. She reached into her handbag and pulled out a notebook. He eyed it with distaste.

'Is that really necessary?' he questioned acidly.

'I'm afraid so. You wouldn't be very happy if I forgot everything you told me, would you? And so far you haven't told me anything.'

'But you look like you're interviewing me—and we're in a restaurant!'

'Well, you chose it.'

'I know I did—but would you have agreed to dine in my suite if I had asked you?'

'Not a snowball's chance in hell.' She looked at him, daring him to defy her. 'Presumably you wanted me to be a captive audience?'

Hashim's eyes narrowed as he considered her quickfire responses. Smart. And sassy. No matter how good an actress she was, she couldn't play smart unless she really *was* smart. 'Captive?' he mused. 'Yes, perhaps I did.' He imagined her tied to his bed with black satin ribbons, wearing nothing but scarlet underwear and a pair of matching high heels, and he felt the heavy stab of an erection.

'So, is it going to be a big party?' Sienna asked, cutting into his erotic thoughts.

'Party?' With a distracted movement of his shoulders Hashim brought himself back to the subject in hand with an effort. 'No. Very small. A private dinner party for ten.'

'And the guest list?'

'One of my assistants will organise that side of it. I am afraid that most of my guests will refuse to deal with a stranger.'

Defensively, Sienna picked up her water glass. 'In that case I'm surprised I'll be any use at all.'

'But that is where you are wrong. You will be responsible for the event itself,' he said. 'I'd like you to organise the music—I thought perhaps a string quartet. And the lighting—I like lots of candles, by the way. And the wine and the food—of which there must be an interesting and imaginative vegetarian selection. The mood of the evening will be down to you, Sienna. Everything you need you must ask for, and it will be supplied.'

How effortless everything was when you were rich! You snapped your fingers and got what you wanted. Sienna allowed herself a small smile. Well, not quite *everything*. He couldn't have *her*.

'And what kind of ambience do you want?' she questioned. 'Is there any particular reason why you're giving this party?'

There was one brief moment of hesitation. 'As a thank-you,' he said smoothly, running the tip of one finger reflectively along the soft linen of his napkin. 'For some of the many people in England who have done me favours.'

Bizarrely, Sienna found herself wondering if that

included sexual favours—but since his dark, lean looks were attracting all kinds of predatory glances maybe it wasn't such a bizarre thought after all. 'Have you thought which of the hotel's function rooms you'd like? There are several.' She looked at him expectantly. 'Or do you just want to me to choose?'

He stared at her. 'But that is the whole point, Sienna,' he said softly. 'I don't want it held here—or indeed in any hotel. A hotel is too impersonal for the needs of this particular event. I want you to find me a house.'

Sienna looked up from her pad and met the dark steel of his eyes. 'What kind of house?'

'A fine country house—with gardens and a view— a very *English* house. It should have at least ten bedrooms, so that my guests can stay overnight should they so desire it. There should be a lake which will magnify the light of the moon and double the number of stars. Somewhere that symbolises everything which is beautiful about your country. Can you do that for me, Sienna?'

The poetry of his words momentarily threw her, as did that fleeting, dreamy look which had softened his hard face, and she swallowed. 'How long have I got?'

'A month.'

'A *month*? That isn't long. Certainly not to find the kind of house you're looking for.'

'Are you saying you can't do it?'

'Oh, I can do it,' she said. 'But you might have trouble getting your guests there if they've only got four weeks. Important people have busy diaries—especially the kind of people I imagine you'll be inviting.'

He gave a low laugh. 'Please do not concern yourself on that score. They will attend,' he said softly. 'If I so wish it.'

'By royal command?' she mocked, resting her wrist against her water glass and enjoying the sudden cool sensation. 'Tell me—just out of interest—have you spent your whole life getting exactly what you want?'

'Material things, yes. That is, I imagine, what you meant?'

'It wasn't, actually.'

'No?' He studied the dark shadows beneath her eyes. Was he responsible for those? Or had some lover shared her bed last night—making use of her body and denying her sleep? He found himself unprepared for the dark jealousy which twisted his gut, and his voice hardened. 'Money is the preoccupation of most women,' he said harshly. 'Surely not even you would deny that?'

How cynical he sounded. Sienna felt a wave of something like regret wash over her—for she had only helped to convince him that women would do all kinds of things for money. She wished the food would arrive, so that she could eat it and go. Yet wasn't there a tiny part of her which was revelling in the opportunity to be this close to him again? To feast her eyes on a man she had once loved to distraction—and told him so.

Briefly she closed her eyes as she remembered whispering it to him, on that last, terrible evening. And the way he had just ignored her trembling statement.

Try and obliterate the past, she told herself, but she stared down at the food on her plate without really seeing it.

'You aren't really hungry at all, are you, Sienna?' he said, his silken voice weaving its way into her troubled thoughts.

He breathed her name in a way she remembered him once breathing it in passion, putting the emphasis on the last syllable and holding it in his mouth as if it were a mouthful of fine wine.

'Not really, no.' He was looking at her in a way which was making whispers of longing tiptoe over her flesh—and she had to snap out of it.

She needed to protect herself against his enchantment, and she found herself wondering how other women coped. Surely she couldn't be the only woman he bewitched with his curiously old-fashioned air of mastery and chauvinism? And women weren't *supposed* to be bewitched by qualities such as those. They were supposed to look for tolerance and compassion—not simply the desire to be swept off their feet by a flashing-eyed Alpha man.

She laid her fork down and pushed her plate away. 'Well, since we've tied up the business side of things, and neither of us looks as if we're about to tuck into the food, then you'll forgive me if I take my leave—'

'No.' The word was emphatic. 'I will not. You aren't going anywhere because I haven't finished with you. Not yet.'

Did he mean to make her sound disposable? she wondered. Like something he could just crumple up and throw away? And suddenly it wasn't easy not to be intimidated, to take charge and be calm and un-flappable—all the things she had learnt to do in order to survive and succeed.

Maybe this was one conversation she couldn't get out of having, and maybe it was a waste of time to try. Like having a tooth pulled—wasn't that ravaging moment of pain worth it just for the blessed relief you felt afterwards?

'Well, fire away, Hashim,' she said, using her last bit of bravado. 'And get whatever it is you want to say off your chest.'

He traced a thoughtful forefinger along the edge of his lips. 'I simply cannot understand why you chose obscurity,' he said.

She stared at him. 'Excuse me?'

He gestured towards her, as if he was about to in-troduce her to someone at a party. 'Oh, there is no doubt that you have become successful—'

'Why, thank you,' she said drily.

'But only in a purely *relative* sense.' His gaze was very steady. 'It puzzles me that you have stayed working in hotels.'

'Lots of girls do.'

'But lots of girls do not look the way you do.'

'Hashim, *please—*'

'You could have earned a fortune by capitalising on your body, and yet you chose this. So tell me…' His question hung on the air and Sienna waited breathlessly. When it came out it was disguised with the silken cloak of civility, but the look of disgust which hardened the ebony eyes told its own story. 'Why did you never pursue your career in topless modelling?'

CHAPTER FIVE

WHY did you never pursue your career in topless modelling?

With Hashim's critical question ringing in her ears, Sienna felt like someone who had put a piece of expensive lingerie away in a drawer, only to pull it out and discover that it had become faded and moth-eaten. He made her feel cheap. Tawdry. Something she hadn't felt for a long, long time, and she glanced around them, as if the other diners might have overheard.

'You worry that people might be listening?' A cruel smile curved his lips. 'So you have not boasted of your days working in *glamour*?' The word dripped with contempt. 'You are concerned about what others think, perhaps? I cannot believe *that*, Sienna—for why reveal your body if you are afraid of people finding out about it? Why allow men to feast their eyes on your nakedness if you then act coy about it?'

'I'm surprised you bother asking me questions to which you obviously have all the answers,' she said quietly. 'Or rather, you have *decided* you know the answers. You think I am a certain kind of woman—so why don't we just leave it at that?'

'Because I am…curious.'

Yes, of course he was. He was fascinated in the same way that people couldn't help themselves looking at a roadside crash—they didn't want to be part of it, but something compelled them to watch. 'Why do you think I didn't pursue it, Hashim?'

He shrugged. 'Because I suspect you saw that in the end it would work against you. Would spoil your greatest ambition of all.'

'And what ambition would that be?' she asked faintly.

The tip of his forefinger rested thoughtfully against the dark shadow of his jaw. 'I think that you saw the seamy side of the industry, as girls who expose themselves often do. You anticipated that real dangers existed—and so you decided to work in the real world instead. An honest though a much harder living. But I suspect that you found it even harder than you imagined, and so you looked for an escape—an easier way—easier even than taking your clothes off.'

Sienna flinched. 'Go on,' she said, in a pinched kind of voice.

'You realised that you had an extraordinary gift which few are given. The gift of beauty.' His voice became cold as he recalled how he had fallen for the oldest trick in the book. 'Sirens had it, and lured sailors to their death. Men are driven mad by beauty. And you decided to use it as women have used their youth and their looks since the beginning of time. As a bargaining tool.'

Sienna swallowed, willing herself to float out from

her body—to hover suspended in the air above them, looking down at this horrible little scene to hear the words of vitriol which were spitting from his lips.

'With you, presumably?'

He shrugged. 'With me, yes—or with anyone else who happened to fit the bill at the time. I do not flatter myself that I would not have been moved aside if somebody even richer than I had stepped into the frame. You wanted a wealthy benefactor and for that you decided to play the Cinderella role. You chose a humble job as a receptionist, where your beauty stood out like…' He frowned, as if he was trying to remember something, the ebony brows knitting together, and then his face cleared. 'Ah, yes! Like a diamond in the rough,' he said softly. 'Hoping and praying and plotting that someone would sweep in and take you away from all that.

'And I must say that you were very good,' he continued, eyeing her thoughtfully. 'Even I was taken in by your deceit. You really did come over as an innocent and unspoilt girl. In a way, I suppose I should commend you for your acting ability!'

'Your English is quite perfect, Hashim,' she said unsteadily.

'I know it is,' he agreed arrogantly. 'I had an English tutor as a young child, and I am as fluent in your language as I am in my own. But why do you change the subject, Sienna?'

'Why do you think?' She felt as she imagined battered wives might feel. That after a while the punches no longer seemed to hurt. Insult someone enough and eventually the slurs would simply run off their skin like water. Let him rant and have his poisonous say, and then it would be over.

He narrowed his eyes at her. 'And still you do not contradict me?'

'What's the point? You are the worst kind of bigot—for you do not open your mind to the possibility that you might be wrong. You have made your mind up that something is so—and therefore it must be. I'm a topless model without any morals, and now it seems I'm an old-fashioned gold-digger to boot! Nothing will change the way you view me—so why should I even bother trying?'

'Because you have no defence against what I say!' he accused.

'We aren't in a court of law!'

'No, but that is where you might have ended up!' he declared hotly. 'In the end you *did* make the right choice—even though you have had to work hard for a living. But the women who continue along that path so often end up compromised. Next time—or the time after that—the photos that you agreed to do would not have been so tasteful. You would have got older, and as your youth faded you would have become more desperate. Soon you would have accepted less and less for more and more. And one day you might have ended up fully naked on some garage mechanic's wall in one of those explicit shots—'

'You *bastard*!' she hissed.

'But that is where you are wrong, Sienna. Your barb does not offend me because it is untrue—my birth was completely legitimate. Whereas what I say to you *is* true. The facts are indisputable.'

Sienna lifted a hand to the waiter who had begun to hover anxiously on the periphery of her vision. 'A glass of red wine, please.'

'Yes, madam.'

'You did not storm off,' he observed. 'As I suspected you might.'

Sienna shook her head. Her legs would not have carried her anywhere. She took the wine from the waiter and drank a large mouthful. Gradually its warmth and vitality began to seep through veins which felt as though they had been injected with ice.

'Why does it bother you so?' she questioned. 'Haven't you had girlfriends with questionable pasts before?'

'Of course I have. But they did not pretend to be something they weren't.'

There had been women who had made no secret of their hunger for his body and his money. And there had been actresses, too—of course there had—including one who had starred in a film which had broken the mould at the time. Some of the critics had called it soft porn. But none of that had mattered—they had just been cheap flings. What he'd seen had been what he'd got, and he had accepted that.

With Sienna it had been different—or at least he'd thought it had. They had been much more serious about each other. And when the sordid truth had been revealed to him he had felt outraged. It had made him question himself—he who had never had to question anything.

To a man impervious to self-doubt it had been a hard lesson to learn—that his judgement was not infallible—but ultimately it had made him stronger. And if there had still been one small fragment of his character which had believed in the fantasy of the perfect woman, then she had banished it for ever. He would never make that mistake again.

'What if…?' Sienna hesitated, feeling as if she was fighting for more than just her self-respect. She couldn't bear it when he looked at her that way— with such cold condemnation written in his eyes. 'What if you could understand my reasons for having done the photos?'

'Greed is never difficult to understand!'

'You have to understand that it wasn't like that— it really wasn't! I needed the money urgently.' She sucked in a breath and it felt like hot fire scorching down her throat. Would he believe her? 'To pay for an operation for my mother.'

There was a pause, and then he said, 'Bravo!' He gave a small silent handclap and then looked around, an expression of mock amazement on his face. 'But what has happened to the violins?' he taunted sarcastically. 'I can't hear them. Are there hordes of orphans at the door, too—waiting for you to put food in their mouths?'

'It's true, I tell you—it's true!' She wanted to stand up and rush round and drum her fists against his chest. To shout and to rail against him despite all that she'd vowed. But she couldn't—was that another reason why he had chosen the restaurant? To protect himself from an emotional scene? To enable him to insult her as much as he liked, knowing that she wouldn't be able to fight back?

'Whether you choose to believe me or not is up to you—but I'm not lying to you. Why don't you have one of your henchmen run a check on me?'

His eyes narrowed. 'What kind of operation? Cosmetic surgery, perhaps? Was she once as beautiful as you, Sienna, and could not accept that time was bleeding her of her beauty?'

Oh, how he must despise her! *Don't rise to it. Fight your corner with pride and with dignity.* Sienna bit her lip as she remembered her mother's pain and—nearly as bad—her worry. 'It certainly wasn't vanity, but neither was it a matter of life or death. Though maybe in a way it was. She needed a hip replacement—she runs a riding school, you see. Without the operation she faced disablement and the closure of her beloved business.'

Sienna looked down and realised that her hands were shaking, but that was nothing compared to the unsteady racing of her heart. She looked again, and this time there was appeal in her green eyes. *Just believe me!* they said. And never had a sense of injustice burned so strong.

'She was at her wits' end, Hashim, and so was I. So I took the easy way out—I admit that. I had once been told that I could make a lot of money—that I wasn't tall enough for the catwalk but that my face and figure could make my fortune. I wasn't at all interested at the time, but I remembered it when I needed to. And I did it. A one-off which I never repeated nor ever would.' She stared at him, braving that dark-eyed look of censure. 'And that's the truth. I swear it.'

There was silence for a moment while he brooded on what she had told him. An interesting development—if it was true. And if it was then perhaps it made her actions slightly less contemptible. But did it actually change anything? Make him forgive her for what she had done?

Never!

In the world Hashim inhabited women were modest and demure, and it was unimaginable to think of them posing naked for money and men's pleasure. He closed his mind as he pictured the calendar as clearly as if someone had just put it down on the table in front of him. Because they weren't just nude shots— no matter how 'artistic' the photographer had tried to make them. She looked…she looked… He felt an involuntary shudder run through his big body and the pooling of lust in his groin.

She looked as if she was begging the viewer to drive himself between her silken thighs!

And no matter what had motivated her it didn't change the fact that she had posed for the erotic shots.

But neither did it change the fact that he wanted her—and he would not rest until he had lost himself in that exquisite body. And only when he had done that, could he cast her aside and forget her.

He was calm again when he spoke. 'And your mother—she approved of your actions? Condoned them, perhaps?'

'Of course she didn't! She didn't know. Not until afterwards.' Sienna shrugged and stared down at the fish congealing on her plate. She wanted to say that she had regretted it bitterly ever since—but that wouldn't be true. She had been glad to help her mother—the only bitterness she had felt was against Hashim, and the way he had made her feel about herself. But even that could not seem to rid her of her longing for him.

Stupid, hopeless longing. How was it possible for this man to deride her, to criticise and pour scorn on her, and yet she was still drawn to that dark, lean body, wanted to see those black eyes soften with passion once more? 'So that's it. Subject closed.' She lifted her eyes and met his stare with a steady gaze. 'So now you know—can we please just forget about this whole farce? You can't possibly want me to work for you—not really. Get someone else to arrange your wretched party for you.'

The corners of his mouth lifted upwards in a cruel imitation of a smile. She still did not get it! Oh, foolish, foolish woman. 'On the contrary, Sienna,' he said softly. 'I do not want anyone else. It is you I want and you that I shall have.'

And Sienna began to tremble.

CHAPTER SIX

A MONTH was no time at all—but in a way Sienna was glad that Hashim had demanded such an outrageously short time to arrange his party. If it had dragged on over weeks, then what kind of state might she have found herself in?

As it was, she had her work cut out to find a venue—and there certainly wasn't time to think about his thinly veiled threat, or the sensual way he had looked at her.

Determinedly, she put him out of her mind and holed herself up in her tiny office at her home in Kennington and rang round, using every contact she'd ever made until at last she struck lucky. She could have the use of Bolland House, set in a hundred acres in the glorious Hampshire countryside. She had driven down to see it and had pronounced it perfect.

She had found a local acclaimed chef who cooked using fresh organic produce sourced from nearby farms. She had chosen flowers, and was bussing in her favourite sommelier—though she had warned him that some of the guests might not be drinking alcohol and asked him to provide a wide selection of soft drinks which were rather more exciting than orange juice!

In fact everything was now in place…and with just three days to go it felt a bit as she imagined the atmosphere in one of the giant space stations just before they sent a rocket into flight—the tension of the countdown was almost unbearable. Especially in this heat.

'I'm making coffee!' called a voice from the kitchen. 'Do you want some?'

'Love some!' Sienna called back, and sat back in her chair and sighed. It was funny how circumstances could change out of all recognition in such a short time. Up until that meeting with Hashim, Sienna had been utterly contented. She had her little terraced house in Kennington, which she had bought as a neglected and nearly derelict wreck. She had spent every spare minute doing it up—stripping the walls, sanding the paintwork and painting it in light colours, filling it with mirrors to make it seem bigger and brighter. She had saved up to have a new bathroom and kitchen put in and had painted the front door in a deep, dark blue.

When the house had been habitable, she had taken in a lodger to help with the mortgage—Kat, who was now in her last year of studying languages at a nearby university. And only then had Sienna given herself the luxury of turning her attention to the garden and the challenge of making something pretty out of the small square of ground which had looked like a builders' yard.

'Coffee's ready!' called Kat.

'Coming!'

Sienna got up and went through to the kitchen, where Kat was just putting the cafetière and mugs onto a pretty spotted tray, her red hair falling over her shoulders. She looked up as Sienna came in and smiled. 'Shall we drink it in the garden?'

'That would be lovely,' said Sienna, but she could hear the flatness in her own voice as she went out into the sunshine.

She felt like an outsider to the rest of the world. Usually she revelled in pride and pleasure at the small oasis she had created in the middle of the city, but not today. She could see the sunlight dappling through the honeysuckle, but she couldn't seem to smell the fragrant blooms, nor appreciate its simple beauty. Hashim's reappearance in her life seemed to have sucked the vibrancy out of everything except the memory of his dark and cruel face, and his hard, virile body.

She took the coffee that Kat poured for her and stared into the cup as gloomily as someone with a fear of heights being told to do a high dive.

'Are you going to tell me what's wrong?' said Kat.

Sienna looked up. Her teeth gritted into the bright, cheery smile which she had become rather good at perfecting. 'Oh, just work. You know. It's frantic at the moment.'

'You don't usually complain,' observed Kat, her eyes narrowing. 'You're usually glad when it's like that.'

'Well, it's hot, too. Isn't it?' Sienna wiped her damp brow with a jokey and exaggerated gesture—because how could she tell Kat what was troubling her, and *what* could she tell her?

Oh, I had a fling with a sheikh until he discovered that I'd done some topless photos, and then he…he…

Little beads of sweat studded her forehead and she wiped them away with an angry hand. How awful it sounded when pared down to the basic facts.

She wouldn't tell Kat. Because if she told Kat about Hashim then that would give him an identity which would live on for ever. Kat would want to know all about him—who wouldn't? No, she wouldn't tell anyone. She would do what he wanted her to do and then hopefully he would leave her alone.

Hopefully?

That was part of the trouble, too. He had forced her into this corner and yet a part of her wanted to impress him. To engineer the most wonderful dinner party for him and dazzle him—leaving him with an altogether better memory of her than he currently had.

And wasn't there another part of her—a stubborn and stupid and romantic one—which wished that she could just go back and rewrite history?

Sometimes she started thinking about how it might have been if she'd never done those photos—but then she made herself stop. Thinking like that was a pretty pointless exercise. If she hadn't been able to come up with the money quickly then her mother's life would have collapsed around her—and how could she have lived with *that*?

And even if he hadn't found out it would never have been anything more than a fling—for how could it have been? What had she been imagining—that he'd buy her a whopping great ring and marry her, take her back to Qudamah as the Sheikh's wife? Sienna took a mouthful of too-hot coffee and winced.

'Steady,' warned Kat, only half jokingly.

'Oh, listen—there's that wretched phone again!' Sienna leapt to her feet and gave her housemate an expression which said sorry. But in truth she was glad to get away—to keep herself busy instead of fending off Kat's concerned questions.

'Posh Parties,' she said as she picked the phone up, and then gripped onto it with whitening knuckles.

'Hello, Sienna,' Hashim said softly.

He had the kind of voice which made your skin shiver in spite of yourself, and Sienna closed her eyes in despair. She hadn't spoken to him since that night in the restaurant, and sometimes she had half imagined that she'd dreamt the whole thing up.

But life was rarely as kind as that.

'Hello, Hashim,' she said calmly.

Most people might have asked if it was convenient to talk, but not him.

'It is done?' he questioned, watching as a blonde on the other side of the foyer crossed one slim, silk-stockinged leg over another and slanted him a smile.

'Everything is arranged,' she said mechanically. 'You got my photos of the venue?'

'Yes.'

'And you are happy with the menu plans?'

'Perfectly happy.'

'Drinks seven-thirty to eight, dinner at eight-thirty.' She hesitated. 'Obviously I will be down there earlier, to oversee everything—but do you…do you want me to stay until the end?'

'Most assuredly I do,' he said smoothly, and unseen a slow smile of anticipation curved the cruel line of his mouth. 'And you will dress to party, Sienna. I want you to blend in. Or stand out,' he added mockingly, a jerk of longing arousing him as he imagined her baring her white and perfect breasts. And she would. Oh, she would…. 'The choice is yours.'

She opened her mouth to tell him that she didn't need advice on what to wear—until she realised that antagonising him would get her nowhere. Grit your teeth and bear it, and it will soon all be over.

'I shall look forward to it,' she said crisply.

Hashim's smile became hard-edged. He could see the blonde sliding her tongue wetly over her lips but he turned away. He had never been turned on by the very obvious—and besides, his thoughts were given over to one seduction alone.

'Let's hope it lives up to our expectations,' he murmured, and his black eyes dilated, like a cat's. 'I'll see you on Saturday.' Abruptly he terminated the connection, before the sultry throb of desire could be transmuted to his voice. Because he wanted her to be relaxed, her guard down.

Sienna replaced the phone and stood staring at it for long, countless moments. After Saturday it would all be over.

And suddenly she couldn't wait.

Clunking up the grand drive in her battered old car, Sienna arrived at Bolland Hall just after teatime and let herself in.

'Hello!' she called, but there was no response. She walked through the arched hallway into the dining room and saw the table laid for dinner. She was unable to resist a smile of satisfaction. It was perfect.

Beside Georgian silver and priceless crystal, crisp damask napkins were folded into pristine rectangles and tall candles were ready to be lit.

Everything was as it should be.

There was a stunning floral centrepiece. Fragrant flowers of pink and ivory, dotted with the occasional yellow rose—chosen especially because they were the Sheikh's colours. The colours his jockeys wore. The colour of the Qudamah flag—pink and cream, with a tiny splash of gold in one corner. She breathed in their scent appreciatively.

Similar arrangements of flowers were dotted around the place, and Sienna made her way through the silent house, briefly wondering where all the staff had disappeared to—but they were probably having a well-earned break, since they had clearly been busy.

In the vast kitchen, berry-dark and luscious individual summer puddings lay cooling in the fridge, along with marinades and champagne. Crisp meringues sat snowy-light on a tray next to a bunch of perfect grapes and a dish of white peaches. Several bottles of claret had already been decorked, ready to be carefully poured into the eighteenth-century crystal decanters.

Sienna smiled again. Let Sheikh Hashim Al Aswad try to find any fault with her arrangements!

She heard the crunch of gravel on the drive and wondered if the staff were back. She glanced at her watch. Probably. But as she glanced out of the window she saw a low and screamingly expensive black sports car drawing to a halt. Well, if that was one of the staff then she needed to switch career—and sharpish!

She clip-clopped her way into the hall as the doorbell rang and pulled open the door, her face and her body freezing as she saw Hashim himself standing there, a lazy smile touching the corners of his lips.

Sienna swallowed. She had somehow expected to see him clad in an impeccable dinner jacket, with black tie and snowy white shirt, and dark, tapered trousers which would make his legs look endless. The Western style he seemed to favour the majority of the time.

But he was not. Tonight he was dressed in clothes which heralded far more exotic climes…in fine silk the colour of a pomegranate which clung faintly to hard muscle and lean sinew. It provided the perfect backdrop for his rich black hair and golden-dark skin, but it reminded her of another time—a bitterly erotic one. She felt shame and desire and regret bubbling up inside her, but most of all she felt longing—felt it with an intensity which took her breath away.

Please don't let it show, she prayed silently.

Hashim saw the play of conflicting emotions which crossed her features, and an emotion which was almost alien to him caught him in its silken snare.

Excitement.

'Hello, Sienna.'

'Hashim!' she said softly, in a tone he couldn't quite work out. 'You're…you're early.'

She stood bathed in the soft yet fierce light of the setting sun and he thought that he had never seen her look more beautiful—that thick, shiny hair caught up and woven with glittering clips, making him aware that her neck was classically long and swan-like.

Her dress was made of some light, delicate fabric, layer upon gossamer layer of it, in swirls of rose which made him think of the petals of her mouth. The dress was modest by anyone's standards, even his— and yet he was struck, not for the first time, by how the hint of a body could inflame the senses far more than if it was on show.

As if his senses needed any inflaming!

But he kept his face calmly impassive. This had, after all, been a long time in coming—and he was a master at keeping his feelings hidden. He must not strike until he was certain...

'Aren't you going to invite me in?' he queried mockingly.

She knew she should tell him that it was not her place to invite *him* in—that this was his party, and his money paying for it—but all those thoughts just flew straight out of her mind. For his proximity was making her head spin. She shrank back as he passed by her—as if that could make her immune to the raw virility which seemed to radiate from him. But nothing could make her immune to him.

The black eyes were studying her face as a fox's might just before it devoured a chicken—whole—and a smile was playing around his lips. A smile that made her feel hot and prickly and distinctly...*odd*.

'Do...do you want a drink?' she questioned. 'Or to have a look around—check things out?'

'No.'

She wished he wouldn't stare at her that way, and yet she never wanted him to stop doing it. Pull yourself together, Sienna, she told herself. Remember who he is.

'I'm afraid that the staff have gone off on an extended break,' she said, trying for something light, something to dispel the atmosphere which was fraught and heavy—building into something she didn't recognise nor even want to acknowledge.

And maybe that was why she relaxed and didn't

see it coming. But even if she had would she honestly have been able to stop it? Or *wanted* to stop it?

Because Hashim suddenly pulled her into his arms without warning and anchored her firmly against the full length of his body. His smile hardened.

Don't, she told herself weakly as she felt the musculature and the power. Fight him.

But she did not fight him. She trembled.

And Hashim briefly closed his eyes as one arm encircled the slender column of her waist, sighing with soft triumph as he felt the instinctive flowering of her breasts crushed to his chest. What he had desired for so long would soon be his. It was going to be easier than he had even dared anticipate.

He tilted her chin with the tip of his finger, his black eyes glittering with an inner fire, and she smouldered beneath his scorching gaze. 'Who cares about the staff?' he drawled, and his lips began to move towards her as if a magnetic force compelled them to.

'But—'

'Shh.' His lips grazed hers, touchpaper-sure. 'There are a thousand things I wish to do and show to you, and we must waste not a second.'

Time froze. Her heart seemed to thump out a million beats in those few seconds. His face swam before her, shifting in and out of focus, and she drifted her eyes over it greedily, drinking in the hard, flat planes, the thin, jagged line which ran down the side of his cheek and scarred it.

But most of all it was the mouth which tempted

her—the voluptuous cushion of the lower lip contrasting so markedly with the cruel hard line of the upper one. She could see the gleam of his white teeth and the soft pink of his tongue. It was as if all the time in between had never happened, as if nothing existed nor ever had except for what was here and what was now. In this room, in his arms, in the heightened and fragile atmosphere, with the unsteadiness of their breathing and the scent of the flowers.

'Hashim,' she whispered, but she never knew what it was she intended to say, for his eyes had hardened in tune with his body and he bent his head to blot out the world.

CHAPTER SEVEN

A KISS could be a question and an answer. It could take or give. But Hashim's kiss robbed Sienna of everything except her own helpless response to it. Somewhere at the back of her mind a thousand voices screamed out their protest, but she silenced them as ruthlessly as if they had been her enemies. Instead, she opened her mouth beneath the hard, seeking warmth of his lips. And was lost.

Hashim gave a low laugh of delight at the ease with which she pressed her lips so eagerly against his—it grew in the back of his throat and came out like the small groan of a playful lion cub.

'Oh, yes,' he murmured into her mouth, and she murmured back, something muffled and incoherent—the mindless sound women sometimes made when they were ready for sex.

But Hashim was careful, and although he felt his heart pounding, desire hardening him with its exquisite torturous heat, he knew that this seduction must be a cold-blooded one. One wrong move and she might flee from his arms. One incautious word and all would be lost.

He knew which buttons to press—for his experience of women was encyclopaedic. He knew when to cajole and when to demand. When to lead and when to follow. But with Sienna it was different. She had stated her resistance to just this act, and while her body might be responding at the moment the mind could be a powerful deterrent. Particularly in a woman's case.

It was, he realised, as he drifted his mouth away from her neck and began to kiss softly at the line of her jaw, the very first time in his life that he'd had to actually *seduce* a woman. Normally he had to fight them off. Vaguely he remembered something he had read when schooling himself in the art of love, as royal males of Qudamah did when they reached the age of fifteen. That when a woman was uncertain, you must take it slowly. Very slowly. You must make her believe that you do not have love in mind until it is too late for her to stop. And women did not so easily reach that place of no return as men did.

His mouth was featherlight—provoking and enticing—and Sienna's head fell back. '*Hashim,*' she breathed, and all her hopes and longings were focused on that one little word.

He leapt on the spark of assent and sought to fan the fire with sweet words of his own. 'What is it, sweet Sienna? Sweet, sweet Sienna,' he whispered. His lips touched the base of her throat, teasing it with the tip of his tongue—an erotic and neglected area, or so he had been told—and her little moan told him that his information had been correct. At the same time he began to stroke his fingers down the curve of her hips, taking great care to avoid the obviously erogenous zones. 'That pleases you?'

She felt the pulsing of her blood, felt the words spill from her mouth as if she had no control over them. 'Oh, yes!' she gasped. 'Yes!'

Unseen, he smiled, now risking the flat of his hand lightly skating over her bottom, and in silent answer to the unspoken progression of his movements he felt her squirm against him. The smile disappeared as he let it skate right back again, to cup the pert globe with possessive fingers. Of course she was responsive! Was he forgetting what kind of woman she was? But he dampened his anger down, for it made him harden even more. And it was not his wish to just rip her panties off and drive into her. He would make her eat her defiant words of the other day in the most delicious way possible.

And she would beg him to do it to her!

He teased her and excited her, drifting his fingertips along her thighs, skittering them over the hungry fork of her, but, like a man spoilt for choice at a feast, he deliberately stayed away from her breasts. His mouth hardened. Those he was saving until last.

'Hashim!' she gasped in wonder, as he tiptoed sensation all over her skin, ignited it where he touched, leading her down a path so unbearably sweet that she could scarcely believe this was happening.

His mind worked more quickly than his fingers. If he sought out the classic place of seduction—a bed— then it might allow time for reality to snap into focus and break the spell. He felt himself grow taut, tense, tight, hard as he realised that it was going to have to be here. *Here!* Like a schoolboy with no place to go—but the thought of that, too, excited him. Making do was not something he had ever encountered before, and as always the novel had an intoxicating power all of its own.

When he touched her leg she made no objection. He could feel her impatience and he rewarded it with the slow slide of his hand beneath the filmy layers of her delicate dress, circling the cool satin of her inner thigh to the sound of a tiny moan made at the back of her throat.

'You like that?'

What could she say? Especially as his fingertips were now skating over the moist silk of her panties. Her skin was blazing, her heart was thundering, and warmth and longing overwhelmed her. For only Hashim could make her feel this way—this alive—this wonderful. Like one of those statues brought to life at the end of a play, able to live properly at last. 'Y-yes.' She shuddered. 'You know I do.'

'Then hold me, Sienna,' he urged. 'Hold me.' And as her hands fluttered up to catch hold of the broad bank of his shoulders he gave a grim kind of smile. That was not exactly what he had meant, but for now it would have to do.

Exulting in the freedom of actually touching him again, Sienna was aware that the tips of her fingers were pressing into the fine silk which covered the infinitely finer silk of the skin beneath. Her nails began to scrabble cat-like against the slippery material, as if she wanted to rip it from his body, and he gave a low laugh of delight.

'Ah, yes,' he murmured appreciatively. 'Much better! I see that time has done nothing but hone your appetites.'

His words should have warned her, or stopped her, or cautioned her, but she was in a golden fog of wanting as he began to touch her with a slow, expert caress, and too bewitched to stop him, wanting more, far more.

He pushed aside the damp fabric of her knickers and touched her intimately, where her heat seared against him, and he felt the warmth of her and now he, too, groaned.

'Hashim!' she cried out, startled by sensation—like someone who had jumped out of a parachute after a long absence and forgotten just how mind-blowing it could be. And it had been such a long time…

'You like that?' he teased.

The word was wrenched from her. 'Y-yes.'

'What else do you like?'

'You know,' she breathed. He seemed to know *everything*.

Amid the clamour of his senses he had one last thought of clarity. That the bodyguards stationed at the end of the drive and on the outskirts of the surrounding farmland could not completely guarantee his privacy. Rogue photographers from the hated press might be hiding in the undergrowth—and what a story this would be!

Sheikh caught in flagrante with employee!

Ruthlessly, he continued to move his fingers against her, until, glancing down, he could see that she was lost. Her eyes were smoky and she trembled like a leaf. Was she as receptive as this with every man? he wondered grimly, unprepared for the poisonous snake of jealousy which coiled around his heart. His black eyes scanned the hallway and the dim, dark corridor which ran from the far end of it. Along there they would be unseen.

He felt her stir restlessly and kissed her again, for he knew that a kiss held more power than anything else. That women could be made to fall in love under the spell of a kiss—for they read into it all their secret desires and needs. He felt an infinitesimal moment of hesitation before she melted right into him, and he knew then that her capitulation was certain.

He picked her up in his arms and carried her towards the cool flagstones and the muted colours of a long, silken rug which softened it, lying her down on top of it. Sienna's eyes fluttered open as if she had suddenly just come out of a coma and realised where she was.

'What are you doing?'

There was a strange kind of startlement on her face which almost moved him—until he reminded himself that disingenuous questions like *that* one were sometimes asked out of habit more than necessity. Had she learnt somewhere along the line that men were turned on by innocence? But he would play along with the game if it eased her conscience.

'What do you think I'm doing?' he said softly, as he lay down beside her—*he*, the *Sheikh*, lying on the floor with a woman. 'I am fulfilling my wildest dream and fantasy.'

And hers, too.

'Really?' she questioned tentatively.

'But of course,' he said smoothly, taking her into his arms, knowing that his embrace would dispel any lingering doubts. 'I want you, Sienna. My beautiful Sienna. Indeed, I have never stopped wanting you. Did you not know that?'

She shook her head, her mind a whirl of confusing thoughts. 'But you—'

'Shh.'

His face was close to hers, his breath warm on her face, and all she wanted was for him to kiss her again. She felt the ground hard beneath her back, and the hard body pressing against hers, and fleetingly she wondered how and why she had allowed this to happen. But it was only very fleeting, and suddenly it didn't matter. She couldn't stop. She didn't want to stop.

Once—a long time ago—Hashim had given her a taste of passion and it had branded and spoiled her for ever. The men who had tried to get close to her subsequently had had an impossible act to follow, even if they hadn't been aware of it at the time. And might not this single act help her to exorcise a ghost which was all too real, to move on and break free of his enchantment?

She licked at her dry lips. 'We do not have very long. Wh-what about the staff? The...the guests?' she managed.

Hashim stilled, his eyes narrowing. If there had been any tiny vestige of guilt at his cold-blooded seduction then she had banished it with her words. She knew *exactly* what she was doing. She was sexually hungry, as he was, and probably almost as experienced. Well, then—let her see who was the most magnificent lover of all her conquests!

For he too had been enchanted by the sense of nearly. Of something unfinished and incomplete. In his anger—with himself as well as with her—he had sent her packing before he had properly had his fill of her, and that sense of aching and burning frustration had never quite gone away. Well, now it would— and it would be gone for ever.

'We have long enough,' he said, and the stark note of hunger made his voice sound hollow—as if it came from a long way away—and for a moment he scarcely recognised it as his own.

And hunger made his hands tremble, made his need to join with her overwhelm him with a desire which banished all his carefully conceived plans. Forgotten was his long-nursed wish to feast upon the magnificent breasts which she had displayed for all the world to see. Instead—unbelievably and inexplicably—he found that he didn't want to wait. No—*couldn't* wait.

With a groan, he rucked up her skirt and found himself ripping off the delicate panties. She made no protest, her legs parting for him instantly. His robes were not encumbered by belts or buttons or zips. He could slither off the light silk of his trousers with ease until he was free at last, sliding on the necessary protection with the impatient fumbling of a schoolboy. And then he was touching and nudging against her with a restrained and magnificent power. At last! Such sweet torture, this moment of expectation, but a torture to be treasured and savoured until he could bear it no longer.

'Now,' he whispered—not a question but an emphatic statement, and in answer her lips pressed into his shoulder, opening against him, closing around his flesh. He could feel the wet of her tongue and the sharp graze of her teeth and could contain himself no longer. He drove hard into her.

There was one moment before he realised, a split-second as he worked out what was happening but by then it was too late. He saw the screwing up of her eyes, the way her little white teeth bit down on her bottom lip, and then he knew. By the mountains and the rivers!

'Sienna!' The word was torn from his lips even while her body became taut, like a bow stretched around him, before the arrow of his desire pierced through to the very heart of her. 'Sienna!' he said again, but this time it was on a note of wonder.

'Oh,' she breathed, the word a little feather which drifted away as the pain became transmuted into a growing and indescribable wave of pleasure and he began to move inside her.

He had planned his own release with little concern for hers—not like the first time—but now it was different. Now it was a virtuoso performance. Never had he taken so much care with a woman as he thrust all the way inside her—but then, never had the weight of such responsibility lain so heavy on his shoulders.

He found himself being gentle with her—an odd and unfamiliar kind of gentleness which made what was taking place seem to do so in slow motion, like a film viewed through a gauzy lens.

'Ah, Sienna.' And her name came out on a long, shuddering sigh.

He was slow for as long as he needed to be, and then a little faster. He held back for as long as he needed to, and then he drove in again, harder and then harder still. He teased her when she breathlessly began to beg for more, relentlessly retreating to take her further along the inexorable path, and just when he thought that he could withstand no more of this exquisite self-control he felt her begin to convulse around him.

Her cries split the air, her legs splaying and her back arching as her sweat-sheened face fell back, and she was calling his name in wonder and in disbelief.

And then—oh, sweet, sweet desire—then he let go himself, in an orgasm which rocked his world on its axis—which took him completely out of his body. It was a slow drift back to earth, and he fought it every bit of the way.

It had been the most mind-blowing sex of his entire life—but that should not have surprised him, not really.

After all, he had been waiting for this for a long, long time.

CHAPTER EIGHT

THROUGH the soft darkness Sienna became aware of her heart as it beat within her, strong and loud and steady. And then she became aware of another beat and another heart—so close to hers that it almost felt as if it was inside her. She felt warm and complete—as if she had been made whole at last—the slight aching deep inside her a glorious physical reminder of what had seemed like a perfect dream.

Opening her eyes, she took in the scene with something approaching disbelief. It had not been a dream. She was lying on a carpet in a dim, cool corridor in Hashim's arms, her dress around her hips, and he was staring down at her. Impossible to read what was in those glittering black eyes, but his question gave her some idea.

'Why didn't you tell me?' he asked quietly, his voice as deadly as the silent snakes which glided around the foothills of Qudamah's mountains.

'Tell you what?' she teased.

'Do not play games with me! You are a *virgin*!'

She heard the accusation in his voice and the pink bubble of contentment began to dissolve. 'I was,' she corrected.

He shook his dark head. 'I cannot believe it!'

'I'm afraid you have incontrovertible evidence, Hashim.'

'But...how?'

At any other time his incredulity would have been almost laughable, but now...now it just hurt. 'Surely you don't need me to tell you that?' she questioned quietly.

His mouth tightened. He was still reeling from this one incredible piece of knowledge which had rocked his world just as surely as his orgasm had. For the fact of her innocence had blown all his preconceptions out of the water. And it had done something else, too....

From the start his instinct about her had been that she was innocent, but the existence of the calendar had convinced him that her innocence had been a sham. But if *that* instinct had been correct then what about the other ones which had crowded in on him at the time? The ones which had left him muddled and confused making him wonder if he had found in her something which he had not thought possible?

And hadn't he been glad to abandon those feelings by seizing on her questionable past with something like relief? As if he found it easier to live in a state of cynicism rather than one of hope and longing, like other men.

He shook his head again, dazed and angry, too. 'It should not have been like that.'

She wanted to tell him that it had been perfect, but something in his attitude was puzzling her. He was acting as if something *shameful* had just taken place—rather than the something wonderful it had been. She stared up at him. 'What was wrong with it?'

'Wrong?' A frown creased his brow as he studied her face, rather as a scientist might intently bend over a test tube. 'Nothing was *wrong* with it.' How could she fail to understand? 'But it would never have happened if I had known. Why did you not tell me, Sienna?'

Because she hadn't been thinking of anything except the touch of his lips and the hard, strong embrace of his lean body. She had found it impossible to stop something she had wanted for so long—even though she had denied wanting it. Had told herself that it was wrong to want it.

'We weren't having much of a conversation at the time,' she said, aware that her voice sounded flippant.

'Your first time should not be with a casual lover on the floor of an anonymous house,' he said, and his deep voice was tinged with regret. 'Your virginity is a gift which you have clearly treasured, as every woman should. You should have saved it for a man you love. Who loves you.'

And with those sad words he smashed all her foolish hopes and dreams. He made her feel as if she had offered him fresh flowers at dawn—still wet with the morning dew—and he had taken them and carelessly tossed them into the gutter, to be ground underfoot into dust and crushed petals.

He seemed so far away, even though he was right next to her. A moment ago he had been kissing her over and over again, but he was not kissing her now. The hands which had wrought such sweet magic were not touching her now. It was done. Finished. And Sienna felt the dull ache of dawning realization, which eclipsed the deeper aching in her newly awakened body.

She had allowed...no, she had been a more than willing participant in *allowing* herself to be brought here. To lie with him on this hard stone floor and to...to... She would not use the words 'make love', for it had not been that. It had been nothing to do with love. He had just told her so.

So why were erotic and tender images still jostling for position in her mind? The way she had called out his name in breathless wonder. The way her body had shivered its pleasure, and the way that pleasure had grown and surged and taken her into a place where the senses reigned supreme. And she had stupidly allowed herself to believe that for him it meant more than simply pleasure. That his whispered words of encouragement and pleasure had been voicing some deeper emotion than mere desire—a longing more precious than lust. But in that she had been totally wrong.

Sienna swallowed, forcing the memories away, for they would soon bring nothing but pain. It was too late for regret, but not too late for pride. 'Well, there's no point in having a post mortem, is there?' she said, hearing the false brightness in her tone.

He was silent for a moment, and then his eyes imprisoned her—searching and seeking to know. 'Why has there been nobody else?' he demanded.

It was a question she had asked herself many times—and, oh, how it would feed his monstrous ego if she told him what she suspected was the truth: that he was the only man she had ever remotely imagined making love to. Men had tried, but they had failed. Or was it she who had failed—to abandon foolish hope and try to make the best of an ordinary life?

'You make it sound like a fault on my part that there hasn't been,' she said bitterly.

His eyes narrowed. 'What happened between us that last time. The way I behaved. Did that put you off men?'

'In a way.' But not the way *he* meant.

'You should have told me,' he said, and now his voice was angry. 'Back then you should have told me. But now—*now* when you are older and more independent, a true woman at last—you should have said something!'

'Would you have believed me?'

Another silence.

'Would you?' she persisted.

'No,' he said eventually. 'I guess I wouldn't have.' He felt like a man who had been swimming towards a familiar shore only to discover that he was headed for a strange land of which he knew nothing. None of it made any sense to him. How could it? She? Of all people? A *virgin*?

'Because you'd already made your mind up about what kind of woman I was. The photos proved that I must be some sort of slapper!'

Hashim's eyes narrowed, his English for once deserting him. 'Slapper?'

'The kind of woman who will just sleep with anyone. You didn't look further than skin-deep, did you, Hashim? You just made a judgement about me. But people are a lot more than they appear to be on the surface. Not cardboard cut-outs but living and breathing flesh and blood, with flaws and strengths all their own! Don't you realise that?' she finished.

'I'm afraid that my position sets me apart,' he told her coolly, seeking a familiar refuge behind the invisible barrier of his royal status. 'I do not have the luxury of the time to dig deep beneath the surface.'

'Or the inclination to even try?' she challenged.

'Maybe not,' he admitted, for it was impossible not to answer that lancing question in her green eyes.

Sienna nodded, forcing herself to voice the bitter truth. She had allowed passion to cloud her vision, but now that passion had passed it was achingly clear. 'You see women as commodities,' she whispered. 'To be used for passing pleasure but little else, other than maybe one day motherhood.' And she felt a stupid great yearning as she realised that Hashim would never put her in *that* category. Not in a million years. A woman who had allowed herself to be photographed in that way, a woman who had fallen oh-so-easily into his arms, was merely a woman to be discarded. And the aching sense of longing for something she could never have washed over her in a bitter tide.

He could feel her retreating from him—not just mentally, but physically, too, and that reawakened the desire which had been obscured by his startling discovery. He was used to calling the shots, and by rights *he* should have been the one to distance himself from her now. Or not.

'Ah, Sienna,' he murmured, and reached out his hand to cradle her face. 'What is done is done. Is it not a little late in the day for words of recrimination?'

Involuntarily Sienna trembled—for the touch of his skin was soft and warm and exquisite to behold. It had the power to lure her back into that place of unimaginable pleasure. But at what cost? She shook his hand away and sat up.

'Yes, you're right, it is. I should have said all this before.'

'But you could not!' he breathed triumphantly. 'For you were as much in thrall to me as I to you! What just happened between us was as inevitable as the passing of night through to day. I knew that.'

'Well, we're all entitled to make mistakes,' she said woodenly. 'And anyway, we're wasting time, sitting around here talking. Your guests will be arriving very soon and I suggest that we both of us try to tidy up.' She reached up her hand to feel the bird's nest mess of her hair, wondering how the hell she was going to tame it down.

She was surprised that he wasn't leaping around fretting. He hadn't once mentioned the no-show of the staff. Or the fact that his guests would be upon them shortly. And then something else occurred to her—dripping into her thoughts like slow poison—something which in its way was almost as bad as what she had just let happen. She could feel the heavy plummeting of her heart as everything clicked into disturbingly sharp focus.

Oh, no.

How could she have been so *stupid*?

Slowly, she turned her head to stare at him. 'But there aren't going to be any guests—are there, Hashim?'

He met the accusation in her eyes but he did not flinch from it. 'No.'

'There were never going to be any guests, were there?'

'No.'

She geared herself up for the next blow, knowing the answer to her question before she asked it. 'And the staff? The staff I so carefully vetted and booked but who didn't bother to show?'

'I allowed them to prepare for the dinner, so that your suspicions would not be alerted, and then I cancelled them.'

'You cancelled them,' she said slowly, feeling sick-ened by the sheer cold-bloodedness of his plan. 'Just like that?'

He shrugged. 'It was not difficult. I paid them in full.'

'*You paid them in full?*' she repeated, her voice shaking, haunted by the thought that she had followed suit. Fallen into line and done exactly what Hashim had wanted. What he had planned. He had lured her into a sensual trap which she had embraced with all the enthusiasm of the convert. She felt the hot sting of hurt but she would not allow it to be converted to tears. She would *not* cry in front of him.

'You snapped your fingers and everybody jumped, I expect. You and your damned money and your damned power,' she whispered. He had tricked her into organising a party just so that he could seduce her—how low could a man sink? And how could she have let him? How *could* she? The true extent of his deception brought fire into her voice.

'You think you can just pick people up and use them, move them around like pawns and then throw them off the board when you've finished with them?' she raged.

Hashim listened, waiting patiently for the storm to pass. Let her rage be spent, and then afterwards let her see sense. Realise that what had passed between them had been magnificent and that to let it go would be a waste of the highest order. Why, he could take her upstairs to one of the magnificent bedrooms, where they could continue to take their pleasure. Her anger would soon be forgotten after a night in his arms!

'Sienna—'

'No!' she said fiercely, pushing away from him and scrambling to her feet. She had seen the brief darkening of his eyes, and she might be new to this game but she knew exactly what it meant. And did she trust herself around him? No, she did not. Her spirit might be fighting all the way, but around Hashim her flesh was as weak as it could be.

She moved as far away from him as possible. There was no dignified way of adjusting her dress and her panties, but she did her damnedest, raking her fingers back through the hair which had tumbled in untidy tendrils all down the side of her long neck.

And at least she had the enjoyment of seeing *Hashim* get to his feet and begin to rearrange his clothing, his face now tight with obvious displeasure and a simmering kind of anger. Or was it merely frustration?

She walked out into the hall, all the warmth and comfort and pleasure evaporating from her body like raindrops on a scorching pavement. And then she caught a glimpse of herself in the mirror and recoiled at the sight of her flushed cheeks and mussed hair— the definite look of someone who had been rolling around the place.

How could she? Oh, how *could* she?

She picked up her handbag and a silken voice stopped her in her tracks.

'Where do you think you are going?' he questioned softly.

Composing her face, she turned round, and suddenly she didn't care *what* he tried to threaten her with. Just let him try. Nothing could be worse than what she had just allowed to happen, despite all her supposedly good intentions. 'Home,' she said crisply. 'Where else?'

'You could come home with me.'

Sienna almost choked. 'I'd rather spend the night in a lions' cage! And anyway—I wouldn't call a luxury hotel suite a *home*! It isn't yours, it's anonymous—just like this place. There's nothing of you there, Hashim. A luxurious room with no soul. And that's your life. Empty.'

For a moment a dark shadow passed across his heart. She dared to say this to him? To accuse him of an empty life? He, who had palaces and oil fields and people scattered all over the world who were eager to do his bidding? No woman had ever dared say such a thing to him. She was daring to look at him and speak to him as no woman ever had before...almost as his *equal*. Again he felt the sensation of being on unfamiliar territory, and his mouth hardened in anger.

'I forbid you to go!'

'Well, you can't. You don't own me. You don't even employ me any more. I've done what you asked and now I'm leaving.'

His eyes narrowed as he glanced around the carved

wooden interior of the airy hall. 'And what of this house and your obligation to it?' he demanded.

'It's not my concern. Not any more. *You* sort it out! Here!' And she flung the keys at him.

He caught them one-handed, realising that she meant exactly what she said. She was leaving! Walking out on him even though she had been sobbing out his name only moments before. And suddenly he was filled with a reluctant kind of admiration which only renewed the subtle throbbing of desire. 'Has anyone ever told you how beautiful you look when you're angry?' he questioned softly.

'Fortunately, most people have a more original line than that!'

'But it is not finished yet, Sienna,' he said evenly. 'I tell you that quite unequivocally. You have but tasted the pleasures I can give you, and soon you will be greedy for more.'

'Oh, but you're wrong. So wrong.' She stared at him. 'After all, we're even now. I deceived you, and now you've paid me back by deceiving me. We can call it quits. I just want to forget you and your fake party. In fact, I want to forget all about you.'

He shook his head and his mouth curved into a cruel smile. 'You still don't understand, do you, Sienna? Those are not *my* wishes—and the Sheikh always has *his* wishes fulfilled.'

He wasn't listening to a word she said! Frustratedly, she turned away, and his dark laughter was still ringing in her ears as she slammed her way out of the front door, running down to where her beaten-up little wreck of a car was parked beside his smooth, dark sports model. And if she needed some concrete evidence of the insurmountable differences in their lives she had only to look at their two contrasting cars.

It's over, she told herself fiercely.

So why did she look up into the driver's mirror to see his tall dark figure, the silken pomegranate robes whispered by the breeze to caress that hard, honed body which had made such sweet and unforgettable love to her?

She turned the key in the ignition with an angry jerk. It was over.

CHAPTER NINE

HASHIM rang her. Repeatedly. Sienna kept the phone on 'divert', but once she picked it up without checking and heard his voice, and quietly terminated the connection with a trembling hand.

He sent her a cheque—such a grossly inflated cheque that the businesswoman side of her momentarily weakened, until she allowed her righteous fury to put it in an envelope and send it back to him. She supposed she could have torn it up—but returning it might help to get the message through loud and clear.

He even tried flowers—and for some reason those riled her more than anything. How *dared* he think he could buy her off with a bunch of flowers?

'They're lovely,' Kat said wistfully, sniffing at the lily-of-the-valley and freesia and roses.

'Have them—they're yours!' And Sienna unceremoniously dumped the monster bouquet into her bemused lodger's arms.

Her work, which had previously fulfilled her, suddenly seemed a chore, and her life felt like a punctured balloon, coloured grey. Kat had taken to asking if she was sickening for something, and Sienna knew that she really was going to have to snap out of it. She had a business to run and she couldn't divert her phone for ever. And Hashim seemed to have got the message at last, since he had left her alone for nearly a week.

She was sitting in her minuscule office, trying to concentrate on an engagement party which seemed to mock her with its celebration of love, when the telephone on her desk rang. Tiny hairs on the back of her neck began to prickle as she heard a disturbingly familiar dark, silken voice, and she wavered for a second. She could hang up, of course—or she could have the courage to tell him to leave her alone. And she couldn't keep running away for ever.

'What can I do for you, Hashim?' she questioned coolly.

'Why have you failed to cash my cheque?' he demanded.

'Because I don't want your money!'

'Ah, Sienna,' he purred, like a trainee lion cub. 'Don't you realise that resistance turns a man on?'

Especially a man who wasn't used to being resisted. 'That isn't why I'm doing it,' came her icy reply.

He knew that. As a ploy it would have failed, because he would have seen through it. As a genuine wish it excited him. Greatly. 'I want to see you,' he said softly.

Images of his dark mocking eyes swam into her unwilling memory. 'Well, you can't.'

Did she not realise that he could hear her breathless note of hesitation—and the reluctant longing which matched his own? His voice dipped into a mocking caress as he felt the hot, hard jerk of desire. 'Then say it like you mean it.'

Sienna closed her eyes, but that only made it worse. Now the images were of a hard body entering hers with almost heartbreaking sweetness. 'There's no point,' she said wildly.

'On the contrary. There is every point. I have a proposition to put to you.'

'A proposition?' Suspicion crept into her voice. 'Planning another fictitious party, are you?'

He gave a low laugh. 'Now, that's an idea! Meet me and I'll tell you all about it.'

'Have you listened to a word I've been saying? I don't want your phone calls or your flowers, and I certainly don't want to *see* you, Hashim!'

'Yes, you do,' he murmured. 'You know that and I know that. You are unsettled and so am I. Why keep fighting it? Your work will suffer, for a start.'

And he was right, damn him! She had almost more work than she could reasonably cope with, and—ironically—no inclination to do it. It had taken every bit of concentration she had to prevent herself from sitting staring into space and thinking about the dark Sheikh, trying to school herself away from wanting him, but in reality… Oh, the reality was so different.

'If I meet you, will you promise to leave me alone?'

He gave a wry smile. How had she managed to get

so far with such an appalling sense of logic? 'If that is what you desire,' he said carefully.

Desire. What a dangerous and provocative word that was. Sienna clenched her fist as she felt the empty little tug of her heart. 'Name a time and place.'

'Now.'

'Now?'

'I am very close to your house. I will be waiting.'

'You *are* joking!'

'What's the matter, Sienna?' he mocked. 'Are you never spontaneous?'

She was wearing her oldest jeans and a T-shirt which one of the football team had given her at college. There was a rip at the hem and a stain on it which she thought might be *crème de menthe*, but she wasn't entirely sure. She glanced in the mirror at her unwashed hair, which was caught back in a ponytail. Maybe if he saw her like this—the real, basic Sienna—then he would get the message.

'Okay,' she said slowly. 'I'll meet you.'

'Five minutes,' he clipped, and hung up.

Pausing only to brush her teeth, telling herself that she would have done the same no matter who she was meeting, she slid on a pair of old flip-flops and let herself out of the house, wondering where he was waiting.

She didn't have to wonder for very long. A shiny limousine with tinted windows was parked at the end of the road—presumably because the road was so narrow it could go no further. In front of it and just to the rear were two leather-clad outriders on powerful motorbikes. It was like a scene straight out of a film, and Sienna could see a couple of curtains twitching as she walked towards it.

My neighbours will never look at me in quite the same way she thought, as a chauffeur stepped out of the driver's seat and opened the door for her.

Telling herself that she could hardly be rude to Hashim's employee, she had no choice but to slide into the soft-cushioned luxury of the back seat. It took a few seconds for her eyes to become accustomed to the dim light, but she could see Hashim sprawled negligently on the back seat, watching her.

Today he was wearing Western clothes—not a shimmer of soft silk in sight. An immaculately cut dark suit, with a snowy shirt and a tie which gleamed dully in the reduced light. Sienna could feel her heart begin to pound.

'Nice of you to get out of the car yourself,' she said.

'I was thinking of your reputation.'

'Liar.'

He laughed. 'Your assessment of me is wholly and completely wrong, Sienna—my honesty has at times been described as almost brutal.'

Brutal. Yes. There *was* a brutal side to his nature. And yet it contrasted with the extraordinary gentleness he had displayed when she had lain so helplessly in his arms. She felt the drying of her lips, and as if he had read her thoughts he leaned forward and touched his mouth to hers in a barely-there kiss which started her senses sizzling.

'Don't,' she said weakly.

The same cold skill and calculation which made him a world-class poker player made him kiss her for long enough to hear her sigh, and then he stopped and leaned back against the seat to study her. He pressed a button by his side and said something she did not understand. The car began its powerful acceleration.

'Where are we going?' she questioned, in alarm.

'Just driving around—we will draw less attention to ourselves that way—this car tends to attract sightseers.'

'Why don't you travel in something less ostentatious, then?' she questioned acidly.

'Because I cannot,' he said simply. 'It needs to be bullet-proof.'

And—perhaps for the very first time—Sienna allowed herself to see the downside of his life. Hadn't there been part of her which had somehow thought that the bodyguards which accompanied him were simply for show? As some kind of indicator of his power and lofty position? She had never actually stopped to think that someone might want to *shoot* him, and now that she had she found her stomach twisting over in anxiety.

'Now, let us both be honest,' he said quietly. 'Can you do that?'

'You don't take any notice of me when I am.'

But he shook his head. 'No, Sienna—I am talking about *real* honesty. I do not mean that you should say what you feel you *ought* to say, but what is truly in your heart.'

'Then I'm at a disadvantage—for *you* don't have a heart!'

He paused, for it was not the first time this accusation had been flung at him. 'Have you thought of me?'

She opened her mouth to say no—but something in his eyes stopped her. 'Yes.'

He nodded his head. 'And for me it is the same. I have thought of little else. The way you felt in my arms. You haunt me, Sienna—for I cannot forget the great gift which you gave to me.'

'Which you took, you mean,' she corrected him quietly. 'You set me up and seduced me—as you had intended to do right from the start.'

'Yes,' he said bitterly. 'Of that I am guilty—I robbed you of your greatest virtue. But I would not have done it had I known that you were innocent, and that innocence has changed everything.' He paused, studying the lush fullness of her mouth, and when he spoke his voice was almost reflective. 'What passed between us was not enough—not for me, nor for you. You were beautiful and responsive, but your initiation into the pleasures of the body should not be limited to a single session on a cold floor, our bodies not even naked.'

She was glad then for the dim light, for she began

to blush and he saw. His eyes narrowed and she wondered if he was remembering—as she was—that very first blush such a long time ago. 'It's over,' she said, aware of how lacking in conviction her words sounded. Was that because she didn't *want* it to be over?

He thought how strange it was that a woman could still blush with innocence, even when that innocence was gone. 'Ah, but that is where you are wrong,' he whispered. 'It is not over. Indeed, that was only the beginning.'

Sienna blinked, because suddenly the picture had shifted, changed focus. Was he asking her to be his *girlfriend*? 'What are you saying?' she whispered.

'You came to me untutored—a beautiful novice,' he said huskily. 'And yet, in a way, it was as new for me as it was for you.' His black eyes glittered. 'You see, I had never had a virgin before.'

He made himself sound like a jockey who had attempted a higher than usual jump, and his matter-of-fact words fractured the tiny flicker of hope which had begun to spark into life. But maybe that was a blessing, because the very word 'virgin' was charged with emotion—and emotion could, she realized, be character-changing in every sense of the word. It could make you weak when you most needed to be strong. 'Am I supposed to be flattered by this remarkable statement?'

'Yes,' he said simply. 'For I am admitting to you that I found the experience profoundly moving.'

As an admission it bordered on the arrogant, and if it had been anyone else then Sienna might have said so. But something stopped her. Maybe it was the look in his eyes. As if he had lifted away a veil and allowed her to see a whisper of contrition. And the unexpected glimpse of this gave him the fleeting shimmer of vulnerability, reminding her that deep down he was just a man—that all the rest was just packaging.

'Go on,' she said steadily. 'I'm intrigued.'

'I want to teach you everything there is to know about the art of love.' His smile was edged with hunger. There was the briefest of pauses before he spoke again. 'I want you to become my mistress,' he said softly.

Sienna stilled. *'What?'*

'I am choosing you to become mistress to the Sheikh.'

He made it sound so...*mechanical.* 'Is there a new vacancy, then?' she questioned acidly. 'Or will I be sharing the post?'

Hashim was so used to complete compliance—to grateful and eager acceptance from adoring women—that for a moment he was taken aback by her flippant attitude. 'I do not think you realise the honour I am affording you,' he said icily.

'No, I probably don't,' said Sienna gravely. 'Perhaps you could tell me a little more about what this exciting position entails?'

Because no one ever made fun of him Hashim did

not recognise the mocking tone in her voice. He had never had to persuade or to entice a lover before, and such coercion did not come naturally to him.

'You will have an open charge account.' His black eyes flicked disparagingly over her jeans and stained T-shirt. 'And in future you will buy clothes that please you and please your Sheikh.'

'Do you have any particular requests?' Sienna questioned meekly. 'Favourite colours? That kind of thing?'

Hashim's eyes narrowed suspiciously. Was she agreeing without further argument? Damn the woman—why did she keep coming out and surprising him? 'Obviously what you are wearing today is thoroughly unsuitable.'

'Obviously,' she agreed steadily.

'I should like to see you in silks and satins from now on,' he said coolly. 'And velvets and lace. Nothing *man-made*.' He shuddered. 'You should dress to please me, for when I am pleased then it follows that you shall be, too.'

'How delightfully simple you make it sound,' Sienna murmured. 'Anything else?'

His black eyes gleamed with anticipation as he imagined clothing her in delicate underclothes—and then ripping them off! 'As you know, I spend the majority of my time in Qudamah, but I frequently travel to the major cities to conduct business on behalf of my country, and when I do I wish for you to fly out to join me. I will send my private jet for you,' he promised silkily.

She ignored the airborne carrot he dangled. 'But what about my job?' she questioned seriously.

'Your job?'

'Or rather, my career,' she corrected. 'I've built it up from scratch and worked hard—I can't just abandon it to flit off to all the corners of the globe on a whim.'

Hashim gave her an impatient look. 'Your job will no longer be necessary. You will have all the money you need. You can give it up.'

Give it up? Sienna could not hold her feelings in any more. Did he have no idea how real people lived their lives? She supposed that he didn't. 'I'm not doing any such thing!' she declared. 'I take pride in my work, Hashim. I have a number of big contracts in the pipeline.'

'Sub-contract them.'

'No, I will not.'

'Sienna, you are stretching my patience!'

'And you're stretching mine! Do you imagine for a moment that I can be bought?'

There was a moment of silence. 'Everyone can be bought—you of all people should know that.'

'Are you still on about those wretched photographs? Can't you just let it go?' She stared at him and then reached for the door. 'I won't be insulted by you any more. And I don't have to be. You've had your pound of flesh, Hashim—just be satisfied with that.'

Suddenly he found himself wishing that he could bite the words back. 'Sienna. Don't go.' He caught her arm and began to caress it with his fingers. 'Please.'

She closed her eyes, her inner turmoil lulled by the touch of his hand, recognising that his plea was an unfamiliar one. She had made her stand and demonstrated her independence and her pride—but nothing could change the effect he had always had on her, and still did. The melting way he made her feel inside whenever he touched her. The way his very presence made her feel so *alive*. If she took that out of the equation there would be nothing to consider, but it was far too powerful to disregard.

She opened her eyes again. 'It's not all about what *you* want, is it, Hashim? It's about what I want, too.'

He had been almost certain that she was—incredibly!—going to turn him down, and it was Hashim's turn to be surprised. Was she playing games with him? 'You mean you are giving consideration to my proposal?'

'Of course I am. A woman would have to be pretty stupid not to, wouldn't she? It isn't every day that she is offered a chance to play the starring role in Cinderella!'

But, inexplicably, his triumph was now tempered by a fleeting sense of disappointment—for it now ap-

peared that she was going to give in, and he had been
enjoying doing battle with her. 'So you will agree?'

'Only if you agree to my terms.'

'*Your* terms?' he repeated, outraged.

'But of course. Why should it all go your way?'

Because it always had done—all his life! 'Name
them,' he snapped.

'Well, you can forget the idea of a charge card, for
a start—I don't want it, thank you all the same. I don't
earn a fortune, but what I do has been honestly come
by—and I usually manage to scrub up well enough
without the benefit of costly clothes. And I will only
fly to see you if it is convenient. To me.' Because
soon it would be over, and when it was she would
need her livelihood just the same as she always had.
'I will continue with my life as normal—if you want
to see me then you will have to fit in around me.'

'But what you ask of me is outrageous!' he protested.

She shrugged. 'Then forget the whole idea. In fact,'
she added truthfully, 'that would be much better for
me in the long-term.'

'But in the short-term you do not want to forget it,'
he murmured, pulling her into his arms. 'Right now
your body is screaming out for me. You know that I
am growing hard even now, just as you are wet with
wanting. Aren't you?'

'Hashim, you're…you're…' But her words were
forgotten, for he had put his hands underneath her
T-shirt to cup the aching mounds of her breasts.

'No bra?' he questioned shakily, torn between excitement and disapproval as he felt their velvet weight against his palms.

'I never wear one when I'm working at home. Oh!' She gasped as he bent his mouth to one hardened nipple and began to suckle it. His hand was skimming the narrow indentation of her waist, which led down to an unforgiving waistband. And now his hand had moved to the fork of her thighs, and he was touching her through the denim…touching her and touching her. 'Hashim, wh—what do you think you're doing?'

'Guess.'

'But…but we're in the car.'

'The driver can't see. Do you want me to stop?'

She squirmed with pleasure beneath his touch. Not yet. Just a couple of minutes more and then she would stop him. 'We can't actually *do* anything if I'm wearing jeans, can we?' she asked breathlessly.

'Can't we?' He laughed, skating a featherlight fingertip over the most intimate part of her.

How could she feel this way? As though he was touching her flesh instead of the thick material of her jeans. 'Hashim—'

'Shh. Let go,' he urged, excited now as he watched her. 'Just let go.'

And to her eternal shame she did just that. Forgot the fact that she was writhing around in the back of a car in the middle of heaven only knew where. Forgot that she might have salvaged a little pride by returning his cheque and refusing his calls. She just went right along with the demands of her body, allowing herself to be carried along by the sweet and irresistible torrent.

'Oh!' She half sobbed as he increased the movement of his finger.

'Yes,' he murmured. 'You are so close, Sienna. So beautifully close. Let me watch you as I give you pleasure. Let me see you orgasm in your blue jeans.'

And then that feeling was upon her again—that out-of-this-world, flying-to-paradise feeling was sweeping her up and away, orchestrated by the relentless and expert caress of his fingers. And suddenly she had begun to cry out—little cries of astounded pleasure—until the fierce pressure of his mouth blocked out the sound and her body shattered into a million beautiful pieces.

For countless seconds she felt the spasms of her body shuddering to a slow halt, the sticky warmth of contentment. She was aware of Hashim stroking away the hair from her sweat-sheened brow.

'How can that have happened?' she whispered, half to herself. 'How?'

Unseen, he smiled. How little she knew—and how much he had to show her! He lifted her chin so that he could stare down at her with black eyes which mocked and lanced. 'Ah, Sienna,' he said softly. 'Do you see how much you have to learn?'

Lying curled in his arms in the aftermath of her orgasm, she was at her most vulnerable. 'Perhaps I do,' she agreed drowsily.

Maybe when you first gave your heart to someone it was difficult to claw it back again. With Hashim there had always been a sense of something left uncompleted—hadn't he said so himself? Maybe this really was the answer. If she saw more of him then mightn't it diminish some of the magic which surrounded him? Which made her see him as she failed to see other men?

'So you will agree to be my mistress?'

She turned her face up to his and opened her eyes very wide. 'Only on a strictly informal basis.'

'And will you come back to my hotel now and let me give you dinner?'

And, presumably, bed. But that was what a mistress *should* do—and who was she to complain if it meant that Hashim would make love to her?

'I'll need to go home and get showered first.'

He gave a slow smile of anticipation. 'We'll have a bath together,' he said. And he would send out those disgusting clothes of hers to be laundered.

CHAPTER TEN

Six months later

'You are late,' Hashim said coldly, as Sienna walked into the hotel bedroom.

'Only a little.'

'I have been waiting,' he said ominously, 'for over an hour.'

'Sorry, darling.' Sienna slipped off the soft green cashmere coat she had allowed him to buy her for Christmas, its emerald *faux* fur collar gleaming in the pale winter sunshine. It was the *only* thing she had allowed him to buy—and then only because it was Christmas. Even though—as she had teasingly pointed out—he didn't actually *celebrate* Christmas.

'But *you* do!' he had growled.

In a way, it frustrated him that she had steadfastly refused to be showered with the gifts which he thought were her due—but then, he didn't have a monopoly on frustration. She had discovered early on that it went hand-in-hand with the pleasures of being a mistress.

It was such an unreal existence.

So many of their meetings were conducted in secret—behind the closed doors of hotel rooms—while

128

they lost themselves in each other's arms. Sometimes they would slip out to a discreet restaurant for a meal—though always shadowed by the ever-present bodyguards.

It was easier in Paris or some of the Spanish cities—which afforded more anonymity—but being abroad only increased Sienna's sense of unreality. The certainty that this relationship could not last, and her fear of when it would end. Whether it would be less painful if it happened sooner rather than later.

It was as though what they had between them was so fragile that any kind of analysis might shatter it. And it wasn't even something she could talk to her girlfriends about—and certainly not her mother. When you had an ordinary relationship—were having those ordinary fears about where it was headed—then friendly advice was yours for the taking.

But being a mistress was an indeterminate occupation, frowned on by society in general—both his *and* hers. For it flew in the face of the family values which most people believed in, deep down.

Only in her case she was not strictly a mistress. Hashim didn't have a wife waiting at home. Instead he had a country—which was far more demanding.

She turned to watch him as he pressed a button on the wall and the heavy drapes slid silently to a close, blocking out the daylight and enclosing them in their own private world.

Hand provocatively placed on her hip, Sienna raised her eyebrows as he turned round. 'You complain that I've kept you waiting, and yet you haven't even kissed me hello yet!'

Exasperated and turned on, he pulled her into his arms and kissed her. 'Hello.'

'And hello to you, too.'

He rubbed his forehead against hers. 'How you love to make me angry, Sienna.'

'No, I don't,' she said seriously. 'It's just that you work yourself up into a complete state when I don't do exactly what you say.'

'But you never do what I say.'

'Ask me something—anything—and I will!'

He took her face between his hands and looked down at her. 'Will you kiss me again, my non-compliant and informal little mistress?'

She lifted her lips to his, winding her arms around his neck, giving a little yelp of pleasure as their mouths collided in a kiss which this time was much more than a greeting. It was a hard, hungry and frustrated kiss. She hadn't seen him in nearly a month, and he wasn't supposed to be here for another fortnight.

But he had sandwiched in an extra trip to London on the way back from the States and called her at the last minute. Sienna had decided not to play games for the sake of it and had agreed to change her diary around. And bought a new set of underwear.

In between the frantic unzipping and unbuttoning of their clothes there were fractured bursts of conversation.

'I've missed you,' he groaned.

'Good.'

He reached down and slid off first one high-heeled shoe and then the other, caressing a silk-clad ankle on the way. 'You're supposed to tell me that you missed me, too.'

'That…oh!' She shivered as he rippled his fingers up over a stocking-top and circled the satin flesh above it. 'That is what I would call fishing for a compliment.' She gulped.

His hand halted. 'So you didn't?'

'You've only been gone a month.'

'Only?' he questioned ominously.

She reached down and guided his hand back again. 'Yes, yes, yes—I've missed you. I've thought about you constantly and dreamt of this moment! Is that better?'

'Much better,' he murmured. 'If it is true.'

Oh, yes, it was true, she thought as he carried her over to the bed and put her down in the centre of it. She had missed him more than he would ever know and more than she would ever tell him. She might have been a novice when she started her affair with Hashim—but she was growing to learn the rules. And the number one rule seemed to be always keep something back.

She had recognised early on that her Sheikh was a natural hunter—and that like all hunters he enjoyed the thrill of the chase. He was never more passionate than when she didn't leap into line. It wasn't the hardest psychology in the world to work out that a man for whom the world jumped would be fascinated by someone who didn't.

And for Sienna it was less about game-playing than protecting herself. Stopping herself falling deeper in love with a man who could never reciprocate the emotion. But holding back love wasn't as easy as playing hard to get. Love was like sunlight outside the dark of a barn—there were always cracks and crevices for it to come flooding inside.

She pushed the thoughts away as he took off her dress, her bra and her panties—though he left her stockings and suspender belt on. Lying back against the cushions, she watched as he removed his clothes, peeling off his suit and shirt and skimming off his silken underwear until he was formidably and powerfully naked.

Sometimes she touched herself while he undressed, as he had taught her to—rubbing at her breasts or teasing him with the tantalising stroke of a finger between her legs. Sometimes he even liked to watch her bring herself to orgasm—but today she could see a tight tension in his muscular body, and she frowned and did not tease him.

When he came to lie beside her she noticed the dark shadows beneath his eyes and lifted a finger to touch them. 'You're tired,' she observed softly.

'Then make me untired.'

'Is there such a word as untired?'

'There is now.' He closed his eyes as she licked

with her tongue from nipple to belly and then beyond, to where he was unbearably hard. 'Ah, Sienna,' he groaned. 'Where the hell did you learn to do that?'

'You taught me, Hashim,' she murmured, before taking him slowly into her mouth. 'Remember? You taught me everything.'

Afterwards he thought that he had taught her perhaps too well... She was like a whore in the bedroom—as a woman should be. She was everything he had ever dreamed of—and more. And one day another man would benefit from his tutition—perhaps sooner than either of them had anticipated. Another man would see her head bobbing up and down on his lap, her mouth working sweet spells while she took him to paradise and back. His lips twisted as a sting of pain caught him unawares, but then fatigue wrapped him in its gritty arms and he slept.

When he awoke it was to see Sienna lying propped on one elbow watching him, her hair spilling down all over the rosy flush of her breasts, and in that hazy moment between sleep and waking he gave an instinctive smile—for this was the place in which he most liked to find himself.

She thought that he looked like a lion who had temporarily sated his huge appetite. A fleeting look of contentment before the relentless and ruthless search for sustenance once more. He drove himself, she had realized, more than most men would even be capable of doing. And, whilst he had a huge capacity for hard work and long hours, she had never seen that weary tinge to his smile before.

She touched his lips with a gentle finger. 'So, is it jet-lag?'

'Maybe.' He kissed the finger. She was so easy. So perceptive. Sometimes it was hard not to tell her the things on his mind, but he rarely gave voice to his innermost thoughts. For a ruler it was preferable to keep your own counsel, but sometimes—in the aftermath of making love to Sienna—he found himself wanting to offload his problems, as other men apparently did. He wondered what had changed, and when it had happened.

Something had crept up on him unawares. Maybe it was like the shadow on your jaw. You didn't notice it—and it wasn't until your chin was grazed with the dark rasp of stubble that you remembered it was well on its way to becoming a beard.

Sienna brushed away a lock of the dark hair which had tumbled onto his forehead. Against the white sheets his body looked so golden and erotically dark—like a rich oil painting brought into vibrant and glowing life before her eyes. 'You don't usually suffer from jet-lag,' she observed quietly.

'No.'

There was silence for a moment, and Sienna knew that she could do one of two things: she could get up and go into the plush kitchen of the hotel suite and make them both a cup of the iced jasmine tea he so loved and which she had learned to love, too. She could put on soft and soothing music and run him a deep, deep bath and then join him in it. And later they would make love again. And again. That was what a mistress would and should do.

Or she could venture onto the always precarious path of finding out just what was going on in that clever, quick mind of his. Six months ago she wouldn't have dreamed of contemplating it—but hadn't Hashim been softer of late? Didn't the enigmatic and formidable side of his nature sometimes seem less dominant, so that sometimes he seemed much more *accessible*?

'So, do you want to tell me what's wrong, or do you want me to run away and do womanly things?'

'Like what?'

'Oh, you know…tea, a bath, music.'

A smile edged the hardness away from his mouth. 'No, don't go. Stay here. You've just done the most important thing a woman can do for a man.'

There was another silence, and Sienna tried hard not to read too much into his words. Just because he had sounded uncharacteristically tender it did not mean anything. He was basically applauding her rapidly improving skills as a lover and thus his own skills as an expert tutor—that was all. Or he was being slightly more affectionate because they hadn't seen each other for a few weeks. There were any number of reasons.

But the shadows were still beneath his eyes; the weariness still outlined his mouth. She thought about what he had taught her, and about her refusal to just jump when he snapped his fingers. Hashim respected that, she knew. What he would not countenance was fear or timidity.

'Are you going to tell me what's wrong?'

He shifted position a little, so that he was lying gazing into the huge green glitter of her almond-shaped eyes. The breasts he had once been so obsessed with now seemed just a part of the beautiful whole of her, but still their pert rosiness reminded him of how she had used them, how that could never be undone—at least not for him.

'Just tired. It's nothing,' he murmured—which was true, though only part of the story. There was growing opposition in Qudamah to his Western lifestyle—a demand from some factions that he settle down and embrace completely the culture of his ancestors. There had been views expressed that his trips abroad should be curtailed, with all his energies focused on his homeland.

And didn't Sienna herself exemplify everything that the more traditional elements in his country loathed about the West? Hadn't Abdul-Aziz increasingly been hinting that the liaison was damaging his credibility? That things would blow up if some resolution were not reached? And Hashim knew what that resolution should be.

'It's nothing,' he repeated firmly.

Sienna did her best not to let her face crumple with disappointment. She had asked him and he had closed up—she could tell from the shuttering of his face. Well, that was up to him. It had been her choice to ask and his not to tell her. Asking was one thing, and perfectly acceptable. Prying was something completely different.

She took his words at face value, as he clearly wanted her to. 'So, when did you last have a holiday?'

'A holiday?' he questioned, as surprised by the choice of topic as by her sudden change of subject.

She laughed, pleased to have perplexed him. 'Yes, a holiday. That's the thing that most people do when they're tired and they want to relax.'

He screwed up his eyes. 'I don't remember,' he said.

'No recent bucket and spade job in Spain?' she teased.

'Bucket and spade job?' He frowned.

'Have you never built sandcastles, Hashim?' she questioned.

He laughed. 'Sand is not a big deal in Qudamah—not with so much of it around. We tend to escape from it rather than build our leisure time around it,' he added drily.

'I'd never thought of that.' She snuggled up to him. 'So what kind of holidays did you have when you were a child?'

He frowned. 'You don't really want to know.'

Which meant he didn't really want to tell her. But a woman could not exist on sex alone, no matter what her status. 'Oh, yes, I do!' she said firmly.

And Hashim found himself smiling as he allowed himself a rare dip into nostalgia. How long ago a childhood could seem, and yet how astonishingly clear the memories if you opened the floodgates on them. 'My male kin and I used to take our falcons up into the forests, where we trained them to kill.'

'Nice!'

Idly, he circled the pad of his finger around one of her nipples, feeling it instantly point and peak, and he felt the heavy stir of desire returning. 'There we learned to be men,' he said dreamily.

'No women?'

'Not one.'

'But what about your mother? Didn't she want to go along?'

He remembered the very first trip, being torn from his mother's arms. He had been just five years old and had cried his eyes out. How remorselessly the others had teased him! And his father had told him that the painful separation was all part of the process of learning to be a man. He could imagine what a Western psychologist would say about *that*!

'Females were not part of the endeavour,' he said thoughtfully. 'Their place was at the Palace.'

'And didn't they mind?'

He hesitated. 'My mother *did* mind, as it happens,' he admitted. 'And she made vocal her concerns. It caused a great deal of conflict between her and my father—but she was determined that the women of Qudamah should make some of the changes which women over the world were initiating at the time. Nothing like burning their bras, of course,' he added hastily.

Sienna laughed. 'Well, no.'

'But through her efforts the women of Qudamah were gradually granted small freedoms.'

'Such as?'

He shrugged. 'Oh, they were allowed to walk in the capital unaccompanied by a man—though many still prefer not to.' He saw her face. 'To you this probably means nothing—a woman who has grown up with personal freedom and takes it for granted probably cannot comprehend that in my country it was a kind of revolution.'

'She sounds like an amazing woman,' she said.

'She is.' The words *I should like you to meet her* hung unsaid on the air. For, no matter how true they were, how could he possibly utter them in the circumstances?

Sienna was quiet for a moment. She had heard the deliberate omission and she wouldn't have been human if it hadn't hurt her. What a different world he painted, and how his words emphasised the huge gulf between their cultures. If she had never understood his extreme reaction to her calendar shoot she certainly did now. If it was considered a mighty advance for a woman to go out on her own, then how must the baring of her breasts for an erotic calendar have seemed to a man of such a traditional upbringing?

But if ever she succumbed to the hopeless temptation of thinking *what if*—then all she had to do was remind herself of the insurmountable differences which had always been there and always would. No matter what they did—it was *doomed*.

And Sienna had realised something else, too—Hashim might have been bordering on the brink of love all those years ago, but his feelings—and hers—had been nothing but a violent rush of emotion which had nothing to do with their real lives. Even now nothing had really changed. Their brief time together was spent in a vacuum.

He saw the clouds which had shadowed her eyes, but he did not enquire what had caused them. He had a pretty good idea, and some things were best left unspoken. Why go out and find hurt when it waited like a shadowy figure just around the corner? Instead, he touched her cheek. 'And when did *you* last have a holiday?'

'Last year. I went to Australia to visit an old schoolfriend. She's settled down there—married an Aussie.' The spark of an idea began to form in her mind. 'Wouldn't it be lovely to have a break together, Hashim?' She looked around at the lavish yet soulless bedroom. 'Somewhere that wasn't in a hotel?'

He played along with her fantasy as she had played along with so many of his. 'And where would we go?'

Sienna put her head to one side and considered. 'I guess we'd stay in England. Travelling abroad would be too much hassle, and you travel too much anyway.

It would be somewhere you could be completely in-cognito—completely free.'

'Does such a place exist?' he mocked.

Sienna nodded. 'I know of a beautiful old con-verted farmhouse—it's right in the middle of no-where. I hired it once for a rock star's fortieth birth-day and everyone was raving on about it.'

'But where would my bodyguards stay?'

'There's a cottage in the grounds. Not too far and yet far enough…'

Her voice tailed off and he read the erotic promise in her eyes. An unbearable temptation crept over him. Something was going to have to give in his life soon, and he knew that it was going to be his relationship with Sienna. But before it did…

Couldn't he have the briefest taste of what it was like to be 'normal'? Just an ordinary man taking a holiday with a woman who excited and calmed and provoked and stimulated him in dizzying succession? Someone who was part of his past and now his pres-ent, but could never be part of his future…

'Can you arrange it?' he questioned suddenly.

Sienna blinked. 'You're serious?'

'Yes.' He did a quick calculation in his head. 'I can manage next weekend, if that fits in with your job?'

She was too excited to notice the faint sarcasm in his voice. Or to question whether two weekends on the trot was not pushing their luck.

She nodded. 'Well, yes—of course I can. If we can

get it. It's quite short notice—but it should be fine. I mean—who in their right mind wants to holiday in the English countryside in the middle of February?'

'Well, I do.'

They looked at one another and Sienna started giggling.

'So do I.'

CHAPTER ELEVEN

THERE was a huge fireplace, an ancient-looking kitchen, and a bed in the main upstairs room which looked exactly as it must have done a century before.

The bodyguards were settled in the cottage by the main gate, with a widescreen TV and the promise of a huge, no-questions-asked bonus, and Sienna and Hashim were finally on their own.

'It is like stepping back in time,' Hashim murmured, his black eyes fascinated as he glanced around him. 'And it's freezing.'

'Yes, it is.' She turned to him. 'Can you light a fire?'

His smile touched on the arrogant. 'Naturally.'

'Well, then—over to you. I'm going to make us something to eat.'

But he shook his head. If they were playing honeymoon—which he rather imagined that they were—then there was something far more pressing than food or fuel on the agenda. 'You want to eat food?' he murmured. 'Or to eat me?'

'You are outrageous!' she protested, but only half-heartedly, for his hands had slithered underneath her sweater and were making her nipples grow very hard indeed. 'We…we ought to draw the curtains,' she said breathlessly.

She went and yanked across the faded chintz and he came up behind her, skimming his hands down over her hips. 'Mmm. I am pleased to see that you are wearing a skirt.'

'Because my Sheikh does not like jeans,' she said demurely, and closed her eyes as she felt him reach beneath it to graze his fingers over her searing heat.

'You are ready,' he observed, on a slight note of surprise.

'I've been ready for hours,' she admitted, hopping and almost stumbling in her eagerness to help him take off her panties.

'So have I,' he admitted huskily.

They only made it as far as the big, old-fashioned sprung sofa, where Hashim kicked off his trousers and then pulled her down onto his lap, guiding her slowly over his aching shaft before plunging deep inside her.

'Oh!' she moaned, as he filled her completely, moving her up and down until she thought that she could bear it no longer. Almost before she could believe it to be happening she felt herself begin to dissolve.

And Hashim felt it, too—shatteringly and simultaneously—and as her body began to convulse out its pleasure so did his follow, in almost complete harmony. And in those few last seconds before the power of it temporarily obliterated consciousness their eyes met, locked and held.

'Sienna!' he gasped as she began to shudder around him, and her name seemed to be torn from his soul.

'Hashim!' she breathed brokenly, her fingers digging into the rich silk of his skin. *If only I could tell you how much I love you.*

For a while they stayed just like that, Sienna still astride him, gazing down and stroking her hand along the rugged outline of his jaw.

'What are you thinking?' he questioned softly.

That what should never have happened had done so. That the falling in love was complete. That it was too late to stop herself and protect herself. And it had happened just at the time when she suspected it was all coming to an end.

'You should never ask a woman something like that after making love to her.'

Not when she's vulnerable enough to tell you something you won't want to hear. She shivered a little as the flush of passion on her skin began to fade.

'Better get that fire going,' she said lightly, and climbed off him.

Escaping into the kitchen while he built the fire, she made soup from organic vegetables and served it with chunky wholemeal bread, and cheese which had come straight from the nearby farm. They quenched their thirst with elderflower water and then drank scented tea, sitting on a furry rug in front of the gradually roaring fire.

'Do you like that?' she asked.

'Perfect,' he said, but there was a sudden heaviness in his heart.

They watched a video of Sienna's favourite film— an old musical which soon had her sniffing like a hay-fever sufferer.

'You're crying!' he accused.

'No, I'm not—it's just a corny old film,' she said crossly.

'Come here,' he said.

And, even though it made her heart ache, she went.

They spent their time doing simple things. Wrapping up warm before walking over the crunchy morning frost which hardly had time to melt before a setting crimson sun turned the fields into fire every afternoon.

His bodyguards seemed quite content to be doing their own thing, and there wasn't a peep out of his phone. Once they even ventured into the small local pub for lunch, and if anyone wondered why there was a big, dark car sitting gleaming in the car park, no-body bothered asking.

The real world seemed such a long way away, and part of Sienna fervently wished it could stay that way. If it weren't for his position they could live a life like this all the time. He was right—she *had* always taken her freedom for granted—and never had she cher-ished it more than during this weekend.

She watched him relax. Saw the dark shadows melt away from beneath his eyes and the tiny, fan-like creases at the corners of his black eyes ironed out as if by magic.

And for Hashim it was a provocative glimpse of a life he could never really know. He had not felt as unencumbered as this since those long-ago days of falconing in the mountains of Qudamah.

'Ah, Sienna,' he said on their last morning, when they sat eating pancakes for breakfast. 'Don't you wish that life could always be this simple?'

She smiled, knowing full well that there was no point in coming out with a stock phrase like: It *could* be like this. Because it couldn't.

She put the lid back on the golden syrup. 'Do you want to listen to the radio?'

Hashim frowned. 'What for?'

'Well, Qudamah seems to have been in the news a lot lately.'

Funny how you could look for an opportunity to say something and then find, when it came, that you wished you didn't have to. He gazed down at the clear amber of the delicate tea. 'There is going to be an election very soon—and elections always demand a lot of my time.' He looked at her. 'I am going to have to fly back tomorrow.'

Sienna nodded. 'I know you are.'

He drew in a deep breath. 'And I'm not sure when I'll be back.'

She felt the tendril of long-held fear finally wrapping itself around her heart. 'I know that, too.' Don't make him have to say it. Accept what is inevitable.

Make it easy on yourself. 'Hashim, it's okay. You don't have to say it. I know it's over.'

He didn't deny it, but the dark eyes which he lifted to her face were troubled. 'I do not wish this, Sienna—but increasingly I recognise that my place is in my homeland, not here.' He gave a restless little movement of his shoulders. 'There are obligations I now need to fulfil. And I don't want to tie you down to a relationship which can never go anywhere. Or to make you a promise I am unable to keep. If this fades into failed intentions and meetings which never happen then all that we will have left to remember is bitterness.' His voice grew hard. 'And I cannot face that. Not for a second time. Not when...'

The words were there in his mouth, just begging to be said. But words could be dishonest—even if you meant them. They could open up all kinds of unrealistic expectations. If he tried to explain how much she had come to mean to him then would that not tie her to him anyway—no matter how much he tried not to let it? What if she started seeing them as star-crossed lovers instead of just getting on with her life?

She saw the discomfiture on his face and jumped in to rescue the situation—or rather to rescue herself. She had had more with him than any woman could have hoped to have, and she would ensure that he remembered her with dignity.

'It's been wonderful. Gorgeous. It was a fine affair,' she said softly. 'But now it's over.'

His eyes narrowed. He had expected...what? That

she might at least shed a tear for him! Or that her face might indicate some feelings of dejection! His pride was hurt, yet his pain came from deeper feelings than pride. He pushed them away with an instinct borne out of self-protection. 'You seem almost pleased about it,' he observed coolly.

'Oh, Hashim,' she said impatiently. 'Of course I'm not *pleased* about it—but I recognise that it has to be, so what's the alternative?'

Women had begged him before—many times. They had shed tears and clung to him. Hadn't there been a selfish side which had thought that Sienna might do the same? For if she behaved like all the others, then wouldn't that make it easier for him to walk away from her without another thought?

But there had never been another relationship like this one, he recognised. Nor ever would be again. His destiny would not allow it—for his flings and his freedom must now be curtailed. The luxurious but weighty doors of his royal prison were waiting to clang shut on him, and if he took himself down the path of useless and indulgent analysis then what good would it do him? Or her?

'Come here,' he said simply, and opened his arms.

Sienna didn't need to be told that this was the last time. It was written in his eyes and spoken in every lingering kiss and caress. His hands and his fingers seemed as though they were discovering her for the first time, and yet bidding her farewell as they did so.

'Oh, Hashim,' she said, in a choked kind of voice.

'Let us lie once more in that old bed,' he whispered, and she nodded.

He carried her up the rickety staircase towards the room they had shared, bending his head so as not to knock it on one of the dark beams, and put her down as carefully as if she had been a cherished and delicate piece of filagree.

Their undressing was slow and silent, and as she sank back into feather pillows his dark body moved over hers. She thought about how many couples had lain in this bed, like this. How many children had been conceived—maybe even born here? Ghostly generations of long-ago lovers joined them—wordlessly entering the indefinable space between past and present. For at what point did the present become the past?

Their climax would bring an end to it all, and the sex would become just a memory. As would the rest. She trembled as Hashim thrust into her with a hunger and a poignancy which made hot salt tears slide from beneath her eyelids.

'Ah, Sienna. Don't cry,' he said afterwards, wiping the tracks away with his finger.

They lay there for a while without sleeping, and then Sienna stirred. Be the first to make a move, she told herself. Don't put yourself in the position of being the deserted one.

'I'd better go and pack up the kitchen.'

He tightened his hold on her waist. 'I can have one of the guards come over and do it.'

But she shook her head and prised his fingers away as if she was removing a clam from the side of a rock. 'No, Hashim—that will defeat the object of our ordinary weekend. I'll go and chuck all the leftover food away—you can wash the dishes.'

He was torn between outrage and humour. 'Yes, Sienna,' he murmured, but his heart was heavy.

They were quiet in the car on the drive back, even though the driver was firmly locked away behind soundproof glass. It had begun to rain, and through the tinted windows she could see droplets battering against the glass, as if the heavens themselves were sobbing.

It was only when they were approaching South Kensington that he laid one dark hand on hers.

'You will come back to the hotel with me?'

'No.'

He asked for no explanation; but then he had known what her answer would be. 'Sienna?'

She turned her head back to face him and her green eyes were sombre, but there was a soft dignity about her which took his breath away. He thought about how often in the past he had been able to persuade her to do something against her will just by the sheer power of the sexual chemistry which existed between them, but he recognised now that nothing he could do would change her mind. Not this time.

Something had changed. In her. In him. In them both. For not only would she refuse to succumb to him, he would no longer make an attempt to have her bend to his will. Somewhere along the way they had become equals, and for Hashim it was a bittersweet awakening. An awareness that it had come at the wrong time—but could it have ever been the right time?

Not with Sienna, no.

He bent down to the Qudamah-crested dispatch box which accompanied him everywhere and pulled out a slim leather box. He held it out towards her but she shook her head, the thick dark hair flying like a storm.

'No, Hashim!' She would not be paid off—have him bid her farewell with the expensive baubles she had previously refused to accept. 'Whatever it is, I don't want it. I don't want your diamonds or your emeralds, thank you very much! I told you a long time ago that I could not and would not be bought, and I meant it!'

He laughed softly. 'I know you did, my fiery Sienna,' he murmured. 'And I think that your expectations of costly gems are a little wide of the mark.' He put the box in her hand and closed her fingers around it, his black eyes washing over her. 'Please. Open it.'

Something in his manner made her obey him, her fingers trembling as she flicked open the catch to see a necklace lying against indigo velvet. But it was no ordinary necklace. The chain was as fine as a sliver of light and in the centre of it lay a tiny golden bird.

'H-Hashim?' she questioned shakily.

'Here.' He lifted it from the box and placed it into

the centre of her palm, where the fine chain lay coiled like an elegant snake, the small charm gleaming like the sun.

'What is it?'

'It is an eagle—a golden eagle. She flies on the flag of Qudamah and is the symbol of my country—for she represents freedom and power. This is the only time you will ever see her chained.'

Like him. The thought flew unbidden into her mind. Freedom and power and never to be chained. She studied it intently, focusing fiercely on the workmanship because at least that kept the tears at bay.

'It's…beautiful.'

'Shall I put it on for you?'

Sienna nodded, unable to speak for fear that she would blurt out words which could never be taken back. Words of love which would mortify him and make their parting even more painful.

He slid his hands around her neck, wanting so much to linger there—to raise the heavy weight of her hair so that he could kiss the soft nape and then turn her head to take her lips, coaxing their luscious warmth into eager response.

'I thought you were going to put it on?'

Her faintly bemused voice disrupted his troubled thoughts. 'So I was.' He clipped it in place. 'There.'

For a moment their eyes met, and the pain which smote at her heart made her feel dizzy and weak. Turning her head to look out of the window with the desperation of a drowning woman struggling towards the surface for light and air, Sienna saw with relief that they were at the end of her road.

'Well, here we are! Thank you, Hashim.' She leaned forward. The touch of her mouth against his was fleeting and the pain increased. 'Take very good care.'

He touched her fingertips to his lips and as she pushed open the car door said something in his native tongue to the driver, who got out and removed her one small bag from the boot.

The tinted window slid silently down and all she could see were glittering black eyes—the only thing which seemed truly alive in the tight mask of his face. She flashed him a smile, and then she turned away.

Somehow she made it inside without crying, but once there the tears began to pour down her cheeks without stopping. Kat was away and she was glad, because it gave her time to get over the worst, to recover on her own like a wounded animal.

There was no one to tell her to eat. No one to question why she couldn't sleep. No one to tell her that it was wrong to shed her tears and that there were plenty more fish in the sea. Maybe there were—but none like Hashim.

By the third day she had begun to feel a little better. Her heart was aching, but she knew that Hashim would hate it if she became one of those women who let their whole lives collapse around them because a love affair hadn't worked out.

She bathed and washed her hair, and was just pull-

ing on a big black sweater which virtually came down
to her knees when the doorbell rang. She wondered
if it was Kat back, having forgotten her keys.

She opened the door, completely unprepared to see
the batallion of photographers who were jostling for
position, jerking back in alarm as the multiple flash
from their array of cameras temporarily blinded her.
Someone thrust a phallic-looking microphone under
her chin.

'Miss Baker!' called a TV-trained voice. 'Sienna!
Is the Sheikh of Qudamah aware that you used to be
a topless model?'

CHAPTER TWELVE

THE startled doorstep photo made the first edition and the second—only it ran alongside a much larger photo. There was her sand-sprinkled and sultry image plastered over all the tabloids.

Even the serious broadsheets gave it house-room—justifying their usual no-breasts policy with weighty pieces on the changing morals of the Middle East. And a censored version of it was beamed into homes the length and breadth of the country as an add-on to an otherwise boring television news show.

'And finally, the Sheikh of the fiercely traditional State of Qudamah is rumoured to be dating a British glamour model. Stunning brunette Sienna Baker...'

Female leader-writers took up the case in their mid-week columns, asking righteously: *What would you do if* your *son brought a topless model home?*

Trapped inside the house, unable to go out without fear of being accosted, Sienna was sitting in the kitchen at the back of the house with the blinds drawn down when Kat came in and handed her the telephone with a look which said everything.

She pressed the phone to her ear. She wasn't aware she'd actually said anything, but she must have made some sort of sound because she heard his deep and silky voice.

'Sienna?'

She bit her lip. Closed her eyes. She wouldn't cry. She *wouldn't*. But the sound of his dear voice was almost more than she could bear. 'Yes, it's me.'

'Are you all right?'

'Ask me another. How about you?'

He ignored that. 'The press are still there?'

'Well, not so many of them. I think they got fed up because I refused to say anything.'

'Good. If you feed a story it only grows.'

'Oh, Hashim—how the hell did they get hold of it? How did they even find out about it?'

Hashim's mouth tightened into a grim and forbidding line. He suspected that someone in Qudamah must have informed the foreign press about a juicy piece of gossip in their Ruler's life. In the power-play that was his life Sienna's past had become a weapon. And he must protect her from the fall-out.

'These things have a habit of getting out,' he said slowly. 'That's the way the world works.'

He sounded almost weary, as if he had seen sides of the world she did not know—and of course he had. She couldn't imagine what it must be like to be a sheikh, but she was fairly sure that it would be very hard to trust people's motives towards you. 'Yes,' said quietly. 'I imagine so.'

The silence between them seemed huge. 'I am sending some people to look after you, Sienna. If I come myself it will only add fire to the story. Is there somewhere you can go?'

She was suddenly and acutely aware that this conversation was a purely practical one, and not personal at all. He didn't want to talk—not *really* talk—and besides, what was there left to say? This was damage limitation time.

She bit her lip. Where did she always turn when she wanted an escape route? Who would always accept her with open arms and no questions asked? Who wanted the best for her no matter what. 'My mother wants me to go to her.'

'Then go. Let me arrange it.'

'Hashim—you don't seem to understand!' she said frustratedly. 'I have existing contracts to fulfil. And the phone hasn't stopped ringing with work requests—I've never been so popular. I think it's the curiosity factor,' she added acidly. 'Having your party planned by a so-called "Glamour Model." But some of the calls are from journalists pretending to be clients. I'm certain of it.'

He felt the dark dagger of self-contempt as he remembered that he too had done just that. Pretended. Masqueraded. Finally got his way by seducing her— and now what had happened? Had she ever deserved this because of some rash youthful decision made with all the best intentions? 'I'm sorry,' he said quietly.

She shook her head as if he was in the room, hating to hear his apology—so stilted and formal—like one stranger talking to another. 'It isn't your fault, it's mine. I should never have done it in the first place—I just didn't realise it was going to come back and haunt me in such a big way.'

'But that is down to me. To your relationship with me.'

The most precious thing in her life. *Past tense*, she reminded herself. She sighed, wanting to lean on him yet knowing she shouldn't. And anyway, she couldn't—not really. He was at his Palace, thousands of miles away, and she was holed up in her tiny terraced house in Kennington. There were no arms to hold her, no heart to beat next to hers, no hand to stroke her hair.

'Can you get someone else to honour your existing contracts and ignore all the others?' he demanded.

'And who is going to pay my mortgage in the meantime?'

There was a moment's silence, and Hashim chose his words with fastidious care, knowing that he trod on very sensitive ground here. 'That is simple. You must let me help you, Sienna.'

She froze. 'What do you mean—*help* me?'

He could hear the bristly defensiveness which spiked her voice and, while he silently applauded her fierce pride, he knew that it would not and could not serve her well—not in circumstances such as these. 'Just hear me out without interruption. That is all I ask of you. Please, Sienna, it is vital,' he said softly.

'If I took care of your mortgage for you—would that not free you up to get away for a while?'

'I'm not letting you pay for me!' Her voice lowered. 'You must be able to see why I stand so firm on this issue.'

For a moment he had to control the instinctive lash of his tongue. Stubborn woman! Could she not see that he was only trying to help her?

Drawing on diplomatic reserves he had never had to call on before, he tried again. 'Sienna,' he said patiently. 'I admire your independence and your spirit, but this is not some showering of expensive baubles on a mistress—this is me trying to help you get out of a bad situation which is mostly of my doing. To make some kind of amends. Will you not let me do that for you? Would not all that has grown between us be completely worthless if you will not allow me to behave as any true friend would towards another?'

There was silence. How appalled he would be if he knew that her thoughts were not of indignation that he was trying to buy her out of something but instead had fixed upon a word which resonated cruelly round and round in her head. Who would ever have thought that the acknowledgement that he was her *friend* could have unwittingly caused so much heartache?

'Will you let me?' he said.

What choice did she have? To brazen it out in London, aware of the eyes which followed her? The curious glances? Women looking down their noses at her and men looking…? Well, she didn't even want to go *there*.

'In a few weeks all the fuss will have died down,' he continued smoothly. 'The news will have moved on. That's what happens.'

And, stupidly, that upset her even more—for once it had died down it really would be over. And wasn't there a part of her—ever while loathing all this fuss and attention—that was secretly glad because it had brought Hashim back into her life when she'd thought that he had gone for good?

'All right. I'll go to my mother's,' she said.

At the other end of the phone, Hashim closed his eyes with relief. Outside his private study the court was in uproar, and Abdul-Aziz was prowling round the palace like a starving tom-cat, but Hashim didn't care. She was safe. She would be safe—he had the resources to protect her.

'I will have a car sent immediately,' he said, glad now that he could rely on action, for this was something he always felt comfortable with. 'And body-guards will be placed at the entrance to your mother's home.'

She opened her mouth to say that he didn't even know where her mother lived, but then shut it again. Of course he did. He knew everything—and if he didn't he could get someone to find out for him. Hashim could get anything he pleased.

'Thank you, Hashim,' she said.

'Don't thank me,' he said fiercely. 'Just stay strong.

Can you do that?' He nearly said *for me*—except that in the circumstances he knew he had no right to ask.

She allowed herself to picture him, and knew she would not crumble. 'As an ox,' she said huskily.

Hashim closed his eyes. 'Or an eagle,' he whispered.

'Goodbye,' she whispered back, and put the phone down before she began to cry. Because although the structure of her life had been torn apart it didn't even register on the pain-scale.

Nothing touched her and nothing could—other than the heartbreak of not being with the man she loved.

CHAPTER THIRTEEN

'DARLING, calm down, sit down, and drink that cup of tea before it gets cold!'

Sienna sniffed and smiled, and took a sip of the fragrant Earl Grey. How some things never changed!

'That's better,' said her mother approvingly, brushing some mud from the leg of her jodhpurs and dunking a digestive biscuit into her own tea.

'Mum, I'm so sorry—'

'Oh, fiddlesticks!' said her mother cheerfully. 'It's done my reputation no end of good locally—I'll never be asked to judge the prize cauliflower section at the village show again!' She sighed. 'I was getting rather bored with it, if the truth were known.'

'No, I'm serious.'

'And so am I, Sienna,' said her mother firmly. 'In my opinion you look rather lovely in those photos— and if you compare them to some of the nudes in our national galleries, why, they're positively tame! It's all a question of perception. I admit that when you first did it I was angry—but not for long. How could I be when the money you earned from it meant that I could have my operation? I thanked you then from the bottom of my heart and I still do.' She finished her biscuit and edged her fingers towards another.

'Better not. Now, what I really want to know is— what's this young sheikh of yours really like?'

This, in a way, was even harder than explaining that for the time being there were two hefty body-guards stationed at the front gate.

'He's not young, Mum,' said Sienna. 'He's thirty-five.'

'Oh, positively ancient!'

'And he isn't…' No, this, *this* was the hardest part. 'He isn't mine. Not any more. He never was, really.' She put her cup down and stared candidly at her mother. 'I just had a relationship with him,' she said defiantly.

'Well, thank heavens for that!' murmured her mother. 'I was beginning to wonder when you'd find yourself a boyfriend.'

'*Mum!*'

'Well, you never seemed really interested.'

There was a question in her mother's eyes, and for the first time in her life Sienna spoke to her not as a mother but as another woman. 'I went out with Hashim years ago—a couple of years after I did the photos, actually,' she said quietly. 'And he was a pretty hard act to follow.'

Her mother replied in kind. 'I'm not surprised,' she said softly. 'He looks absolutely gorgeous.'

'Well, he is—but he just happens to be a sheikh and there's no future in it. He comes from a fiercely traditional country and anyway—he doesn't love me.'

'Are you sure he doesn't?'

'Of course I'm sure!'

'He didn't have to go to all the trouble of arranging protection for you, did he? Or deliver that gorgeous hamper and massive bouquet of flowers for me.' She stared happily at the massed display of blooms which were currently making the sitting room look like a florist's shop.

How could her mother ever begin to understand that for a man of Hashim's untold wealth such gestures were mere drops in a limitless ocean? 'He feels guilty,' she said flatly. 'This would never have erupted if it hadn't been for his position. That's all.'

'Have it your own way, darling—if you want to be stubborn, then I can't stop you. Now.' Her mother beamed at her. 'Do you want to see if you can fit into your old jodhpurs and give me a hand in the stables? A bit of good old-fashioned fresh air and exercise is just what the doctor ordered. Then later I've asked Kirsty over for tea. Cara is *three* now. Can you believe it?' She smiled. 'It only seems a minute ago since you and Kirsty were toddling off to nursery together at the same age.'

Sienna smiled too, because the thought of seeing her old friend was strangely comforting. It was all too easy to let friendships slip—though time and distance played their part. Sometimes she wondered what would have happened if she'd taken Kirsty's path in life—stayed around and married a local farmer, then started producing a brood of children. Would that have guaranteed her personal happiness?

It wasn't that easy, she decided, as she struggled into her old riding clothes. It wasn't the place you chose or the job you ended up doing—it was all to do with the man you ended up falling in love with and the path that took you on.

And she had just had the misfortune to fall for someone who wasn't taking her anywhere.

But her mother was right—the fresh air and exercise *did* work their own kind of magic. Physically, at least. The aching in her heart needed the kind of remedy which never provided instant healing. It needed time.

She got up at first light and went down to the stables. She did all the mucky stuff and some of the fun stuff too—for there was nothing more rewarding than watching fearful children grow in confidence as they began to master the skill of riding. Life suddenly seemed very simple—and her busy London existence like something which had happened in a past life.

She had thought she would miss the networking and the hectic pace of making people's party dreams come true, but she didn't. She just wished that she had the power to fulfil her own personal dreams, but she didn't. Besides, you shouldn't rely on a man to make you happy, she told herself. Everyone knew that.

And Cara was a delight—homing in on Sienna straight away, her eyes wide when it was explained that Mummy and Sienna had been just the same age as her once upon a time!

She had a habit of sticking her little tongue out of the corner of her mouth when she was thinking.

'Can I play with Sienna, Mummy?' she asked one day.

Kirsty shot her a glance. 'Oh, Sienna's far too busy—'

'No,' said Sienna firmly. 'No, I'm not, and I want Cara to come and play. We could make cupcakes one day if you like?'

'With chocolate chips?'

'Yes, darling—I *love* chocolate chips—and we can use those little silver balls too, if you're very good.'

At least there was plenty to keep her occupied—leaving little time for wafting around the house missing her lover. But probably the hardest part of all was accepting that it really *was* over. Because in a way things seemed just the same. Their feelings hadn't changed and they normally had weeks in between seeing one another anyway.

If only they could have rowed—or stopped speaking entirely—then she might have found it easier to believe that it was over. Easier? Well, maybe not. That was asking too much. What's it going to take to forget him? she asked herself. An announcement that he's going to marry someone else, as one day you know he will?

Sienna was making more cakes with Cara one afternoon when her mother came rushing into the kitchen.

'One of the bodyguards has just knocked!' she babbled excitedly. 'There is a visitor on the way to see you!'

Sienna's heart missed a beat. She held the wooden spoon in the air as if it was a magic wand—and, oh, how she wished it was. She would wave it, and…

'Is it Hashim?' she breathed.

'Oh, darling, no—I'm afraid it isn't. It's a man called…' Her mother frowned as she concentrated on saying his name correctly. 'Abdul-Aziz.'

Sienna hoped her face did not betray her disappointment. 'Then you'd better show him in,' she said courteously.

Abdul-Aziz swept into her mother's low-beamed kitchen as if he owned the place. It had been a long time since Sienna had seen him, and in his way he was no less formidable—his eyes still looked like raisins which had been created in the Arctic and his mouth was set in such a way as to show he meant business.

But some of the hardness of his features had dissolved, and Sienna found herself wondering if that was down to the calming effects of married life. Or was she in danger of attributing her own wistfulness to other people?

Five years ago she had been utterly intimidated by him, but a lot had changed since then. For a start she had grown up—but, more importantly, she had shared something very special with Hashim. He had given her confidence and belief in herself as a woman—and nothing could take that away from her.

Abdul-Aziz's eyes narrowed as he saw her, and Sienna was aware that she could not have looked worse—old clothes, no make-up, covered in cake mix, with a tiny girl clinging onto her apron and demanding to know, 'Who's that cross man?'

'It's someone I know,' she whispered, and looked at her mother. 'Would you mind finishing the cakes with Cara while I take my visitor into the sitting room?'

Cara snuffled a bit, and her mother looked disappointed that she wasn't going to get a ringside seat to hear whatever the 'cross man' had to say, but Sienna felt strangely serene as she led Abdul-Aziz across the hall and into the chintzy room. The worst had already happened and Hashim was not with her. Nothing could touch her now.

She looked across the room at him, and she'd have been lying if she hadn't admitted deriving a little pleasure from the look of perplexity on Abdul-Aziz's face. Had he been expecting her to be lolling around in some over-the-top boudoir, wearing nothing but a pair of racy stockings and suspenders?

'Would you like tea, Mr Aziz?' she asked politely. 'I'm not quite sure how to address you.'

'You can call me Abdul,' he said grudgingly. 'And, no, I don't want tea. Thank you,' he added, as if he had just remembered something.

Like his manners, thought Sienna wryly—for he gave the distinct impression of a man who was struggling to contain himself.

'What can I do for you?' she murmured.

'That child.' He cocked his head in the direction of the door. 'She is your child?'

Sienna started to say of course not—but there was no 'of course' about it—not in his eyes. If she suddenly produced a spellbook and started chanting incantations she didn't think he'd bat an eyelid.

'No,' she answered quietly. 'She is the child of my schoolfriend.'

Now he was staring at the tiny golden eagle which dangled around her slender neck and which she never took off.

'And my Sheikh gave you this?' he demanded.

'I suspect you already know the answer to that one. Yes. He did.'

He tossed his head back like a stallion about to rear up. 'You must renounce him!' he declared dramatically. 'Unequivocally and immediately!'

Sienna stared at him. 'I beg your pardon?'

'You have not heard?' he demanded.

'I haven't got a clue what you're talking about.'

'He has not told you?'

This hurt. 'No.'

'Sheikh Hashim is planning to go on State television and make an announcement!'

'What kind of announcement?'

Abdul-Aziz's mouth tightened. 'He refuses to say…stubborn boy!…but I know in my heart what it will be.'

'You do? You're some kind of mind-reader, are you?'

'He is going to declare his love for you!' he hissed.

Sienna's laugh was genuine, but it was tinged with sadness. 'You'd never make money out of clairvoyancy, Abdul,' she said. 'It's over between me and Hashim—he's not in love with me.'

'He isn't?' His suspicious look cleared and was replaced by an expression of bright hope. 'You are certain of this?'

'Yes.'

'Then what is he plotting?' questioned Abdul-Aziz to himself thoughtfully.

'Don't you think you should come right out and ask him yourself?'

'I have. He would tell me nothing.'

'Then it's very *disloyal* of you to come sneaking over here behind his back, trying to find out things he obviously doesn't wish to tell you.'

He glared at her. 'While your loyalty to the Sheikh is admirable, I am not used to being spoken to in such a way, Miss Baker. Especially by a woman.'

'How come I'm not surprised?' Sienna murmured.

'Will you try to stop him?' he persisted.

'I wouldn't dream of it,' said Sienna calmly. 'And even if I wanted to, I couldn't. He is a man in charge of his own destiny.' She stared at him. 'As we all are.'

An odd, calculating light came into Abdul-Aziz's

strange, cold eyes. 'Yes, indeed we are,' he said. 'You are a strong woman, Miss Baker.'

Was she? At that moment she felt a mixture of strength and weakness, but her strength came from her unwavering love for Hashim. And so too, in a way, did her weakness. 'Thank you, Abdul.'

The cold eyes narrowed. Had they softened fractionally, or had she just imagined it? 'You have a message for him?'

Tell him I love him. Tell him I can't stop thinking about him. Tell him that if I really did have magical powers then I would use them all to protect and guard him from evil for the rest of his life.

'Just tell him Sienna says hello.'

'Hello?' he echoed faintly, and then nodded, giving a deep bow before leaving the room.

Sienna felt as if she was operating on some kind of autopilot as she continued with the ritual of decorating cupcakes with Cara. She realised that she was waiting for something, but was not quite sure how she knew—or what, indeed, she was waiting for.

But then her mobile phone rang, and she knew who it would be even before she saw 'Hashim' flashing on the screen. Her heart started beating fit to burst.

'Sienna?'

'Abdul has been to see me,' she blurted out.

'I know he has.'

'You didn't think to warn me?'

'Did you need me to?' he questioned coolly.

'He says you're going to broadcast to the nation.'

'Indeed I am.'

'He wanted me to try and stop you.'

'And are you?'

Sienna laughed. 'It would be like trying to stop the sun from rising if you had your heart set on something.'

Oh, how true her words. Hashim smiled. 'Good,' he murmured. 'I am glad that we understand one another.'

'Hashim…' Sienna hesitated. 'You aren't going to do anything *foolish*, are you?'

Well, that was all down to which way you looked at it. But that was not the answer she needed to hear right now. 'No, Sienna.' His voice sounded strangely controlled, but there was a hint of mockery underpinning it. 'If I send a jet for you then will you fly out to Qudamah?'

Her world spun. A jet? To Qudamah? 'Why?' she breathed.

There was a pause. 'My mother wishes to meet you.'

CHAPTER FOURTEEN

SIENNA'S first sight of Hashim's palace was against a backdrop of stars—like a distant castle in a fairy tale—and she touched her fingers to her lips in disbelief and a growing sense of wonder. As if this could not be happening. Not now, and not to her.

But it was.

She was summoned to a room all golden and sapphire-blue, but she was scarcely aware of the lavish and opulent décor for only one figure dominated her line of vision. As he always did. Tall and lean and proud—the beautiful-ugly face tense. His flowing white robes made him look like a stranger, but his eyes were oh-so-familiar. Burning into her like smouldering coals that heated her skin and warmed her heart.

He nodded when he saw her, as if she had just confirmed something in his mind, but Sienna was terribly aware of protocol and of the presence of his servants—even though they had their eyes averted. And so she simply nodded back—as if they were two commuters who passed each other on the train platform every morning.

With a curt, clipped statement in his native tongue he dismissed the servants, and after the room was emptied he stood staring at her for long, countless seconds.

'Now come to me,' he commanded.

She went like a woman willingly sleepwalking. Towards him. Summoned by her Sheikh. Into his arms. The place where she most wanted to be.

There was no kiss, just a fierce embrace which seemed to force all the breath out of her lungs. He clasped her against him and pressed his face to her scented hair. His words were muffled.

'You know that I love you, don't you, Sienna?'

Sienna pulled away and stared up at him, her eyes blinking rapidly, certain that she must have misheard him. 'Hashim?'

'Can't you feel it in the beating of my heart?' He placed her palm over his chest, where the rapid thundering of his life-blood made her eyes widen in dawning realisation. 'It is no good, Sienna—for I have tried. By the mountains and the rivers, I have tried! I have attempted the impossible and have failed. To forget you. To imagine life without you. And I cannot. *I will not.*'

'But *love*?' she whispered.

'Yes, love.' He smiled. 'More powerful than the eagle—a force as powerful as life itself—can you not feel it gathering strength, Sienna—as the bird itself does just before flight?'

He waited.

But Sienna felt tongue-tied and strangely humble—and scared too, in these imposing surroundings. A declaration she had longed for and never thought to hear—and now that it had been made she was shaken. It was as if dust had turned to gold before her eyes, and she was terrified that it would change back to dust again.

Yet he was right. She could feel the strength emanating from him—waves of it washing over her barely believing self. She touched her fingertips to the charm at her neck, as if it could give her the courage to say the words to him. Words she had once had tossed back in her face. Words she had grown inside her for so long, all the while trying to deny them.

'I love you too,' Hashim,' she said brokenly. 'I have done right from the very start, and it never changed—never dimmed—even when I prayed that it would.' She stared into the black eyes which had softened now. 'But you knew that, didn't you? You could read it in my eyes.'

'Yes.'

'And it doesn't actually *change* anything, does it? Not practically. You're still a sheikh and I'm still a—'

'No!' He cut her words off with brutal force. 'Do not say it! You are more and then much more—but you are not that! A youthful folly does not define a person for the rest of their lives!'

'But that is how I will be perceived.'

'And that,' he said grimly, '*that* is why I am making the broadcast. They are setting up cameras in the small Throne Room.' He tilted his head—handsome and irresistible. 'Will you come in with me?'

'What are you going to say?'

'Will you come in with me?' he repeated inexorably.

'Yes.'

'And I must ask you something else, Sienna—and this is important. The life you live in England is incompatible with mine. My home is here. My place is here—increasingly more so. Could you renounce much of the freedom you enjoy in England? Is your love for me strong enough to embrace my life here? For if you decide to, you must do so without reservation. There can be no trial period, no waiting to see whether or not you can adapt. It must be a leap of faith and nothing less. You must decide whether your love for me is strong enough to commit to me, and to commit for the rest of your life. When you marry me,' he finished deliberately, his gaze fixed firmly on her face.

'*Marry* you?' she echoed, genuinely shocked.

Wry amusement vied with outrage in his black eyes. 'You think that I would contemplate any alternative to marriage?' he demanded. 'That I should not want you as my wife? Assuming,' he added arrogantly, 'that you wish to be my wife? But if you do then you will be taking on more than most women do, and you must be certain in your heart that your destiny is beside me.'

Sienna licked her lips. She thought of the eagle which hung around her neck—powerful and fearless—the symbol of his country. This strange land with a tongue that was foreign to her. A place so very different from all that she had known—and yet it contained the only thing which was important to her.

Hashim.

Was she fearless enough in her love to grasp it tightly and never let it go? To make her vows to him and mean them? Never to leave his side? To promise to be true, no matter what life threw in their path? But wasn't that what *all* marriages were supposed to mean?

'Oh, yes,' she whispered. 'Yes, yes, and a million times yes.' There was an odd kind of lump in her throat. 'But will your people accept me?'

'If they want me as their Ruler, then they will have to.'

'Do you want to take that chance?'

'I can't not,' he said simply. But he knew that he could never rule—nor would be fit to rule—if he allowed his people to prevent him from seizing his heart's desire. Because any man who turned away from one of life's greatest mysteries could never be a complete man.

'But...' Sienna bit her lip, not wanting to destroy the beautiful magic his words of love had created, but knowing that she must not hide behind her fears, must face them head-on—even if expressing them might put paid to all her future happiness.

'But what, my beautiful Sienna?' he prompted softly as he saw the hurt and the pain in her eyes.

'The photos.' It came out in a bitter sigh. 'What if

your people see that calendar—how on earth would they ever accept me then?'

'They shall not see it,' he breathed. 'Not now and not ever.'

He sounded so certain that she stared up at him in bewilderment. 'How can you be so sure?'

'Because I have bought up all the rights to those photos—they are now exclusively mine. No newspaper will ever publish them, the calendar shall never be reprinted, and the negatives have been destroyed. I have even made sure that they will never appear on the infernal internet,' he finished grimly.

She opened her mouth to ask how, but then changed her mind. When you were as rich and as powerful and as determined as Hashim, then Sienna supposed anything was possible. Instead, she gave a rather wobbly smile, needing something more than words or reassurance now. Something which she had missed so unbearably. She was aching to have him touch her again. 'Won't you please kiss me?' she whispered.

He felt a strange kick to his heart as he bent his face to hers. Was it a kind of weakness for a man to be so in thrall to one woman? 'You wish your Sheikh to go before the cameras in a state of arousal?' he murmured.

'Oh, Hashim—I never thought of that! I've got so much to learn. Maybe we'd better not...'

He gave a low, rumbling laugh. 'And you think that I have not been aroused since the moment you first

walked in, my love? That I can look at you without
wanting you? Then, yes, you still have much to learn!
Now, come here.'

It was a brief kiss, fuelled by a sense of coming
home rather than passion—though that was bubbling
away beneath the surface as his lips brushed over
hers.

'Now,' he said firmly, and, bending down, rang a
small golden bell.

A stream of people began to appear. Men in flowing robes who bowed briefly to her and then deeper
still to Hashim. And then they were walking along
cool marble corridors towards the 'small' Throne
Room—which seemed pretty vast to Sienna, but there
again she hadn't had much experience of them.

She had been in TV studios before, but never when
everyone had been behaving with such genuine deference towards the interviewee.

Hashim settled her in a chair at the back of the
room and she watched while the camera lights lit up
his face like the brightest sunshine. And then the red
light flashed and the cameras began to roll, and suddenly he was speaking live to the nation.

She watched on the screen, so that she could read
the English subtitles, and much of it she missed, because her heart was beating so fast with nerves and
excitement and protectiveness.

But key phrases would stay in her mind and her
heart for ever.

'I have been charged with the running of our coun-

try.' His face grew very serious at this point. *'An awesome responsibility which I have always embraced and cherished. But your Ruler must be allowed to fulfil his own personal destiny in order to best discharge his duties to his homeland.'*

He sent her the briefest of looks before continuing. *'In Qudamah, your Sheikh is permitted by law to have a harem of up to sixty women.'*

Sienna sat bolt upright. She hadn't known *that*!

'But I do not wish to have sixty women. I wish for only one, for I believe in monogamy.'

There was an unmistakable ripple in the room—as if he had just come out and declared that he had converted to cannibalism!

Now his eyes were on her, and they were very steady.

'For I have found my very own houri, and I intend to make her my wife.'

Later, Sienna would discover the significance of that particular word. A houri was a beautiful young woman but—far more crucially—she was a *virgin*. He was telling his people that he had found a bride who, although she might not at first appear so, was actually a suitable bride for their Sheikh.

She would also learn that Abdul-Aziz had travelled to England with the intention of attempting to bribe her with unimaginable riches to stay away from the Sheikh. But then he had seen her playing with Cara in the homespun tranquillity of her mother's house.

'I realised that I had never allowed myself to think beyond the stereotype of what I believed you to be,' he told her. 'And of course by then I realised that my Sheikh had grown to love you—and suddenly I could see why.'

And it didn't take long to realise that Hashim's mother wanted only her son's happiness.

For when it all came down to it palaces and different cultures counted for very little. In the end, the human spirit was the same the world over.

EPILOGUE

A DOLLOP of mashed banana landed in a slimy lump on the back of her hand and Sienna giggled as she wiped it away, looking up into the bemused black eyes of her husband as he surveyed the breakfast scene before him.

Hashim smiled. How his life had been transformed! Gone was the starchy formality and the slow glide of numerous servants who catered to his every whim. Instead, there sat his beautiful Sienna, with their gorgeous wriggling son on her lap.

'What a merry dance he leads you,' he observed ruefully.

'Ah, but what wonderful co-ordination he has,' cooed Sienna. 'Only eight months old, and he's practically feeding himself!'

'Indeed,' he murmured diplomatically, as another dollop of fruit was relayed across the linen table-cloth by the lively Prince Marzug.

Hashim had long given up trying to get Sienna to bring their son up in the conventional manner of royal princes, and she had resolutely refused to have child-care except when strictly necessary.

'No one can love a baby like his mother,' she had

told him firmly. 'Or his father,' she had added imp-
ishly.

And in that he could not argue with her—though
he enjoyed trying. For Marzug had stolen his heart
the moment he had made his first lusty bawl. There
was so much love in Hashim's world now. His senses
were raw and on fire with it. And Sienna had started
it all. He looked at her.

Hard to believe as she sat in this scene of cosy
domesticity, despite the grand dimensions of the
room, that last night she had stunned the visiting
French Ambassador at a reception given at the Palace
in his honour. Hashim had watched with pride and
love and lust as she had danced—slender and graceful
as a flower swayed by the summer breeze. And alone
afterwards, in the glorious privacy of their apartment,
she had…she had… Hashim swallowed.

'Are you all right, darling?' Sienna questioned in-
nocently, her words cutting in to a train of thought
which was probably not advisable when he was due
to inspect the Qudamah army in a little under an hour.

'Yes, my beauty,' he murmured, watching her pick
up a cream sheet of paper. 'What are you reading
now?'

Absently, Sienna dropped a kiss onto Marzug's
curly black hair. 'Oh, just a request—asking if I will
be patron of the new children's charity which is being
set up in Nasim.'

'*Another* charity?' Hashim frowned. 'But you do
enough already.'

'I know. But some of the work is extra-special, and...' She put the letter down on the table, out of Marzug's reach, and smiled at him. 'I'm just flattered to be asked,' she said simply.

And he understood. Perfectly.

Because it hadn't been all plain sailing to get to where she was today. Sienna had had to work hard to get the people of Qudamah to accept her. Some of them hadn't—certainly not straight away—but she had understood their doubts and fears about their beloved Sheikh marrying a woman from so far away, who knew little of their culture.

And there were some who had not finally thawed until she had produced the plump and bouncing olive-skinned infant Prince and fireworks had lit up the skies behind the Palace. Then they had finally taken her into their hearts.

The wedding itself had been a bit of a challenge, too—there had been a civil ceremony and then a religious one, after her conversion to Hashim's faith. She'd had to memorise all her vows in Qudamahesh and she had spent the night before the marriage saying them over and over again, until she was word perfect. Learning the ancient language was something she had immediately set about doing—and was even more of a challenge!

But she was young and bright and eager to learn. And she was in love. Just as she was loved. And that put everything in its proper perspective.

She had been a bag of nerves before her first meeting with Hashim's mother—for the Princess was deeply revered by all who knew her. But their shared love for one man had been enough to unite them in a harmony which had soon grown into genuine regard.

She was both a wise and a perceptive woman. She had allayed some of Sienna's fears—recounting the tale of one of Hashim's ancestors, who had married the daughter of his fiercest enemy despite much opposition. 'So, you see, there is nothing new under the sun, Sienna,' she had said softly. 'No matter where they live, nor what they do, people are the same; they never change. They fall in love and they fight for that love, and that is just how it should be.'

Sienna knew that what Hashim's mother had told her was important. Not to compare, no—but to realise that life was very precious and very short. Once, she had wondered when the present became the past, but now she realised that it was happening all the time. Their wedding was already in the past, and their life would whizz by as everyone warned it did. They just had to make the most of it.

She pushed the bowl of banana away and Hashim judged it safe enough to reach out and ruffle his son's hair. 'Will we swim together later?' she questioned eagerly. 'In the Palace pool? Just the three of us?'

'Yes, my love,' Hashim murmured indulgently, wondering what the fabled Special Guard of the army might say if they could see their Commander-in-Chief being such putty in his wife's hands! 'And later we will have dinner alone.' His eyes glinted. 'Since our diaries are free. And at some point we must discuss your mother's visit, and the gift of the stallion I intend to make to her.'

'Oh, Hashim, she's going to be over the moon.'

He took her hand, briefly rubbing the shiny gold wedding band with the pad of his thumb and then lifting her fingers to his lips, licking them provocatively. His eyes captured hers with sensual allure. 'Well, then,' he said lightly. 'That makes two of us, doesn't it?'

'Three of us, actually.' She smiled. 'Well, four if you count Marzug.'

'Always.'

Their eyes met and Sienna's breath caught in her throat. She wanted to hold that moment in her heart for ever.

She had to remember that it didn't last long—and to say the things that counted.

'I love you, Hashim.'

His eyes were tender. 'I love you too, sweet Sienna.'

And Sienna put the baby in his highchair and moved into her husband's arms, wrapping herself close enough to feel the powerful beating of his heart.

STOLEN BY
THE SHEIKH

by

Trish Morey

Trish Morey is an Australian who's also spent time living and working in New Zealand and England. Now she's settled with her husband and four young daughters in a special part of South Australia, surrounded by orchards and bushland, and visited by the occasional koala and kangaroo.

With a life-long love of reading, she penned her first book at age eleven, after which life, career and a growing family kept her busy until once again she could indulge her desire to create characters and stories, this time in romance. Having her work published is a dream come true.

Visit Trish at her website at www.trishmorey.com

Don't miss Trish Morey's exciting new novel, *Forced Wife, Royal Love-Child*, available in April 2009 from Mills & Boon® Modern™.

CHAPTER ONE

SHE knew it without turning.

The sudden flush to her skin, the disconcerting prickle that crawled the length of her spine, told Sapphy Clemenger that whoever had just entered Bacelli's Milan salon was no ordinary customer. In an atmosphere that suddenly felt superheated, instinct screamed that no way was this one of her usual clients rushing in five minutes before evening closing time to search for the perfect outfit to woo her husband, or even her lover.

Her muscles strained and tensed, her senses heightening so much that even the hushed click of the cushioned door closing registered to her senses as significant.

Battling the sensations that continued to skitter up and down her back, she blinked away the weariness bequeathed by her 3 a.m. mornings leading up to this week's successful fashion-week show and swivelled right, a smile of welcome at the ready, only to have her eyes jag on blackness.

His power hit her first.

Like a rush of electricity she felt his impact surge over her. He was a wall of power, a wall of authority. Black roll-neck sweater, well-cut black jeans topping hand-stitched black boots. Even his hair glossed blue-black in the beam from the ceiling's downlights.

But it was his eyes that reached across the room and snared her. Dark and fathomless with a glint that came and went like a shooting star in the night sky, their midnight quality reeled her in.

Was it possible to feel your pupils dilate? *Yes*, if what she'd just experienced was any indication. And given the sensory heights she seemed to be suddenly subjected to in the last few seconds, maybe she shouldn't be surprised.

He said nothing as he moved towards her, never taking his eyes from her face and leaving no doubt in her mind that he hadn't just stumbled upon the salon.

He'd come to see her.

She shivered, instantly regretting letting Carla, the salon's permanent assistant, go home early. This was no time to be alone. But still she didn't move. Not that she was certain she could. It was all she could do to swallow as he devoured the distance between them.

'*Buona sera,*' he said, his voice rich and deep and containing so many influences she couldn't place his accent. 'Or would you prefer I speak English?'

His lips curved slightly yet lacked any real warmth in a face that seemed all harsh angles and planes. She felt her eyes narrow. So he knew she wasn't Italian. What else did he know about her? *And why?*

'Thank you. English will be fine.' Her voice sounded remarkably steadier than she felt as she readily accepted his offer to use her native tongue. After four years working in Italy away from her Australian homeland, she spoke fluent Italian, but here, in this man's presence, she didn't trust herself to think and speak her adopted language without tripping over her tongue. 'How can I help you?'

'You are, I presume, Sapphire Clemenger? The designer?'

Still she couldn't place his accent. It held touches of English, a trace of American and more besides. He wasn't Italian, of that she was sure, even though his dark features could have passed for Mediterranean. Yet he was too tall, too broad in the shoulders.

And much, much too close.

The heat came off him in waves. She felt herself flush, her mouth desert dry. Finally she nodded in answer to his question, incapable of forming the words.

'I suspected as much,' he continued. 'I understood you to be quite beautiful. Of course, until now I had no idea just how much.'

She blinked slowly as something lurched inside her. How could just a few words affect her so deeply? She was used to the flattery and attention she received from the local males. They had a reputation for appreciating the feminine form and they certainly lived up to it. But it was always given in good spirit and in a way that was more lighthearted than serious.

This man's words resonated on another level entirely. Maybe it was something to do with the way his eyes continued to scrutinise her face as if drinking in every detail, to rake over her body with the hot power of a blowtorch.

And still she didn't know who he was.

She straightened her back, pushing herself taller and battling to damp down her own mounting temperature. She'd had enough of being on the defensive.

'You seem to have me at a disadvantage, Signor…?'

'Call me Khaled,' he said, offering her his hand.

She took it and almost immediately wished she hadn't, sensing her new-found courage melt away. For now, with his long, tapered fingers enclosing hers, their latent strength seeping into her flesh, she felt as if he'd somehow taken charge, as if he somehow possessed her.

And that was crazy.

She didn't belong to anyone, least of all to this dark stranger. Even Paolo, whom she'd been seeing on and off for more than two years, didn't instil this sense of possession in her.

She tugged on her hand, aware the stranger had been holding on to it for much too long, and stepped around him, focusing on steadying the rhythm of her breathing as she headed for the salon's lounge area. *If she didn't have to concentrate on standing up, maybe she could think more clearly.* She indicated an armchair while she glanced over to the door, willing someone, *anyone,* to enter the store. 'Please,' she said over her shoulder, 'tell me how I can help you.'

He watched her panicked retreat and her longing glance at the passing pedestrians with some entertainment. He'd been right to wait until now to make his move. It was late and unlikely anyone else would visit the salon and interrupt them. Unlikely anyone would come to her rescue.

She turned and looked at him, the questions laid bare in her large blue eyes. He could see her vulnerability and how she was fighting it. He could feel her suspicion, warring with curiosity.

He could taste her fear.

She was much more interesting than he'd been led to believe. And more beautiful. Even with tell-tale smudges of tiredness around her eyes, they shone with life and promise in features arranged perfectly on her face. Her dark-gold hair was swept up into a sleek curve that exposed the smooth sweep of her neck.

The face of a model and the body of a goddess. Paolo couldn't have chosen better.

She would do perfectly.

'What can I do for you, Signor Khaled?' she asked as he curved his length into the plush Venetian-style chair opposite her own. 'Are you looking for something for a special woman?'

He smiled, more to himself than outwardly. 'You could say that. Your designs are the talk of Milan. Your show was an outstanding success. For a foreigner you have done remarkably well in breaking into such a competitive market.'

'I've been very lucky.'

'You are very talented,' he said. 'Otherwise you would not be where you are.'

'Thank you,' she said quietly, her cheeks surprisingly tinged with pink, almost as if she was unused to compliments. 'Was there something in the collection that particularly interested you?'

'It is all of interest. But that's not why I'm here. I want you to make a dress.'

He saw the interest flare in her eyes. 'Certainly. That's not a problem. I do commission work for many of my clients.'

He could see by her body language that she was finally relaxing as they spoke, back in the familiar territory of what she did best. Her shoulders looked less rigid and, by the steady rise and fall of her chest, her breathing appeared more under control. She assumed he was just one more customer. This would be almost too easy.

'This will be no ordinary dress,' he continued. 'I am to be married in four weeks. I want you to design and construct a wedding gown for my wife-to-be.'

A wedding dress. She loved all of her design work but always the greatest satisfaction, the greatest thrill, came in designing wedding gowns, a woman's most important dress for her most important day. A dress that complemented, that accentuated while it minimised and made the most of the bride as it transformed her into a princess; Sapphy loved nothing more than to make it happen. But he was cutting it fine.

'A wedding gown in just four weeks? Usually we would recommend at least three times that for something so special.'

'With your talent, I should not think that will be a problem.'

Her pulse raced at the opportunity he was offering while her mind was busy negotiating the difficulties that still stood in the way of accepting the job. 'Thank you. You pay me a huge compliment by even offering me this commission. However, as much as I am tempted, I do have other responsibilities and other clients I must consider before I can accept.'

He pushed himself from the chair and loomed over her. 'But you have just shown your latest collection. That is completed. You *will* design this dress.'

She felt her eyes widen, taken aback as much at his physical presence before her as his bold statement. Until now he'd given the impression he specifically wanted her to design the wedding gown. Could it be that other designers had already turned down the commission? Maybe desperation was forcing his hand and he'd run out of options.

Besides, as tempted as she was to take on any wedding-gown design project, she would be mad to promise something she could not deliver. Especially just because it was demanded of her. 'I'm still not a free agent. I do have my own line now, it's true, but I still work within the House of Bacelli.'

'I have already spoken with Gianfranco Bacelli. He will release you.'

'I see.' But she didn't see. She bit down on her lip as she considered his revelation. This was no ordinary commission, not if it had already been squared away with the ageing designer who headed the Bacelli house. Whoever this Khaled was, he was a man of influence. And he obviously expected her to fall in with his plans.

He took a step closer. 'You will be compensated well.'

She stood up, forcing her five-feet-eight frame taller, wanting to show him she would not be the pushover he expected, though she still conceded a good six inches to his height. 'Be that as it may, you have left things very late. As you are no doubt aware, I work to the highest possible standards and that means it may simply not be feasible to do the dress justice in the time available.'

'Name your price, then.'

She drew back, offended by the implication. 'Signor Khaled, you misunderstand me. I wasn't angling at securing a higher price for my services, merely pointing out that the time is very short even to complete the design to the satisfaction of the bride, let alone to construct the dress.'

He waved away her umbrage with a flick of his wrist, almost as if he was bored. 'This dress will be your design. You are the designer.'

'But surely the bride will want to have her say? Perhaps she'd like to come in, we can talk about it together, get some ideas down on paper?'

'No!' He glowered down at her. 'That will not be possible.' He turned and strode to the window. 'She knows your designs. She would have no one else design her wedding dress. You will design it yourself.'

She shook her head. 'I'm afraid that makes the job

almost impossible, then. At a minimum I need to know the bride's tastes and preferences. I need to know what colours best suit her and what styles complement her figure.'

'You cannot meet her. At least—not yet.'

'But why? What bride doesn't want to be involved in organising her own gown?'

His dark eyes narrowed. 'She is…indisposed. The wedding will be challenge enough for her. She doesn't need the additional stress beforehand.'

'Oh, I see.' Sapphy's mind whirled with the possibilities. What could be the problem? Unless she was ill, too ill to handle her own wedding plans. That might also explain the rush…

Her heart filled with compassion. It all fitted. His bride was ill, perhaps seriously, and they wanted to marry while they still could. No wonder he was so desperate to retain her services. No wonder he seemed so angry with her.

'I can tell you all you need to know,' he said. 'I can answer all your questions. So, will you design the gown?'

She swallowed, trying to ease the sudden constriction in her throat. If she was right about the circumstances of this marriage, there was no way she couldn't help. There was no way she could let a bride in such circumstances down. But likewise she wanted more than anything for the bride to be delighted with her dress and, without the usual input, how could she be sure she could pull it off?

'This is a heavy responsibility. I would need to be

sure the bride will be satisfied with the gown. I would hate for her to be disappointed in any way.'

'I guarantee, she will love it.' He suddenly pivoted to face her, as if something had occurred to him. 'All she asks…'

Sapphy's ears pricked up, eager for anything that would give her some indication of the bride's preferences. 'Yes?'

He smiled, his teeth white against his tanned skin and his eyes shining in the glow from the downlights. 'All she asks is that you imagine that this is your wedding, that you imagine you are the bride and that this is the gown of your dreams. Only then will she be happy.'

Her eyelids fell shut, long and purposefully, as the tingles she'd thought long gone resumed their samba along her spine. A client was paying her the ultimate compliment, letting her decide everything about the dress's style, fabric and design. It was an unbelievable opportunity to showcase her talent. Yet something still didn't feel right.

And part of it was in imagining this was her wedding and the resultant picture that flashed through her mind's eye. She was walking down the carpeted aisle towards the man waiting for her. But something was wrong. The man was wrong.

It wasn't Paolo waiting for her.

It was Signor Khaled.

She shuddered and forced her eyes open, staring out into the busy Via Monte Napoleone in an effort to banish the unwelcome pictures from her mind.

He was nothing to her. Nothing but another client and one who was marrying another woman—a sick woman if the indications were correct. So why would she imagine even for a second the thought of marrying such a man? And why did the images persist?

She had to focus on the bride and her gown. This would be her day and Sapphy would do all she could to make it the most special day in the world for her. 'I'll still need to meet her at some stage, of course,' she said, turning away from the traffic at last. 'I'll need to do at least some fittings.'

'We will deal with that in Jebbai. I have organised a studio for you. You can start work as soon as you arrive.'

'In Jebbai?' Warning bells rang loud in her mind. 'But that's somewhere out in the desert. You expect me to go there?'

'Jebbai is an independent state. You have no need to fear. You will be safe while you are in my care. I guarantee that.'

'But why can't I do the job here? I have clients who will need me, I have access to all the fabrics…'

'Gianfranco Bacelli has taken care of all that.' He smiled, or was it just the way he tilted his head? 'And you do want to meet the bride, don't you?'

She paused, licked her dry lips. 'I still haven't agreed to do this.'

'No?' he asked, as if he believed she had no choice. 'Then you have until Sunday to decide. We fly out Monday.'

CHAPTER TWO

SAPPHY let herself into her apartment, tired but at the same time exhilarated. While her body was tingling from her unexpected meeting with Signor Khaled, her mind was weighed down with uncertainty.

The proposal had come completely out of the blue, but given that her current collection and the shows were complete, the timing really couldn't be better. Nevertheless, it would still be tight, designing and completing something special within four weeks.

If she agreed to go to Jebbai.

Jebbai.

Just the name was enough to conjure up exotic images of endless golden sand and swaying palm trees. But what did she really know about the desert kingdom other than that it was a small independent Arab state, landlocked by sand and that it had made its fortune with its rich oil reserves?

She flicked through her small pile of mail, finding nothing there compelling enough to open immediately and distract her thoughts, so she put the letters back down and moved to the glass doors overlooking her small balcony. She stepped out into the cool air, leaning her forearms on the railing, watching the people in the square below enjoying the surprisingly mild February evening, milling about talking to friends or drifting off to one of the restaurants lining the small square.

The commission was tempting, the location alluring, but there was something wholly unsettling about the man, something intangible that seemed to reach out and grab hold of her.

It wasn't just his sultry dark looks, though now at last they were explained. She could see the Arab influence in his features and his bearing and even in the golden glow to his skin. As if he was made for the desert.

In normal circumstances his looks would have been enough to get him noticed, though they were hardly unsettling. What rattled her more was his brooding presence and the way his whole attitude spoke of thinly veiled contempt.

Why should he be angry with her? Unless he was driven by desperation to obtain the services of a designer in time for his wedding and her failure to immediately acquiesce to his demands had displeased him. No, thinking back, he'd seemed angry even when he entered the salon.

Angry and demanding.

Did she really want to fly off to some desert state with him? Did she want to be trapped with him in a vessel as small as a plane? He'd burned up the atmosphere in the salon. Sucked the air dry. Even a plane as large as a seven-four-seven would be hard-pressed to hold enough oxygen for them both.

As much as she was tempted by the commission, by the chance to experience the desert and of designing a wedding dress like nothing she'd ever done before, she certainly wasn't keen on spending another moment in Signor Khaled's company.

She hugged her arms to her, the night's chill finally registering, and stepped back inside, pulling the doors shut behind her. Out of the corner of her eye, she noticed a tiny flashing light. A message on her answer machine; maybe Paolo had called…

She punched the play button but it was Gianfranco's gravelly tones that filled the room. 'Expect a new client,' he said in his rich Italian voice. 'This will be very good for your profile and for the House of Bacelli. I expect you to take this commission.'

The machine beeped its conclusion as nerve endings tingled. There was no getting out of it now. She wasn't fooled by Gianfranco's use of language. What Gianfranco 'expected', invariably happened. So where did that leave her now?

Most likely on a plane to Jebbai on Monday.

Which meant the one thing she didn't want to deal with. She shivered. She wouldn't be travelling alone.

Signor Khaled would be on the plane with her.

She wandered around the living area, retrieving the pile of mail and slapping it firmly against her hand, jolting herself back to reality.

What the hell was wrong with her? As if she'd have to spend time with him once they arrived in Jebbai. He was obviously a person of some wealth to be able to employ at such short notice one of Milan's upcoming designers from one of its leading houses. And he was setting her up in a workshop so she could perform her duties. Clearly he wanted her to complete the gown as soon as possible so that he could marry his fiancée, no doubt during which he had other more pressing duties to attend to.

There was little risk she wouldn't be able to complete the dress in time. While the four-week timetable would be tight, being relieved of her other workload and able to work on the dress full-time made meeting his deadline that much more achievable.

And hadn't she secretly been attracted to the idea of visiting the desert state? Maybe a visit to Jebbai was just what she needed to infuse some fresh ideas into her designs.

Already she could imagine the light of the desert land—the sun would be bright, perhaps even more bold than the harsh sun she knew back in Australia, but she wanted to experience its heat, she wanted to see its dipping rays burn the desert sands red. Colours in Jebbai would seem more intense, fabrics sheer and silky and lush with embroidery.

There would be different fragrances, different textures and sensations. She'd be crazy to miss out on such an experience, surely.

She looked around back into her modest apartment. Her modest, *lonely* apartment. There was nothing holding her here. Even Paolo was still in the States, working on a complex international lawsuit. A case likely to take months by the sounds of it.

Meanwhile she could be exploring a new part of the world. It would almost be like a holiday.

Goodness, after the hours she put in for Gianfranco, she could do with one of those.

Halfway through her opening her neglected mail the doorbell rang. Her insides lurched on a reflex.

Signor Khaled!

But it couldn't be. He didn't even know where she lived. Although from what she'd seen of him to date, a mere technicality like that was hardly likely to stand in his way.

She made her way to the door, heart pumping in anticipation of once again seeing one person who had so dominated her thoughts since their meeting. Tentatively she pulled open the door, only to be pulled into the arms of the man waiting on the other side.

'*Sapphy, bella!*'

'Paolo?' Trepidation melted into surprise as she found herself being pulled into a firm embrace and on the receiving end of a kiss. 'I didn't expect to see you.'

He relaxed his grip, holding her away a fraction and looking down at her curiously. 'What's wrong— aren't you pleased to see me?'

She laughed, apprehension turning to relief as she stood in the arms of the good-looking Italian, and she hugged him in return. 'Of course I am. I've missed you. It's just that it's such a surprise—a nice surprise. Come in.'

He followed her into the apartment as she hit him with a barrage of questions—*When did you get back? How long can you stay? Has the case finished?*

'Enough,' he said with a smile, holding up one hand as he accepted with the other the glass of wine she'd poured as her questions continued to spill out. 'The case is in recess while the defence prepares to introduce some new evidence. I don't have long, it was just too good an opportunity not to visit, seeing I missed your show. I hear you were a great success.'

She looked up at him and swallowed the disappointment he'd just awakened. He hadn't made it to her show, hadn't been with her on the most successful night of her career. And while she'd known there was little chance he'd make it, part of her knew that at one time in their relationship he would have moved heaven and earth to be there.

'After not seeing you for six weeks, I'm just glad you're here now,' she said honestly, curling into him on the sofa and breathing in his familiar cologne. 'We haven't had much time together lately.'

She sipped from her own glass and knew that in her tired state she'd soon need some food to counteract the wine or she'd be asleep in minutes. 'Are you hungry? Would you like to go out somewhere for dinner?'

'No,' he said, almost too quickly. Then he gave her shoulders a squeeze. 'It's been a long day and I have to head to the Villa tomorrow to see my family before I fly back to the States. So why don't we have dinner here, have a quiet night? What do you think?'

Sapphy nodded and settled into the curve of his arm. It was just so good to see him again, she'd eat anywhere.

And even if he wasn't jet lagged, she'd half expected his response. In the weeks prior to his departure for New York, it seemed everywhere the couple had gone together they'd been besieged by the paparazzi, anxious to find a match between the famous international lawyer and the upcoming fashion designer. She'd lost count of the number of articles citing her as the 'imminent Signora Mancini'.

The articles didn't bother her overly much but they'd obviously had a different effect on Paolo. When she'd jokingly asked Paolo if he could take a hint, his reaction had been to withdraw from public life altogether and from her almost as much. She'd seen less and less of him, until finally he'd announced he was handling the New York case himself and had disappeared for who knew how long.

But he was here now. She put down her glass and let go a breath, feeling the tension from the day disappearing as she relaxed back into him again.

'Difficult day?' he asked.

She considered her response, his adjective immediately bringing to mind the salon's final visitor. 'Um, it was long. And interesting. Actually it's lucky you dropped by this weekend. It looks like I'm going away for a few weeks to work on commission for a new client.'

'Sounds interesting.'

'Gianfranco is pushing me. He says it will be good for my career. And, of course, for the House of Bacelli. I'm to design a wedding gown. Should be away four weeks.'

'Where are you going?'

'Somewhere out in the desert. A place called Jebbai.'

She heard the breath hiss through his teeth, felt his muscles tense beneath her, so tight it was almost as if he'd turned to stone.

'Sapphy,' he said, his voice barely more than a husky whisper and with a note that immediately alerted her. 'What's the name of your new client?'

She laughed nervously. 'Why? What's wrong?'

'Tell me!'

Her laughter dried up and she swallowed. 'His name is Signor Khaled. But why? Do you know h—?'

She'd barely finished the words before Paolo had shrugged her from his shoulder and exploded from the seat to circle the room, pacing wildly. 'Khaled! After all this time. I knew it. I knew something was wrong.'

'What did you know? What are you talking about?'

'It's lucky I came when I did. You can't go.'

'Paolo, what on earth are you talking about?'

'Just that you mustn't go.'

'But Gianfranco's expecting me to take this commission. I can't let him down.'

'Tell him you're sick—tell him your mother's sick—tell him anything, but don't go to Jebbai.'

'This isn't making any sense. Give me one good reason why I should turn this job down. More than that, why you'd expect me to lie to get out of it.'

'Because your new client is not what he seems. I know him.'

'What? Are you implying Signor Khaled is some kind of criminal?'

'There's no "Signor Khaled" about it. Didn't he even tell you his full name?'

'His full name? I—'

He snarled. 'Your Signor Khaled is none other than Sheikh Khaled Al-Ateeq, ruler of Jebbai.'

A sheikh? Sapphy absorbed the revelation with interest, searching for the significance that Paolo obviously placed in the news. It made some sort of sense, certainly, as his whole aura spoke of power. But still she failed to see why his identity should change anything. And it was hardly a crime to protect one's title. He'd certainly made no attempt to hide his name, after all.

'So he's a sheikh? That probably explains why Gianfranco is falling all over himself to ensure I take the job. But does that change anything? What I do know is he's getting married and he's engaged me to design his bride's wedding dress. And you haven't given me one good reason why I shouldn't do it.'

'Listen to me,' Paolo said, his hands on her shoulders. 'Whatever's going on, you can't trust this man. I have no idea what he's up to, but I doubt there will even be a wedding.'

She shivered, his tone as much as his words frightening her. She tried to cover her anxiety with a laugh, but the sound came out brittle and false. 'That's ridiculous. Then why would he go to the trouble of commissioning a designer for a wedding gown?'

'To get you there.'

This time there was no covering up the tremor that rocked her. 'You're frightening me, Paolo, and I don't understand why. What makes you say these things? How do you know?'

'I just do.'

'No,' she stated, needing facts to back up this fantastic story he was building up. 'That's not good enough. If you're going to scare me with stories like this then I need some kind of proof. Why shouldn't I go? What do you have against this sheikh?'

He spun away from her, fists clenched. 'I can't tell you.' She was about to tell him that he'd have to when he wheeled back to face her. 'Except to say, he's the most ruthless man I've ever met and I know he'll stop at nothing to get what he wants.'

The client's eyes came instantly to her mind, dark and relentless as they'd all but pierced their way into her skin during their heated scrutiny. Yes, he was no doubt ruthless, but so too could Paolo be, along with half of his colleagues. You didn't make it to the top ranks of international law partnerships by being anything less.

She turned on him, protesting, 'I don't understand. If you feel this strongly about the man, why is it you've never so much as mentioned him before?'

'What happened was long ago. Before I met you.'

'Then maybe he's changed. Whatever differences you had back then probably don't exist any more.'

He shook his head. 'No. You don't know him like I do.'

'And you don't know what I do. There is a bride. I'm meeting her just as soon as we get to Jebbai.'

She knew she was stretching the truth, but with the mood Paolo was in, there was no way he wouldn't jump on the news that Khaled had prevaricated over her meeting the bride, whatever his reasons, and use it to add fuel to his arguments to stop her going.

And she wanted to go, even if it had taken her a while to convince herself. There were good business reasons for her to go. It wasn't as if Paolo would be waiting for her at home while she was gone, after all.

'Then are you so sure that she's willing to marry this man?'

'Oh, for heaven's sake. What are you suggesting? This is the twenty-first century after all. As it happens,' she added, if only to stop Paolo's wild accusations in their tracks, 'they need to get married quickly. The bride is desperately ill.' Then she added for effect, 'It's really quite romantic, don't you think?'

He watched her, saying nothing, though the fierce rise and fall of his chest spoke volumes about how he was feeling. There could have been a ten-gallon drum of romance in the situation and still it would have eluded him.

'Look,' she said softly, moving alongside and placing a hand on his rigid forearm, 'this *Sheikh Khaled*, whoever he is and whatever problems you've had with him in the past, in all likelihood has no idea that

I even know you. He just wants to commission a dress. And I'm only going for four weeks—*four weeks*, I might point out, when you won't even be here. So it's not like you're going to miss me.'

His arms sliced passionately through the air, a gesture that spoke of both his power and frustration. 'You know I have no choice. I have to go back to New York.'

'And *I* have to go to Jebbai.'

'Don't do this.'

'Don't do what? Make my own decisions? This is my career. This is my passion. You know I love more than anything to design wedding dresses. This is a wonderful opportunity for me and I can't afford to miss it, certainly not on the basis of some "secret men's business".'

'You can't go.'

'I'm sorry, Paolo, but listen to yourself. Your arguments and accusations hold all the characteristics of a tired grudge. You're angsting over some apparent wrong committed so long ago that no one other than you probably remembers or even cares.'

'I won't let you go!'

'It's not up to you. You're not my husband. Even if you were, you couldn't tell me what to do.'

A muscle in his face twitched. 'You still haven't forgiven me because I wouldn't talk about marriage?'

'Paolo,' she whispered on a sigh, 'please try to understand, I'm not angry with you. I just don't understand why everything between us changed when the media assumed we were an item. One mention of marriage and suddenly you seemed to find reasons for us to be apart.'

He moved closer, sliding a hand behind her neck. 'You know I care about you.'

'I once thought you loved me. Now I don't know what to think.'

He pulled the hand away, raking it instead through his hair. 'I know. Things back then got—*awkward* for a while. But if what you say is true, and Khaled is getting married, why don't we talk about things some more after the wedding?'

She tilted her head up to his, studying his face for any hint of what was going through his mind. What was he offering her and why would some desert sheikh's wedding make a difference to their relationship?

'Why can't we talk about it now?'

'Because we can't. You have to trust me on this. Just as you should trust me enough not to go to Jebbai.' He gazed back levelly into her eyes. 'You know you mean a lot to me.'

'It's okay,' she said on a sharp intake of breath as she turned to stare out the window again, the sky now dark and the lights of the square bright and inviting and wholly jarring with her mood. 'I care for you too. And I appreciate your advice. Truly I do. But this is something I need to do. So I'm going. Come Monday I'm leaving for Jebbai.'

CHAPTER THREE

HE WAS waiting for her at the airport. One glance at
him through the tinted limousine windows was
enough to send the courage she'd found to disregard
Paolo's warnings scampering for cover. Standing next
to the jet, Khaled seemed taller, even larger than he
had done in the salon, his dark eyes fixed searchingly
on the approaching car.

Why was she here? What if Paolo was right? What
if Khaled was as dangerous as Paolo suggested?
Would she have cause to regret defying him?

Already she regretted their argument. He'd left
soon after, not staying for dinner, let alone for the
night, and she hadn't heard from him all weekend.
No doubt he'd already be winging his way back to
the States.

She hated that they'd parted this way. She'd never
defied him so openly or so vehemently before, but
then he'd never tried to stop her from doing anything
either, certainly for no valid reason. If only there'd
been some sound basis to his objections, she'd have
had no compunction in taking more notice.

But no, Paolo was wrong and he'd have to admit
it when she returned in four weeks. Not that he was
likely to be around to welcome her home, whatever
his vague offer was to sort things out between them.

And even if he was, things were going to be different between them. It was just as well he hadn't stayed the night. Right now she wasn't sure what she felt for Paolo, but it sure as hell wasn't the happy-ever-after love she'd once assumed their relationship to be heading for. Things had changed between them over the past months and not for the better. A change of scenery would give her a chance to get her scrambled thoughts in order.

The driver pulled up alongside the private jet sending her thoughts into further disarray. Why on earth had she imagined they would be flying to Jebbai on a conventional airliner? Of course, she hadn't known back then that he was a sheikh. Naturally he would have his own plane, more than likely an entire fleet of them.

Then her door was opened and her insulated world in the limousine's interior was invaded by the unfettered brilliance of daylight, the roar of engines and the high-octane smell of jet fuel. In the time it took to blink he was there, at the door, offering her his hand.

'Signora Clemenger, I am so pleased you have decided to accept my commission.'

Even over the whine of engines his cultured voice flowed over her, warm and rich in a way that somehow curled into her senses.

She stepped from the car to be greeted by the wind, whipping at the loose tendrils of her hair, and his half-smile, tugging at her self-confidence. Dark eyes shone down on her, a degree of self-satisfaction plainly evident.

She bristled. He didn't have to feel smug about her compliance; it was only a job after all.

'Did you ever doubt it, *Sheikh* Khaled Al-Ateeq?'

If she hadn't been searching his face she might have missed it, that tell-tale tiny tic in his cheek, the jolt of realisation that caused his eyes to narrow fractionally.

'I see you have discovered my little secret.'

'So it would appear,' she rejoined. 'Although I very much doubt that I have discovered them all.'

He laughed, throwing his head back and taking her completely by surprise. She'd wanted to warn him, to let him know that she was no *ingénue* heading off into the desert with a stranger. Paolo's fears were way off base, she was sure, but in any event, it paid to let him know that he would have to earn her trust.

Yet he laughed in a way that sounded as if he was truly delighted. And she liked the way it sounded. Even more so, she liked the way he looked. His pale blue fine-knit sweater hugged his torso without stretching, the colour contrasting vividly against his deep olive skin, especially where the shallow V-neck revealed a tantalising slice of his chest. Fitted black trousers accentuated his firm abdomen, showing off his long legs to full effect.

There was no doubt about it; he was going to make one dashing groom. She made a mental note for her design plans—if she didn't do the right thing by the bride, Sheikh Khaled was likely to steal the show.

His head tilted back towards her, catching her frank appraisal and making her wish her eyes had found themselves a safer occupation while he laughed. But she resisted the temptation to turn them away; instead letting them stay locked on to his. He might be drop-dead handsome, but she was no teenaged schoolgirl who could be embarrassed simply by being caught out looking at a man. And he was her client after all. It wasn't as if she was interested in him for herself.

'Come,' he said at last, a smile lingering in his eyes as he ushered her towards the steps, 'we'll take care of the formalities inside.'

She took one last look around her, bidding farewell to the now familiar mountain range towering over the hangars and planes to the north of Milan's Malpensa Airport. Already her life working with Gianfranco Bacelli seemed distant as she climbed the steps into the plane, a sense of excitement building in her veins at this new adventure that not even the too-close proximity of the sheikh at her back could dispel.

He liked what she was wearing, the soft rose-coloured fabric of her dress contrasting with the blue of her eyes and her dark-gold hair, and the style was feminine without being flowery. But what he liked best was the way it moulded to her shape, showing off the roundness of her behind invitingly as she climbed the stairs.

In her wake her clean scent, a hint of perfume, light and summery, was a refreshing relief from the fume-laden air. She smelled fresh and ripe, with not a trace of the fear she'd projected when he'd offered the

commission. There was something though—a wariness? Certainly her comment on greeting him had
been nothing short of a challenge.

So, she suspected there was more to him than met
the eye, yet still she was here. The woman had courage. So much the better. He liked nothing better than
a challenge himself.

His eyes followed her progress upwards. It was a
long time since he'd had a woman. Too long. He
could feel the ache building even now as he watched
her ascend, the natural roll of her hips accentuating
the curve to her slim waist. Much, much too long.

But he could wait four weeks for this one.

She would be worth it.

And she would be his.

The *Gulfstream V* took off smoothly and ate up the
miles through the air with a five-star efficiency that
mirrored its internal opulence. Sapphy nestled into the
soft leather upholstery of the armchair, taking a brief
break from the preliminary sketches she was working
on, knowing that she'd never look at air travel in quite
the same way again.

The cabin had been fitted out to ensure the comfort
of its passengers. The few seats were all large and
luxurious, the dining setting where she was now sitting large enough for a silver-service menu, and to
the rear was a business office complete with computer and fax facilities made possible by satellite-
communication links. There were other rooms too,

she could tell, closed off to the rear. Space, speed and luxury. Sheikh Khaled obviously travelled in style.

And so far he'd been the perfect host. He'd handled the outgoing formalities with aplomb, seen her settled and comfortable for their take-off and then he'd excused himself, retiring to the cockpit to talk to the pilot. Meanwhile the attentive stewards ensured she was supplied with everything she needed and more.

If this was a taste of how things would be in Jebbai, she had nothing at all to fear from Sheikh Khaled. Just as she'd rationalised, he would have plenty enough to keep him occupied and she'd need hardly ever see him.

The cockpit door swung open and Sapphy's eyes felt compelled to follow the movement. Khaled emerged and seemed to pause, mid-step, as his eyes met hers. Breath jagged in her chest as she saw something pass through them, something hot and hungry and real…

And then it was gone, and the corners of his mouth kicked up and he resumed his progress towards her. She turned her face back to her sketches, making random lines with her pencil, knowing the sudden burst of internal fire she was experiencing would be splashed vividly all over her face.

So much for feeling relaxed.

Then his hand was on her shoulder and her pencil jerked in her fingers as every muscle inside her clamped shut.

'Lovely,' he said, close enough to her ear as he bent down to look at her sketches that she could feel his warm breath on her cheek and there was no way he couldn't hear the pounding of her heart. She didn't dare glance sideways—he was too close, way too close.

She licked her lips, trying to focus on the sketches. 'They're just some rough ideas at this stage, but I was wondering if you have any idea which kind of style you think your bride will prefer? I don't even have a clue as to her measurements yet, so some of these may not be appropriate.'

He stayed silent for a few seconds, seconds where his hand remained on her shoulder and his breath curled against her skin. Seconds that dragged long and interminable.

'I like this one,' he said at last, pointing with his free hand to a graceful princess-line dress, scooped over the shoulders and neck and falling to a full skirt with cleverly designed pleats that revealed a complementary underskirt. 'What do you think?'

From her peripheral vision she knew he'd turned and was looking at her, waiting for her response. She breathed in, licked her lips and nodded. That particular design was her own personal favourite from the half-dozen scattered over the table. It was elegant, stunning in its simplicity, and yet regal enough for a princess.

'If you think it will suit her,' she offered, turning her head fractionally towards him at last, while still directing her eyes anywhere but on his face.

'Oh, yes,' he said, his voice low and husky. 'I think it will be perfect…'

She lifted her eyes to his and her mouth went dry. 'Just perfect.'

He was close. Too close. So close she could taste his breath on hers. So close she could see herself reflected in the dark mirror of his eyes. So close she had cause to wonder whether Paolo's warnings hadn't been somewhere near the mark. This was no ordinary man. Had she done the wrong thing by coming after all?

Yet why did she seem to freeze when she should be doing something—anything? And he wasn't pulling away. If she wasn't mistaken, he was getting even closer…

This wasn't happening! She jerked her head away and leaned forward, scrabbling with the papers on the table in a poor interpretation of organising them. 'That's great,' she said. 'I'll keep working on that design if it suits you. And as soon as I have some measurements, I'll make some real progress.'

She knew she was babbling but it kept her mouth busy and right now that seemed the most important thing on earth. The way he'd looked at her lips. Surely he hadn't been going to kiss her? He was a man about to get married after all.

She must have been imagining it. Paolo's words had poisoned her. Was it possible to suffer altitude sickness in a pressurised aircraft?

She was aware of him standing upright and his hand left her shoulder at last. Strange, it had been there so long, it almost felt cold now that he'd removed it.

'This calls for champagne,' he said, gesturing to the stewards. He sat down in the chair alongside her as if nothing had just happened as a steward delivered two champagne flutes and an ice bucket containing a chilled bottle of sparkling wine. She recognised the label instantly.

'Australian wine?'

He dipped his head a fraction. 'In your honour. I thought you might like a taste of your homeland, seeing as I was taking you away even from your adopted city.'

A swell of warmth moved through her as she was strangely touched by the gesture. She'd expected, from the luxury of the plane, that for him it would be *Dom Perignon* or nothing. To choose an Australian wine, a simply stunning Australian wine none the less, was something she'd never expected. And he'd done it to make her feel at home?

How did he do this to her? How could he make her feel so on edge one minute, so considered the next?

The sparkling wine was poured and he handed her a flute. 'I propose a toast,' he said. 'To a gown that is going to be as breathtaking as the astonishing woman who designs it.'

He raised his glass to her, his eyes half shuttered, smiling at her purposefully before lifting the glass to his lips. His eyes never left her, even as his chin kicked up, his eyes stayed with her, dark, intent.

She swallowed before even taking as much as a sip as her feelings of comfort rocked into uncertainty again. Maybe it was time to remind him of another woman who would play a part in this wedding, a woman who, it now occurred to her, he barely spoke about.

'Thank you,' she said softly. 'And if I may, I'd like to propose a toast to the woman who will wear the dress, for without her, the dress is nothing. To your bride.'

She took a sip from her crystal flute, satisfied that she'd put their relationship back into some kind of perspective. Whether or not he'd intended to kiss her just then, he'd at least know that she wasn't likely to forget he was about to marry another woman.

But, watching him over the rim of her glass, she could see her words didn't faze him in the least. If anything, they just served to increase the width of his smile, the dark intent in his eyes.

'Absolutely,' he said. 'Let us drink to the woman who will be my wife. To my bride.'

He raised his flute and held it up to her again, still smiling, holding her gaze firm and square, and just for one moment she sensed she was missing something.

Something had happened—oh, yes, he'd acknowledged his bride and he'd done it without missing a beat. But there was something else, curious and intriguing, that she couldn't quite pin down. Something that didn't feel quite right.

Her glass moved to her lips mechanically and she had her first taste of the sparkling wine, the tiny bead bursting with the essence of yeast and fruit and neither too sweet nor too dry. But her appreciation of the wine came a poor second to the continued machinations of her mind. Just what was Sheikh Khaled about? She didn't want to give credence to Paolo's concerns but there was something about him that disturbed her on the deepest level.

And yet she'd never been in the company of royalty before. Was it any wonder he was complex and guarded? It was probably bred into him, along with his power. Was it any wonder he was different from other men?

Paolo's words were rendering her too suspicious, too sensitive to the merest inflexion of Khaled's voice and too ready to think the worst.

Sheikh Khaled was clearly a gracious host. She should relax and enjoy the experience. That way she would prove Paolo's fears groundless.

A steward leaned over and whispered something in Khaled's ear, his eyes widening a fraction before they narrowed on a razor-sharp gleam.

'I apologise,' he said, putting down his glass. 'Something has arisen which I must attend to urgently. Please excuse me.'

She looked over to the business workstation, where two uniformed officers were already gathered around the computer screen. 'Is anything the matter?' she asked.

'It is a trifling matter, nothing to concern yourself with,' he assured her, nodding before turning and withdrawing to join his staff. Where had his officers come from? She hadn't noticed them on the plane earlier, although it no doubt made sense for someone of a sheikh's standing to travel with his own security.

Whatever the 'trifling matter' was, it was taking some time. And emotion. Every now and then the sound of raised voices and urgent instructions drowned out the constant hum of the engines and the sudden noise would pull her out of her designs once more to wonder what was going on. But the men were engaged in rapid-fire discussions between themselves and someone at the end of the satellite phone line and there was no way her curiosity would outweigh her good sense. She was staying right here.

Besides, it was a welcome break to have time away from Khaled's presence, his dark, challenging eyes and his unreadable expressions.

A slight change in the feel of the flight told her they'd started their descent. She looked out of the window to the ground some forty thousand feet below. They were crossing a coastline, the blue waters of what she took to be the Mediterranean a stark contrast to the white line of the coast and the wide expanse of yellow-brown interior beyond.

She turned back to find Khaled lowering himself into the seat next to her.

'It won't be long now,' he said.

'Is everything all right?' she asked, with a glance to the rear of the plane, but the two officers had disappeared again.

'It is now,' he said, noncommittally.

It wasn't long before the sleek aircraft gently touched down on the runway at Jebbai's airport, a short distance, Khaled explained, from the capital, Hebra. Sapphy stepped from the plane into the clean, dry heat of a Jebbai afternoon. She paused for a moment at the top of the steps. It was so different from Milan—with no mountains to shadow the small but modern airport. Instead the land was flat, reaching in all directions around, one endless golden dune after another, leading on to the horizon and broken only by a long strip of bitumen, the highway leading to the capital.

The middle of nowhere.

Never had the phrase been so apt. She gulped down a fortifying lungful of air.

Never had she felt so alone.

Khaled's hand squeezed her shoulder, as if reassuring her. 'Welcome to your new home,' he said. She was halfway down the stairs and the moment gone before she realised what he'd said.

They transferred to the waiting limousine for the thirty-minute drive as day was beginning to fade. The heat of the day lingered, the warm air clean and dry under a sky that seemed to go on forever.

They said little for the first few minutes, Sapphy content to gaze out of the windows and drink in the view, finding even the passing dunes and rock formations fascinating, barely able to contain her excitement at the harsh beauty of the landscape. Even the presence of Khaled by her side wasn't enough to quell her enthusiasm. Already she was brimming with ideas about colour, patterns and texture. The landscape was like a breath of fresh air.

'What do you think of my country?'

'It's beautiful, just beautiful.'

'Never take the desert for granted. It's harsh and dangerous and unforgiving.'

She looked over to him, surprised by his words. 'Of course, but isn't the danger what gives it the edge over, say, a landscape of green hills and valleys? There the land is lush and fertile, beautiful in its own way, yet soft and safe. Whereas this place has colour and drama and magnificence that goes hand in hand with danger. Even more,' she licked her lips, searching the view outside her window for the right words, 'there's almost a timeless quality about it. Almost like it's waiting for something…'

She turned back to him, still struggling for the right way to finish her sentence, only to have the breath snag in her throat as a shudder rippled through her.

His eyes trapped her, ensnaring her in a blistering gaze that burned and sizzled her to the core. Whatever she had been going to say was incinerated in raw heat.

His heat.

He moved closer, reaching out a hand to cup her jaw. She flinched at his touch but his fingers held her firm, scorching the skin of her neck and chin. 'Your eyes blaze when you talk of such things. They reflect the light like the facets of a well-cut stone. How appropriately they named you.'

She swallowed, a vain attempt to lubricate her ashen throat.

'Such beautiful eyes. Tell me, is their beauty like your green landscape, lush and fertile, or is it a dangerous magnificence that shines within them? Which is it, I wonder?'

She shook her head, the little she was able, her tongue attempting to moisten her lips. 'I don't know.' She raised a hand to his forearm. 'I've never thought about it.' *Maybe she could brush him away...* Then her hand met his arm, the sheer strength of his limb clearly evident through the fine-knit fabric. His arm was like steel, sculptured tensile steel.

There was no brushing this man away.

His head tilted to one side, his lips turned up into a lazy grin, as if amused by her attempts to rescue herself from his grasp. His grip relaxed.

'Yet your prose suggests you are very perceptive. You see qualities in the desert that others miss. I find it difficult to believe you would not have the same talent when applied to people.'

No question which type you fall into, she thought in a rush. *Tall, dark and dangerous.* 'I really don't see how this is relevant,' she murmured on a breath, closing her eyes for a second and wondering if he could have heard her over the hammering in her veins. 'And I'd prefer it if you didn't touch me.'

He raised his eyebrows in a way that suggested he didn't believe her, but still he shrugged and relaxed his grip on her jaw.

'As you wish,' he said.

Her chin kicked up in relief, but it was to be short-lived as his large hand didn't pull completely away but continued to sweep slowly down the line of her throat, searing a trail of scorching sensation. His fingers spanned the open neck of her dress, skimming lightly under the cross-over neckline before his hand finally withdrew.

She sucked in a breath as naked sensation skittered through her, a charge so electric that her breasts tingled and firmed.

She didn't want him to touch her, didn't want him anywhere near her, so why did her senses continue to hum, her breasts continue to swell, when his hand was long gone? The view out of the window stared blankly back at her, offering no answers, but there was no way she'd risk looking anywhere but outside the car, at least not until her breathing and pulse were back under control. Once they were in the palace she would have to stay right away from Sheikh Khaled. He was far too unpredictable, far too compelling.

Far too dangerous.

Yet a good measure of that danger came from within herself. There was no way she could deny she was attracted to him. His physical presence was enough to rock her to her foundations.

His touch was something else.

She'd just have to stay right out of his reach.

Something ahead caught her interest. There were buildings appearing in the twilight, low flat dwellings at first and then higher-rise, with balconies and the muted shadows of palm trees swaying against their walls. Domes of mosques and minarets interrupted the otherwise predominantly horizontal skyline until the approaching city-centre skyscrapers changed the aspect to vertical. And there were people, gathered along the road, the lights from cigarettes like tiny fireflies spinning in the gathering darkness.

She was just about to turn and ask Khaled if they were in Hebra when their world exploded.

CHAPTER FOUR

THE car rocked with the noise and the force of the explosion as dazzling red and white light turned the interior of the car into a crazy frozen snapshot. She shrieked and jumped across the divide between them, throwing herself into Khaled's arms and burying her head in his chest as a barrage of noise rained down on them.

His heartbeat sounded calm and steady in her ear; already she felt safer with his arms wrapped tightly around her, protecting her, keeping her safe.

More colours lit the sky, green, blue, as cheers from the onlookers filled the spaces between the blasts. Children squealed, not in terror, but in delight.

Fireworks, she realised the instant after she'd plastered herself to his chest; she was getting scared witless over a few fireworks.

And look where it had got her! She was practically sitting in his lap.

She wrenched back her head, away from the comforting rhythm of his heart, the rock-steady safety of his chest, trying to peel herself away without further touching him. If only he'd relax his arms!

'You make it difficult for me not to touch you,' he said with a kernel of humour that had been noticeably absent in his voice until now, 'if you insist on throwing yourself at me like that.'

'I thought… I mean…' It would sound so stupid that she couldn't bring herself to say the words. She pushed back against the circle of his arms, still painfully aware that fabric didn't count for much when your thighs were pressed this close to his. 'Please, you can let me go now.'

'And have you get frightened again? Maybe you should relax,' he suggested. 'Enjoy the fireworks.'

She looked up at him, the strong planes of his face thrown into sharp relief by the crazy colours exploding in the sky. 'What's going on?'

'My people are welcoming back their sheikh.'

'You're kidding. They do this every time you come back?'

He laughed, rich and soft, a sound that reminded her of the smoothest coffee and cream. 'My people are very excited about the wedding and their new queen. This is the start of a month-long celebration in Jebbai.'

'Then I suggest,' she said, levering herself further away from him, 'that it's not such a great idea for your people to see you like this with your bride's dress designer.'

'I wouldn't worry too much,' he said, releasing her all the same so she could scramble back to the opposite side of the wide leather seat. 'My people are under no misapprehension as to who you are.'

She looked at him sharply. He was speaking in riddles again and she didn't want to play his game. She stayed silent as they continued through the city, amazed at the contrast of the old and the new; the ancient-looking mosques, timeless and elegant, the piercing skyscrapers, modern architectural master-pieces—Hebra had it all.

Eventually the car slowed to a crawl outside a pair of massive timber and iron gates swinging slowly open, which thudded resoundingly shut behind them as the car pulled into a large courtyard. A small wel-coming party stood waiting.

He took her hand and squeezed it gently. 'Welcome to my home,' he said before the doors both sides were pulled open and he dropped her hand to alight.

She stepped out onto the ancient cobbled courtyard before the tall palace that was to be her home for the next four weeks. It was magnificent even in the dark of night with spotlights strategically placed to illu-minate the walls and the towers. In the light of day it would be spectacular, its creamy walls studded with mother-of-pearl and tortoiseshell, giving a sumptuous appearance and texture.

Khaled's hand pressed against the small of her back, and she let him guide her to meet the small group waiting for them. A tall man in traditional dress, his face lean and hollow, his beard greying and neatly trimmed and his eyes bearing a strong resem-blance to Khaled's, stepped down to greet them.

'Saleem,' said Khaled, embracing the man, 'let me introduce you to the famous designer, Sapphire Clemenger, from the House of Bacelli in Milan. Sapphy, this is my cousin, Saleem.'

Saleem took her hand, bowing over it graciously before he raised his head and looked up at her, the sudden glint in his eyes sending ice-cold spiders crawling down her spine. 'Welcome to Jebbai,' he said, his mouth curved into what she supposed was intended to pass as a smile.

She'd never experienced anything less welcoming, but managed somehow to crack the layer of ice he'd submerged her under enough to dredge up a smile of her own and murmur her thanks before the rest of the party was briefly introduced. Finally a shy-looking young woman was presented to her.

'This is Azizah,' Khaled told her as the girl bowed. 'She will be your maid.'

She smiled again, much more genuinely this time, and took the girl's hand. 'So you are to help me with the dressmaking?'

'No,' interrupted Khaled, before the girl could respond. 'You will have a staff of ten to help you construct the dress. They will be here first thing in the morning for your instruction. Azizah is your personal maid. She will do whatever you ask.'

'That's hardly necessary,' she protested. 'I won't need an entire staff to make one dress.'

'You have only four weeks and you were the one who thought that was not enough time—remember? So, you have staff. Now, let me show you to your accommodation.' His hand at her back, he urged her up the wide steps to the large keyhole-style opening leading inside.

'Surely the girl can show her to her quarters,'

Saleem's heavily accented English broke in. 'There are matters of state to discuss.'

Khaled wheeled and turned on his cousin. 'Five minutes will make no difference. I will show Miss Clemenger to her quarters. *Then* I will meet you in the library.'

She shuddered as he directed her inside the palace. 'Are you cold?' he asked, surprising her by even noticing.

'No.' The palace interior's temperature was even and comfortable, the air sweet with the faint hint of incense. No doubt thick walls would keep the interior bearable on even the hottest day.

'Then what's wrong?

'Tell me,' he insisted, when still she hadn't answered. 'You're my responsibility now.'

'It's probably nothing—it's just your cousin, Saleem; I get the impression he doesn't like me.'

'He will have to get used to you.'

'Do you think so? In just four weeks?' Khaled glared sharply down at her as he led her through a wide marble pillared reception hall.

'Well, if he doesn't like me now, I'm not sure what I can do to change things in barely a month.'

'It will pay you not to upset Saleem. He is family. Things are different here to how they are done in Milan or even in Australia.'

Sapphy opened her mouth to protest that Saleem already seemed upset enough with her without her doing a thing, but then snapped it shut before uttering a word. What was the point? He was right. Things were bound to be different here. It would just be easier if she didn't feel such an intruder—Saleem had made it crystal clear that he didn't welcome her presence.

But it was only for four weeks after all, maybe less if she could complete the dress early. So the sooner she got stuck into making the wedding dress, the sooner she could return to Milan.

After walking along passageway after passageway, Khaled finally showed her into a reception-cum-sitting room, large and spacious. 'This is your study,' he said, waving his arm over the luxurious lounge suite and the substantial desk, complete with paper and writing tools. 'And this,' he said showing her through into an adjoining room, 'is your workshop. I trust you have everything you need. If not, just ask.'

Sapphy's eyes opened in wonder as she followed him. The room was enormous, at least twice the size of her apartment in Milan and then some. Worktables were arranged at intervals, many topped with sewing machines, all serious industrial models, she noticed as she wandered between them, not simple home dressmaking machines. Bolts of fabric lined the walls—silk, satin, brocade and laces in every bridal colour and tone imaginable. Tubs of beads and sequins, pearls and buttons were stacked on a bench. She'd seen fabric shops with less stock.

'It's incredible. How did you know?' she asked, her eyes still wide with wonder as she attempted to take it all in.

'Gianfranco told me what you might need. It was then a simple matter to have it delivered.'

'No,' she said, turning her eyes up to his. 'How did you know I would come? You couldn't be sure I would agree until today.'

Something fused, deep in his eyes, as he eliminated the distance between them with three quick-fire steps. All at once she was craning her neck up to where he stood before her. A muscle worked in his jaw as he reached out a hand. For a moment she flinched, not wanting him to grab hold of her as he'd done earlier in the car, but this time his touch was feather-light as he traced a slow line from her forehead to her jaw with just the pads of his long fingers.

'*I* was sure. I knew you would come.'

His voice was low with a husky new quality that sent tremors through her, compounding the sensations he'd stirred in her skin. She sucked in a breath that was too light on oxygen, too heavy on raw male sexuality. The pad of his thumb brushed over her lips and she tasted him, his salty heat further stirring her senses into disarray.

Her mind was a mess. Thoughts came and collided with no hint of logic or resolution. How could he have known she would come to Jebbai when she hadn't even known herself? How could he have been so certain?

And why did just one look from his dark eyes make her feel so liquid?

His fingers tilted her chin, so there was no way she could avoid his searing gaze, no way she couldn't notice his wide lips, slightly parted, no way she couldn't imagine what they would feel like on hers.

Anticipate them on hers.

'What I didn't know,' he said, his breath curling around her in the space between them, warm and hypnotic, 'was just how perfect you would be.'

She read his last words on her lips as his mouth descended over hers, warm and gentling, and the contrast in the man struck her. He appeared so strong and hard, upright and defiant, he looked every part the ruler of his kingdom, and yet his kiss was so tender, so sweet, it seemed to squeeze something from her even as it rocked her to her soul. The power was there, lurking just below the surface, but there was so much more besides, so many nuances, so many textures to experience—the softness of his lips, the nip of his teeth, the rasp of his shadowed chin...

She felt her internal thermostat reset itself to slow burn as his mouth gently plundered her own, exploring, manipulating.

She felt his hands at her shoulders, behind her neck, down her back, their gathering touch strangely compelling. They invited her closer and she complied, leaning into the kiss and feeling the press of his firm chest against her own tight breasts.

Then he was gone from her and she blinked, swaying and throwing out a hand to the neighbouring table to steady herself, embarrassed and ashamed as she realised just how easily she'd let herself be manipulated into that kiss. Hardly the mark of a professional on her first day on the job.

'That was a mistake,' she whispered, her voice unusually thick, her hand covering lips still excruciatingly sensitised.

'We had to stop,' he said, one side of his mouth kicked up in a lazy grin. 'Saleem is waiting for me.'

'No!' She spun around, hugging her arms to herself. 'It was a mistake to kiss me. You're getting married. I have a b… I have a boyfriend. It's wrong.'

'You appeared to have no trouble forgetting your so-called ''boyfriend'' just then. Or do you just make a habit of forgetting him whenever it suits you?'

'Of course not!' she insisted. She had never been unfaithful to Paolo, never even thought about another man until now, when their relationship seemed stalled and their differences all the while harder to broach.

Though that wasn't the entire truth. She'd never considered any other man until Khaled had stormed onto the scene and into her life, all rampant testosterone and masculine force. 'Although you make a veritable art form of regularly forgetting you will soon have a wife.'

He came up quickly behind her and by the time she'd turned in surprise he had one arm planted firmly either side of her, trapping her against the long workbench. 'I don't forget,' he said, leaning into her, his voice tight and betraying a rising sense of fury. 'If you must know, I'm very much looking forward to it.'

He dropped his arms and wheeled away, leaving her breathless and dizzy, her mind scrambling to make sense of his words.

'I must meet with Saleem. Afterwards we will dine together—Azizah will show you the way. Meanwhile there is one more room,' he said, thrusting out an arm to indicate a door opposite. 'Do you wish me to show it to you?'

'What's in there?'

'Your bedroom.'

She swallowed, feeling solid colour infuse her cheeks. 'No, thank you. I'll manage.'

She could still recall the amused look on his face at her prim response, long after he was gone.

Dinner was a subdued affair. Saleem ignored her for the most part, directing most of his conversation at Khaled, which suited her just fine. Not that she was interested in chatting too much to Khaled either. While there were questions she wanted to ask, about his family and the history of Jebbai, she was still too shaken by the episode in the workroom. The last thing she needed to do was show him any encouragement.

It was easier to look more interested in the food. The array of spiced meats, salads and dips was laid out invitingly on the low table between them as they reclined on colourful silk cushions. She tried to focus on the spread, to sample the different tastes, all the while biding her time until she thought it was safe to excuse herself and withdraw to bed.

But her thoughts were elsewhere. She'd flung her relationship with Paolo in Khaled's face, a convenient defence in fending off his unwelcome advances, but she'd stumbled over the word 'boyfriend' as if it had been an effort. Why didn't that bother her more when it hinted that the problems they'd dredged up during their argument were more deep-seated than she'd thought? Why was it so hard to even think of Paolo as her boyfriend now?

They would talk some time after her return, he'd promised. She should hold that thought. Instead, on some deeper, instinctive level, she suspected their relationship was already beyond salvage.

Her thoughts in turmoil with the stresses of the last few days, she allowed herself one tiny cup of thick, sweet coffee before she sensed her opportunity to excuse herself. She stood, hoping to make a smooth getaway.

'Sapphire, you're not leaving us already?'

'I'm sorry, Khaled,' she replied, trying to ignore the long, hard glare she earned from Saleem, 'it's been a long day and I wish to get started early in the morning.'

'Of course,' he said, 'I should have realised. Is there anything else that you need?'

'Only some idea when I might get to meet your bride. It would be good to at least talk to her about the design before I get too far along the process.'

Saleem uttered something rapid-fire and urgent in Arabic. Khaled answered simply and briefly in English, 'No,' at which response Saleem's nostrils flared and he rose from the cushions, muttering a few more words in his cousin's direction as he stormed out without another glance at her.

'Did I say something wrong?' she asked, recalling Khaled's warning not to upset his cousin.

He shrugged. 'Saleem is…anxious, as are we all, for the welfare of the bride. Now is not a good time. I will let you know when she is available.'

'Is she in the palace?'

'Oh, yes,' he said, his eyes sparkling. 'She is already here, but she is not yet ready for the excitement of the wedding. It is too early. I will tell you when.'

'But it will be soon?'

He nodded. 'Indeed, it will be soon.'

It would have to do. She bade him goodnight and turned to go. Work on the dress would have to commence as best it could. And some time soon she'd have to hope for a series of fittings, while there was still time to make any adjustments if necessary.

'Oh, and one more thing.'

'Yes?' she said, looking over her shoulder.

'Everyone who is a guest of the palace receives a gift.'

'That's not necessary,' she said, shaking her head. 'I'm working here—'

He held up his hand in a stop gesture. 'It is necessary. You are still my guest. And you will receive traditional Jebbai garments as your gift. You would not think of offending Hebra's finest dressmakers surely? They are most honoured to be designing something for you, a famous designer from the fashion capital of Milan.'

'No,' she conceded. 'Of course I wouldn't want to offend them. Thank you.'

'Good,' he said with an air of finality. 'Someone will be sent to measure you for them tomorrow morning. Goodnight.'

CHAPTER FIVE

SAPPHY threw herself into her work over the next few days. She organised her staff, planning a schedule and putting those she could to work immediately. She'd never had so many people to work on her designs so in one way it was luxury, in another it was a challenge keeping them all occupied and coordinating what they were doing.

But they were excellent. It was clear straight away that Khaled had supplied her with top dressmakers and seamstresses, expert at sewing and beading. Some she'd been able to set tasks immediately, to work on the delicate veil, or bead the intricate panels that would be inset later into the dress. Even the language difficulties she'd expected didn't eventuate.

And while she hadn't been permitted to meet with the bride, she'd been provided with a set of measurements, allowing her to draft the pattern and run up a model in a simple fabric to test the design. And now, one short week after her arrival in Jebbai, the dress itself was starting to take shape.

Her new life was taking shape too, already assuming some kind of pattern. In the mornings she took breakfast in her suite, usually fresh fruit with dates, dried figs and creamy yoghurt, while she arranged her schedule for the day.

Then she would work solidly until four or five o'clock, depending on the day's progress. While her staff took a midday break she inspected their work, which was for the most part faultless, and that ensured better than anticipated progress.

Azizah would let her know when it was time for the evening meal and, as she had on the first evening, she would join in a shared meal with Khaled and Saleem. Khaled would ask after her health and seek a report on the dress, and she would tell him what he wished to know.

She was still reluctant to open up and talk freely with Saleem present—somehow she didn't feel comfortable with him knowing anything about her and it was clear he didn't welcome her input. So for the most part she left the two men to discuss matters amongst themselves and she'd then excuse herself after coffee, removing herself while doing her best to ignore Saleem's frosty glare and Khaled's hooded gaze.

It wasn't exactly pleasant, but at least now she was becoming used to the routine and learning not to feel so uptight in their presence.

Tonight something was different though. She looked around the dining room at the appointed time but no cold stares returned her own. Khaled sat alone amidst the plump cushions.

'Come,' he said, beckoning her to join him.

'Saleem?' she asked, lowering herself opposite.

'Is away.' He poured her a glass of tea. 'I'm afraid you're going to be stuck with just me for tonight.' He handed her the small glass and held on, even when she'd moved to take it from him.

Her eyes found his and caught the crinkle at the sides.

He was laughing at her.

'Lucky me,' she said, wresting the glass from his grasp, suddenly ruing Saleem's absence. His resentful disposition seemed suddenly preferable to Khaled's unwelcome jibes. 'Tell me,' she said, looking to wipe the smug look from his face and regain the initiative, 'how is your fiancée?'

With coffee came Sapphy's chance to make her usual quick exit.

'Are you in a hurry to leave?' he asked.

'Not at all,' she lied, when all she wanted to do was escape. Dinner had been tense after their early jibes and more than once she'd caught his brooding eyes fixed on her, surveying her. But why?

'Then come,' he said, rising from the cushions and holding out his hand. 'I want to show you something.'

'Where are you taking me?' she asked, as he led her into a part of the palace she'd never been before. He'd taken her through a seeming labyrinth of passageways, up and down short stairways and turning this way and that, so much so that she wasn't sure she'd ever be able to find her way back by herself.

'You'll see,' he said, finally leading her through a large, richly decorated doorway. She followed him through and stepped into another world.

Lush greenery surrounded her, softly lit with

torches flickering shadows against the ferns, palms and vines. Scented flowers perfumed the air, sweet and rich. They were in a large courtyard, completely enclosed by the palace, but the foliage was so tall in places that you could imagine you were miles from civilisation. From somewhere unseen came the splash of water, setting a musical backdrop, while the exotic call of birds settling down for the evening provided an accompaniment.

'It's the most beautiful garden I've ever seen,' she said as she wandered along the marble-paved walkways lined with clipped shrubs and stone. She recognised a few of the plants and bushes—myrtle, bay trees, even a grove of orange trees, their coloured fruit standing out against the foliage as brightly as ornaments on a Christmas tree.

He reached up alongside her and plucked one of the oranges from the tree and handed the heavy fruit to her solemnly.

'The best oranges either side of the Tigris,' he said before he twisted off another for himself, studying it, weighing it in his hands as he talked.

'This was my mother's favourite place. My father had it planted for her as a wedding present.'

She looked up at him. It was the first time he'd ever referred to his parents. Apart from Saleem, she knew nothing at all of his family. She touched his forearm gently.

'Tell me about them.'

Even in the muted light, she saw the darkness swirl in his eyes, felt the tension in his corded arm, and for a moment she thought he wasn't going to respond. Then he uttered a deep sigh and turned down the path, taking her with him.

'My mother was a Frenchwoman, a model turned successful actress. And very, very beautiful. My father saw her on the screen and fell in love with her at first sight. He went to Paris and wooed her and brought her back to be his wife.'

A French mother. An Arab father. And no doubt a university education in Europe somewhere. His blend of accents suddenly made sense. No wonder he'd been so difficult to place.

'What happened to your mother's film career? Did she continue making movies?'

'Not once she married my father.'

'She gave it all up? She left everything behind, her career, her stardom, to come here and be someone's wife?'

'Does that surprise you? My father was a very good-looking man. He was also very persuasive and he wanted her.'

'But what about what she wanted? Times might have been different then, but didn't she get some say in it?'

'She wasn't a prisoner here. She could have left any time. But she fell in love with my father and they were married. They were very happy together. Very happy.'

She matched his steps along the marble flagstones, marvelling at the constantly changing views at each turn, feeling the magic of the garden permeate her soul. It was so peaceful here, so beautiful. Was it enough, though, to make someone abandon their former life?

'She must have loved him very much,' she said at last and he nodded silently, seemingly lost in his own thoughts.

Yet for all the apparent romance, there was clearly no happy ending to this story. She could sense it in his mounting tension, she could sense it in the air that fairly crackled around him.

'What happened to them?'

He brought her to a halt alongside a large tiered fountain, staring without focus at the marble animals, the deer and antelope, the birds and the fish, playfully squirting streams of water from their mouths. It was a work of art but she could tell he saw nothing of the artisans' skill, nothing of the beauty of the piece as his mind fixed on another event, another time. 'They were killed by an avalanche,' he said, his voice strangely flat. 'They were supposed to be in London but there was a sudden change of plan.' He paused. 'They ended up going to the Alps instead...'

His words trailed off, lost in the burble of the fountain.

'That's terrible,' she said. 'I'm so sorry.' She knew it was painfully inadequate but there was nothing more she could offer.

'They should have been in London,' he asserted, the volume in his voice rising. 'If they'd been in London, they would never have been swept away. They would never have been killed.'

His vehemence tipped her off. For whatever reason Khaled obviously held himself responsible for his parents' change of plan. 'You mustn't blame yourself,' she offered.

His eyes blasted cold fury down onto her, his face all brutal angles and harsh planes in the soft light from the torches.

'That's where you're wrong,' he muttered through clenched teeth. 'It's not me that I blame.'

He turned and stormed off, leaving the sharp tang of orange peel piercing the turbulent air in his wake. A flash of colour on the ground caught her eye. It was his orange. She picked it up, assuming he'd dropped it in his rush to get away.

Until she saw the imprints left by his fingers, the angry wounds caused by his nails, puncturing the skin and pulverising the flesh with such force that, compared to hers, the inside of his orange was no more than pulp.

It had been a mistake to take her there. Instead of making her feel more at ease with him, all he'd done was dredge up the hate from deep inside him until it spilled over, fetid and rank.

But he would have his revenge. It was now so close he could taste it. And it would be sweeter than he'd ever imagined.

The dress was nearing completion. It was going to be magnificent, without a doubt the most beautiful wedding dress she'd designed. Even the champagne-coloured silk dress she'd whipped up for her own sister, Opal's, wedding in Sydney two years ago and that she'd been so proud of couldn't hold a candle to this design.

All it now needed was a fitting or two and the seams could be completed, the length tweaked and the finishing touches made. And all Khaled had to do was agree to her request to allow her just one hour with the bride, instead of continually frustrating her with excuses and deferments.

He'd hardly spoken to her since that strange night a week ago in the gardens when his barely restrained fury had been a palpable thing and his cryptic words still haunted her. For some reason she'd upped the ante on his emotions that night in a way that made her feel that somehow, in some strange and inexplicable way, *she* was responsible for the death of his parents.

But that was crazy. She'd grown up on the other side of the world. She'd never had anything to do with the royal family of Jebbai. It didn't make sense.

She tried to push these thoughts aside as she sat at her desk, writing postcards in the hour before lunch. She'd sent her staff home early as, until Khaled agreed to a fitting, there was nothing more for them to do. She'd already completed brief greetings for her family, her mother and sisters back in Australia. It was the last postcard she wavered over.

What should she say to Paolo?

Her mobile phone was useless out here and in a way she was glad. She wanted Paolo to contact her first. But he hadn't made any attempt. They hadn't spoken since their argument in Milan and somehow 'the weather's fine, wish you were here' didn't cut it. So why couldn't she think of anything to write?

Part of her wanted to reach out and repair the damage to their relationship. The other part of her was still angry with him. He'd scared her half mad with his predictions of disaster in Jebbai, done his best to put her off going. And without offering a shred of evidence to support his crazy claims.

Without a doubt Khaled was a force to be reckoned with. Certainly he had issues with the tragic death of his parents, but was that so unusual?

Whatever, surely it should be easier to recall exactly how Paolo looked while she attempted to write this postcard? Instead her thoughts were infused with the shadow of a tall, dark-eyed man, brooding and magnetic, emphatic and compulsive. Why did he come to mind so easily when pictures of Paolo were proving so difficult to summon? Why was it so hard to forget about him?

A knock on the door interrupted her thoughts. 'Come in,' she called without looking up, expecting Azizah to be returning from some errand or advising her that the midday meal was ready.

'Am I interrupting you?'

Her head snapped up to where he stood inside the door, looking down at her. She shivered. He hadn't been in her rooms since the day she'd arrived. Somehow the large room seemed shrunken with him in it. He strode closer to the desk, pouncing on the postcard she was toying with. She hadn't managed to get further than the address and 'Dear Paolo'. A nerve in his cheek twitched. Her heart jumped wildly in her chest. They'd never discussed Paolo by name so how would Khaled react to seeing her postcard addressed to him? And would he recall their differences as clearly and as vehemently as had Paolo?

'Missing your boyfriend?'

Her blood formed an icy crust. 'Who said he was my boyfriend?'

His eyebrows lifted. 'Fair question,' he said. 'Maybe "lover" would be more appropriate.'

Her knuckles tightened as she screwed her fingers tighter around her pen. 'I haven't finished that.'

'On the contrary, you haven't started it. Nothing to say after so long apart?'

She kicked up her chin. She wasn't going to discuss Paolo and their relationship with anybody, least of all with Khaled. 'The dress is just about complete,' she said, switching topics. 'When are you going to agree to my request for a fitting with the bride?'

He flicked the card back down onto the desk. 'She knows what you're doing. There's no rush.'

'On the contrary,' she said, reiterating his own words for emphasis, 'there's every reason to rush. You have two weeks until this wedding and if I can complete this gown now, that's one major thing out of the way and then I can go home. I need just one fitting with the bride and my work is almost done.'

He lunged towards the desk and spread his arms down wide around her, his face dipping closer to hers.

'Are you in such a hurry to return to your lover? Why so, when he has made no attempt to contact you in all the time you have been here?'

'How do you know he hasn't?'

'Has he?' he challenged.

She refused to let her gaze fall. She would not be drawn into whatever game Khaled was playing.

'The dress is almost ready,' she repeated. 'When do I get my fitting?'

'Show me,' he said.

She was grateful for the opportunity to get up from her desk and burn up some of her nervous tension, if only by walking to the next room. She led the way into the workroom, where the almost completed garment sat on the model set up according to the measurements provided. Even on something as inanimate as a headless arrangement of metal and padding the dress was sensational. She felt a surge of pride just looking at it. Together with the team that Khaled had assembled for her, she'd turned a rough sketch into a dress that would turn its wearer into a princess. It would be perfect.

Or it could be, if only she could be guaranteed a fitting before the big day.

'Here it is,' she said. 'Now, when do I get my fitting?'

'When I say so.'

'*I* am the designer here and I say that I need to have a fitting now.'

'The bride is not ready.'

'This is crazy. If your bride cannot manage to turn

up for a fitting, how can you be so sure she'll turn up for the wedding?'

'She'll be there.'

'You think so?' She hesitated, almost afraid to put to voice the thoughts her mind was now throwing around. 'You know, I thought she must be desperately sick, that's why the secrecy, that's why her non-appearance for a fitting and her complete non-involvement in this wedding. Yet you don't act like the husband-to-be of an ill woman. Something's not right. She's not sick, is she?'

'I never said she was ill.'

'You let me believe she was.' It was an accusation.

He shrugged. 'What you choose to believe is up to you.'

'But then, why else would she be so invisible? What other reason can there be for her not wanting to be involved in her own wedding?'

Her mind churned, wheels turning as the fight she'd had with Paolo came into sharp relief. He'd warned her that things weren't right. The shudder that moved through her chilled her to the bone. She gritted her teeth to prevent them chattering as the knowledge of what he was doing seeped into her consciousness.

'I have to question whether there even is a bride,' she whispered, when at last the tremors in her body had stilled enough for her to talk. 'That would explain why she's not exactly champing at the bit to walk down the aisle with you. I've been here for two weeks without catching a glimpse of her. Nobody talks about her and I don't even think she's got a name. You've certainly never mentioned it. There's no bride and no wedding and no reason for me to be here. Yet I don't understand—'

'There is a bride!'

'Oh? Then maybe Paolo was right. I should have listened to him. He warned me this was on the cards, that even if there was a bride, she might be less than willing.

'Is that closer to the mark, then?' she continued, her voice lifting in her own certainty. 'Is that what you're worried about—that your reluctant bride has to be dragged kicking and screaming to the altar because she's being forced to marry you? Is that why you can't let her have a fitting, because the poor girl can't bear the thought of wearing the dress on her wedding day, let alone any other time? Because she can't bear the thought of marrying you?'

He spun towards her, reaching out, cold fury gathered like storm clouds in his eyes, the lines of his golden skin drawn and tight around his mouth. His hands clenched down on her upper arms like iron claws, manacles for her arms, pinning her to the spot with a white-hot grip.

'You think your Paolo knows everything? Obviously he could not or you would not be here.'

'Wha—? What do you mean?'

'You really want to meet my bride? You so desperately want this fitting?'

She swallowed, tasting his fury on her tongue, swirling in the heated fog of his proximity. Yet even in a rage she felt his raw sexuality reach out for her.

Even in her fear she felt her own body react, her breasts achingly firm, her thighs soften and pulse within.

She battled to focus on his words when his lips were so close. Too close. She could bury herself in his heat, lose herself in his power.

He could make it happen and she would be powerless to stop him.

She wouldn't want to stop him.

She wouldn't even try to stop him.

'Well?' he demanded, dragging her thoughts back into focus. 'You want this fitting?'

She sucked in a breath too low on oxygen and too highly charged with the scent of him and tried to forget how much he affected her. 'All she needs is to try on the dress. Just once. That's all. And then I'll be happy.'

He scoffed. 'Then you'll be happy?'

Her chin kicked up, reclaiming some measure of defiance. 'Just one fitting. It's not too much to ask, surely?'

'Okay,' he said, almost discarding her as he let go his grip and wheeled away. Two strides on he turned back, the fury in his eyes replaced with something else—*boldness*? 'You win. You get your fitting.'

At last. She let go a deep breath she'd been holding and rubbed her arms where the touch of him lingered like a brand. She would finally get the fitting she'd been asking for, then she could complete the dress and get on the next flight out of here. It wouldn't be soon enough. 'So when? How soon can you arrange it?'

'Right now.'

There was no way she would miss the opportunity. 'About time. Would it be best to take the dress there?'

'No need for that. We can do it right here.'

'What do you mean—you'll bring her here?'

'No,' he said, the spark in his eyes taking on a victorious gleam. 'You wanted a fitting with the bride—you've got one.'

'But I don't understand.'

'So put it on.'

'What?'

'Put-the-dress-on!'

CHAPTER SIX

'No!' COLD fear crashed over her, a drenching wave that left logic spluttering in its wake. 'This has to be some kind of sick joke.'

His eyebrows lifted in response, his mouth curling dangerously into a bare grin that held no trace of humour. He took a step closer. 'You will make a beautiful bride.'

She shook her head, inching backwards as she kept her eyes fixed on him, willing him to keep his distance as her mind battled for reason.

He moved closer still.

'You're just trying to scare me, because I insisted on this fitting. You're just trying to get back at me.' She felt the worktable behind her, clutching on to it with tight fingers for support, praying for its solidity and strength to supplement her own.

'Are you going to try it on?'

'No, of course not.'

He stopped just inches away, looking down at her, and she waited for the moment when he would reach out and touch her, searing her again with his hands.

It was crazy. What he was saying was crazy, yet still the anticipation of his touch threatened to wipe out logical thought. And she needed to think straight, needed to harness every shred of reason that she could muster in order to fight her way out of his onslaught.

'You were the one who insisted on a fitting.'

'It's not my dress.'

'Isn't it? Then whose measurements do you think were provided to you? That dress was made to fit you like a glove. That dress was made for you.'

'How?' she asked even as the realisation hit her— they'd taken her measurements her first morning here. *She'd let them take them.* 'You tricked me. You said those were so they could make some sort of gift. You lied to me.'

He shook his head. 'I did not lie. Your traditional Jebbai garments have been made for you. I just did not tell you all of the truth.'

'This is mad. I'm not your bride. I won't be your bride. You can't make me.'

'I won't need to. You'll come to me willingly.'

She laughed, her tension betrayed in the short, fractured sound. 'Now you kid yourself. Why the hell would I do that?'

'Because,' he said, curling one hand around her neck, while the other snaked its way around her waist, pulling her close and extinguishing the space between them, 'you want me.'

She fought the pressure of his hands, not allowing herself to be collected as easily as he might wish. 'In your dreams.'

'I do dream, as it happens,' he said, his voice low and close to her ear, so that his breath curled against her skin, the sensation assailing her senses. 'And I dream of you, in my bed, under me, on top of me, bucking with me. Every way I dream of you and your eyes flashing blue as you explode in my arms.'

Her breath stuck fast in her throat as his lips caressed the skin under her ear while the very same pictures played wide-screen in her mind.

It wasn't just her then.

The attraction she'd felt, the pull, the magnetism— if what he said was true it wasn't just one-sided. He felt it too, this allure, this desire.

Clothing faded to insignificance as she was dragged into contact with him, from her chest to her thighs, and, for all the protection they gave her, her clothes might not have been there. His arousal pressed firm and hard into her belly, proof of his own attraction and upping the gears on her own need. Involuntarily she squirmed against him, driven more by passion than by common sense.

He uttered something in Arabic, something primal and guttural, a low roar that spoke of his own desires, as he lowered his head, meshing his mouth with hers.

Her senses blurred in the rush of blood, the bloom of hotness that came at the touch of his lips, as his mouth moved over hers. *Intoxicating.* How could one mouth feel so persuasive, so magical?

The urge to comply with the sweet demands of his lips was almost irresistible, the urge to let her own mouth open and blossom under his overwhelming. He tasted of intensity and power, of the timeless desert sands, and he tasted so right. He felt so right. Her body was already preparing itself for more, wanting more.

But he wasn't right.

He was wrong.

Wrong about her—wrong for her—just plain wrong. And she would be making the mistake of her life to give in to his sensual onslaught.

How could she believe anything he said or did? This was a man who'd brought her to Jebbai under false pretences. This was a man who'd got her here by claiming he was marrying another, only to think he could claim her for his bride.

This was a man who had lost his grip on reality.

And she would not be part of his fantasy!

She wrenched back her head, fighting off the band of his arm around her neck, pushing him away at his shoulders.

'No,' she breathed, her mouth dodging his searching lips. 'Let me go.'

He caught her hands in his, trapping her forearms against his chest. 'You want me, don't try to deny it.'

'No. I don't want you,' she insisted, her voice defiant, even though she knew she was hardly telling the whole truth. 'Why would I? I have a boyfriend.'

Strangely he smiled. It was the last thing she'd expected and his cool reaction to her words stilled her fight.

'Ah, of course. Paolo.' In her motionless state he transferred one wrist to join the other. With his free hand he drew a slow line from her forehead to her chin. 'The newspapers seemed to suggest he was more than just a *boyfriend*, though. Wasn't there talk of marriage between you?'

Her veins turned to ice even as his fingers seemed to sear her soul. How would he know that? Just how long had he been watching her?

'All right,' she said, putting aside the complications of her relationship with Paolo in the disturbing warmth generated by Khaled's touch. 'Yes, I have a fiancé. And if I'm going to marry anyone, I'd prefer it to be him.'

He laughed, sudden and loud and as if he was truly enjoying himself. Yet there was unmistakably a hard edge she heard there too.

'Tell me, then,' he asked, 'do you think Paolo will rush to your rescue? Do you think he would marry you himself, just to save you from me? Is your lover that much of a hero?'

'Of course he would marry me,' she maintained, stiffening further in his arms, certain that, for all his recent and inexplicable inability to commit, he would never let her suffer the indignity of a forced marriage to anyone, let alone someone like Sheikh Khaled. 'And he will, just as soon as I get out of this place.'

She kicked her chin up defiantly. So it wasn't exactly the truth—Khaled didn't need to know that, and Paolo *had* said that they would work out their differences on her return. But if it brought Khaled to his senses, so much the better.

He paused and frowned, and something indefinable intruded into his dark eyes. 'You love him that much you would believe that?' he asked, his dark, clouded eyes searching hers.

The sudden tender note in his voice took her by surprise. Did he really care how much she felt for Paolo? 'I... Of course—'

He didn't wait for her to finish stumbling over her sentence. He let her go, lifting his hands from her and stalking away, raking one hand through his hair.

'He won't marry you,' he said softly.

She wasn't sure she'd heard right. 'Pardon?'

'He won't marry you.' This time louder so there was no mistaking his words.

'You can't know that,' she accused, her voice amazingly steady while all the time her mind screamed, *How do you know?* How could he sound so sure, so certain? There was no way he could know something like that.

His eyes told her he did.

Warning bells sounded in her head. 'What's this all about?' she asked, trying to connect the dots between Khaled's crazy intention to marry her and Paolo's deep-seated resentment. She wasn't sure what it meant, but somehow there was a connection. There had to be. 'Why me? Why did you pick on me to be your bride?'

He shrugged. 'I saw a picture of you. I heard about your reputation. Everything I learned about you fascinated me. I had to meet you. And when I met you, in the salon, I knew you were the one for me.'

She surveyed him coolly. 'That's too unbelievable for words.'

'Why? Don't you believe in love at first sight? It happened to my father. Why shouldn't the same thing happen to me?'

'Because unlike your mother, I already have a boy-friend. I'm not looking for a husband.'

'Paolo won't marry you because he can't.'

Something inside her snapped. She'd had enough. She threw her hands up in the air in exasperation. She didn't want any more of his mind games. She didn't need them. Now that he'd let her go she had better things to do with her time—like pack her suitcase and get out of there.

'I don't have to listen to this. I don't know what you think you know and I don't really care. I'm leaving.'

She turned for the door and his words came after her as sharp as a dagger. 'Didn't you hear me? It's not possible for him to marry you.'

'I'm not listening,' she said, shaking her head as she reached for the workshop door to slam behind her. 'I don't care.'

She gave the door one hell of a swing, thinking her energies could have been much better directed at connecting her fist with one particularly arrogant sheikh's jaw, but there was no resounding slam, no satisfying conclusion. She turned, growling in frustration, only to see him right behind her, blocking the space the door should have filled.

'Don't you want to know why?'

She put her hands over her ears as she headed for her bedroom. 'No. I don't want to hear what you think you know. Don't you understand? I just want to get out of here. I just want to get away from you!'

'Then you should care,' he said, nonchalantly tracing her steps. 'Because it's obvious that, for someone apparently in love with you, he hasn't been totally honest.'

That got her attention! She swivelled around where she stood, buried in the walk-in wardrobe, her suitcase in hand, already in flight. Just her luck that when she finally got to enjoy a dressing room large enough to swing a suitcase, she would have been more than happy to hit a few walls, or one particular sheikh, just for effect.

'Oh, that's rich, coming from you.' She flipped open the suitcase on the floor, started tearing clothes from hangers and flinging them in while the prick of tears stung her eyes, blurring her vision. But there was no way she was giving in to them. No way. 'What would you know about honesty? You've lied to me from day one.'

'But I never pretended to be in love with you.'

Her frantic movements stilled, her hands midway to the next item, as the fury inside her reached meltdown. 'You're mad!' she said, dragging the shirt free from its hanger at last. 'You must be, to think that I would stay here to be your bride. To even talk about love in such circumstances is a joke. I don't want you as a husband and I certainly don't want your love.'

She collected up the few remaining items from the shelves and tossed them on top of everything else before pushing past him to get to her bathroom and gather up her toiletries. She jammed the zipper bag on top and then bundled the whole pile to somehow fit the suitcase's confines.

'Where do you think you're going?'

'Where do you think? I'm going home.' She flipped out the case's handle, set it right side up on its wheeled base and puffed out her chest defiantly. 'And then I'm going to marry Paolo.'

She pushed past him, unsure of how exactly she was going to get to the airport and how long she'd have to wait when she got there for a flight, but determined to get out now anyway.

'That's *after* his divorce comes through, I take it.'

She kept walking with barely a hitch, her heeled sandals clicking on the cool tiled floor, suitcase rolling behind. 'Well, if that's your trump card,' she said without raising her voice, knowing he was still close enough to hear every word, 'you just blew it. I'm afraid you've got the wrong Paolo. My fiancé has never been married.'

'Oh, he never shared that piece of information with you, then?'

'On the contrary. He had nothing to share. Like I said, you've got the wrong Paolo.'

'Paolo Eduardo Mancini? Married an English student, Helene Elizabeth Grainger, in Paris on March twenty-fifth twelve years ago. Funny that he'd never share that news with you, his lover, his fiancée.'

Okay, so what that he had Paolo's name right? She bit down on her bottom lip and forced herself further along the hallway. No way was she going to show him he was rattling her. It couldn't be true. It just couldn't.

Although it could explain why Paolo had been so cagey…

No!

She trusted Paolo. She had no reason at all to doubt him. Whereas she had no reason to trust Khaled. No reason at all.

'You'll have to do better than that, I'm afraid,' she tossed over her shoulder with a wave of her free hand as she kept walking.

'Then maybe you'd appreciate seeing the wedding video? Or perhaps the photographs. I have an extensive collection.'

Video? Photographs? This time her steps faltered as the air evaporated in her lungs.

'Why should I believe you?' She didn't turn and her voice was barely more than a croak. Surely it couldn't be true? And if it was, why hadn't Paolo told her?

All this time!

All this time they'd been dating and seeing each other and not once, even just once, had he intimated that he was already married, that he already had a wife. Why the hell wouldn't he have admitted to something like that? *Dammit*—he should have told her!

'In the end it's not about what you believe. It's about the truth. Your *fiancé* has already been married for twelve years.'

She squeezed her eyes shut as her head dipped to

her chest. 'Then I want to call him,' she said before sucking air deep into her lungs and looking back at him over her shoulder. 'Now!'

Five minutes later she was holding on to the receiver in Khaled's office, clutching the phone with white-knuckled fingers, waiting while the phone rang in an apartment somewhere in New York. She couldn't sit, nervous energy wouldn't let her limbs relax.

She had to stand, shifting impatiently from one foot to the other as she waited for the call to be picked up halfway around the globe, all the while trying to ignore the arrogant Jebbai ruler who sprawled unconscionably in the well-worn leather armchair opposite. He obviously had no trouble relaxing and that only added to her fears. The one hope that he'd back down on his crazy claims at her insistence on phoning Paolo drizzled away. He must be so certain that what he was saying was true.

She turned her back on his smug demeanour and glanced at her watch. What time was it in New York now? Some time in the night—he had to be there— she had to discover the truth now—or she didn't know what she'd do.

Eventually the phone was picked up and Paolo answered. 'Yes?' came his voice, thick with sleep and husky as if he'd tumbled straight out of bed to answer the phone. Something squeezed in her heart as she clamped her eyes shut, trying to staunch the flow of tears still so closely threatening. She knew that voice, had once rejoiced in it as he'd held her in his arms, had whispered to her how beautiful she was and that she was the most important person in the world to him.

But now it wasn't love she felt, love to warm and sustain her and hold her true. Now it was icy panic clamping her inside, compressing her last frantic hopes.

'Who is it?' More alert now, she could tell.

'Paolo,' she whispered, her voice set to break.

'Sapphy, *bella*. Is that you? What's wrong? Has something happened?'

The once oft-used term of endearment sliced a cold path through her with ruthless efficiency. If what Khaled said was true, she'd never been his darling, his sweetheart. Someone had held that place long before her.

'Sapphy? Are you still in Jebbai? What's Khaled done?' There was fear in his voice too, laced heavily with alarm. Was this just the normal concern of a person woken in the middle of the night to what could be devastating news, or did his reaction signal a deeper dread?

She swallowed back on a sob. 'Nothing's wrong,' she lied, feeling her whole world splitting apart as easily as fabric snipped at the edge and ripped in two. 'Just tell me one thing…' She hesitated, knowing this moment was about to change her life, change all her perceptions about living and love, and teach her about betrayal. This moment would be the start of her new life, in whatever form that took.

'Is it true—are you married? Do you have a wife?'

Silence met her questions, a damning silence that fractured whatever threads of hope remained intact. They were gone, shattered, smashed in his soundless affirmation of the truth.

'It's true, then,' she said on a sniff. 'You should have told me.'

'Sapphy, listen to me. I couldn't tell you—'

Even though his silence had already screamed the truth, his words cemented the facts with a cold, hard reality that shook her.

'I have nothing more to say to you,' she uttered with finality, her voice as chilled as her heart. 'Goodbye, Paolo.'

'Sapphy, listen to me—'

She dropped the receiver back onto the cradle. 'Goodbye, Paolo,' she whispered, shivering now, her arms hugged closely to her chest as the shock of deep sudden loss took hold.

Strong arms surrounded her and pulled her close. For a moment she wanted to struggle—what was this? The victorious barbarian staking his claim? But she sensed none of that with his warmth. Instead she felt compassion, even some kind of understanding, and she sagged gratefully into him, welcoming the solace and comfort he offered.

His strong heartbeat thumped loud in his chest, its rhythm steady and firm and as rock-solid as the man holding her.

'It's okay,' he whispered against her hair. His lips brushed her scalp in the barest of kisses and the warmth from the contact radiated down through her as her breathing steadied, her heart rate calming to match his.

And it hit her then.

Her life hadn't changed when she'd discovered the truth about Paolo. It had changed the moment Khaled had stepped inside the Milan salon. He'd been the catalyst, the trigger that had turned her life upside down.

When Khaled had kissed her that first time in the workroom, he'd forced her to face up to her ambivalence in her feelings for Paolo. She could never have betrayed someone she loved deeply by falling into the arms of another man. Now it had been Khaled again who'd proved her relationship had been a sham from the beginning.

Whatever his motives were for doing it she had no idea, but she certainly didn't have to thank him for it.

It was time to regain control of her life.

She peeled herself away from his chest, aware of his reluctance to let her go and dipping her head so she could wipe away the traces of tears before he could see them.

'I'm sorry you had to find out that way.'

'Are you?' she snapped. His gentle words did nothing to ease her pain and everything to cement her resolve. 'It seemed to me you were only too happy to throw that knowledge in my face.'

'It was time you knew the truth.'

'Why? What does it have to do with you anyway? Did you think I would be so devastated by the news that I would happily fall in with your crazy plans to marry you? I've just rid myself of one lying man. Why the hell would I launch myself straight into the arms of another?'

His jaw looked as if he was grinding his teeth together. Then he whispered, low and menacingly, 'Never put me in the same category as Paolo.'

'Why the hell not? Why are you doing this? Paolo said you two had been involved in some feud years ago. I told him he was being crazy, that no one probably even cared any more. But you do, don't you? You care so much it's like a poison in your system. Tell me, what did he do? Why do you hate him so much?'

Anger set the planes of his face hard and cold. 'You're upset,' he said, his voice revealing a barely controlled fury.

So he was mad, good for him. It was *nothing* to how she was feeling.

'Damned right, I'm upset,' she said. 'And I'll stay upset until I get out of this place. You don't have to become the barbarian. For the most part you appear to be a civilised man. You have no need to act like some petty despot. And if you have any respect for me at all, if you think anything of me, you have to respect my wishes. Let me go. I have to go.'

He looked down at her, the depths of his dark eyes swirling, his brow knotted, and her hopes lifted. Was he relenting in his mad desire to make her his wife? Had he realised he'd inflicted enough damage on her already?

'I can't let you go.'

Fury blasted through her. 'Then I'll go in spite of you. I'll find some other way of getting to the airport and I'll go anyway. Because I won't stay here.'

She stormed her way to her suitcase propped up near the door and grabbed purposefully at the handle.

'You're not going anywhere.'

'I'm not staying here. I'm definitely not marrying you.'

'So you keep saying, but that changes nothing. You cannot leave Jebbai now.'

'You can't keep me here. I want to go home.'

'But not today,' he said. 'Not for at least twenty-four hours.'

'I have to get away,' she said, half-demanding, half-pleading.

'You have no choice, as it turns out,' he snapped, his voice cold and imperious again. 'The airport is closed.'

CHAPTER SEVEN

'YOU'RE lying.' Her voice seemed surprisingly level under the circumstances. 'This is just some pathetic attempt to keep me here. But it won't work. I'm leaving.'

'Unfortunately it's true. Insurgents from neighbouring Jamalbad have been stirring up trouble along the border. This is the second such infraction in a few weeks—the first happened while we were *en route* from Milan. It seems someone thought that my absence then was an opportune time to stir up trouble.'

She thought back to the plane flight, his sudden disappearance, the urgent discussions going on around the communications equipment.

'I remember,' she said. 'Yet in spite of that danger, you still brought me here.'

'I would never have brought you here if I'd thought it was serious. My guards believed they'd dealt with the problem. It now appears they missed the ringleaders. They've still been out there, stirring up trouble. We've closed the airport as a precautionary measure.'

'For an entire day?'

He shrugged. 'It is best to be prudent—perhaps it will be closed for less.'

She looked ruefully down at the suitcase and let go

of the handle. It was like letting go of a lifeline. He'd told her she would be safe here. Now she couldn't get away even when she wanted to.

And how she wanted to.

She wanted to be as far away from this desert ruler as possible. Her previous life had never seemed calm—the fashion industry was madness as well as maddening, but compared to the way her feelings and emotions were being tossed about now it was a cakewalk.

She didn't want to stay near Khaled. If his scheming methods to get her here weren't frightening enough, his quiet declaration that he didn't have to force her to marry him and that she would come to him of her own accord scared her even more.

He was kidding himself! Not that she wanted to hang around to prove his theory wrong. But neither did she want to stay and be subjected to the pull of his fiery magnetism.

She couldn't trust herself to resist it.

'I'm sorry,' he said, 'but I promise you will be safe. That's why I came to see you today. I wanted you to hear it from me, to assure you that we are dealing with the problem and that Jebbai will soon be returned to its former peaceful existence.'

'And what of my former peaceful existence?' she said. 'When will I be returned to that?'

She looked so fragile right then, her blue eyes foggy with vulnerability and defeat, and he felt her anguish deep inside, in a place he'd long thought shrivelled and empty.

She did that to him. Touched him in ways no one ever had. Why else would he have risked his whole plan by revealing the truth so soon? Her constant goads, her insistent demands, they had been bad enough—nobody had ever defied him the way she did. But it was the way she seemed so desperate to return to her deceitful lover that had forced him over the edge of reason.

So he'd spilled his intention to take her as his bride much earlier than he'd planned and in doing so he'd threatened the entire scheme.

But maybe this way was better. Maybe now he would secure a far more effective payback.

Already he'd exacted a measure of revenge upon his former foe. He'd smelt the fear coming down the phone line as clearly as one felt the blast-furnace heat of a Jebbai midsummer day. Half a world away Paolo would know that this was his doing, he would know that he had brought this on with his own precipitous actions so long ago. He would wear the guilt like a heavy burden he could never shrug off. He would bear the pain forever.

As for Sapphire? Her anguish at her so-called fiancé's betrayal was palpable. He'd felt her despair like a knife thrust under his ribs; it touched him deep inside and instinctively, *bizarrely*, he wanted to make it better.

He had thought it would be easy—to take the woman of the man he hated as easily as stealing one of his possessions. Yet this woman was no cold chattel, no inanimate property. She was warm, and human and so responsive.

And he wanted her.

Oh, how he wanted her.

He wanted to feel more of her responsiveness, more of her body curling into his, more of her body melding with his until she was part of him, until they were part of each other.

And he wanted her now.

Even now, when she looked so lost and lonely, the urge to possess her, to ease her pain by obliterating any trace of Paolo in her mind and stamping his own claim on her, was almost primal.

He moved closer to her then, her hands clasped nervously in front of her like a young schoolgirl unsure of her next step in the world or where it would take her. If he had any say in the matter, that next step would take her straight to him, but this time it was up to her.

This time she would decide.

He wouldn't take her. She would give herself to him.

And then his victory over Paolo would be complete.

He lifted her chin with his hand and watched her large blue eyes reluctantly rise to meet his, the dampness in them rendering her long lashes heavy and dark.

'I will take you to the airport,' he said. 'When it reopens and when it is safe, I will take you there myself.'

He watched her nervous swallow, followed the movement in her throat, and fought the urge to drop his mouth and cover the pearly skin there with his lips.

'You'll let me go?' Her breath was choppy and hesitant; her bottom lip plumped and reddened with the tracks from her teeth.

'If that's what you want.'

Her eyes grew wide with hope and expectation and he accepted the challenge. He would make it his duty to change those expectations before it was time for her to leave.

'If that's what you *really* want.'

'Of course it's what I really want.'

'Then that's what will happen,' he asserted. 'We have a deal.'

'How…' she started unsuccessfully. She licked her lips as if searching for the courage. 'How do I know I can trust you?'

'I assure you my word is my honour—' he smiled when he noticed her sceptical expression '—although I understand you may not entirely agree. But perhaps you are right. Perhaps in deference to your concerns we should seal our bargain. We could shake hands—' his free hand surrounded her own, squeezing it reassuringly on feeling her electric reaction '—or we could seal our agreement with something much, *much* more satisfying…'

He saw the panic flare in her eyes, felt her instant reaction for flight as she pulled back. 'Just a kiss,' he promised. 'No more than that.'

He tugged her gently closer with one hand, tilting her towards him while he directed her chin with the other, until his mouth slanted over hers. He felt the shudder move through her as his lips meshed with hers, as if her internal resolve was being rocked and tested. He felt her sigh into the kiss, as if knowing she had no choice.

And she hadn't.

She might as well get used to it.

His tongue traced the line of her lips, tasting, examining, cajoling, and at the precise moment, at the tiniest hint he felt she was responding, he pulled away, letting go of his hold on her in the same instant.

Her eyelids batted open, her cheeks were flushed and her lips red and plumped.

It was enough for now.

He could have continued, God, but it had taken every shred of control to pull himself away when all he wanted to do was bury himself deep inside her. And he would. He would erase from her mind all thought of Paolo, every last memory of his lovemaking, every last aching pain of his deceit. He would have her. But not yet. Not just yet.

He would not take her.

He would make her come to him.

'So, do we have a deal?'

She reeled, knowing that once again he'd taken her to that place where she forgot herself, forgot who he was and even forget that she wanted to get away from there. How did he do that? And why did she feel so cheated that he'd stopped?

'Sure.' Her voice came too soft and sultry for her liking, so she tried again, searching for more resolve. *'Definitely,'* she said, adding a nod of her head for emphasis. 'You'll take me to the airport when it re-opens.'

He looked down at her, half smiling. 'If that's what you really want.'

'Oh,' she said, 'I want.'

I think.

She dropped her eyes so there was no chance he'd catch even a glimmer of her inner turmoil, and moved to collect her case, doing her best to distract herself from wherever her thoughts were about to take her. She'd return to her room. Think about practicalities. Focus on doing her packing a little more thoroughly.

And forget all about uncertainty.

'One more thing,' he said as she reached the door. 'I must attend a meeting with the desert tribes this evening. It will mean an overnight trip. I'll be leaving later today.'

Surprise mingled with relief mingled with disap-pointment. She wouldn't see him again before he re-turned to take her to the airport. Their time together before she left would be limited to a short ride in his limousine, if that. She should be happier about that, given the experience he'd put her through, surely?

'Is it safe for you to travel away from Hebra, under the circumstances?'

One of his eyebrows arched. 'Now you are con-cerned for my safety? You do surprise me. A moment ago I think you would quite happily have thrown my body out for carrion.'

She blinked, her lips tightening. 'If I show concern it's for the poor people you will no doubt drag along with you on this desert sojourn. It's their safety that concerns me.'

His lips turned up in the barest smile. 'Of course. But it's perfectly safe. I'm headed to the opposite end of the country.'

'Yet you thought it was safe when you brought me here. That doesn't say much for your risk-assessment analysis.'

'I assure you, I've assessed the risks,' he said, his eyes narrowing to a dark gleam, 'and I'm willing to take them on.'

Heat flooded her senses. She'd experienced enough of his double meanings to realise there was little doubt his words were aimed squarely at her.

But he had no chance. In one day, no more than two at the outside, she'd be gone. There was no way now that she could fall any further under his spell. Her own risk assessment told her she was just about home free.

'In that case,' she said, lifting her chin and finally feeling as if she was turning today's events around, 'I only hope you're not disappointed.'

'How could I be disappointed,' he asked, 'when you're coming with me?'

CHAPTER EIGHT

'No,' SHE said without a moment's hesitation. 'I don't think that's such a good idea.'

Whatever her see-sawing emotions were telling her, her brain was still screaming that she should get out of Jebbai as fast as possible and, failing that, to stay right away from Khaled. On that basis, going into the desert with him overnight was simply not an option.

'Why not,' he asked, 'when you have seen little or nothing of my country? You've buried yourself in that workroom. This would be the perfect chance to explore wider afield, before you return home.'

'Go with you, into the desert, when only minutes ago you were telling me I was to be your bride? You must think I'm mad or stupid to wander off into the desert with you when all I want to do is go home.'

'You will go home, if you wish. I gave you my word.'

'You got me here under false pretences. You lied to me all the way. You even let me believe in a bride that was an entire fabrication. I have to wonder what your word is really worth.'

He looked up, surprised. 'I'd hardly describe you as an entire fabrication. Besides, I thought we'd sealed that particular deal.'

'That was your concept of sealing a deal, not mine,' she threw at him.

'I see,' he said. 'You think we should seal the deal with something more…' his eyes took on a predatorial gleam '…*comprehensive?*'

Heat suffused her skin in an instant, a heavy, longing pooling low down in her belly. *'More comprehensive.'* The images his words conjured up sprang ready formed into her mind. A shock of tangled limbs; his smooth, sweat-slickened skin slipping over hers; his mouth, hot and hungry at her breast…

She forced the pictures back down, all of them, back to where they couldn't betray her any more than the hardened peaks of her nipples already did. It was bad enough he was so painfully arrogant without her body responding to his taunts.

'Don't expect me to sleep with you, simply to get out of the country.'

'I don't,' he said, swooping down to pick up her case. 'When you sleep with me I expect it to be for much more basic reasons.' He caught the look of shock on her face and smiled. 'Of course, I meant *if* you sleep with me.'

His instant correction did nothing to reassure her.

'I… I'll stay in the palace.'

'No. You're my responsibility. I won't know you're safe unless I take you with me.'

'I'll be safer here, surely. There are rebels, you said, insurgents out there somewhere. Why wouldn't I be better off here?'

'This palace is my home. I have doubts they could get this far, but if someone is after me then this is the first place they'll look. I won't leave you here alone.'

'I have Azizah.'

'And Saleem…'

Mention of his cousin stilled her protests. Saleem would hardly accept the role of her protector. He didn't like her, no matter how much she tried to stay out of his way and not upset him. The resentment was there, the mistrust clear in his eyes. He gave every impression that he hated her, but why? What had she ever done to him? And did she really want to endure his cold glares for two days alone?

'Wouldn't Saleem go with you?'

He shook his head. 'He has other matters to attend to. He must stay here.'

'Oh.' Saleem was staying in the palace. That put a completely different slant on things.

'You still don't like him?'

'I don't know—he just makes me feel uncomfortable, unsettled.'

'Saleem is my cousin. You should not feel that way.'

'I know. I just don't feel that I can trust him.'

'Like you don't trust me?'

Not like that at all. Khaled's simple question came with a simple answer that only complicated her thoughts. Her mistrust of Saleem was whole and entire and every cell in her body reacted in the same adverse way to his presence. He made her cringe, he made her flesh creep. She just didn't want to be anywhere around him.

Her mistrust of Khaled was completely different. She doubted his motives, she resented his arrogance and his duplicity in getting her here for reasons still not clear to her, but it was her body that she mistrusted the most. It was her body that reached out for him at the very same time her brain repelled him. It was her body that wanted him.

And she couldn't trust herself to deny him. Maybe staying in the palace with Saleem was the lesser of two evils after all, even though the thought chilled her to the bone.

Khaled didn't wait for her answer.

'Then I will not let you stay. You will come with me.'

Panic welled up inside her. 'But—'

'Sapphire,' he said, the sound of his voice strangely soothing, like a parent convincing a child, 'it's only for one night after all. What can possibly happen in one night?'

In less than two hours they were on their way out of the city and heading into the desert, the narrow strip of bitumen their only link to modern life. Sapphy travelled in the first Range Rover with Khaled choosing to drive. Half a dozen staff followed in the second.

The terrain at first was much like it had been driving into Hebra, stark, sandy flats broken by the occasional thorny plant, the air dry and clear, but gradually the landscape changed and the sand formed dunes, low and barely distinguishable at first, growing higher as they headed deeper and deeper into the desert.

Sculpted by the incessant winds, the red sand-dunes billowed all around them, creeping over the road in places and making the going tough. She sat quietly alongside Khaled as he drove, avoiding talk as far as possible and letting the landscape speak to her.

She couldn't regret coming here. Even after all that had happened, she'd learned so much visiting Jebbai, experiencing palace life in Hebra, cool and insulated and heady with the ever-present scent of incense; visiting the city souks with Azizah and the colourful market stalls with their wares both simple and exquisite. Even his mother's garden at the palace had been an experience that had fed into her psyche, enriching her experience of this country.

And Khaled? She looked over to him, his profile as majestic as the country he ruled, his strong features sculpted in his face like the lines carved by the wind in the dunes. With the white sleeves of his shirt rolled up to his elbows, his lean forearms worked at the wheel over the uneven territory and the occasional sand drift with strength and skill. Even some part of Khaled, whether it was his power, his arrogance or his dark and dangerous eyes, would feed into her work, she was sure. There was no way she would be able to divorce him from the experience.

He looked over, snaring her gaze.

'You're very quiet,' he said. 'Are you finding the journey too tiring?'

'Not at all,' she answered truthfully. Khaled had been right. She'd concentrated so much on completing the wedding dress that she'd barely been out of the workroom. In many ways it was exciting to be out of the palace and away from the city. 'Jebbai is much bigger than it looks on the map.'

He smiled, showing his even white teeth. 'We are

one of the smaller independent states, it is true, though the desert certainly makes the country seem much larger. There is more to see in terms of civil-isation to the south, where the oil fields are situated. Here it is very empty, apart from the occasional tribe.'

'Well, at least you have four-wheel drives to get around these days. Beats the heck out of doing it all by camel.'

'Is that experience talking, or supposition?'

'Of course I've ridden on camels, lots of times.' She brushed her fringe out of her eyes. 'Nothing to it.'

He looked quickly over at her again but this time as if he didn't believe a word she said.

'Really. There are loads of camels in Australia, out in the outback. Leftovers gone wild from the eigh-teen-hundreds when they used them for transport. Now they catch them and the handlers bring them into the cities and use them to take kids for rides at the beach or at the annual shows. It makes a change from pony rides.

'Our nanny used to take us all to one of the beaches every year for an outing and we'd have a ride to-gether. Opal, our older sister, loved the ponies the best. But with Ruby, my twin sister, and me, it was always the camels.'

'I'm impressed,' he said, a note of approval creep-ing into his voice. 'You're quite a multi-talented woman.'

She pressed her lips together and shook her head. 'Okay, you can laugh. But it was fun anyway.'

'Who said I'm laughing?' he said with all seriousness. 'You just never know when a skill like camel riding will come in handy.'

Behind her sunglasses she rolled her eyes, before turning them back to the endless dunes. 'Sure,' she said, dismissing him yet secretly pleased that in just one small way she'd managed to surprise him. He seemed a different person when they could touch on neutral topics, when whatever grievances he brought to their other dealings could be put aside.

It was at least twenty minutes before either of them spoke again. The road had all but disappeared under the drifting sands and her seat was getting less comfortable, the bumps were getting more pronounced and she was generally sick of the vehicle's grinding progress through the dunes.

She reached for her bottle of water and took a swig. 'How far now?'

'We'll be stopping soon.'

'We're nearly there?'

'Wait,' he said, the unexpected smile on his face warming her. 'I think you're going to like this.'

It wasn't long before she found out what he meant. They pulled into a relatively flat area, really no more than a space between dunes and dominated by an ancient and squat mud-brick building. It was the end of the road, literally, and what there was to like about it was anyone's guess.

The vehicles parked side by side under a lean-to and men started unloading the supplies.

'You might want to take this opportunity to freshen up,' Khaled suggested. He reached behind the front seat. 'And here, you might want to put this on. It will protect you from the sun and the sand.'

She took the bundle he held up to her. 'Why should I need this now?' she asked.

'Our journey is not quite over,' he said.

'What do you mean?'

He focused on something behind her. 'See for yourself,' he said.

A protesting bawl told her what she'd see before she turned.

'Camels!' she cried.

The man leading the first camels, his coiled-turban-framed face all leathery wrinkles from years of exposure to the desert sun, broke into a wide grin at her delight, revealing just three remaining teeth.

She reached up and stroked the nose of the first camel. It looked down at her, its thickly lashed, doe-like eyes considering her briefly, before lifting its head and letting out another loud bawl.

'You weren't kidding,' Khaled said, suddenly appearing at her side, his hand low on her back, the other stroking the neck of the camel. 'You really don't mind camels. Many people are not so keen, even afraid.'

'Camels get bad press,' she said, trying to ignore the pressure of his hand. He was barely touching her yet all her senses seemed to focus on that one point of contact, the warmth that built deep inside, pooling into longing. It was a struggle to pull herself back to the topic.

'But I've learned,' she continued, licking lips already losing moisture to the arid conditions, yet more so, as if edged with the heat emanating from him, the heat flowing from his gentle touch, 'that once you get to know them a little, it's clear their reputation has been unfairly earned.'

'Indeed? And do you think that observation might have its parallel with the human species? Do you similarly find that there are those people whose reputation has been unfairly attributed?'

He had to be kidding. She paused momentarily, considering him carefully and wondering if he was ever going to remove his hand. 'Your actions to date go far beyond mere reputation, Sheikh Khaled.'

'And does that then render me beyond redemption in your estimation?'

'When compared to camels, you mean?' She allowed herself a smile at his arrogance and shifted sideways out of his reach. 'Let's just say you're starting off from a much lower base.'

He threw his head back and laughed, the sound rich and mellow. She liked the sound of it when he laughed; she liked the effect it had on his features and the warmth it stirred inside her. Something let go in the muscles of his face and the harshness softened, the angles smoothed. She liked him like this, when he seemed less autocratic, more human.

A feeling akin to regret spiked her consciousness. If only things were different...

The camel bawled into her ear, spiking her out of her thoughts. What the hell was she thinking? Things weren't different. This guy had all but dragged her off to his desert kingdom with the intention of making her his wife. She was glad things weren't different. Now there was no way she could possibly like him.

So what that she'd had to accompany him out here? After tomorrow it wouldn't be an issue. She'd be gone. Long gone. He wouldn't see her for sand.

She felt his gaze settle upon her, hot and expectant, and she deliberately avoided it, focusing instead on the camels. She needed a distraction. She needed to think about something safe. Camels were just the ticket.

They were dromedaries, or one-humped, the same kind she was used to riding with her sisters on their childhood jaunts to the beach, but these wore different saddles. Instead of the double seat she remembered sharing with her sisters, this saddle was arranged over the hump, higher off the ground and more daunting. Not that she was about to admit that to Khaled.

'Which one is mine?' she asked, looking forward to the separation their mounts would bring. She could do with some distance from Khaled right now.

'This camel seems to like you. I think we will take this one.'

We will take this one? Impossible. That was so obviously a saddle built for one. If she had to share it with him, she'd be sitting literally in his lap, brushing against him, feeling his body rock against hers every step of the way. She swallowed.

'You mean, this one is for me.'

His lips curved into a grin. 'We're one camel short. You'll have to share with me.'

'Can't you get another one?'

He looked up at the sky. 'Too late. The track is

steep. We must leave now if we are to make the meeting place by nightfall.'

'But we won't both fit. There's nowhere for me to sit. It's not fair to the camel.'

'The camel can handle the slight addition of your weight. As to the rest, let me take care of that.'

Suddenly she wished she'd stayed back at the palace. Even the sullen moods of Saleem were less threatening than the prospect of spending time within Khaled's grasp.

'Can't I stay here? Wait for you to get back?'

'And miss the experience of a lifetime? A meeting with one of the few remaining Bedouin tribes—you would never forgive yourself for that, surely.'

Was he being obtuse or was he just teasing her? It wasn't missing the experience she was worried about. Couldn't he see that? Or did he see it too well?

She sucked in a breath, firing up her resolve. He hadn't got the better of her yet and she wasn't about to let him now. It would take more than a simple camel ride to make her change her view of Sheikh Khaled.

'Okay,' she said with a sense of bravado that surprised even herself. 'Let's do it.'

As it turned out, a few minutes later when they were ready to disembark, there was nothing simple about it. From the moment she'd been hauled into Khaled's arms she knew she was in for a rocky ride.

'Hold tight,' he warned her as the handler urged the camel upright, back legs first, threatening to plunge her forward into the sands if not for the steel-like bands of Khaled's arms surrounding her. Then the process was reversed as the camel raised itself on its front legs, forcing her bodily against him.

Then the five camels set off, with Khaled in the lead, padding their way over the soft desert sands. The side-by-side motion of the camel was familiar. The feel of his body so close to hers was not. She was nestled into the space between his thighs, pressed close to the wall of his chest, her head perilously close to his shoulder, feeling the friction between them increase with every step. His scent, woody and masculine, surrounded her, spiking subtly with the motion, adding to the cocktail of sensory impressions.

And there was no way she could hold herself aloof. There was no way she could keep her distance. If she wanted to stay on she had to cling to him, and cling tight.

Not that she was likely to fall off, not with the band of his arm circling her waist. Every breath she took, every rise of her chest brought his arm closer, tighter. But she dared not squirm. Already heat gathered low inside her, alluring, seductive. To wriggle in the cradle of his thighs would be to invite disaster.

'Are you not comfortable?' he asked, bending his head low to her ear. 'Maybe you should try to relax.'

Relax? Like that was on the cards. 'Why couldn't we take the cars? I would have thought that with four-wheel drives and helicopters, camels would have been a thing of the past.'

'Out here they still have some uses. There's an escarpment coming up. We could drive around but the camels will take the most direct route and save us hours of travel.'

'And helicopters?'

'Not half as much fun, wouldn't you agree?'

Her dark silence seemed to amuse him and his chuckle welled up, rippling through his chest. 'Besides, have you forgotten? The airport is closed. Such a shame.'

She gritted her teeth. 'A damn shame,' she muttered.

The ground became rockier. Pebbles took the place of sand and she became aware they were climbing, gradually at first, until they reached the escarpment and began the steep climb up the ancient track. Now she could see why they couldn't bring the cars. The narrow path was barely wide enough for a man, let alone a camel. A vehicle had no hope.

Below them the desert sands were spread out like a golden blanket, rippled and shadowed, warm and seductive in the fading light. It was beautiful and already she felt her life enriched, more textured by the experience.

The camel's movements became less rhythmic, more unpredictable as it ascended. Somewhere near the top of the escarpment, one plate-sized foot slid sideways on loose gravel and the camel lurched, jarring her out of Khaled's lap and threatening to launch her over the side, but his strong arms only tightened around her, reeling her back in close to him again.

She huddled close to his chest, waiting for her breathing to calm, her heart still racing from her narrow escape, but it was another rhythm that caught her attention. Outwardly he was so composed, so in charge. Yet inside she could feel his heart thumping wildly.

Had he been taken by surprise as well?

'Do not be afraid,' he whispered as she clung on to his arm. 'I would never let you fall. I would never let you get hurt.'

Tremors shook her body, though whether from relief or the impact of his words she couldn't be sure. For somehow she knew what he said was true.

'I'm okay,' she replied, thinking he might release his tight grip a fraction once he knew she was all right. But his arms stayed vice-like around her, even after they'd reached the summit and were finally nearing the collection of tents that made up the encampment. She couldn't wait to get down. The dust of a day's travel had worn into her skin and she was sure the smell of the camel had done likewise. But now she wouldn't have long to wait.

Small dark-haired children ran towards them, smiling and laughing, their long robes flapping around their bare shins and feet. A herd of goats looked up momentarily, checking out the latest distraction before losing interest.

A taller youth met the camels, his eyes alert and intelligent, his smile genuine. Excitement fired his features as he pulled on the nose ring of the lead camel and urged him to sit. Sapphy felt herself rocked forward as the camel dropped to its knees but Khaled's grip never let her fall. Then the camel was down. He released his hold enough for her to slip out of his grasp and onto the earth before he, too, dismounted.

'Majeed,' Khaled said, embracing the boy.

'Good day, Sheikh Khaled,' he replied formally, obviously working hard at his English. 'You have brought my new teacher?'

'Of course, Majeed. Didn't I promise?'

Moments later she noticed the youth leading away one of their fellow travellers. She wanted to ask Khaled about the exchange—she'd assumed their several accompanying riders were all guards—but she was surrounded by the young children, hanging on to her hands and chattering non-stop.

'You might want to clean up now,' he suggested to her, ruffling the children's hair as he steered her through the throng and towards the camp. 'Your bag will have been delivered already. I will show you to your tent.'

He turned back to the children and rattled off something fast in his language. They all scattered immediately, heading for the tents like shot from a gun.

'What did you say to them?'

'I told them to tell their mothers the doctor will be ready to see them shortly.'

'A doctor came with us? I thought those men were guards.'

'We had one guard with us, it's true. But guards won't do my people much good. They need practical help if they want to keep this way of life for as long as they can. They need medical help and immunisation clinics. It is much too far for them to travel into the cities for such luxuries.'

'Is that why you brought the teacher?'

He nodded. 'Exactly. The boy, Majeed, is very

bright. He has already surpassed his previous teacher's level. He needs new challenges and to learn new skills.'

'Couldn't he go to school in Hebra? Don't they have boarding-schools in Jebbai?'

'Of course. But then how could he help his family? He will go to university, when it is time and when his brothers are older. But his father needs him now and this way he can both study and help with his family.'

'I see,' she said, even though she didn't. Oh, it made sense all right. But this was a completely different side of Khaled. She was used to the ruthless, authoritarian side of him, the Khaled who acted out of anger, with no thought to the feelings of those he trampled with his unreasonable demands.

This was a different man. A real leader of his people, who ensured their ongoing existence in the style of life they had been accustomed to since ancient times. He could have forced them to abandon their way of life and move to the cities in the name of progress, simply by not supplying them with modern medicine and education. Yet he was ensuring the continued existence and preservation of their separate and special way of life. And from his reception here he was clearly well loved and respected as their leader.

How could someone who was so considerate and generous towards his people act so unreasonably towards her? It made no sense. No sense at all.

In the gathering dusk she noticed the women emerging from tents, their long robes flapping in the light breeze, babies in slings on their backs, many with young toddlers following in their wake.

They converged on a small tent set to one side, where one of the men who had travelled with them—the doctor, it was now clear—was setting up his equipment. It couldn't be an easy life for these people, always wandering and rarely settled, but they looked happy and healthy as they collected outside the tent, waiting for the doctor to attend to them.

'After you,' Khaled said and she realised he was holding open the tent for her. She stepped inside. It took a few seconds for her eyes to adjust to the lantern-lit interior and then her first reaction was to gasp.

The tent's interior bore no relation to its plain exterior. The floor was lined with carpets, woven and richly coloured. Curtains lined the walls, silks and gauzes softly draped in vivid jewel shades, and cushions lay scattered around, inviting and sumptuous. Perfumed candles scented the air, sweet and fragrant. Beyond an open silken partition she could just make out a large bed, presumably her bed, given what looked like her bag placed on top.

It was every little girl's fantasy. And despite all the dreams she'd had from way back to be a fashion designer, she could even believe it was hers. She'd grown up surrounded by luxury, been raised in the most exclusive boutique hotel in Australia, but this somehow went beyond mere fantasy. This was pure magic.

'Will you be comfortable here?'

She spun around slowly, trying to take it all in. 'Oh, yes. It's beautiful.'

His hand reached for her shoulder, stopping her right in front of him. His other hand tilted her chin. 'Though nowhere near as beautiful as you.'

Her breath caught as his face hovered above hers, his golden skin glowing and shadowed in the lamplight, a magic prince for a magic setting.

It could have been a fairy-tale.

Except she had no place in this story. She had already chosen her course. She would leave Jebbai, return to Milan, and before long all this would seem no more than a dream.

She raised one hand to his chest, uncertain of whether she was trying to stop him or merely giving in to the temptation of touching him again, of tasting his muscled torso with her fingers, of reading the strong beat of his heart.

The hand on her shoulder moved to cover hers, wrapping her fingers in his. His eyes still locked on hers, he lifted it from his chest and pressed the palm of her hand to his mouth. She sucked in air as his warm lips, his heated breath danced over her skin, as the merest trace of his tongue spread liquid warmth coursing through her.

'And now,' he said, his voice low and thick, 'relax a while. The women will help you. I have business to discuss with the men and then we will dine together.'

Women? She looked around to see two women near the bed unpacking her bag. Unfamiliar blue fabric shot with gold floated over one woman's hands. Sapphy frowned.

'That's not my bag,' she said, stepping towards the partition. 'It can't be.'

'You will find it is,' Khaled responded.

'But none of this…' The women moved aside while she checked the bag—it looked like hers, yet nothing inside was familiar. She dug her hands through the gossamer fabrics, the golden tassels and belts, the heavier cloaks. She didn't own these things. Yet, underneath everything else, there was her toiletry bag. It didn't make sense.

And yet all of a sudden it did.

Icy realisation filled her veins. This was just the sort of thing she should have expected from someone who had frustrated her at every move. She turned, barely able to restrain the mounting hostility within.

'What have you done with my clothes?'

CHAPTER NINE

KHALED dismissed the women with a flick of his hand.

'You don't like your new garments?'

'These things aren't mine. What have you done with the clothes I packed?'

'I promised you a gift—the garments made by Hebra's best seamstresses. Do you agree they are quite beautiful?'

'I want my clothes.'

'Your clothes were not appropriate for the desert. This isn't Milan or Sydney or even Hebra. Aren't you going to try these on? See how well they fit? See how well they become you?'

'Why the hell should I?'

'Because,' he said, his dark eyes shiny with victory, 'you have no choice. You have nothing else to wear.'

'Then I'll wear what I've already got on.'

His nostrils flared. 'It is entirely up to you if you wish to offend our hosts. For while we value the camel for transport, it is not a beast we would choose to eat with.'

She spun away from him, determined that he wouldn't see that she knew he was right. From the moment they'd arrived at the encampment she'd looked forward to the prospect of washing off the baggage of a long, dusty trip and changing into clean clothes. But her idea of clean clothes had more to do with a linen skirt and fresh blouse than the silky nothingness of the fabrics now contained in her suitcase.

'You need not be concerned,' he said, almost as if he could read her thoughts. 'It makes no difference what you had planned to wear as no one would see it anyway. The women will provide you with an *abaya* and *hijab*, a cloak and scarf to cover your garments and head, and a *burka* to hide your face, as is the custom here in the tribes. All anyone will see of you is your eyes. So you see, you really have nothing to get upset about.'

'In that case,' she said at last, 'it would appear that I don't have much of a choice.'

'No,' he said, 'you don't.'

And then he was gone, leaving her and her resentment simmering in his wake.

All night long the blue eyes had captivated him. All night he'd wished for a halt to the seemingly endless cups of coffee, the conversation that lingered interminably, when all he wanted to do was be alone with her.

Even covered from head to toe she stood out. There was simply no way Sapphire would blend in by dressing her in the local garb. There was no way she would not be noticed.

All anyone could see was her blue eyes, clear and warm, shining from behind her cotton *burka*. Yet he could see the way they lit up when she laughed, the way they creased at the corners with delight, the way they reacted when others told their tales of desert wanderings or their children, the way they would fill with compassion when the story was sad.

Most of all he liked the way they stilled when his gaze locked on hers, smoke suddenly swirling in their depths before they dropped or turned away.

All he could see was her blue eyes and even they were enough to hold him transfixed. Yet the promise, too, of what was under the dark *abaya* intervened in his thoughts. He wanted to strip away the cloak, to find the woman under the dull garb, to explore her feminine shape and hidden curves.

And now, when their hosts had finally called an end to the evening, now he finally had his chance.

She clutched the sides of the *abaya*, avoiding looking at him directly as Khaled walked her to her tent, the soft maa-ing of the goats carrying gently across the crisp night air. It was cooler now although feeling warm didn't seem to be a problem for her. Not given the way Khaled had made her feel through dinner.

Tonight he looked more like a sheikh than ever. For the first time he had put aside the western garb she was used to seeing him in and that was so much a part of business in modern Hebra and instead he wore the traditional robes of the region. In the fine white shirt, the traditional headdress with its double cord of woven goat-hair and sheep's wool, and the long black robes edged with gold braid, Khaled looked larger than life, a real desert king.

She'd seen the way he'd watched her tonight, had

felt his eyes on her, and on those times she'd been
unable to resist looking his way she'd been held by
the authority of his features, the sheer power of his
eyes, the potent message they contained.

He wanted her.

Sure, she'd known it before, she'd felt his need on
his lips and in his kiss, but never had it taken on the
significance it had now, the way it rocked her as they
made their way almost silently across the pebble-
strewn sands to her tent. He knew she was leaving
yet still he wanted her.

Under her long robe a multitude of sensations beset
her. Silk slid across her skin at every move, the metal
belt shimmying softly over her hips, and tiny bells
jangled softly on her ankles. She felt ultra-feminine,
exquisitely sensual and sexy in a way she never had
before.

Was it the garments that lay hidden under the
abaya or was it the way Khaled had looked at her
through dinner, as though he was already slowly peeling off her clothes, that made her flesh tingle and gave
her such a rush of moist heat?

It didn't matter. What suddenly did was the realisation that she could no longer deny.

She wanted him too.

It made no sense. She was leaving soon. Returning
to her fashion-industry life in Milan and leaving the
desert far behind her. She was getting what she really
wanted, wasn't she? Escape and freedom. Whereas
Khaled meant the exact opposite. Khaled would keep
her here forever. Even though his crazy marriage

plans had been aborted, she knew he would possess her if she let him. How then could she even imagine that she wanted any part of him?

But imagination didn't come into it. What she wanted was real.

They reached her tent, and he followed her through the opening, the heaviness of her need threatening to swamp her, to drown all rational thought. Suddenly she didn't want to say goodnight. Suddenly she wanted to prolong this moment, this time out here, in the soft lamplight of a lush Bedouin tent.

He placed one hand on her shoulder, angling her towards him. 'You have the most expressive eyes, did you know?' He lifted the other hand to her mask, tracing her cheek through the fabric. 'You didn't mind wearing this? It must seem strange to you.'

'It's all right,' she said. Her voice sounded clouded and thick. 'It's the custom here. I don't mind.'

'Well, you have no need of it now,' he said, his hand reaching behind to release the tie that held it in place. It dropped to the floor at the same time he removed her scarf. Automatically she reached up a hand to smooth back her hair, suddenly nervous, expectant.

'Your cloak too,' he said, his voice heavy with need. 'If you wish.'

She hesitated fractionally. It was only an outer robe, but by taking it off, what was she saying to him? The silken garments that she wore beneath hardly constituted a barrier between them. But then, the way her body was humming, her need accelerating, maybe it was time the barriers came down.

Her fingers fumbled their way to the closures that ran from her neck to her waist, undoing them in turn. Only when she had finished, her hands unsure of where to go next, did he put his hands to her shoulders, parting the robe and peeling it down her arms, finally letting go and allowing its weight to drag it to the floor, exposing her to his gaze.

She held her breath.

Breath hissed through his teeth. After the severity and relative shapelessness of the *abaya*, he had expected that her feminine shape in the garments his seamstresses had prepared would please him. But his thoughts and preconceptions had in no way prepared him for this.

She was a goddess.

The blue skirt hugged her low down on her hips, the golden threads of the fabric winking in the lamplight with every tiny movement, the shadow of her long legs an enticing promise beneath. More gold bound her breasts, concealing even as it accentuated her womanly curves, leaving bare the exquisite skinscape of her midriff.

She might not have been happy about having her clothes swapped but right now she didn't look as if she held it against him. He'd wanted to strip away all the shackles of her previous life, to let her absorb and enjoy the full experience of the desert without the barrier of western clothes to hide behind.

And, if he was honest, there was more than a modicum of self-interest involved. He'd longed to see her out of her usual attire, her well-designed yet far too tailored attire.

Now he had, he was sure he would never have his fill. She was a feast for the eyes. His body reacted in the only way possible. Inside him the hunger cranked up a notch, the need to possess her all-consuming.

When he didn't move she lifted her eyes fractionally, afraid of what she might see in his. She wasn't disappointed. Hot appreciation, vivid and intent, blazed out of their dark depths, his chin set rigid as if he was holding himself tightly under control.

Sparks ignited inside her, sparks that fired messages to nerve endings that tingled and buzzed. Flesh responded, exposed skin goose-pimpled, breasts peaked and firmed.

Then his mouth slanted over hers and the feelings were magnified, intensified, as his need fed into hers. She tasted coffee, the desert and passion, the power that was Khaled alive in his kiss as his lips moved over hers, as his tongue explored her depths.

His arms curled around her, pulling her in close to him, his hands warm on the dip of her spine, the flare of her hips, the curve of her breast.

Pressure mounted inside her, pressure that turned the dull ache between her thighs into more like a pulsing imperative. Her hands tangled through the metres of cloth that made up his robes, wanting to feel not his clothes, but his body, firm and hard, next to hers.

And close up she could feel his strength, feel the

power of his need as she pressed herself against the firm ridge of his erection.

His head drew back on a shudder as his arms loosened and she looked up, confused, missing his heat already.

'Sapphire,' he said, his voice a bare rasp, his breath fast and choppy.

And instantly she was reminded of the times before, when he'd kissed her and pulled away, leaving her reeling and hungry for more and resentful of his control, and she knew that no way was he doing that to her again. She couldn't bear it.

This was most likely her last night in Jebbai. Her last night with Khaled. Her last chance to satisfy this reckless desire that flared whenever he was near.

Soon she'd be back in Milan, alone in her apartment, no Paolo to console her, nothing to ease her regret for missing out on what she could have had.

So this time would be different. This time he wasn't leaving her cold. This time he could damn well finish what he'd started.

She anchored her arms around his neck and pulled herself tight up against him. 'Khaled,' she whispered, her lips close to his ear, pressing tiny kisses along his throat, nipping his skin with her teeth and pressing her breasts into his chest. 'Make love to me.'

CHAPTER TEN

HE SEEMED to hesitate a moment, almost as if he didn't believe what he'd heard. But only for a moment.

Then his eyes sparked white heat and he uttered something low and guttural, the words indiscernible to her but his intentions clear. He collected her in his arms and lifted her out of the circle of her discarded robe, breaching the distance to the bed in three long strides.

He laid her down, amongst the soft covers and tasselled cushions, and knelt beside her, his chest rising powerfully, drinking her in with his eyes.

'Magnificent,' he said, his words curling into her senses, feeding the fires inside, as he shrugged off his cloak and tore his headdress away. Then he dipped his head and reefed his long shirt over his back and shoulders, balling it in his hands before flinging it across the tent.

She didn't see where it landed. Her eyes were on him, on the golden skin of his chest, glowing warmly in the soft lamplight.

His shoulders were broad, his muscles well defined, his skin satin-smooth. She reached out a hand to touch him, spreading her fingers, relishing the feel of his firm abdomen, anticipating what lay below the loose white trousers that were his only remaining garment. Her fingers dropped to the waistband, slipping inside.

Breath hissed through his teeth as one hand whipped out, snaring hers. And what she saw in his eyes—desire, raw and urgent, naked and demanding—edged up her own hunger. He pushed her arm down onto the bed, stretching himself out lengthwise alongside, his leg situating itself between hers, dipping his mouth to hers once more.

Then she was lost in his kisses, lost in his touch and in the heat he generated inside her. There were too many sensations, too much to assimilate, such that all she could think of while he explored her body, setting fires wherever he touched, was that he felt so good.

He felt so right.

His hand cupped her breast, his kisses trailing down her neck until his mouth too was there. Even through the fabric his hot breath hit home, her nipple budding tight between his teeth.

He moved suddenly and reached around her. Then her top was slipping down her arms and cool air met her exposed breasts. Cool air and his hot gaze. He made a sound like a growl, low and deep, before his head dipped first to one nipple, gently lapping, suckling, rolling the nipple, before turning his attentions to the other.

It was torture. Her head rocked from one side to the other. *Exquisite torture*—but still it wasn't enough.

His hand ran down the length of her leg, floating

down the silken layers of her skirt, and then up again, this time shucking the filmy fabric out of his path. Nerve endings screamed along the length of her body, sending off needle-like charges that speared direct to just one place.

She felt liquid inside, molten, as his hand caressed her thigh—close, so close—and then he touched her there and her back arched as light like a flash bulb went off in the recesses of her closed eyes. His touch was gentle, sensual, erotic and she felt herself responding to him, opening, yielding.

Yet still it wasn't enough.

'Khaled,' she pleaded, her hands tangled in his hair, wanting an end to the waiting, an end to the anticipation. 'Please.'

He lifted his head from her breast and looked up at her, his dark eyes smouldering, so heavy with intent that it rocked her.

'Nothing could give me greater pleasure,' he said, raising himself up to his knees and tugging down his cotton trousers. Her eyes followed the motion, held captive by the sheer beauty of his form, unable to tear her eyes away from his sculpted torso, his flat stomach and down further, where the cotton fabric provided no restraint…

And then he was free and anticipation gave way to apprehension.

He was magnificent.

She swallowed, suddenly less sure of herself. But he allowed her no chance to reconsider as he leant over, his mouth meshing with hers, telling her in no uncertain terms that whatever her concerns, he had none.

She lost herself again in his mouth as he pressed himself close to her and in a few deft moves she realised that her skirt had been efficiently despatched and her legs laid bare. Then his fingers slid under the lace of her thong until even that was slipped away and awareness and expectation washed over her like a tide.

Thigh against thigh. Breast against breast. Skin against skin. They rolled together on the bed, a tangle of limbs, and with the hot promise of more. And with the last barriers gone, there was nothing to stop them. She was glad. She wanted him inside her, so he could be part of her, so they could be part of each other.

He rolled away suddenly and she felt cold, exposed, until she realised what he was doing. But by then he was back and her mind processed his sensible actions with gratitude and appreciation.

And it meant, oh, it meant that soon there would be an end to this endless aching need.

He held her face in his hands, kissing her tenderly on her eyes, her cheeks, her chin as the seconds spun out in the suspense of waiting for the inevitable.

Inevitable.

Ever since Khaled had entered Bacelli's salon, this moment had been unavoidable. Even from that first moment the attraction between them had been apparent. And ever since then it had been building, smouldering away, gathering force in spite of all that had happened to force them apart, despite all she had done to protect herself.

This moment was her destiny, her fate.

He took her mouth again as he raised himself up onto his elbows, positioning himself above her. His eyelids were heavy, his brow glossed satin with sweat.

She felt his weight, settling at her entrance, testing, probing, and instinctively she lifted her hips to welcome him with her own slick need, wanting him closer still, needing the completion, needing to have him deep inside.

And then he was. He plunged full length, driving his hips into hers, throwing back his head as if in triumph as his back arched over her.

Time stood still. She was unable to breathe, unable to think, unaware of anything beyond the exquisite sensation of him stretching her, of him filling her completely.

And then he moved inside her and a new wave of nerve endings came into play. Slowly he withdrew, only to fill her again and then again, and with each thrust the sensations grew, the pleasure mounted, wave upon wave of sheer ecstasy, building, always building.

She could feel his tension in his corded arms, she could sense his own battle for control, she could feel her mounting need for release mirrored in his own as the waves rolled in, the rhythm quickening and threatening to carry her away.

And then he took her there himself, with one final

thrust that sent them both spiralling, shattering out of control, sending a tidal wave of sensation crashing over them, violent and primal, until it left them sweat-slickened and panting, their bodies spent, like so much driftwood left on the shore.

It was enough. She came to slowly, her pulse steadying, her body humming, dimly aware that, while it was still late at night, this was a brand-new day; and that, although she was still Sapphy Clemenger, on another level she was a stranger, even to herself.

She looked at him, settled into her shoulder, his eyes closed, his steadying breaths warm on her breast, his beautiful body majestic even in repose.

He'd changed her.

Never before had she experienced such need, such desire, and never in her wildest dreams had she imagined that lovemaking could be so mind-blowingly spectacular. Not that it had been bad before, just that in hindsight it seemed as though making love had been on another level, almost as if some vital ingredient had been missing.

If this night gave her nothing more, she would indeed have some warm memories to keep her company during her lonely nights back in her apartment in Milan.

Milan. She sucked in a breath. She'd be back there in less than two days, assuming the airport reopened as planned. And for all her desperation to escape from Khaled and return to Italy, the city itself had lost some of its appeal. Somehow she couldn't see herself slotting straight back into work. Even involved in the crazy, fast-paced fashion industry, it was going to seem strangely dull after her visit to Jebbai with its enigmatic ruler.

Maybe first she should take some leave, go home to Australia and visit her sisters and Pearl and check up on her baby niece. She was owed some time and it wasn't as if she couldn't start sketching up designs for the next collection while she was travelling. She'd talk to Gianfranco as soon as she was back in Milan.

His eyes blinked open and she realised she'd been staring at his face the whole time. He smiled and reached out a hand, stroking it down the side of her face and brushing away the loose strands of hair.

'You look...deep in thought,' he said, his voice rich and low enough to make her toes curl all over again.

She flicked her gaze away. He didn't need to know she was having second thoughts about returning straight to Milan. It wasn't as if it had anything to do with him. 'I was just—thinking about my family.'

He rolled closer, pressing his lips to her neck. 'You don't talk about them much, apart from when you went camel riding with your sisters. Tell me about them.'

She tried to ignore the feeling of his mouth leaving tiny kisses along her collar-bone, although the sensation was strangely soothing while at the same time it seemed highly erotic.

'I haven't seen them for far too long.'

'You're not close?'

'We used to be closer.'

'What changed things?'

She drew in a deep breath and rolled over, away from the distraction of his mouth, to somewhere bland she could direct her words, like the pillow in front of her. 'Oh, it was nothing bad. My mother came back…'

He said nothing for a few seconds. Then, 'I don't understand.'

She turned her face back to him. 'We thought she'd died when Ruby and I were four. It turns out she'd been living in exile at that time—banished by our father.'

'How did you find her?'

'Opal's husband, Domenic, tracked her down to where she was living in England. He took her back to Sydney. She lives there now, in the family hotel that Opal runs. Dad died a couple of years before. He was always busy when we were young and it was usually just the three of us girls growing up with the nanny of the day. But Opal was our big sister. She looked after us better than anyone.'

'You don't like your mother?'

'Oh, no. Don't get me wrong. Pearl is lovely. It's just hard to come to grips with the idea that I have a mother at all. For years we thought she was dead. And now she's there and it's just not the same any more. Opal has a baby girl, Ellie, who's toddling now, and Pearl and Opal are very close. And Ruby works in Broome and is just so very far away.'

He curled his arm around her shoulder, gathering her in close to his chest, stroking her hair.

'I see,' he said, softly kissing the top of her head. 'You've gained a mother, yet it feels like you've lost your sisters.'

She blinked against the warmth of his skin, surprised that he understood so much. 'Yes. That's exactly how it feels—except it's still not like I can even accept her as my mother. She was gone too long. And now I don't even know my sisters. Does that make sense?'

'It makes sense. It is never easy to lose the ones we love,' he said, his words trailing off, his hand stilling in her hair.

She almost groaned out loud when she realised. Here she was feeling sorry for herself and Khaled had known *real* loss. Both his parents, killed in tragic circumstances. He'd probably give anything for his mother to be alive. And yet she was acting as if her mother's return had ruined her life.

'Khaled,' she said, lifting herself up so she could see him, 'I'm so sorry. I didn't think.'

Even in the dim lights, his eyes shone bright and glossy, their dark depths granite-hard, his chin set rigid as he stared unseeing at the ceiling. Then he looked at her and something inside them slowly peeled away.

It wasn't her fault. He looked into her concerned blue eyes, his hand resuming its stroking motion of her hair, and knew that, despite her associations, it had nothing to do with her. It was Paolo who was to blame, it was Paolo who would pay. Already he would be suffering, his imagination no doubt conjuring up all sorts of despicable ways in which Khaled would be taking advantage of his one-time fiancée.

He allowed himself a smile. It was almost funny. How much worse was Paolo going to feel when he discovered the truth—that he hadn't needed to take her by force? That it was Sapphy who'd asked him to make love to her. How much worse would he feel when he discovered that she was not a prisoner—but that she had decided to stay in Jebbai, as she surely now would, of her own accord?

No doubt the irony would not be lost on Paolo.

But then, in another way, it didn't matter what Paolo thought. For right now he didn't matter. Sapphire was here with him now, it was his scent she would smell on her, it was his body holding hers.

'It must have been a dreadful time for you,' she said, the breath behind her words falling like warm caresses on his skin. He sucked in a breath. She was much too special for anyone else. He could listen to her gentle words all day. He could watch the way her rounded breasts, her nipples peaked and taut, brushed against his chest forever. That was, unless he was doing something much more satisfying.

'It wasn't a good time,' he agreed, feeling his need rising with the sudden urge to do something much more satisfying. He flipped her over onto her back again, enjoying her whoop of surprise and the way her eyes widened first with shock and then with anticipation.

'But right now is a whole lot better.'

He made love to her then, slowly, deliberately, taking his time, exploring her body and sharing the initiative with her when she chose to explore his. And this time was even better than the first, more tender and yet more passionate, more exploratory and yet more focused. She was everything he thought she'd be as a lover and more.

And only when finally they'd both tumbled over the edge of reason again, only when he'd seen the blue facets of her eyes spark and flare into a fire that consumed them both, did he follow her into sleep.

The goats woke her—with their early-morning bleating for attention and the soft jangle of their bells as the first hint of dawn light permeated the tent's walls, reminding her of where she was. But once awake, it was the heated body of the man who slept alongside her amongst the tangled sheets and the musky scent of their lovemaking that proved the distraction.

She propped herself up on one elbow and drank him in. He lay on his stomach, his head to one side, his arms high on the pillow. The remnants of one sheet was slanted across his thighs, so that his well-defined back was exposed from his broad shoulders to his tight waist and even tighter mounds of his rump below. She sucked in a breath.

How could he do that? How could he look so damned sexy when he was still asleep?

Memories of the night's activities came flooding back in a rush of heat, bringing a smile to her mouth. Hot memories. Her flesh quivered at the images playing over in her mind, at the same time rarely used muscles ached their protests, bringing to mind more of Khaled's seductive night moves.

Her muscles would recover. In a day or two they'd forget and be back to normal. Not so her. Last night would be a night she'd remember for a long time to come. And after last night, *normal* was going to seem exceedingly dull.

What would it be like to have Khaled in her bed every night? To share passion and desire with him, night after night and then to wake up with him alongside her every morning? What would that be like?

She'd thrown away the chance to find out.

Realisation hit her like a cold shower. If she'd agreed to become his wife she could expect that—Khaled in her bed, every night, every morning, *every way*.

She'd had the chance and she'd thrown it away when she'd thrown his crazy marriage plans back in his face.

She sighed and eased herself back down onto her pillow, staring up at the tent's ceiling. She'd done the right thing. It had been a crazy marriage plan—he'd been way out of line, scheming and conspiring to make her his wife in his own version of an arranged marriage—and she'd had no choice but to refuse. Any sane person would.

Why had he ever imagined she'd go along with it? It didn't make sense and the more she came to learn about Khaled, the less sense it made. He was a strong leader, respected and loved by his people. She'd seen this with her own eyes, he was both fair and good in dealings with them. He was no petty despot.

And with his good looks he could have his pick of women to be his bride. So what could possibly have driven him to choose her?

None of it made sense. So she *had* done the right thing. She knew it. Despite the sex. Even if she couldn't imagine ever tiring of feeling the way he'd made her feel last night, sex just wasn't enough. For since when did compatibility in bed constitute a sound basis for marriage anyway? It wasn't as if they were in love with each other after all.

Oh, she'd miss him when she returned to Milan, that was true. She'd miss catching his hooded gaze upon her when she looked up, and his brooding magnetism setting her nerve endings alight. She'd even miss the verbal sparring between them and the endless mounting tension.

And there were times she even liked him. Though that was hardly the same thing as love.

Hardly the same thing at all…

On impulse she leaned over to him, his face still turned into the pillow. Holding back her hair with one hand, she dipped her head and kissed him.

His eyelids batted open and he smiled, uttering a low growl as one arm came down and circled around her.

'Thank you,' he said.

She smiled back. 'I think it was my pleasure.'

'It was our pleasure,' he purred, nuzzling her ear. 'You are so beautiful. I cannot understand why any man would be crazy enough to choose another over you.'

She went rigid. Paolo hadn't even entered into her thoughts and right now was hardly the time to bring him up. Not that she felt guilty. It wasn't as if they were still involved in a relationship and she'd betrayed him by sleeping with Khaled, not given her last phone call to him that had signalled the end of their relationship.

But still she didn't want to think of Paolo when she was in another man's arms. The shock of Paolo's deception was still too raw, too painful. She didn't want to be reminded of it now. She didn't need to be reminded of it now.

Tell me you enjoyed making love to me, she wished; *tell me it was worth it. But don't remind me that someone else thought I wasn't.*

He cursed under his breath. What was he thinking? He had done what he had set out to do. He had made her want him and then he had made her his own. But his victory over Paolo was for his satisfaction—he should never have mentioned his name. Not when she was probably still mourning the loss of their relationship.

He pushed himself up, scooping her into his arms, kissing her averted cheek. 'I'm sorry,' he said. 'That was a stupid thing to say. But there is one thing I'll never be sorry about.'

A blink of her eyelids, the soft parting of her lips on a sigh, was her only response.

'I could never be sorry that you are here, in my arms and in my bed. I will never be sorry for that, for as long as I live. I don't think I could ever have enough of you.'

She took a deep breath, her chest rising in a way that could not escape his attention. He couldn't resist. He dropped his mouth over the closest nipple, rolling it languidly between his lips with his tongue, to be rewarded almost immediately with her gasp of pleasure as the nipple peaked in his mouth. Then he lifted his head fractionally, blowing softly on to the tip, fascinated to watch it pebble and firm.

She trembled in his arms as he drew closer to the other nipple. 'Prove it,' she invited.

The capital was bustling with afternoon crowds and swirling traffic by the time they neared the palace. She sat quietly in the Range Rover, the return trip having gone all too quickly for her liking, and she cursed the invention of the internal combustion engine that saw her sitting in a luxurious leather bucket seat, so far from Khaled's reach, when a century ago she might have been sharing his saddle the entire journey.

The journey on camels from the encampment back to the vehicles had been the best. Almost every part of her felt tender, her aches a welcome reminder of their night of passion, and she'd let herself relax into his body, had even found ways she could inveigle herself closer still, pressing her face to his chest, relishing the scent of man, rich and raw, as it fed into her senses.

Even after a night and morning of passion she was still burning for him. She couldn't help it. Back home in Australia his touch would come with a government health warning—it was dangerously addictive. And after a night spent revelling in his touch, and a ride together through the desert dunes on a loping camel on their way to meet the cars, the more addicted she'd become.

It was going to be more of a wrench to leave than she could ever have imagined. Surprisingly more of a wrench, given yesterday she'd been demanding to be taken to the airport so she could leave the country immediately. She'd been so sure then, so absolutely driven to escape the first chance she had.

Why now, then, was she in two minds about leaving? Why, barely more than twenty-four hours later, was the thought of heading for the airport so much less compelling?

What had changed, other than they'd made love, out there in a tent amongst the desert sands?

Unless this wasn't just about sex? Unless…
No way!
There was no way. Between them there was just sex. It was just a physical thing. There could only ever be just sex.

So why did the thought of leaving Jebbai, of leaving Khaled, seem to tear a hole right through her? Seem to gut her completely? Why did the closer she got to saying goodbye for ever make her less and less comfortable? It couldn't only be put down to the best sex she'd ever had, surely.

'What's wrong?' said Khaled from the driver's seat.

'What do you mean, what's wrong?' she asked, suddenly aware that she'd been shaking her head from side to side.

'You don't look happy. Would you have liked to stay longer in the desert?'

Heat suffused his words and swirled the depths of his eyes and she saw the pictures he must be thinking, she could feel his touch on her skin. 'Oh, no,' she lied, her voice shaky as the bottom fell out of her world with the power of her discovery. 'It was an interesting trip, but it's such a relief to be back.'

Her voice choked up on the last word but still she managed to dredge up a bright smile from somewhere. His eyes hardened, taking on a granite sheen as he measured her words, and she wished he'd look back at the road before they veered off it.

Finally he looked to the front again and she felt

her smile crack and slide away. How much longer could she keep this up now that it had hit her? Now that one sight of the reflection in his dark eyes had confirmed what she'd feared was true.

Damn it all. She'd known this would happen if she'd stayed. She'd known she was in danger of falling more and more under Khaled's magnetic spell if she didn't get away.

And it had happened. The worst thing possible had happened.

This wasn't about sex.

This had never been about sex.

She'd fallen in love with Khaled.

CHAPTER ELEVEN

SHE had to get away. Now more than ever. No longer could she trust what she felt and she couldn't even be sure she was thinking straight any more. She'd lost control of her life and she needed time away to try and get it back.

Away from Khaled's influence and powerful spell she could be more objective and clear-headed. A break spent with her family in Australia would give her the distance she needed to get herself back together. She had bridges to rebuild there as it was, with her mother and sisters, before she could consider moving on. Gianfranco had to allow her the leave. He just had to.

But the first step to doing any of that was to get away from Jebbai.

She was quiet as Khaled pulled the vehicle to a halt outside the palace, reluctant to speak until he had shaken off the servants and carried her bag back to her room himself.

'There,' he said, opening the door to her study and putting down her bag. 'Back safe and sound. Didn't I say so?' He looked around the apartment. 'Where's Azizah? She should be here.'

'Maybe she wasn't expecting us back so soon,' she

said, wishing he would go, wishing he would stay, wishing it was all over.

She glanced down at her watch, mentally adding a six-hour journey to the early-afternoon time and thinking it might still be possible to arrange a flight back to Milan today if the security alert was over. Compared to that it really wasn't important where Azizah was in the scheme of things. It wasn't as if she needed anyone to help her pack. And it wasn't as if she could put off the question that had been plaguing her thoughts.

'Is there any news of the airport reopening?'

He stiffened, the long, fluid lines of his body pulling up tall and taut.

'Is that a passing enquiry, or do you have a more specific interest?'

She swallowed back her first response. How could he pretend not to know why she cared?

'Why do you ask? Will it make your answer any different?'

'I want to know. Why do you care whether the airport is open or closed?'

'Because you said you'd give me a lift, remember? You promised to take me to the airport and put me on a plane for Milan, just as soon as it reopened.'

Silence met her words, a fat, incredulous bubble of silence.

Then it burst. 'You're still planning on leaving?' Disbelief turned his words into an accusation.

'Of course I am. I told you I wanted to leave. You

told me you'd take me to the airport yourself. You promised.'

He took two strides towards her. 'But that was before…' His words trailed off.

'Before what?' she demanded. 'Before last night? You think that what happened last night changes anything?'

His eyebrows lifted. 'Doesn't it?'

'We had sex, Khaled,' she said. 'People do it all the time and then they walk away. End of story.' She shrugged. 'It changes nothing.' She turned her head, before he could see the lie in her eyes. Before he could see how her own words tore at her heart. She couldn't let him see what it meant to her, not when she was so vulnerable and afraid and desperate to escape.

'Sex?' The word erupted from him like a cannonball as her forearm was grabbed in his iron-like grasp, pulling her back around to face him. 'Is that what we had? And all the time I thought we were making love.'

'Call it whatever you like,' she said more shakily than she wished. 'You promised to take me to the airport.' She looked up at him, her eyes pleading for him to understand. 'And I'm holding you to it.'

He let go of her arm, wheeling away, raking one clawed hand through his hair.

'I don't want you to go.'

She squeezed her eyes shut, clamping back on the stinging dampness behind her lids. 'We've been through this.'

He spun around to face her. 'No, we haven't.'

'Khaled—'

'No!' he shouted. 'When I made that promise I thought I could let you walk out of my life if you wanted to. I really believed it. But I thought it wouldn't come to that—I thought I would change your mind about leaving—that you would decide to stay here in Jebbai with me.'

She laughed, the sound coming brittle and harsh. 'You thought one night with you would change my mind? You really must fancy yourself as some sort of Arab stud.'

His eyes flashed with danger, his jaw rigid as concrete, and she stepped back, fearing she had gone too far.

'Listen to me,' he hissed, his teeth clenched, his eyes rapier sharp. 'No one has ever felt so right in my bed, such liquid fire in my arms. That perfect moment when we two became one—you could not help but feel that. I know you felt it too. You can't deny it.'

There was no oxygen left in the room, otherwise why was it so difficult to breathe? So difficult to think?

'Khaled, I...'

'I don't want you to go, Sapphire. Even if last night changed nothing for you, it changed the world for me. After last night I know I could never live without you. The last thing I want to do in the world is to take you to the airport never to see you again. I can't lose you now. I want you to stay here and become my wife.'

'No,' she protested, vehemently shaking her head as she tried to dislodge his hand on her arm. 'That's crazy. That's exactly why you brought me here in the first place! Why should this time be any different?'

His free hand cupped her cheek. She flinched, trying to pull away, but his hand remained, and against her own better judgement she found herself nestling into the warm strength of his palm. His face hovered just inches from her own, his eyes suddenly more tender than she'd ever seen.

'Something happened to me last night, while I was out there in that desert tent with you. I discovered something momentous that I should have realised long, long ago.'

She was afraid to blink, afraid to breathe, afraid the sound of her pumping heart would drown out his words.

'*Zafeerah…*' The way he said her name fed into her soul, he might have been worshipping her. 'I'm not good at showing these things, but can't you feel it? I love you.'

Her pulse quickened, thumping in her chest as his words hit home. *He loved her?* How could it be possible, after all that had happened?

'You don't believe me,' he said, 'but you must. I think I loved you from the very first time I saw you in the salon. I wanted you back then but it has taken me all this time to see the truth of what was staring me in the face all along.

'I love you. And that's why I cannot bear the

thought of your leaving. I want you to stay and be by my side forever. I am asking you to become my wife.'

His mouth slanted over hers and she felt his lips, heated, filled with promise and expectation, moving over hers.

She felt her resolve to leave wavering, losing balance in a world she was less and less sure of. So much was changing and all too fast. Her heart sang with his revelation yet at the same time her mind reeled.

She couldn't think straight before he'd made his announcement. How could she possibly think straight now?

He lifted his head, his hands taking hers in his. 'Will you stay then? Will you stay, and become my wife?'

She could tell him now that she felt the same way, that she too had fallen and fallen hard, but there was still too much to think about, too much history to get over, too many things to forgive.

She started to shake her head. 'I don't know.'

'Please,' he implored. 'Please think about it.'

He was so different now. This was a man used to getting what he wanted. All he had to do was click his fingers and people came running. Yet he was asking her now, pleading with her to reconsider.

She could see what this was costing him, could see the pain and uncertainty in his features. It was a different side of Khaled—a much more vulnerable and human side than she'd seen before.

Maybe he was speaking the truth. Maybe he did

love her. But how could she be sure? After all the
half-truths and secrets, it was all too much to process.

'Think about it,' he repeated, sensing her own bewilderment. 'I'll leave you now. Take your time; call
me on the intercom when you've made up your mind.
The airport has reopened. I'll have my jet put on
standby. If you still want to leave, you can leave immediately. On the other hand, if you decide to stay…'

His words trailed off and she nodded. 'Thank you,'
she said, thinking how inadequate that sounded after
such a conversation.

He smiled and pressed his lips to her forehead.
Then he turned and left, pulling the door softly closed
behind him.

It seemed like years since she'd been in the workshop,
yet it was really only yesterday. Azizah had still not
shown up, so there was no opportunity to distract herself with small talk and minor housekeeping issues.
Instead, as she prowled amongst the worktables bearing machines all now empty and silent, her thoughts
kept churning, going over and over trying to digest
the impact of Khaled's surprise declaration, trying to
fit all the pieces together.

He loved her.

She loved him.

He wanted to marry her.

She wanted to get away.

Or did she?

Her reason for leaving was to keep herself safe, to
protect herself from Khaled's influence. But what

would she be saving when she'd already lost her heart? What more was there to risk when her body wanted nothing more than to be pressed close next to his?

Would it be so wrong to stay and marry him? To have him as her partner, in bed and out of it for her entire life? Was that not preferable to turning her back on their love and living without him, alone somewhere and full of regrets for what might have been?

It was still so difficult to think, but maybe this was how it was supposed to be—a decision that should be made not with the head, but with the heart. What could she lose by doing what her heart knew instinctively was right?

In the corner of the room the wedding dress that had brought her to Jebbai still hung on the mannequin, its brilliant beaded and jewelled bodice gleaming even through the clear protective dust jacket. The sight of it brought a smile to her face, even in the midst of her inner turmoil.

If she'd achieved anything in Jebbai, it was this gown. It was beautiful, the most beautiful she'd ever seen and most certainly the most beautiful she'd ever made. The design was exquisite and, thanks to the skill and dedication of her assistants, the workmanship second to none.

And it could still be hers…

Sensation shimmied down her spine at the possibility and she bit down hard on her bottom lip as carefully she peeled back the protective layer, revealing the full splendour of the dress.

It had been made to her measurements, certainly, but with not one fitting. And the real test of any garment was not how it looked hanging up, but how it looked on the person it had been designed for. How well had they transformed a bare set of measurements and metres of fabric into a gown for a real woman? There was still the possibility she might leave Jebbai and never know.

There was only one way to find out.

The dress slipped sensually over her skin, cool and satin smooth after she'd stripped off the cotton shirt and chinos she'd worn for the return journey. There was weight in the gown, much more than was apparent at first glance, but the weight felt balanced in the long skirt that flared out from her hips. She did up as many of the pearl fastenings at her back as she could, thinking it would be so much easier with someone to help her but at the same time thankful there was no one to witness her folly.

There was a full-length mirror in her walk-in wardrobe. And heeled shoes. She hitched up the heavy train and headed for her bedroom, feeling heady with both exhilaration and recklessness.

She saw it propped up against her telephone as soon as she walked through the door into the office. She'd completely missed the envelope when she'd first arrived, too preoccupied talking to Khaled, her back to the desk. But from the door the angle was perfect and she could not miss it.

Who was writing to her here? Unless it was Gianfranco, although it was more usual for him just to send a fax. Curious, she picked up the envelope on the way through to her dressing room. The outside gave nothing away, the typewritten address bland and uninformative. Likewise the absence of a return address.

She shrugged and flipped the envelope down onto her bed as she passed. The letter could wait. First to the shoes. She searched her wardrobe, where her gear had been returned since her aborted attempt to leave yesterday, and hauled out the highest pair of heels she'd brought. They were brightly coloured sandals, hardly a good match, but they'd give her the extra height she needed to get the best impression of the fall of the dress.

She slipped them on, smoothing down the material, impatient now for her first glance in the mirror. She twisted her hair into a knot on the top of her head, took a deep breath and stepped in front of the mirror.

Oh, wow!

It looked—sensational.

The dress fitted her like a second skin, moulding itself perfectly to every dip, every curve, while its exquisite lines spoke elegance. She looked instantly taller, more regal. But if it looked fantastic, it felt even better. Even in this hurried try-on state, without make-up or her hair done properly, the dress felt superb.

More than that, it felt right.

Her teeth found her lip again. It did feel right. Just as making love with Khaled in the desert tent had felt so perfect, as if they were destined to be forever.

Maybe this wedding was preordained too. Maybe it was written in the stars and all she'd had to do was to say yes. Had Khaled felt that all along? Was that why he'd concocted his plan to lure her to his desert kingdom and win her heart?

A bubble of laughter welled up inside her and in her excitement she couldn't hold it back. Neither that nor the mistiness that suddenly filled her eyes. Her hands flew to her mouth as the sheer craziness of what was happening hit home.

Yesterday she hadn't thought it possible. There'd been no way she would have contemplated marriage, despite the attraction growing between them. But yesterday she'd known nothing of his love for her and she'd had even less idea of her own love for him.

She turned this way and that in the mirror, allowing herself one final appraisal. She'd never thought herself a fairy-tale princess, but she sure felt like it in this dress. The only things missing were her veil, a bouquet of fresh flowers—and a handsome prince.

Although she had one of those just waiting for her call.

All she had to do was pick up the phone.

Then he would be here. And she wouldn't even have to tell him—one look at her in the wedding dress and he would have his answer.

She picked up the phone next to her bed and dialled.

CHAPTER TWELVE

Ten minutes, Saleem had told her, Khaled would be along then. Meanwhile he'd seemed more interested in whether or not Azizah had shown up yet.

Deflated and suddenly filled with nervous tension, she paced the room, wanting something to stop her thinking. Now she'd made up her mind, the last thing she wanted was more time to think.

Her eyes fell upon the letter where she'd discarded it on the bed and gratefully she scooped it up. It would serve as a distraction, at least for a minute or two. She tore it open and unfolded the pages as she walked back into the study to wait for Khaled, recognising the handwriting instantly.

Paolo's handwriting.

She wasn't sure whether to be delighted or sad. It was the first letter she'd received from him in all the time she'd been here. Why would he be writing now, unless he was wanting to make amends? She began to read.

Dearest Sapphy,

I realise you may not want to hear from me right now but I could not leave things the unsatisfactory way they were left when last we spoke. For one thing I know I owe you an apology and an expla-

*nation and for another, while it may seem melo-
dramatic to you, I continue to fear for your welfare
while you are in Jebbai.*

Her lips tightened and she rubbed her forehead. If
Paolo was going to wheel out another bitter diatribe
as to why she should not stay in Jebbai it was going
to fall on deaf ears. Paolo obviously had a problem
with Khaled knowing of his secret marriage. Khaled
must have threatened to reveal the secret long ago—
nothing else would explain why Paolo hated him so
much and wished her to have nothing to do with him.
But she knew the truth now and he would just have
to accept that he had made a mistake by not telling
her. Their whole relationship had been based on a lie.

*I realise I owe you a huge apology. I am forever
sorry that I was not the one to tell you of my marriage when I had the chance. I am so afraid the
promise that I made back then to keep my marriage
to Helene a secret has destroyed any chance of
friendship between us in the future. But then, how
could I have told you? I was too scared of losing
you although I wish I'd found a way, as I fear you
must now hate me.*

*But whatever you think of me, you have to know
the truth, now more than ever.*

*The circumstances of our marriage were uncon-
ventional to say the least. More relevant to you,
though, my marriage was to a woman promised by
her family and against her will to another and for*

*that he swore that one day he would have his re-
venge against me, promising that he would one day
steal any woman I intended to marry. And that is
why, more than anything, I fear for your safety.*

That man was Khaled.

Khaled? Revenge? Her gut clenched and cold tremors assailed her as the impact of Paolo's words hit
home. With not a thought to the prospect of creasing
the dress, she let herself collapse into an armchair.

So Paolo had married the woman intended for
Khaled—no wonder he had a vested interest in revealing Paolo's secret.

But as to his suggestion that Khaled had chosen
her because of her links with Paolo... It was crazy.
They had never been officially betrothed—unless he
had believed the speculation the magazines and gossip columns had spouted...that a link between successful international lawyer, Paolo Mancini, and up-
and-coming fashion designer, Sapphy Clemenger,
was inevitable.

Was that what she was doing here? Had Khaled
lured her here with the promise of a commission in
order to 'steal' her from Paolo? It all seemed too incredible. It couldn't be true.

But then, didn't it make more sense than his asser-
tion that he'd fallen in love with her from a photo-
graph and set out to woo her?

She read on, feeling each new revelation like a
body blow. Paulo had married Helene to save her
from an arranged marriage to Khaled. The arrange-

ment was to be in force only until Khaled found another wife. Then their marriage could be annulled and
they would be free to continue with their lives and
the relationships they chose. Neither of them expected
that twelve years on Khaled would still be waiting,
watching, casting the long shadow of his revenge over
them.

What kind of bitterness made someone act that
way?

No wonder Paolo had been frightened of commitment. No wonder he had pulled away from talk of
marriage and the future. He had no choice. Words
blurred on the page as tears pricked her eyes at the
sacrifice he'd made for a friend, the sacrifice that had
cheated him for twelve years of any chance of love.

She blinked the moisture away, clearing her vision
enough to allow her to read the final paragraphs.

*Sapphy, bella, perhaps I'm wrong. Perhaps the
fact that Khaled told you of my marriage is evidence that he's over the past and ready to put it
behind him. Maybe it means nothing to him any
more. I sincerely hope so.*

*I know things didn't work out between us and I
hope you can start to understand some of the reasons why it was so difficult for me to be honest with
you, but I do care for you, Sapphy, I care for you
immensely. So please, I beg of you, be careful in
your dealings with Khaled. Don't take anything at
face value as he has a score to settle with me and
I am afraid he will stop at nothing to do it.*

Her insides were gutted, totally empty, her heart a black empty chasm pulling wider apart with every breath. Her legs lashed out as she kicked off her heels, reading the paragraphs again, tucking her legs underneath her on the chair, curling tighter and tighter into a ball.

Over the past? Not a chance. Khaled hadn't used his information in the spirit of forgiveness, he hadn't shared it with her over a drink and a laugh for old times' sake. He'd used it as a weapon against Paolo, its barbs designed to dig deep and twist and bury his nemesis completely.

As for stopping at nothing—hadn't he told her he loved her? What was that if not just one more attempt to prevent her leaving and ensure the success of his plan?

She let the pages fall to her lap and hugged herself, her breath jerky, her sobs strangely silent, unable to make a sound because there was absolutely nothing left inside.

Nothing—*except anger*. Into the shell where her heart once resided white-hot anger rushed in on a tidal wave—foaming and crashing, filling the space and gaps, its heat fed with the oxygen from every breath she took.

Khaled had played her for a fool all along. But no longer. Her hands formed into fists and she sprang from the chair, energised by the sudden rush of emotion, letting the pages scatter on the floor.

She had to get this dress off. It was a dress for a bride to wear when she wedded the man of her dreams. She'd been kidding herself that she could ever be that bride. She'd been kidding herself that there would ever be a real wedding. Her dream had turned into a nightmare.

Her hands had tackled only the first of the pearl buttons when behind her someone tapped on the door. She swivelled in time to see the door swing open and suddenly he was there.

'I came as soon…'

With one look at her his words died on his tongue. She was wearing the dress. His blood pumped harder, louder in his veins, spiralling warmth and pride through him. Soon, she would be his.

'Beautiful,' he said, his tone almost worshipping. 'Just stunning. The most beautiful bride ever.'

She sniffed, raising her chin and rubbing her cheek with the back of her hand, and it was then that he noticed her eyes, large and luminescent as if he'd startled her with his sudden appearance, yet smudged around the edges, almost as if she'd been crying.

She dropped her arm to the side and brought herself up taller and suddenly her eyes looked less doe-like and more glacial, and set amongst features that seemed to harden even as he watched.

'Do you think so?' she said, her lips tilting into a harsh curve. She looked down at the dress. 'I was thinking of it more as a going-away outfit.'

'What do you mean?'

She turned her eyes back up at him. Back to where their frosty spears could inflict the most damage. 'When were you going to tell me?'

'Tell you what?'

'Were you going to spring it on me before I'd walked down the aisle, or wait until we were hitched? Or even better, maybe you were saving it for a honeymoon treat?'

'Do you mind telling me what you're talking about?'

'It must have been challenging—always finding ways of keeping me here. But you sure came up with the trump card to beat all today. You love me. Yeah, right. What were you going to try if that didn't work?'

Breath rushed out of his lungs on a growl and he closed the space between them, latching on to her shoulders. 'What's happened?' he said.

'Oh, I get it,' she said, wincing, looking pointedly down on his hands. 'You were planning on physically restraining me. Nice touch. No doubt there's a dungeon somewhere down below where I can be kept for as long as it takes.'

He cursed as he flung his hands from her shoulders, pacing to the desk, where he took two steadying breaths before being able to face her again. 'Something's happened,' he said. 'Are you going to share it with me or are you going to make me stand here and play twenty questions?'

She waved her hand in the direction of the letter, its pages still abandoned in the corner, where they'd fluttered down onto the floor. 'Paolo wrote to me,' she said. 'And it made for interesting reading, the story of your vendetta against him.'

Her eyes glittered blue ice, her chin was set and

defiant and inside he felt sick. This was not the way she should have found out.

He crossed the room, snatching up the pages and scanning their contents.

'This whole trip, my whole reason for being here, was simply so you could satisfy your desire for revenge.'

'It wasn't like that,' he snapped, though he knew it was, at the start.

'Oh? What was it like then? Surely you're not going to tell me you stumbled upon me by accident, completely unaware of my connection with Paolo?

'Oh,' she said, throwing her head back, 'I'm so stupid, I can't believe it's taken me this long to work it all out. You planned this whole fiasco from the start. How convenient that I'm a designer. How easy that proved to be to get me here—all you had to do was pay enough to Gianfranco and he just about pushed me onto you. And once here, you had no intention of letting me go.'

He dragged in a short, sharp breath. 'No! Though it's true I have a score to settle with Paolo.'

'And taking me away from him was part of that vendetta.'

'Why should he have you? He doesn't deserve you. Yes, in the beginning, all I wanted was revenge. But that was before I met you. Then I knew he wasn't good enough for you. That you deserved better.'

'And you were supposed to be better? I believed you, you know. I stood up for you against Paolo when he pleaded with me not to come to Jebbai. I actually felt sorry for your *"fiancée"*, too ill to be able to take part in her own wedding preparations, and yet you were using me the whole time. Using me to get back at him.'

'Maybe it was like that at the start,' he admitted. 'But not all the time. I wanted revenge, that's true, but once I met you I knew you were not just some possession of Paolo's that I had to have. I wanted you for myself then, for the woman you are. I had to have you, body and soul.'

She crossed her arms, the expression on her face mirroring her body language and screaming her disbelief. 'Tell me about Helene,' she said. 'What was so special about her that you couldn't bear the thought of anyone else having her?'

His jaw clenched, teeth grating together. The questions were bound to come, he expected it now, but still that made it no easier to deal with. 'She was young and pretty, a student at university, very clever. Our parents supported the marriage, it would have cemented relations between a huge oil conglomerate and a producing nation. It would have been a good match.'

'Did you love her?'

It was a difficult question and so long ago. He was sure he'd thought he'd loved her once, but now, knowing Sapphire and the way she made him feel— maybe he had just liked the idea of being in love. He shrugged. 'I was barely twenty years old.'

'That doesn't answer my question.'

'Then, no,' he said on a sigh. 'I didn't love her.

But I wanted her. It could have been a good marriage, beneficial to both our families and interests. But it was not to be.'

'Because Paolo got there first.'

'He interfered in something that had nothing to do with him,' he said, his voice rising. 'He should have stayed out of it. And for what he cost me I swore I would take something from him, to make him suffer loss even just a fraction of what I had lost. To make him realise the damage he had done and to make him pay.'

'He saved her! He stepped in and did more than a friend should ever be asked to do, he stood up for her and rescued a terrified girl from a marriage she didn't want, and from a man who would ruin her life. And yet you can't see what an heroic thing he did? Then you pursue him for years, *years*, merely because he snatched something you wanted.'

She paused, her face flushed and eyes wild. 'Don't you think it's time you got over it?'

Breath hissed through his teeth as he sought to bring his breathing under control. 'You think that losing Helene is what this is all about?'

'Isn't it? Though I'm sure your pride took a beating too—knowing that someone was smarter and faster than you. I'm sure you'll never forgive Paolo for that.'

His fist slammed onto the desk, toppling items and scattering pens. Pain shot up his arm but it was nothing compared to the hate. To the pure, unadulterated hate for someone who'd cost him so much.

'That's where you're wrong. I could get over him taking Helene. I could even live with him outsmarting me, if that's how you see it. But I will never forgive him for what he did to my parents.'

'Your parents? What are you talking about?' Her brow furrowed, her head tilting to one side.

'On the day they should have been at my wedding, the day they should have been celebrating my marriage to Helene in London—on that very day, on the side of a Swiss mountain, they were swept away by the avalanche that killed them.'

CHAPTER THIRTEEN

HER hands flew to her mouth, covering a gasp of horror.

'My intended wedding day,' he continued. 'Definitely not a day of joy for anyone. It took the authorities three weeks to recover their bodies and those of their two companions, three weeks where I didn't know whether to hope they would be alive or to hope their bodies would just be found as soon as possible. *Three weeks of hell.*'

She stepped closer, placing her hand on his arm. 'Khaled, I'm so sorry.'

'Are you? Then maybe you understand now why I set out to do what I did. My parents had been in London for the wedding preparations but two days before the bride was spirited away to marry someone else. My mother was distraught, my father embarrassed. There was no point them staying in London to sort out the mess. It wasn't their mess to sort out. My father took her to her favourite resort in an effort to cheer her up, only...'

She squeezed his arm. 'Khaled, I don't know what to say—that's a terrible thing to happen. But you have to realise, it was an accident. You can't blame Paolo.'

'Can't I? Their deaths were the direct consequence of his actions. He didn't just cost me a bride. He cost me my parents. He might as well have killed them himself!' He moved away, just far enough away that she had to let go of his arm.

He didn't want anyone touching him, he felt too raw, just as he had when he'd received the visit from the police, their faces glum, their eyes averted, coming to relate the message from the Swiss authorities that his parents had been swept away and they were doing everything humanly possible to save them.

Just like back then it felt that someone had grated the skin off his body—every part of him felt exposed and raw and weeping.

Her heart was breaking, her anger now tempered with sympathy. It was clear what his parents' deaths had cost him. The young prince had lost his youth, had lost his chance to become his own person before being thrust prematurely into the leadership of the sheikhdom of Jebbai against the backdrop of tragedy.

No wonder he'd focused so much on the circumstances that led to his parents' deaths. No wonder he'd dwelt so much on how he could seek retribution. Paolo was the obvious target.

But his words and the depth of his feeling were shocking. 'Khaled,' she said, 'your parents died in tragic circumstances. But don't let that spoil your whole life. Don't let hate consume you. Don't you think your parents would want you to get on with your life and not dwell on the circumstances of their deaths?'

'You do not understand.'

'I understand that it was fate that took your parents

from you, and had it not been that day it might well have been another. What if the wedding had gone on as planned and they were killed in a motorway accident on their way to the wedding—who would you have blamed then, the bride for agreeing to marry you?'

'That doesn't make sense.'

'Neither does pursuing someone to the ends of the earth for something they had no control over.' He opened his mouth to protest and she launched straight into the next sentence without giving ground. 'Yes, he spoilt your wedding plans, but don't you see, he didn't send your parents to the mountains? It was their choice, you said, to go there. They chose to be on that mountain, not Paolo. You can't blame him for what happened next.'

'And you don't blame your mother for what's happened between you and your sisters?'

His words took her by surprise and she reeled back. 'That's hardly the same thing…'

'Isn't it? She comes back from the dead and now you have competition for your sisters' affections and you don't like it. You actually resent her for being alive. Ironic, isn't it, that I would have given anything for my mother to live and you would be quite happy if your mother had remained safely "dead".'

'Khaled! What a horrible thing to say.'

It wasn't true. It couldn't be true. Sure, she wanted things to be the way they'd always been before, but that was hardly the same thing.

He took a deep breath and dropped his head back.

He felt weary and sick. Heartsick. Was that the word for how it felt when your insides ached as though they'd been pulped?

There was nothing for it now. He had no other means of convincing her to stay, no other words he could say. She'd taken his declaration of love as a lie and why should she suddenly change her mind and believe him now? Attacking her just now would have been the last straw.

'I'm sorry,' he said. 'I should never have said that.' He sighed, long and loud, with the aching tiredness of someone who had hated for far too long. 'I think it's best that I take you to the airport right away. Do you need help packing?'

She looked at him, all wide-eyed and pale, barely moving.

'You have no need to fear. I will not stop you leaving tonight. I'll arrange for the jet and crew to be on standby and send someone to pick up your bags in, say, half an hour?'

This time she nodded, her murmured assent the barest whisper. And then he let himself out of her rooms, letting his eyes drink in until the last click of the door the sight of her in the crumpled gown, committing her sweet lines to memory, knowing that he had forever lost the battle to make her his bride.

They were silent on the way to the airport and for that she was grateful. She doubted she could have spoken anyway, her throat chokingly tight, her chest feeling as if someone had squeezed all the air from it, so there would have been precious little anyway to give sound to her words.

Khaled sat brooding one seat's width and yet an entire world away. He had given up and for that she should be happy. No more lies, no more promises or entreaties. No more declarations of love. She'd thought he might try to convince her that at least that much had been true, that he'd fallen in love with her and that there was still a chance for them, still a future together. She'd been expecting it. She'd even *hoped* that much was true.

But there had been nothing and the emptiness inside her grew as did her certainty that that, too, had been a lie.

At least he was letting her go. Now she could return to Milan; now she would be free.

She looked at the land surrounding the airport road, out over the sandy plains and stunted trees, and her heart ached with the impending separation. So much for being free. Part of her would always belong here, in this desert kingdom with the tall, golden-skinned sheikh named Khaled. With the man she could never now tell she loved.

They passed through airport security, markedly tightened since her arrival, the presence of guards a disturbing but necessary reaction to their earlier troubles. Then they were through the gates and onto the tarmac, where the driver pulled alongside the jet, its engines already warming up. And then her door was being pulled open and before she knew it she was standing at the foot of the steps, Khaled's hands surrounding her own, and the moment had finally come to say goodbye.

She looked up at his face, his jaw set, his dark eyes tortured, and she wanted to kiss his eyes then to kiss away the pain. 'Promise me something,' she said.

His jaw eased up enough for him to speak. 'Promise what?'

'Forget about Paolo. Forget about what happened so long ago. Think about your future, as your parents would want you to do. Can you do that?'

'I'll see,' he said with some effort.

She smiled. It was something at least. 'Thank you.'

'What are your plans?' he asked. 'Will you stay in Milan?'

She exhaled a long breath. 'I don't know. I think I have to go back to Australia first. I need to visit my family. You were right, you know; I've blamed my mother too much for what's happened between my sisters and me. And you've made me realise how lucky I am to have her. I'm going to visit and really get to know her and try to put things right between us.'

He smiled himself then. 'I'm glad. But your work?'

She shrugged. 'Maybe it's time I went out on my own. Gianfranco has been a wonderful teacher, but I'd love to have my own business somewhere…'

She left it there. She didn't need to tell him what kind of shop it would be. Neither of them needed to remember right now what had brought her here or to be reminded of the dress that now lay crushed and tear-stained on her bed.

'I hope you get it,' he said.

'Thank you.'

An officer stepped forward and whispered something in Khaled's ear. He nodded and sighed as the officer stepped back.

'It's time to go, then,' she said, feeling a lump in her throat growing larger and larger.

He nodded. 'It's time.'

'Well, then. Goodbye.'

He looked into her eyes and she saw the swirling emotions that were going on in his and his mouth moved, as if he was on the brink of saying something. And just for a moment she got the impression that he was going to tell her again—tell her that he loved her—and she knew that if he did, then she would tell him too. But then he pressed his lips together and when he did speak it was only to say, 'I'm so sorry.'

He squeezed her hands, bringing her just close enough that he could press his lips to her cheek, lingering there momentarily so she felt for the last time his intake of breath against her skin, the rasp of his five o'clock shadow and the warm sensuality of his lips.

And then he took his mouth away and without looking back at her disappeared into the car.

She shivered. Liquid nitrogen would feel warmer than his cold dismissal. Stiffly she turned and clambered up the stairs, pressing back tears behind a wall of resolve that threatened to tumble at any moment. Through a haze of moisture she was shown to her seat. She tried to smile at the attendant but she didn't know if her face was working. She couldn't feel anything. She was totally numb.

Her eyes searched the windows, looking to catch sight of his car, hoping for a last glimpse of Khaled, but already it was moving towards the security gates, the glass too darkly tinted to see through. He wasn't even waiting for her plane to take off. He'd probably already forgotten her.

The plane's engines whined, doors pulled closed, and gradually, smoothly, it started its taxi to the runway, the security gates slowly disappearing from view as the plane angled away. She craned her head around but it was no good. The gates and the car were gone. She slumped back in her seat, paying scant attention now to the changing view of the airport as a sense of loss like she'd never known weighed down upon her.

What was it worth to be free, when you were leaving your heart behind? What was the point of freedom, when you had lost the one you loved?

That was when she saw it coming. Low and flat, just skimming the roofline over the airport hangars flew the helicopter—perilously close, she thought. But then, it was an airport after all and it could have been coming in to land.

She lost interest momentarily, until her brain registered the danger. It wasn't landing. It was aiming right for them and there was someone hanging on the edge of the door. Something protruding.

A gun!

She gasped as the helicopter drew nearer.

The pilot's voice crackled urgently over the intercom— 'Everyone down!'

She didn't have enough time to be scared, it all happened too fast. Barely had she unbuckled her belt when she was ripped from her seat and thrown bodily to the floor, covered almost completely by the large body of a guard. She was winded but it didn't matter as gunfire battered the side of the aircraft, punching holes through the fuselage and thwacking into the upholstery and fittings around her. Something glass shattered, sending a spray of shards over them both, the guard taking the brunt of the debris.

The engines were still whining, one sounding choppy although the plane had now stopped, and someone was yelling in Arabic. 'What's going on?' she gasped.

The guard above her muttered to her in rough English, 'Stay low; the helicopter is pulling away.' And then suddenly she could breathe again as his weight lifted free.

And all her thought congealed to one certain prospect. Unless the helicopter had decided to melt back into the direction it had come, then it must have found a far more attractive target...

'Khaled!' she screamed, jumping to her feet, knowing that his car would be an easy target from the air, able to be picked out easily on the long, lonely road between the airport and the city.

Then smoke began to fill the cabin, dark and acrid and thick. She was aware of doors opening behind her, of escape chutes being deployed and the wail of sirens as rescue vehicles screamed across the tarmac towards them. Escape was at hand but all she wanted to do was get a quick glimpse to see where the helicopter had gone.

But even as she made for a window someone grabbed her hand, the man who'd covered her earlier, quite possibly saving her life, and pulled her back towards the escape route. Blood trickled from under his hairline and from his hands—the shattered glass—but if he felt his wounds, he gave no indication as he bade her to pull off her low-heeled shoes and quickly mimed the escape routine.

She followed his actions, escaping from the plane and reaching the ground, where already the emergency services were gathered to collect the escaping crew. She was hoisted out of the way and rushed to a vehicle as the cabin crew and security guards followed in rapid order from the smoking jet as sprays from a fire engine began to cover it with foam.

That was when she heard it.

The blast that could only mean an explosion—a mighty boom that came from the direction of the highway. She turned and saw the plume of smoke rising above the desert, black and thunderous and speaking of destruction and death, and something inside her burst open on a silent scream.

Khaled's car!

Her gut clenched in revulsion and panic.

But that would mean...

Khaled—*dead*?

It couldn't be possible. It just couldn't. Not when

she'd never had the chance to tell him what he meant to her. Not when she'd never had the chance to tell him that she loved him.

It didn't matter now, what he'd thought of her. Whether he'd lied to her or not, whether he'd loved her or not, he'd had a right to know that she loved him. What he'd chosen to do with that knowledge should have been up to him, but at least he would have known.

She should have told him that much at least.

She let herself be led into an ambulance. Someone held something to her face and she pulled back but the dressing came away red and she looked at it strangely, wondering that the blood could be hers when she felt no pain but for what had happened to Khaled.

Why were they even bothering with her? Why weren't they looking after him? Hadn't they heard it? Didn't they know?

The ambulance sped away from the plane. 'Where are you taking me?' she asked, hoping desperately that one of them spoke English.

She wasn't disappointed. 'Hebra,' the one who'd held the dressing to her face said. 'Hospital.'

'But what about Khaled?' she begged. 'His car…'

The men looked at each other, exchanging glances that shredded what was left of her heart. Did they know or were they just as scared as she was because they didn't?

They reached the perimeter security gates and stopped. She looked around, wondering about the delay—there was a car blocking their progress, trying to get in. A black car. A black car with two flat tyres, blistered paint and smashed windows.

Khaled's car!

Even as she watched a door opened wide and Khaled jumped out, running to the ambulance as his driver backed the damaged car out of the way.

'Zafeerah?' he shouted, half-demand, half-question, and one of the men nodded and pointed to the rear door. Before she had a chance to lift herself from the stretcher the back doors flew open and Khaled was inside, at her side, hauling her into his arms as the ambulance set off again, its siren screaming, as it sped its way to the city.

Grime stained his golden skin, particles of shattered windscreen lodged in his dark hair, but he was alive—gloriously alive.

'Sapphire,' he said, looking at her, 'I'm so relieved to see you.' He touched his hand to her face. 'But you are hurt.'

She covered his hand with her own, relishing the touch of his strong fingers, feeling his heat replace her earlier chill. Feeling his strength renew her own. She shook her head. 'It's nothing. Your guard saved my life. I don't think I need to go to hospital.'

'You've been through a great deal,' he said. 'You should be looked after properly.'

She felt the tremors start then. Tremors from the shock. From the fear of losing Khaled. From the wave of relief on discovering he was alive. He held her tight, rocking her, soothing her fears.

'I was so scared,' he said. 'When I heard the helicopter fire on the jet, I was so damned scared. But you are safe.' He hugged her closer, burying his face into her hair. 'I cannot believe it.'

His lips brushed kisses over her forehead, down the line of her nose.

'I heard the explosion,' she said, her fingers clutching his shirt. 'And I—' She broke off, her voice cracking. 'I was so afraid.'

Something shifted in his eyes, peeling away a layer so that something below shone through, burnished like copper lights, alive with hope.

'The helicopter. It came in close but by then it was already too late. A mortar from the airport guards brought it down. It crashed alongside the road.'

She swallowed. It must have been close, for the car's paint to be blistered with the heat, the tyres all but melted from the rims. She squeezed her eyes shut, trying to banish those pictures. They didn't matter now. Not with Khaled alive, holding her.

'I saw the pilot,' he said. 'I recognised her.'

'Her? Who was it?'

'Azizah.'

She gasped, unable to grasp the concept of her meek servant being capable of committing acts of terrorism. 'I can't believe it. She was so sweet, so helpful.'

He sighed deeply, shaking his head. 'Saleem began to suspect something was not right and he tried to tell me to get rid of her because he was worried for your safety. But I didn't listen. She came from a good family, with a long and loyal history with the palace. I could not believe she would betray us. By the time we had discovered the truth, she had fled.'

Saleem had been concerned for her welfare? And yet she had been so suspicious of him, so afraid of the way he watched her and of his abrupt manner. It was Azizah—timid, shy Azizah—who'd been the real danger. How she had made a mess of everything.

'But why?' she asked. 'What did she have against you?'

'Her parents were my parents' closest aides. It was they who died along with my parents in the avalanche. Azizah was only five years old at the time. We paid a pension and for her upbringing, it was the only thing we could do, and relatives in Jamalbad brought her up. But it seems they never forgave me for what had happened to their family and their hatred fed into her for twelve years until she became their vehicle for retribution.'

He hugged her closer. 'I cannot believe I entrusted you to such a dangerous woman. Can you ever forgive me?'

She shivered, wondering how much further the bitter tentacles of revenge could reach. There had to be an end to the pain, to the anguish. Somewhere the cycle had to be broken.

'I'm so sorry,' he whispered and she trembled again, remembering the last time he had used that expression.

'Do you still want me to leave?' she asked, her voice soft and uncertain.

'What do you mean? You're going straight to hospital.'

'I mean afterwards. The last time you told me you were sorry, you put me on the plane and walked away.' She swallowed deeply, trying to force down the fear of revealing the truth, steeling herself to go on because she knew she had no choice. 'Because if that's what you still want, I'll live with it, but there's something I must tell you first.'

His brows pulled together, his eyes unsure. 'I thought you wanted to leave. I thought you couldn't wait to see the back of me.'

'At one time that was true, but not for the reason you might think.'

'Then why?'

'Because I was scared of the way you made me feel. From the start I felt an attraction to you. Even when I knew I shouldn't. Even though I knew you were marrying someone else. I knew that if I stayed too long then I wouldn't want to leave. I knew that the longer I stayed, the more I came to know you, then the more I was in danger of falling in love with you.'

Silence stretched out between them, tension and expectation heightening against the backdrop of the wailing siren, and she feared she'd already said too much.

'And?' he prompted at last. He sounded impatient, giving her a kernel of hope. Did he really care what she had to say? Would it make a difference?

'And it happened. I didn't want it to. I even tried

to fight it. But it was no good. There was nothing I could do to stop it. Then when the jet was attacked and I feared for your life, I knew I was wrong not to have told you.'

'Hold on,' he said, holding a finger to her lips. 'Take a deep breath. What should you have told me?'

She blinked and sucked in a lungful of air, hoping for a burst of courage to go with it. 'I love you, Khaled. Somewhere along the way, in the midst of all that has happened, I fell in love with you.'

'You did?' He looked as if he didn't quite believe her.

She nodded. 'My pride wouldn't let me tell you. I was still so angry about everything that had happened. But pride and anger are such worthless emotions when so much is at stake. When I thought you'd been attacked and I feared for your life, I knew then that even if you never loved me in return, if you survived, I needed to let you know the truth. I needed to be honest with you.'

'But I don't understand. What do you mean, if I never loved you? I *told* you I loved you. You knew that.'

She gazed up at him. 'I thought you only said that to prevent me from leaving.'

'No.' He touched the tip of her nose with one finger. 'I told you that because I loved you.'

'But that was before I opened Paolo's letter. You never once told me after that—when we argued and you said you'd take me to the airport—you never mentioned it. You made me think it was just another ploy, another tactic to keep me here.'

'Not a ploy.' He gave a sad smile. 'But I understand why you would think so. I have never treated anyone as badly as I have treated you.'

She opened her mouth to protest—there were reasons why he acted the way he did, she knew that now. But two fingers on her lips shushed her.

'I cannot ask for forgiveness, it is too much. I planned to cold-heartedly steal you from one man and take you for my own—'

'No, Khaled, don't.' She brushed his hand aside, only to have him muffle her objections with his kiss.

'Please, let me explain,' he said, finally lifting his lips from hers, asserting his will instead with his dark eyes. 'I need to tell you these things. If you can bear to hear them.'

Her teeth scraped her bottom lip. She'd told him she loved him and he'd confirmed that he loved her. She wasn't sure she wanted to hear any more, certainly not if that risked changing the balance, but she nodded anyway. There must be no more secrets. Just as he needed to tell her these things, she needed to hear them.

'At first I set out to have you because of Paolo, that much is true. I had seen photos, I knew you were attractive and successful, but I had no doubt I could bend you to my will and make you go along with my plan. A month would be all I'd need.'

He took a deep breath. 'But from the moment I met you, my plan was in trouble. I began to want you, right from the start, and not just because you belonged to someone else. It was almost as if there was something between us—a wire—invisible and tightly strung, that pulled tighter and tighter the longer we were together.'

'I felt it too,' she offered. 'I couldn't get you out of my head, even when I thought I was designing a wedding dress for another woman—another bride.'

'You did? Of course, I suspected as much.' His smile turned suddenly serious. 'But still, the way I treated you was inexcusable. Even though I couldn't get enough of you. It was the ultimate irony that the woman I had stolen to get back at another man had gone and stolen my heart.'

He sighed. 'You made me risk the entire plan by telling you two weeks early.'

'I did that?'

He nodded. 'Believe it. You needled and bullied and refused to give in to my excuses for not having a fitting. You drove me so crazy with your demands that I wanted to throw you off balance.' He smiled. 'And I did,' he said, earning him a quick punch in the arm.

'I thought you were mad,' she said.

'It was a form of madness,' he agreed. 'I was so mad for you. And when you said you were going home to Paolo, I just got madder still. How could you prefer him over me?

'And if the airport hadn't been closed yesterday, I would have let you go home then, so deep did you seem affected by the pain of betrayal. Except…'

He paused and she waited expectantly.

'Except what?'

'Except, even then...' his voice sounded tenser, more strung out '...even then the drive for revenge was so strong. I knew that if you came to me of your own free will then my revenge on Paolo would be that much sweeter.'

'If I came to you of my own free will...' Her thoughts shifted her back to the desert tent, where she'd been the one to initiate lovemaking. She'd been the one to make the decision. The one to decide. She could have let him pull away from his kiss and leave the tent but no, she'd been the one to take that fateful step.

'I told you—I've treated you so badly.'

'And I have something to tell you.' She looped her arms around his neck. 'Paolo and I weren't getting married. Certainly not lately and neither, I believe, in the future.'

'But—'

'I know,' she said, 'we were touted as the next great love interest and for a time there I thought that's where we were headed, and while it hurt—*a lot*—that he'd never told me he already had a wife, us getting married wouldn't have happened, whether or not you intervened. He'll always be a good friend but he just wasn't the one.'

He looked at her strangely. 'You mean, after all my planning, I still didn't get to steal Paolo's bride?'

She shook her head. 'No. Does that mean you need

to go steal someone else to satisfy your need for revenge?'

'No.' He broke into a broad grin. 'I ended up with something much better than revenge. I ended up with you.'

'Oh, I love you, Khaled,' she said, pulling him close. 'I love you more than you could ever know.'

He pushed her away and for a moment she resisted. Until she saw his eyes and the love that shone there, deep and true.

'You do? After everything that has happened?'

She nodded, exhilarated at having the truth revealed at last—all of it. 'And things will be different from now on. No more talk of revenge and retribution. The past is gone and buried. From now on it will be love that drives the future.'

'Oh, yes,' he said, 'love for you, my dazzling Sapphire; love between us.'

He broke off the kiss that followed suddenly— much too suddenly, confusing her with his sudden withdrawal. She blinked her eyes open to find his studying hers, their darkness bright with excitement.

'You would not have to give up your work if you stay,' he said, his words coming almost too fast for her to keep up with. 'You mentioned you wanted your own salon. Would you consider having one here, in Hebra?'

She drew in a breath. She hadn't thought about it, hadn't thought through the ramifications of revealing her love, the thrill of finding it reciprocated, the surprise that he wouldn't expect her to give up the career she loved.

But why not Hebra? It was time she branched out on her own and there was nothing now to tie her to Milan. From what she'd learnt, Hebra was a thriving city, its women as proud and as fashion conscious as any in Paris or Milan.

She started nodding, her excitement building, thinking of the stock still in the workroom at the palace and the excellent seamstresses she knew were available. It would be almost too easy.

And it was almost too much to take in—the prospect of having both her own salon and the love of the man beside her. Who said you couldn't have it all?

She smiled and kept on nodding. 'It could work, yes.'

'I knew it!' His words exploded from him in a rush. 'Then so be it. You shall have your own salon and your designs will be world famous.'

'I don't need to be world famous,' she said as his lips moved closer to hers, 'so long as I have your love.'

His mouth turned into a smile, the darkness of his eyes melting to warm velvet. 'Oh, you have my love. You hold my heart and soul forever.'

Sheer bliss welled up inside as his mouth slanted across hers and he kissed her, slowly, languorously, thoroughly, in both a confirmation and a celebration of their love. Finally he drew back his head. 'After all that's happened, I wonder—is this too soon to ask you if you'd do me the honour of becoming my wife?'

'It's not too soon at all,' she answered, unable to restrain the bubbling joy from her voice. 'So why don't you go ahead and ask me?'

He smiled and then his eyes glittered and the smile dropped away to something entirely more purposeful. 'Marry me, Sapphire. Make me the happiest and luckiest man in the world by agreeing to become my wife.'

'Yes,' she said, 'I will marry you!' her laughter welling up with love and certainty, her face pressed brow to brow against his as his lips closed in for another kiss.

'After all, I already have the perfect dress.'

FIT FOR A SHEIKH

by

Carol Grace

Carol Grace has always been interested in travel and living abroad. She spent a year in France and toured the world working on the hospital ship *HOPE*. She and her husband spent the first year and a half of their marriage in Iran where they both taught English. She has studied Arabic and Persian languages. Then, with their toddler daughter, they lived in Algeria for two years.

Carol says that writing is another way of making her life exciting. Her office is her mountain-top home, which overlooks the Pacific Ocean and which she shares with her inventor husband, their daughter, who just graduated from college, and their teenage son.

Don't miss Carol Grace's exciting new novel, *The Sicilian's Bride*, available in July 2009 from Mills & Boon® Romance.

Chapter One

The late spring rain beat down against the window of the bridal shop, I DO! I DO!, but inside it was all white satin, pink roses and plaster of Paris wedding cakes. Carolyn Evans sat behind her desk facing her clients, a young couple who'd come to the wedding consultant to help them plan the "perfect wedding." Of course there was no such thing. There was always something—the ring bearer who tripped as he ran down the aisle and burst into tears, the forgotten boutonniere, the best man's risqué toast, the band that played too loudly or too softly. But one could always dream, always hope, as she did…if not for the perfect wedding, for the perfect groom. But that's all it was so far— just a dream.

Out of the corner of her eye, Carolyn saw a strange man in a dark suit standing outside in front of her window—in the rain—staring in at her. She gave a tiny shiver of apprehension. Was it possible he was a disgruntled suitor out for revenge? No, of course not. She was being ridiculous, letting her imagination run away with her. It was just the rain, the lateness of the hour and her fatigue after a long day of heading off minor disasters like bridesmaid dresses in the wrong color and an irate mother-of-the-bride. The man was most likely a prospective groom, sizing her up, trying to decide if she was up to planning his wedding or trying to decide whether to get married at all. She prided herself on being able to calm both jittery brides and grooms. She gave him a quick, reassuring smile and turned her attention back to the couple.

"At some point in the ceremony," the groom on the other side of her desk said, "I want to present Melinda with a rock as the emperor penguins of the Antarctic do in their courtship ritual. Will that be a problem?"

"No problem at all," Carolyn assured him. No more problem than the hot-air balloon wedding she'd arranged or the underwater ceremony for the professional divers. "I'm here to help you plan a wedding that may not be perfect, but one with your own personal stamp on it. I've never seen a ceremony with a penguin rock-giving exchange, but I don't see why…"

The mysterious stranger in the Armani suit chose that moment to enter the shop. Probably tired of the rain falling on his broad shoulders. All three heads turned in his direction.

"Ms. Evans?" he asked in a voice that matched his appearance. Strong, deep and virile.

"Yes, I'll be with you in a moment," she said, noting that the rain had barely dampened his Italian-tailored suit or his crisp dark hair. He looked like he'd just stepped out of *GQ*. Something told her he always looked that way, rain or shine.

"I can't wait a moment," he said, looming behind the

couple at the desk. "I must see you now." His look was arrogant, his tone was insistent.

Taken aback by this unexpected aggressive approach, Carolyn stood and glared at him. The bride-to-be's mouth fell open in surprise and her groom's eyes widened.

"If you don't mind..." Carolyn began. But it was clear he *did* mind. With a hasty glance over their shoulders at the intruder, the young couple grabbed a handful of brochures from the desk and started for the door.

"We'll come back when you have more time," Melinda said.

"When you're not busy," her groom added before he shut the door behind him.

"That's better," the man said. "Now we can get down to business."

"You interrupted us," she said sternly. "They had an appointment and you don't."

"They can come back another time. I can't. I'm a busy man."

Carolyn choked back a protest that other people were equally busy but they had the time to make and keep their appointments.

"My name is Sheik Tarik Oman," he said, taking a seat and fixing her with his intense dark gaze.

"Sheik..." She sat down as a shiver went up her spine. Wasn't that like a king in some countries? Was she in the presence of royalty? So that's why he thought everyone should drop what they were doing and cater to him.

"It's just a title. It means nothing...in this country," he explained.

She wanted to ask then why he expected special treatment from her? Being a sheik might mean nothing in this country, but she had a feeling it meant something somewhere else. Where people jumped when he told them to and obeyed his every wish. That happened in America too, only they didn't call such men sheiks, they called them dictatorial alpha males and Carolyn had had enough of them to last a lifetime. It was not only his title that gave away the sheik's royal standing, it was the way he carried himself—his shoulders back, his spine like a ramrod, his firm jaw jutting forward.

She sat down. "What can I do for you?" she asked, resigned to the fact that he'd taken over her time and her attention. She ought to order him out of the shop, but her clients had disappeared. She sighed. Once again she'd failed to assert her authority, even after her assertiveness training seminar. She shifted uncomfortably under his perusal, wishing for some unknown reason she'd had time to comb her unruly curls and apply some fresh makeup. After working nonstop since morning, she was sure she looked as haggard as she felt.

"You're a wedding planner," he said. "I want you to plan a wedding."

She automatically pulled out a form and attached it to her clipboard, intending to transfer the information to her computer later as she always did.

"First let me tell you my philosophy of wedding planning," she said. "Just to be sure we're both on the same page, so to speak."

"It's really not important what page you're on, Ms. Evans," the sheik said brusquely. "We'll begin on page one. You may have your own philosophy, I happen to have one of my own. Since I'm in charge of this wedding, we'll follow mine."

She blinked. No one had ever dismissed her philosophy so completely before they'd even heard it. They may have tuned out as she articulated it, but at least they were polite enough to let her expound for a few minutes. It didn't take that long. Life was too short to deal with this kind of man more than once in a lifetime. It wasn't too late to show the sheik to the door before they wasted any more of each other's time. And with this kind of a beginning, she already had a feeling they weren't going to get along. With this kind of groom, she felt sorry for the bride. Destined for a lifetime of being overruled and browbeaten. She'd been the observer of such a marriage for most of her life.

Carolyn took a deep breath. "What about the bride? Perhaps we should hear what she has to say."

"The bride is away at school. I'm paying for the wedding. I'm planning the wedding. Or I have been until now. Now I need help. Professional help. Your help. I'm not too proud to admit it." The way he said it sounded like admitting he needed help was something out of the ordinary for him. And that pride was his middle name. "I hear you're the best in the business," he added.

No use protesting. No use pretending she wasn't good at what she did. She might be the best but she sure wasn't the most successful or the richest. The rent on the shop had just been raised. So much so that she wondered if she and her partner could afford to stay in this prime location. Cash flow was sometimes iffy when clients were late or delinquent in paying. Which made her even more upset to think that this man had chased away her clients, maybe for good. However, one could certainly count on a sheik not to back out on his financial commitments, couldn't one?

She studied his darkly handsome face and his regal bearing from across the table and thought of all the reasons why she should turn him down immediately, before they went any further. One, he was domineering. Two, he was planning this wedding without the bride, always a recipe for trouble. Of course one-sided weddings were not that uncommon. Most brides took the initiative and made most of the plans. Choosing flowers and dresses were hardly something most men enjoyed doing. The participation of grooms at all was a recent phenomenon.

But a man coming in to plan his wedding without the bride was very unusual indeed. So much so she wondered why, how, what and who was the woman who'd snagged the gorgeous sheik and was willing to put up with his autocratic "I'm in charge here" ways. But she didn't ask that.

Instead she asked, "When do you plan to have this wedding, Mr...that is, your excellency, I mean..."

"In one month."

Carolyn gasped. "Planning a wedding in one month is impossible," she said firmly. "I have other clients, other commitments."

"Nothing is impossible. Difficult, yes. Impossible, no. Anyone in business knows that. There's always a way."

Carolyn pressed her lips together to keep from blurting something she'd regret, like go find another wedding consultant. One who doesn't mind taking orders from a dictator.

Oblivious to her dislike of his manner, he continued in the same vein. "I'm here because this wedding is very important to me. To me and my whole family. They're counting on *me* and I'm counting on *you*." The intensity of his gaze made her knees knock together under the desk. Was that how he looked at his fiancée, too? Like he was going to eat her alive?

She had the feeling he was not going to take no for an answer. She had a feeling he *never* took no for an answer. And she was too tired to stay here and argue much longer.

Maybe it was just a small family affair to be held at home, which wouldn't require much work on her part. The least she could do was ask.

Carolyn held her clipboard between her and the sheik as if to ward off the vibrations emanating from the man who must be accustomed to giving orders and having them followed.

"Before I make a decision, I'll need to know some of the details. Now," she said, filling in the first blank on the form. "We have the date. What about the place?"

"Grace Cathedral."

She blinked. "Grace Cathedral?" The most sought-after site in the city for the weddings of the rich and famous. A gothic landmark that sat high above the city on Nob Hill.

"Yes, why not?" he said. "My sister is a convert to Christianity and her fiancé is a Protestant. So I made a sizable donation to the missionary fund and booked it some time ago as soon as we set a date. It seemed like a suitable and convenient location with enough room inside for both families as well as business associates. But that's as far as I've gotten. The rest is up to you."

"I see," she said, picturing the sheik waiting at the altar of the cathedral in his ceremonial headdress, the light shining through the stained glass windows on the bride as she came down the aisle. Carolyn had never done a wedding there but had always wanted to. She could almost smell the fragrant stephanotis she'd place at the end of each aisle, and hear the organ filling the magnificent church with music she'd help choose. She knew it could be the most spectacular, romantic wedding of the year if not the decade. And she'd be the one who planned it. The publicity wouldn't hurt business. Not at all.

Just as a matter of form, she went on to ask about flowers, ceremony, reception, officiant, photography, food, but he shrugged after each question saying he'd leave that to her and that money was no object. She realized that if she took this job she'd certainly be able to put her own stamp on this wedding.

To her surprise, Tarik stood up as if the interview was over, the decisions made and the contract signed. He held out his hand to shake hers. Probably the way they sealed the bargain in his culture. In her culture things weren't quite that simple. In fact, she didn't remember saying she would take the job.

"Just a minute," she said. "A handshake is not quite enough. I'll need you to sign this contract."

He shrugged, sat down again and signed the form she held out.

"One more thing," she said, suddenly overwhelmed by the thought of pulling off a large wedding in a month. "I'll need help. I can't do this by myself."

"Of course you can't," he said. "Where are your assistants? Surely you don't run an operation like this by yourself."

"I have a partner, but she's as busy as I am. We share the office and use the same florists and caterers and so on, but we each have our own clients. Both our calendars are filled up for the next year. When I say help I mean from you or from the bride. You need to at least be in on the decision making or you're going to be stuck with a wedding that doesn't reflect your lifestyle or your personality and you won't be happy. You want this to be a day you'll remember for the rest of your life."

"I'm sure I will," he said. "In every way possible. All right. You want some help. You want my input. You can have it. I can't stay any longer tonight, but if you come by tomorrow morning I'll meet with you before breakfast for one hour because that's how important this wedding is to me.'' He pounded his fist on the table for emphasis.

''That's very considerate,'' she said hoping she wasn't laying on the sarcasm too heavily. ''Some men don't devote even that much time to wedding planning. They leave it to the bride.''

''Perhaps they don't have as much at stake as I do,'' he said.

''Perhaps not. The bride must be a very special person,'' Carolyn said.

''Special, yes. But stubborn and headstrong, too. My sister is also a bit spoiled.''

Carolyn frowned. ''Your sister?''

''My sister Yasmine, the bride who is getting married in one month. I thought I made that clear. That is why I'm here. To hire you to plan her wedding.''

Carolyn stared at him. ''I see.'' But she didn't see, not really. What kind of a woman would trust her brother to plan her wedding? She told herself it didn't matter. She'd agreed to plan it and it was immaterial who the participants were. In one month it would be over, and she'd never hear of or see the sheik again. Something to look forward to.

''She's away at school in Switzerland,'' he explained. ''She has exams coming up so she won't be here until shortly before the wedding. When she arrives, everything will be in place—her dress, her flowers. Everything will go like clockwork.''

''It may go like clockwork. But on the other hand, most brides like to choose their own dress at least. And try it on. They must have wedding dresses in Switzerland. Perhaps she could buy one there.''

"She doesn't have time. And it won't be necessary," he said. "Stand up."

"What?"

"If I'm not mistaken, you are approximately the same size as my sister, which will eliminate the need for her to choose the dress and try it on. Stand up so I can be sure."

Reluctantly she got to her feet. His gaze was cool and appraising but he made her feel uncomfortably warm inside while goose bumps popped out on her skin. Couldn't he have simply asked her what size she was? Or didn't he know his sister's size to compare it with?

"Yes," he said, his eyes traveling slowly from the top of her head to the tips of her shoes, and lingering here and there as if he had all the time in the world. "I was right. You'll do."

Do? she wanted to ask. I'll *do?* Seething under her calm exterior, Carolyn sat down again.

"About my schedule," she said, her face still flushed from his lengthy scrutiny. "I don't know what kind of business you're in, but…"

"Oil."

Arab sheik. Oil. It figured. "Yes, well, in the bridal business we have weddings planned months or even years in advance. I can't just drop everything and concentrate on yours."

"I'm sure you'll be able to handle everything," he said smoothly. "Bearing in mind that my funds are unlimited, and this is a very important event."

"That's the way everyone feels about a wedding in the family. I'll do what I can but I hope you'll understand that I can't work full-time on this wedding. As it happens I *am* free tomorrow morning, shall we say nine?"

"Eight is better. Here's my address," he said handing

her a business card. "You see, there's always a way."
There was so much certainty in his voice that she'd be
there, that she wouldn't back out. Carolyn began to believe
the sheik always got his way. She realized now how unlikely it was that the sheik himself would be getting married. What kind of a woman would marry him? Someone
after his money, no doubt. No amount of money could
tempt her to marry a man who called all the shots. Who
micromanaged his wife's life. Even if he looked like a Hol-
lywood version of a sheik with his exotic dark good looks
and his royal bearing.

She couldn't help but pity his sister who would arrive at
the last minute to put on her dress, chosen by him with the
help of a paid consultant, walk down the aisle of a church
selected by him, accompanied by music, ditto, ditto and so
forth and so on. But who was she to object to her clients'
strange ways. She was there to help them realize their
dreams, even though she doubted the sheik had any dreams
at all, just plans and goals and royal imperatives.

If he thought he was going to get away with one brief
early morning meeting and then bow out and disappear
until the wedding day, he was mistaken. As she said, if he
didn't give her any input, he wasn't going to be happy with
his sister's wedding. And if he wasn't happy with the way
the wedding turned out, she had a feeling she'd hear about
it. Loudly.

After she'd confirmed the appointment for the next day
at his house—actually it was more of a command performance than an appointment—Carolyn set her clipboard
down and stood. She felt like she'd just gone about ten
rounds in the ring while avoiding being knocked out by a
man who'd overwhelmed her with his attitude only to have
the match declared a draw. She knew she was lucky she

wasn't lying flat on her face while he held up his hand in a victory sign. Had he really won or had she? All she cared about at that moment was that it was over, at least for today. Tomorrow she'd be in better shape to cope with this man. To make it clear how decisions would be made.

"Closing up, going home?" he asked.

"Yes."

"It's late. I'll walk you to your car."

"That's not necessary. It's right in back of the shop."

"In back? It sounds dark and dangerous," he said. "I'm certain your husband wouldn't want you out there by yourself at this time of night."

"I always park there, and I've never been attacked yet," she said. "And I have no husband." Now why did she feel obliged to tell him that? It was none of his business. "I assure you I'll be fine. Furthermore I'm concerned your wife will be wondering why you're out so late." There, that served him right for the husband remark.

A brief flicker of amusement crossed his face as he glanced at his Rolex watch. "It's not that late," he said. "And if I had a wife, which I don't, I would still insist on walking you to your car. Any wife of mine would not expect me until she saw me."

"Her role would be taking care of the house, I suppose. Keeping your dinner warm and bringing you your pipe and slippers." She tried to keep her tone light, but a hint of bitterness crept into her voice at the memories of her mother doing just that. Submerging her own interests, her own life, year after year.

"That sounds appealing. But difficult to find someone like that in this day and age," he said.

"Which is why you aren't married, I imagine." She didn't know why she was engaging in this pointless banter with the sheik. It was really senseless to argue with him and though his accompanying her to her car was a trivial matter, she feared it was a bad omen for their future collaboration. Somehow she had to break the pattern of his giving orders and her giving in.

She'd never been able to assert herself while growing up in a house with an egomaniac, but she was grown-up now and in charge of her own life and her own business. She'd excommunicated her father from her life, and she'd learned to stand up for herself and what she believed. Of course putting what she'd learned into practice was another matter. To make things easier, she made it a point never to date a man with a strong will.

Actually she seldom dated at all these days since most of the men she met were on their way to the altar with someone else. She told herself that some day a kind, gentle, caring man who was not otherwise engaged would show up. They'd fall in love and then she'd be glad she'd saved herself for marriage and had never engaged in casual sex like some of her friends had. But with her thirtieth birthday on the horizon, she sometimes wondered when and if it would happen.

Normally she would have taken the time to clear up the loose ends on her desk, check her e-mail and enter the data. But with the sheik standing there watching her every move like a hawk, all she could manage at that point was to grab her jacket, turn off the lights and lock the front door. She felt his hand on her elbow as they walked out the back exit, guiding her firmly as if she was some kind of fragile flower who might stumble without his help. As if she couldn't manage to get to her car by herself, which she'd been doing safely for the past eight years. And if that weren't enough macho male chauvinism for one night, he took her keys

from her hand and unlocked her car door for her. She told
herself he was from a different country, a different culture,
where men were men and women stayed behind tall walls
and heavy veils.

"Thank you," she said stiffly.

"Until tomorrow," he said, lowering his head in a slight
bow.

She nodded and drove away at full speed, though what
she was trying to escape she didn't know. He was only a
client, a man who'd hired her to manage his sister's wedding. In her rearview mirror she saw him standing there in
the alleyway while the rain bounced off his impeccable suit,
a tall, dark mysterious figure watching her until she was
out of sight. She turned her car heater up to high to combat
the chills that suddenly attacked her. But nothing helped.
She was still shaking when she got home. Due to a stranger
who walked into her life tonight. Tomorrow, things would
be different. Even though she'd be on his turf, she'd show
him she was in charge. He might control a whole oil company, but he didn't control her.

Chapter Two

The next morning she drove to his house at the end of a tree-lined street in the prestigious and aptly named area of San Francisco called Sherwood Forest. It was a long, low house on at least an acre of prime real estate overlooking the Pacific Ocean. After driving through the open gate and parking her compact car in the circular driveway, she gave a quick check in the visor mirror, pleased to see the circles under her eyes had disappeared thanks to the cucumber slices she'd placed on them for twenty minutes this morning. A necessity because she'd spent entirely too much time lying in bed the night before tossing and turning and replaying her conversation with the sheik. And wishing she'd said no to him.

The whole situation was too bizarre. It was not just the situation, it was him. As sleep eluded her she couldn't shake the image of the dark ebony hair that matched his dark eyes that seemed to bore right through her, or the sound of his slightly accented deep voice. If someone had to plan the sister's wedding, why couldn't it be their father? If he was around, wouldn't he be a more appropriate person to plan the wedding? She could have dealt better with an old, fatherly sheik who didn't exude such masculine virility. Who didn't make her feel so aware of his overpowering presence.

Sooner or later they were going to come to blows. Not real blows of course, but verbal ones, and Carolyn was not going to give in. Not if she knew she was right. She had the right to conduct her business the way she saw fit and if he didn't like it, he could find someone else. If she'd learned anything after leaving home at eighteen, it was to stand firm on her principles. Confronting the sheik would be the ultimate test. They didn't come any more macho or determined than he did.

By morning Carolyn had come to her senses, realized that the sheik was just a man, a little more virile than most, but certainly nothing she couldn't handle. And more importantly, his sister's wedding was an opportunity she couldn't pass up. This job would be a lot of work, yes, but it would be over in one month. It was a chance to do a spectacular, dream wedding in a beautiful cathedral, which just might give her career the boost it needed. It could lead to other big weddings, ones where they gave her decent notice, like a year in advance. Yes, this was short notice, but with her energy and organizational skills, she ought to be able to pull it off. She had to try. And the first order of business was to find out if the invitations had been sent. She should have asked last night, but her mind seemed to have taken a leave of absence at the time.

At the massive front door, she knocked and pressed the bell. A tall, dark-skinned woman in a graceful silk sari answered the door and looked her up and down for a long moment without speaking a word.

"Carolyn Evans…. I'm here to see Mr. Tarik Oman, I mean the sheik, that is."

"Ah, yes. The wedding consultant." The woman spoke in heavily accented English "Will you come into the library?"

Before she entered the library, Carolyn gaped at the formal living room and the majestic staircase leading to the second floor. She hoped she'd get a tour of the place sooner or later. Instead of going off to fetch the sheik, the woman closed the door behind her and stood with her back to the floor-to-ceiling shelves of leather-bound books.

"I just wonder," the woman asked, "if you know what you're doing."

"Oh yes, I've planned many weddings. I'm looking forward to working on this one. I'm sure it will turn out fine."

"It's wrong. All wrong. It won't work."

"Don't worry," Carolyn assured her. "Of course it's short notice, but I'm sure it will work. It will all come together. Believe me, it always does." Prewedding jitters were nothing new to her, but who was this woman and what was her role in the wedding? Carolyn had started the day with high hopes, planning to get off to a good start with this project, but the first person she'd run into was already voicing her doubts. She had a fleeting thought of her office where she would have been if it hadn't been for the sheik, sipping coffee while she looked through the phone book for a harpist for a garden wedding in May. It was the sheik's idea to have her come at eight. If she'd known he was going to keep her waiting she would have insisted he come to her office.

There was a long silence while the woman closed her

eyes and pressed her hand to her forehead. Carolyn didn't know if she had gone into a trance, was worried about the wedding or just tired. She cleared her throat, and the woman turned abruptly and opened the door.

"Very well," the woman said. "I'm going to make tea. You'll find *him* in the pool room." She waved her hand toward a sliding glass door.

Carolyn stepped lightly across the vast Oriental carpet in the great room and opened the door. There was no doubt who him was. But why was he playing pool at this hour of the morning? Didn't sheiks have anything better to do? Like manage their oil business? At the end of the hall she found herself in a huge glass-enclosed solarium with a retractable roof above an impressive mosaic-tiled swimming pool.

She stopped dead in her tracks at the even more impressive sight of the man who emerged from the pool, his broad shoulders covered with droplets of water, his tanned chest covered with fine swirls of dark hair and the rest of him barely covered at all with a European swimsuit. Oh, my. She felt her cheeks flush. Maybe she was wrong. Maybe she couldn't deal with all this testosterone, at least not this early in the morning.

She jerked her gaze from his lower body and forced herself to look him in the eye as he approached her. She thought she'd prepared herself to see the man today, but nothing could have prepared her for the sight of a partially clad gorgeous man. Why couldn't he have met her in the library, preferably fully-clothed.

"Hello," he said, draping a towel around his shoulders. "Forgive me for greeting you so informally. I didn't know you were here, or I would have met you elsewhere. Ap-

propriately dressed. How did you get in? Where is Meera?"
he asked with a frown.

"A tall woman wearing a sari and a disapproving look?"

"I'm afraid she's angry with me," he said. "She lets me
know it by neglecting her duties. What can I say? She's
been with our family for two generations. She's old and set
in her ways. I'd be lost without her, and she without me,
but sometimes…"

"She's making tea," Carolyn noted.

"Good. That's one thing I can rely on her for. A decent
tea. I shall meet you in the library."

She looked at her watch.

"I know, you're a busy woman. We'll begin our work
shortly," he said. "Do you swim?"

"Not at eight in the morning," she said. Although at that
moment, she could think of nothing more appealing than
to plunge her whole overheated, overstimulated body into
a pool of cool water.

"I see," he said, his gaze once again—for the second
time in twenty-four hours—traveling the length of her
body, lingering on her hips and moving to her breasts as if
he could see right through her suit to her silk, pale lavender
underwear. But this time his appraisal was not as cool as
the one in her office last night. In fact his gaze was down-
right heated this morning. Causing a shiver to move up her
spine. And a slight weakness in the knees. Ridiculous. The
look in his eyes could have nothing to do with her. It was
just his way. After all, she was an underling he'd hired. He
was a sheik. He said he didn't have a wife, but maybe he
had a harem. Maybe he was sizing her up as a future mem-
ber. The idea ought to have had her running for her life.
Instead she stood there, rooted to the spot.

Whether his gaze was personal or not, she wondered

somewhere in the back of her mind whether he approved of what he saw. She'd taken care to choose a tailored suit, business-like, but fitted as if it had been made for her. Her partner, Lily, said it was her Ally McBeal suit with the skirt substantially above the knees. So she wasn't as thin as the TV lawyer, or as muscular as a fitness center model, but no one had ever accused her of being overweight or out of shape.

"And now, if you'll excuse me for a moment. I'll get dressed," he said.

She'd only been there for fifteen minutes and already she was breathing hard as she walked back to the library, seething with frustration. When was this so-called eight o'clock meeting going to take place? This wasn't a job, it was a way of life, and she had her own way of life, thank you very much. One which she was extremely anxious to get back to. To the safety of her shop where *she* was in charge.

Tarik toweled off quickly and dressed, choosing a pair of charcoal gray slacks and a white Egyptian cotton shirt. Everyone he'd spoken to said Carolyn Evans was the best wedding consultant in town, but no one had mentioned she had masses of auburn curls and eyes the intriguing color of the Arabian Gulf during a storm.

No one had told him whether she was married or not either. Why should they? It had nothing to do with her competence. Then why had he troubled himself to find out? Simple curiosity? Or did it have something to do with her alluring body or exquisite legs that went on forever? He knew these were not relevant qualifications for a bridal consultant, still…she'd caught him off guard. He smiled to himself as he remembered her checking his marital status as well.

Frankly, he'd expected someone older, plainer, with glasses and sensible shoes instead of high heels and a snug-fitting suit that hugged her curves in a most captivating way. When he saw her, he actually hoped she had a husband and was off limits. Husband or not, he reminded himself sternly, she was still off limits to him.

Seeing her through the window of her shop last night, he almost turned away, not wishing to be distracted by an attractive woman at this crucial time. Especially an independent American woman. He'd had experience with women of that type when he'd first arrived in this country. With one in particular. He'd been overwhelmed by her vitality, her dazzling good looks and her freedom to make her own choices. So overwhelmed he'd fallen head over heels in love. Or so he'd thought.

When his father learned of his involvement with the woman, he made it clear he was not pleased with Tarik's choice. He warned that marriages of the heart were not advisable for the heir to such wealth and power. Witness his own happy marriage to Tarik's mother, which had been arranged by their parents. His father offered to broker a marriage with a suitable girl, the daughter of his best friend. Blinded by infatuation, and offended by his father's interference, Tarik refused. His father angrily reprimanded him and reminded him of his duty to his family, but Tarik wouldn't listen. Later, he wished he had.

There was no need at this point to tell Ms. Evans there was more to this wedding than the joining of two people in matrimony. He would tell her all she needed to know to plan the wedding. Nothing more, nothing less. If he told her the whole story, she might object, and he didn't want to hear any more objections from the women in his life who didn't understand his position.

He was relieved to see that Meera, however angry she was about the nuptials, had at least provided a tray of mint tea and small cookies and lighted a fire in the fireplace chasing the chill from the early morning air. Carolyn Evans was studying a portrait on the wall.

"My father," he explained, handing her a cup of tea. When his hand brushed hers he felt a slight jolt of electricity. Obviously the combination of dry air and the thick, hand-knotted carpet. She gave him a quick glance, but otherwise she appeared not to notice anything unusual had occurred.

"I see the resemblance," she said looking at the painting.

"Thank you. I only hope I can live up to his reputation. He was an astute businessman and a wise leader."

She took a seat on a leather couch and crossed her legs. He had to drag his gaze back to hers. He must not ogle the wedding consultant's long legs. Especially not on day one when he only had a short time to spend with her. This was business, after all. He had no time for pleasure.

"Will your father be here for the wedding?" she asked.

"In spirit only," Tarik said. "He died two years ago."

"I'm sorry," she said softly. He was surprised to hear there was real sympathy in her voice and in her eyes. After all, she barely knew him.

"Are your parents alive?" he asked.

"My mother is, my father is too, actually, but he's not a part of my life."

He raised his eyebrows. A father not a part of his child's life? He wanted to ask why not. But he could tell by the shuttered look in her eyes she wasn't eager to talk about it. In his world, no matter how old the child, the parents must be respected. It had been a hard lesson but he'd learned it well. Thank goodness he'd learned it before it was too late to reconcile with his father.

"I feel my father's spirit guiding me in business and family matters every day, especially with this wedding. I believe he would be pleased to know you are helping me achieve my goal to honor his memory."

"I hope so," she murmured, gazing at him over her tea-cup with her extraordinary gray-green eyes. It must be the morning light from the windows on the east that made them so luminous.

He set his cup on the table and sat on a low ottoman facing her, his legs stretched out in front of him, tenting his fingers together thoughtfully, unable to tear his gaze from hers. If he did tell her everything, would she join forces with the other women in his life and go against him? Or would she understand his point of view and help him bring about the solution to all his problems? Whether she understood or not, she had to help him. She'd agreed to do that. That was her job. That's what he was paying her for. Heaven knew he needed an ally at this time but this was not the time to confide in a stranger. No matter that she was a beautiful stranger at that. The only thing he wanted from her was to have the wedding go off without a hitch.

"In my culture there is nothing more important than family," he added. "Fulfilling my father's goals and unfinished business has become my highest priority."

Carolyn nodded. As if she understood. It was the way she was looking at him, so intently, her gaze unwavering. He felt hope rising somewhere deep inside, hope that if she did know what was going on behind the scenes she would not launch into a discussion about the importance of love and romance and other female illusions.

"The unfinished business has to do with oil?" she asked.

"Just so," he said. For a long moment neither one spoke. The library was his favorite room, made for quiet contemplation, but today the only thing he could contemplate was Carolyn Evans. He knew it was wrong. He knew she was off limits, that she was a passing attraction, but he wondered if she felt it, too. Never mind if she did. It would lead to nothing. The reason he couldn't take his eyes off of her, the reason he'd dreamed of her last night was just because he was overworked with the upcoming merger of his oil company and the largest privately held refinery in the U.S. She was a distraction, and he couldn't afford any distractions now. Not with the wedding and the merger so close at hand.

Finally Carolyn broke the silence. "I assume you and your sister are very close," she said at last. "Or she wouldn't allow you to plan her wedding for her."

"We've had our differences," he admitted. "Since my father died I became head of the family and her guardian. At first she had a hard time accepting that fact. Perhaps she still does. She's young and has a strong will. They say it runs in the family," he said with a wry smile. "Nonetheless, we agree on most things. Divorce is not an option in our culture. Not the way it is in America where people marry for romantic love then get divorced when they find the thrills don't last."

"Sometimes divorce is the only way out of a bad situation," Carolyn said, her eyes fixed on the tea leaves in the bottom of her cup. "But I'd like to believe that true love can last forever."

"Are you speaking from personal experience?" he asked. "Have you ever been married or divorced?" Or in love? he wanted to ask. But it was none of his business, and it was not an appropriate question to ask a stranger.

"Neither," she said. "I've never been married." She hesitated for a long moment. "I don't believe in divorce either. Not for frivolous reasons. But sometimes there is no other way."

"You speak of true love," he said. "By that I can only hope you mean respect and admiration and not an emotional attachment. Because a marriage based on emotion doesn't stand a chance of surviving. If women ever feel the way they're supposed to feel when they fall in love—that they've been struck by lightning, the pulse speeds up, the knees are weak and the heart pounds—they probably should be taken immediately to the emergency room. They're either having a heart attack or a stroke. Men, on the other hand, are level-headed and sensible and are not susceptible to such phenomena. They marry for practical purposes. To ensure offspring to continue the lineage or for companionship."

She gave him a brief smile that was over too soon. He knew she didn't believe him. He wished he could say something to make her really smile. To see those lips curve upward and her beautiful eyes light up.

"Then you don't believe in romantic love," she said.

"Ah, now you understand," he said. "Love is an exaggerated notion put forth by poets and songwriters. I can understand instant attraction, if that's what you're talking about. A chemical reaction that sometimes happens between two people that produces some of the effects I mentioned. But these feelings don't last." It was a pity they didn't. But there it was.

"Well," she said, opening her briefcase. "Shall we get down to work? I've brought some pictures of some possible locations for the reception."

She spread the photographs on the large dark walnut library table and they stood side by side while she told him the benefits of the Octagon House versus the advantages of the historic gardens at Filoli or the wild Marin headlands.

To be honest, and he was always scrupulously honest with himself, Tarik found himself more aware of the woman next to him than the pictures of the reception sites. It was partly the subtle scent she wore of wild roses that made him want to get closer to her, to inhale deeply and let it permeate his senses. It was partly the way her hair brushed against her cheek that made him want to wrap the curls around his fingers. Finally he had to move away. To clear his head. To reaffirm his purpose.

"What is it?" she asked. "What's wrong? Don't you like them?"

"I like them fine," he said brusquely from the other side of the table. But did he? Did he even know what he'd seen? He began to wish he'd insisted she do this wedding completely by herself. Or that he'd kept looking until he found the other kind of wedding consultant. The older one with thick ankles, a no-nonsense air and iron-gray hair.

Fortunately this meeting would be over soon, and he'd make it clear she was on her own. He'd send her on her way with a few suggestions and let her do the work. That's what he was paying her for. He didn't want to spend anymore time than necessary with her. She disturbed him with her manner, both competent and calm, and her looks, both sexy and subdued. He didn't want to think about her the way he had last night after he left her office. Remembering the color of her eyes and the rose tint of her complexion. Which led to those disturbing dreams of her he'd had. He had to keep his mind on important matters of money, merger and family honor. Both day and night.

He started to usher her out of the house before she could

disturb him anymore today, but before she left she paused in front of a small oil painting of the white-walled family compound on the Gulf of Arabia.

"How beautiful," she murmured.

"Even more beautiful in actuality," he said. "It is where I grew up. The property has been in the family for generations. And now it is mine."

She nodded and finally she left. He breathed a sigh of relief, wishing that her subtle scent did not linger in the library the way it did.

Chapter Three

As Carolyn walked to her car she had the distinct feeling she'd been hustled out of the house abruptly for some unknown reason before they'd barely finished talking through the wedding plans. Even when she lingered to admire the painting, she sensed his restlessness. Was he afraid she'd never leave? Was he suddenly sorry he'd hired her? Had she said the wrong thing? She went over the conversation in her mind. Of their talk about love and marriage. She didn't want to get involved in a personal discussion with the man. But somehow she had.

However personal it had been, however much he'd learned about her, and she'd learned about his family, she still didn't know if he himself had ever been involved with a woman. Or why he was planning his sister's wedding by himself. His explanations just didn't hold water. There wasn't a woman alive who wouldn't stop everything, even in the middle of finals, to at least buy herself a wedding dress. If she was as excited about the wedding as she should be. If she was as much in love with the groom as she should be, that is.

The groom. No one had mentioned him. Who was he? She didn't even know his name. Carolyn had forgotten to ask the most basic questions. The groom's family might want some say in these proceedings. At the very least, she ought to meet them and put them in the loop.

And what about the invitations? Again, she'd forgotten all about them. What was wrong with her? This man had the ability to make her forget everything. Including a list of questions she'd prepared for him. She got out of her car and walked back up to the front door. Before she even knocked Tarik opened the door. As if he expected her. As if he was waiting for her. But he didn't look particularly happy to see her again from the way his eyebrows were drawn together in a frown.

"I...uh...I forgot to ask you if you've sent the invitations."

"That's your job," he said.

"Then I ought to know what name to put on them. You've never mentioned the groom. Who is he?"

"Jeffrey Branson."

Branson. The Bransons were an old prominent San Francisco family. They had made their original fortune from silver mines in the last century. Now they were involved in...what? Refineries, railroads, lumber?

"Do you know him?" Tarik asked.

"No." As if she hobnobbed with high society. "But I've heard of the family of course. What does Jeffrey do?"

"He's involved in the family business."

"Which is what exactly?"

"An independent oil refinery."

"Oil," she said. "Like your family."

"Not exactly. We produce crude oil, the Bransons are in the business of refining and distributing it."

"You must have a lot in common. It sounds like a match made in heaven," Carolyn said.

Tarik nodded. "My feelings exactly."

The way he said it, with a slight emphasis on *my* gave Carolyn a moment's pause. Was this a match made in heaven or somewhere else?

"I gather you like Jeffrey."

Tarik's expression hardened, and she knew right away she'd overstepped some imaginary boundary and intruded into his personal life. "Whether I like him is beside the point and really none of your business. He's a suitable match for my sister, that is what counts."

Carolyn had an overwhelming desire to up and quit right then and there. The man was insufferable. *Suitable match. None of your business.* Of course it was her business to know as much as possible about the bride and groom and the two families involved. But she'd learned that losing her temper in the face of male dogmatism was pointless. Instead she took a deep breath.

"You're right," she said as calmly as possible. "If your sister loves him, that's all that matters."

If she thought that was the tactful thing to say, she was wrong. If she thought that would end the discussion, she didn't know the sheik. Tarik looked like a black cloud had passed overhead. He positively glowered at her.

"I thought," he said, bracing his hands on the solid door frame, "that I'd made it clear how I felt about marrying for love. It's a poor excuse for respect and admiration and duty."

"Yes, you said that, but…"

"But you persist in believing that the decision of a lifetime be made on the feelings of a nineteen-year-old girl and her fiancé. Fortunately I know better. As I said before, it doesn't matter how you feel, Ms. Evans. Your job is to plan the wedding. I remember distinctly your complaining to me about the lack of notice I've given you to come up with this wedding, thus I advise you to not waste your time discussing these trivial, frivolous matters with me when we both have better things to do.''

Carolyn swallowed hard. He was dismissing her in no uncertain terms, dismissing her legitimate concerns and questions as well. It was time to take a stand. She straightened her shoulders.

''May I remind you, Mr. Oman, that I have planned over seventy-five weddings in my career and you, to the best of my knowledge, have planned none at all. I would never presume to tell you how to run your oil business so I would hope you would allow me to do my job as I see fit. It doesn't matter to me who the participants in the wedding are. How they met or why or how they're getting married is not relevant.

''I have done a wedding for trapeze artists under the big top and a hot-air balloon wedding at two-hundred feet in the air and I've never questioned anyone's motives for getting married or their allegiance to each other. What is important to me and I hope to you, is that the wedding goes smoothly and that it meets the expectations of both the bride and groom's families, no matter who is paying. That's my job and I believe I've been reasonably successful at it. Or you wouldn't have sought me out and asked me to take the job. Would you?''

He stared at her as if she'd asked him to swallow a bitter pill.

''Fine,'' he said at last. But the tone of his voice told

her it wasn't fine at all. "Feel free to ask all the questions you'd like. But not now. I have a conference call in five minutes, and I believe we both need a break to think things over. You have your work cut out for you and so do I. I look forward to hearing from you regarding the reception."

"First things first. If you want to fill Grace Cathedral, the invitations must be ordered and sent out immediately. Who's announcing the marriage?"

"I am," he said. "I thought I'd made that clear."

"The bride's full name?"

"Yasmine Noor Oman."

Carolyn reached for a pencil and scribbled on a small notebook she retrieved from her purse. "I'll need a picture of her for the newspaper. I assume you'll want to put it in."

"Of course. And oh yes, don't forget about the honeymoon."

"What?" Carolyn gasped. Plan the honeymoon, too? What next? The christening of their first child?

"The honeymoon. Make the necessary reservations."

"But I can't possibly make that decision, not without…"

"I wonder, Ms Evans, how you've come so far in your chosen field with your negative attitude. Can't is a word I refuse to listen to in my business. I'd advise you to avoid using it. If you really can't make the decision, at least you can give me a list of options. Agreed?"

Back at the shop on Union Street, Carolyn couldn't remember if she'd actually agreed or simply marched away from the house, speechless with disbelief and indignation. She tossed her briefcase on her desk, threw herself into a chair and exhaled loudly, as if to expel all the frustrations she'd been holding back for the past few hours.

"Where have you been?" her partner Lily asked, looking up from a desk covered with papers.

"I've been to a sheik's palace," she said.

"A real, honest-to-God sheik?" Lily asked. She looked impressed, and it was hard to impress Lily. She'd been in the business longer than Carolyn. Seen every kind of wedding and every type of bride and groom. "Was it business...or pleasure?" she asked with a grin.

"Business of course," Carolyn said. "He came in last evening, interrupted a meeting I had about the Trenter wedding and insisted I drop everything and plan his wedding."

"Who is the sheik marrying?" Lily asked. "Not a commoner, I hope."

"No one. No one would marry him. When you meet him you'll understand why."

"Old? Ugly?" Lily asked.

Carolyn shook her head. "Young and handsome. But his personality! He makes my father look like Mr. Nice Guy."

"That bad?"

"Worse. He gives orders like you're his personal servant. Who I actually just met by the way. No, this is his sister's wedding, only he's doing all the planning. Or rather I am. I think."

"How come you didn't turn him down if he's so obnoxious?" Lily asked.

"For one thing it's a plum job, a big society wedding that could put I DO! I DO! on the map for sure. Bring in some good money, too."

"Nevertheless, I can't see you working with a tyrant, Carolyn. You have a problem with authority figures," Lily said.

"But I'm learning, aren't I? At least I thought I was. Until Sheik Tarik Oman walked in here last night. This is the kind of guy to try my patience, to test everything I've ever learned about assertiveness, anger management, you name it. The problem is working with him is likely to set me back a few years. I could end up in therapy for years. What do you think? Should I call and tell him I can't do it?''

She answered her own question. ''It's not worth it. Not for the money, not for the prestige. I didn't tell you but it's scheduled for one month from now, and he hasn't ordered the invitations. Fortunately he has reserved the church, but that's all. No, I can't do it.'' She reached for the phone.

''Sounds like a real challenge,'' Lily said mildly. ''If you can work with this guy, you can work with anybody.''

Carolyn set the phone down. ''You'd do it, wouldn't you? Do you want the job?''

Lily shook her head. ''I'm overwhelmed. Three weddings this month, four next. If I'd been here I would have turned him down flat. But then I didn't see him, did I? I'm just as susceptible to good-looking men as the next forty-three-year-old married lady. What did you say he looked like? Fill me in, I've never seen a sheik before. Does he wear one of those headdresses? Did he ride in on a camel? Does he have a wife?''

''No, no and no,'' Carolyn said, leaning back in her chair. ''I can't imagine anyone marrying him, except for his money. He's got dark hair and dark eyes, and he looks just like your average, everyday sheik.'' She shrugged nonchalantly as if his looks had made no particular impression on her, but they had. She couldn't shake the image of the man in his library, seated across from her, his dark gaze locked on hers, making her feel like she was melting on the inside. Couldn't forget the painting of the villa on the sea or the portrait of his father who looked so much like him, an older, kinder, gentler sheik. A hint of what the young man would or could become. If he mellowed with time. An interesting thought, but not very likely.

"Just an average, everyday sheik, hmmm?" Lily said, interrupting her reverie. "If he doesn't wear one of those white headdresses, what does he wear?"

"Oh, you know, just the usual…" The image of the sheik emerging from the swimming pool in nothing but his Speedo swimsuit barely concealing his masculine attributes caused the heat to flood Carolyn's cheeks, which was not lost on her astute partner.

"I've got to see this guy," Lily said with a smile. "When are you getting together next?"

"I don't know. Honestly, a few minutes ago I would have said never."

"Never say never," Lily cautioned. "You can do it. I know you can. It sounds like a great opportunity for you. Both professionally and personally. Everyone will ask who planned this spectacular event. You'll get your name in the paper, you'll pull in some money and you'll show yourself once and for all that you've got what it takes to stand up to a man with guts."

"Guts? That's putting it kindly." But Carolyn knew Lily was right as usual. Every time Carolyn had shied away from a difficult project, Lily had urged her on. She'd learned a lot from the older woman and her advice was usually right on. But then Lily hadn't seen the sheik.

So Carolyn swallowed her apprehensions and plunged ahead. After all, they had a signed contract. She spent the day on the phone to the printer, researching reception sites, caterers and even honeymoon locations for the sheik's sister. Since the sheik hadn't given her even a clue as to where his sister would like to go on her honeymoon, she decided to plan it as if it were her own. If they didn't like it, they could find their own destination.

As for her, she'd always wanted to go to a tropical island and stay in a thatched hut on a secluded beach that was rustic and luxurious at the same time. Where she and her new husband would make love for the first time under the stars. Where the sensual pleasures of lovemaking would unfold in endless ways on endless days. Where she would know that she was right to wait until her marriage to make love with the man of her dreams.

Who that man would be wasn't clear. Perhaps it would never happen. Maybe he didn't exist. But that didn't take away the vicarious pleasure of planning Yasmine Oman's honeymoon. At five o'clock she said goodbye to Lily and started out the door for an appointment. At the door she was met by his highness, Tarik Oman, looking more regal and handsome than that morning, if possible. If she had a half a brain she'd back out right now and tell him she couldn't possibly do this wedding. All he was doing was standing in the doorway and suddenly her palms were damp and her brain had turned to mush. She could barely remember where she was going. She clutched her briefcase to her side.

"I'm glad I caught you," he said. "I was in the neighborhood and I have some matters to discuss with you. I find face-to-face meetings are always more productive, don't you?" he asked.

"Yes, of course. But not now. I have an appointment...with the printer...now, in ten minutes. She's staying late to accommodate me, so if you'll excuse me...." She tried to edge past him, but he didn't move. Of course she could squeeze by, but if he didn't move it would mean coming into intimate contact with his body, pressing her breasts against his chest.

"Fine," he said, but he still didn't budge an inch. "I'll go along. We can talk along the way. My car is right here."

She was about to say she preferred to take her own car and go by herself because it was more efficient that way when the truth was she didn't want to spend anymore time with him than absolutely necessary, but on the other hand, she really needed him to see the invitations. While they were standing there at an impasse, sizing each other up, Lily got up from her desk and introduced herself.

Carolyn had almost forgotten she was there. That was the effect Tarik had on her. There was something about the man that disturbed her, caused temporary amnesia and attracted her like a magnet at the same time. Something that caused her voice to falter and her surroundings to fade away.

She waited anxiously for Tarik to display some of his arrogant, boorish behavior, just enough to convince Lily and herself that she hadn't exaggerated, but he took the opportunity to turn on his considerable royal charm. Carolyn could tell her partner was eating out of his hand and wouldn't believe a word of what Carolyn had told her. When she finally interrupted their conversation to say she was leaving immediately, she thought Tarik was going to kiss Lily's hand. And Lily would have let him. Honestly, the man was not to be believed.

Before she knew what was happening, Carolyn was ensconced in Tarik's foreign convertible and they were driving down Union Street, which was crowded with cars and pedestrians going to the upscale shops or heading for the many coffee bars in the trendy neighborhood.

She gave him directions to the printer and then crossed

her arms over her waist. "What do you want?" she asked, unable to stop the defensive tone in her voice. He put her on edge, that's what he did. Especially when she hadn't been expecting him, and had no time to prepare herself for the encounter. Now here she was sitting next to him in his expensive new car with a dozen controls in front of her for the sound system, the heater, the air-conditioning, navigation system and whatever else came with a car like that.

"To see you."

"Yes, I gathered that. What about?"

"About the wedding, of course," he spoke slowly as if speaking to a simpleton.

"I've been working on it all day but so far I have nothing definite to report," she said briskly. "Which I would have told you if you'd called first. It would have saved you a trip to my office. I've left messages here and there but I don't have anything definite yet. About the honeymoon…"

"What about it?"

"Can you at least tell me which continent they want to go to, or if they like the beach or the mountains or a big city? Do they do outdoor sports? I can't believe they haven't given you any information."

"Believe it," he said. "They're both busy people. Especially now. Which is why the responsibility has landed on me and by extension, on you. I assure you they'll be grateful to you for all you're doing. What is the customary destination for honeymoons in this country? Isn't it Niagara Falls?"

Carolyn stifled a smile. "Yes, that is a traditional honeymoon destination, or it was some seventy-five years ago."

"Out of date, I see. Well, then, if it were you, where would you want to go?"

"Oh, I don't know," she said nonchalantly as if she hadn't been dreaming about it for years. "Somewhere warm, I suppose," she said, leaning back in her seat as he drove down Geary Street toward the printer. She pictured that tropical island she'd dreamed of, warm sun and cool breezes and bare skin.

"An island, perhaps, like Hawaii?" he asked.

"Hawaii is too crowded, too civilized. I'd want to get away from phones and faxes and traffic. If it were me I'd choose one of those small islands in the South Pacific near Fiji where you can have a thatched hut and a private beach all to yourselves."

"I see. Warm weather so you can act uncivilized and throw away inhibitions, wear very few clothes and have the privacy to make love whenever you like, night or day. Yes, it sounds very appealing."

She felt his eyes on her. Heard the sensual innuendo in his voice and maybe even a trace of longing. Did the sheik have dreams, too? He said he didn't believe in romantic love, but he probably believed in sex. Most men did. She reached for one of the dashboard controls to get some air to cool her flushed cheeks. But she turned on the radio instead. Strains of a piano concerto came from the speakers. He covered her hand with his broad fingers and guided her fingers to adjust the air conditioning as if he knew what she wanted. Just the touch of his hand caused her heartbeat to speed up. As the cool air obediently shot out of a vent, she knotted her fingers in her lap and stared straight ahead. Why did his touch have such a disturbing effect on her? He was just another client, just another man.

"But you don't need to wait for your honeymoon to enjoy a romantic interlude," he said with a glance in her direction. "You Americans do such things without being married."

"I don't," she said firmly. "I intend to wait for my honeymoon."

"Really. Then you are a..."

"Yes," she said quickly before he could say the word that made her so nervous. She turned to look out the side window so he wouldn't see her blush. She didn't know why or how they'd gotten onto this subject. As if he cared. Besides it was a personal decision she didn't share with everyone. Or anyone for that matter. Here she was blurting out her most intimate secret to a client. Not even a friend. What possessed her to tell him?

"That's the printer on the corner," she said.

Actually it was good he'd come with her to proofread the invitations before they went to be engraved. After he'd made a few corrections and she'd made a few suggestions, they agreed on a final version:

Sheik Tarik Oman
requests the honor of your presence
at the wedding of his sister
Yasmine Noor
and
Mr. Jeffrey Philip Branson
at five o'clock in the evening
Saturday, the tenth of June
Grace Cathedral
San Francisco, California
Reception following
Please R.S.V.P.

"Uh-oh," Carolyn said staring at the blank space after Reception following. "We've got to get the reception nailed down right away. When are you sending these to be printed?'' she asked the woman who was helping them.

"They should go tomorrow. You haven't given us much time.''

Carolyn gave Tarik a look that conveyed the fact that it was his fault they had so little time to plan the wedding and not hers.

"Then we'll find a place for the reception tonight,'' Tarik said. "And let you know in the morning.'' He gave the woman a brief smile and with his hand under Carolyn's elbow, guided her out the door.

She ground her back teeth together. She didn't need help walking from the shop to the car. What did he think, she was going to fall off the curb?

"You don't know what you're saying,'' she said, standing next to his car. "This is not how it's done. You don't just go out and find a place for a reception. You look at the list of possible places, study the brochures, which you didn't seem interested in doing this morning, then you make calls, then…''

He opened the car door. "That's your way. Mine is to take action. What about the top floor penthouse of one of the famous hotels? Someplace with a view.''

"That would be fine,'' she said, "but I'm sure they're already booked for months ahead.''

"Get in,'' he said.

His first stop was the famous Mark Hopkins Hotel. When they approached the office of the events director, and they heard the woman say just what Carolyn thought she'd say—they had been booked solid for years—she couldn't help feeling smug that she was right and he was wrong. But Tarik didn't seem discouraged. He simply took her hand and they hurried across the street to the Fairmont Hotel. She didn't want to hold his hand. The less physical contact with him the better.

On the other hand, dashing across California Street with him was an exhilarating experience. With the wind in her hair and the solid warmth of his hand in hers, she felt protected and daring at the same time. What was it about him that made an ordinary street crossing exciting? It was because he wasn't ordinary. Far from it. He was a sheik. He came from a long line of generations of camel-riding, oil-rich sheiks before him. He was raised to assume responsibility, to take care of his family. He was raised to give orders, to have servants and maybe even a harem.

If anyone had asked her yesterday if she would be interested in meeting a sheik, or if she thought sheiks were romantic, she would have responded with an overwhelming no. Today she couldn't be quite so negative. Today she was standing on top of Nob Hill, unwillingly holding hands with a sheik, looking out over San Francisco Bay at dusk. From the looks of him he could be anybody. No royal headdress, no flowing robes, no royal steed in sight. *Yes, he could be anybody,* she thought, a cursory glance in his direction. Anybody who was breathtakingly handsome, dressed with impeccable taste, had his clothes tailored just for him and who exuded confidence. The lights of the Bay Bridge went on as they watched, as if just for them, and the whole scene was transformed into a fairyland. As if he was the prince and she was the princess in the glass slipper.

"It's a beautiful city," he said as if they had nothing better to do but to stand there and enjoy the view.

"Will you stay here in San Francisco?" she asked. "Or return to your country some day."

"It looks more and more as if I'll be staying. With my sister marrying an American and this merger with an American company. San Francisco is our U.S. headquarters. Of course I will return to my home country to visit, but I feel as if this is my adopted home now. Come on,'' he said as if she was the one who was dawdling. ''Let's get this reception settled.''

As much as Tarik used his charm and persuasive powers and money, the second hotel was also unavailable for months. When Carolyn suggested making some calls instead of driving all over town, he insisted once again that his way was best. Face-to-face contact was how he preferred to operate. She pictured the search going on and on into the night until she dropped from hunger and exhaustion.

''You have no faith in me,'' he said as they drove down the steep hill toward downtown.

''I didn't say that,'' she protested.

''But you're thinking it. Your face gives you away.'' He reached over to gently touch her cheek.

Tarik knew he should keep his hands off the wedding consultant. But she was irresistible. Was it because she'd told him she was a virgin that made her so desirable? Every man wants to be the first in a woman's life. To be responsible for awakening her sensuality and teaching her the pleasures of physical love. Or was it just the charming way she blushed? Was it her soft skin and masses of curly hair?

No, it was more likely because they were on a mission together. He needed her and perhaps in some way she needed him. Only until the wedding was planned, then he could go back to business. In the meantime he felt as if he'd been let out of school early, been given a reprieve from business matters, and regained part of his lost youth. Was that all due to this woman? If so, he'd better get a grip on his emotions—the ones he didn't have. And keep his hands to himself.

"Here we are," he said, stopping in front of the hotel to allow the valet to park his car. "The St. Francis Hotel. I stayed here when I first came to the city. Before I bought the house. I ate at the restaurant on the top floor every night. Maybe they'll remember me." He could tell Carolyn was still skeptical by the way she looked at him. It wasn't her way of doing business, but it was his. He wanted to show her that it worked.

The manager did indeed remember Tarik. It could have been because of the generous tips he left. It could have been because they didn't get that many sheiks staying for three months. Whatever it was, he wasn't shocked when he heard the date of the wedding was only one month away. He merely nodded and looked at his appointment book. Then he escorted both of them to a private banquet room on the top floor with spectacular views of the city and the bay. "It's our newest facility," he explained. "I haven't scheduled anything here until July, but for you..."

"Thank you," Tarik said, nudging Carolyn gently. Hoping that she'd finally admit he'd been right.

"I know your family comes from a different part of the world," the man said. "And you say the groom and his family are American. So I would like to suggest a compromise for the reception. Something a little different. Neither American nor Middle-Eastern. I propose a Balinese theme with Gamelon musicians in the background. You'll need a different band for dancing of course, that's up to you."

"Of course," Carolyn murmured.

"The floor panels can slide back," the manager continued, waving his hand at the inlaid wood, "to reveal an oval lotus pool with a bamboo bridge. I suggest orchid and fruit displays by our resident decorator. Then the caterer could provide a sumptuous buffet and a gold-dusted tiered cake in the same motif.''

''What do you think?'' Tarik asked Carolyn.

''It's an interesting idea,'' she said, glancing around the room at the teakwood panels and the small tables decorated with flowers. ''Completely original. But will your sister...''

''Irrelevant. She's not here. We are. You and I are making the decisions.'' Tarik realized that only twenty-four hours ago he'd said ''I'' and now he was saying ''you and I.'' It gave him a strange feeling.

''Then I say yes,'' Carolyn said. ''Considering how little time we have. It sounds original and it could be very beautiful.''

The manager smiled. He asked how many guests and gave them an estimate of the cost. Tarik thought he heard Carolyn gasp at the figure, but to him it was a bargain.

''Won't you stay for dinner in the sky room, as our guests of course,'' the manager said.

Tarik was about to say yes when he realized he should consult Carolyn first. Consulting a woman went against the grain in every way. He was accustomed to giving orders, both in his personal and business life. He assumed he'd be giving them to the wedding consultant but it wasn't working out that way. She was the kind of strong-willed woman who wanted a say about everything, it seemed.

''I really shouldn't,'' she said. ''I have things...''

''It will give you a chance to sample our food. Of course it won't be the same as at the reception, but we're very proud of the quality. I think you'll find it meets your expectations. Our chef is very good,'' the manager said.

''I'm sure he is, it's just...''

Perhaps she had a date. Or perhaps she simply didn't want to spend any more time with him, Tarik thought.

He, on the other hand, wanted to spend more time with her. He knew nothing about her, except that she was a virgin and a wedding consultant and she wasn't married. She was a mystery that he wanted to solve. He also did not want to eat alone. It would remind him of those early lonely days in the city when he knew no one except his office staff. He'd take a file folder of work projects to dinner with him and pore over it between courses in the hotel dining room. He was no longer homesick or lonely but he didn't want to eat alone tonight. He wanted to eat with this woman he'd hired. He wanted to watch her face by candlelight, hear her talk and maybe even coax a smile out of her.

She didn't say anything for a long moment, and he had to stifle the urge to insist. To order her to eat with him. Though he knew it would be counterproductive. If she walked out, if she insisted on leaving, he'd have to go back to the office or back to the huge house where Meera would be cooking some of her native curry for herself. Neither appealed to him. She had to say yes. He wouldn't admit it, but for some reason he needed, wanted to have dinner with her.

"Well…" she said.

"Think of it as work. I know I do," Tarik said. "It's research. Nothing more, nothing less." He deliberately kept his voice businesslike. But he didn't feel businesslike. He felt young again, the way he did before he'd inherited the business, and looking forward to dining with her more than he should.

When she nodded, albeit reluctantly, he felt a rush of excitement as if he'd just hit the bull's-eye with his bow and arrow on his private archery range. It was the same jolt of adrenaline he got when he scored. He told her it was only research, he told her he thought of it as work, but he didn't. He loved his work. He found it satisfying to be a part of an effort to extract oil from the ground, to bring money to his homeland, to carry on a tradition of service begun by his grandfather. But having dinner with an attractive woman, a woman who intrigued him was not the same thing, not at all. It was something else. Something he didn't want to name. "You won't regret it," Tarik said with a smile. He just hoped he wouldn't either.

Chapter Four

The dinner was superb. The cuisine was better than he remembered. The company was better than he'd imagined. The soft candlelight made Carolyn's skin glow and her eyes shine, and he couldn't tear his eyes from her. Carolyn— that was her name, but she hadn't given him permission to call her that, so he hadn't. It probably wasn't a good idea to get on a first-name basis with her. Then she'd have to call him by his first name and where would that lead to? Before he knew it, he'd be asking questions. There were so many things he wanted to know about her. Did she have a boyfriend? Who did she live with? Why was she still a virgin when other American women were not? But if he asked, he would then have to answer her questions. She'd ask if he'd ever thought of marriage, what he was looking for in a wife—things like that—personal questions he didn't want to answer.

As it was, propriety dictated that he keep the conversation on a more impersonal level, so he asked instead about the weddings she'd planned, including the underwater ceremony with the professional divers where she had to outfit the guests with fins and snorkels. Not only did she smile, she laughed along with him when she described another bride and groom who got lost on the way to the reception because the groom, according to the bride, "refused to stop and ask for directions." Then there was the wedding of the bungee jumpers.

"At least my sister's wedding will not be as much of a challenge as theirs was, I hope," he said. "Though I imagine jumping off the bridge at the end of a bungee cord is no more risky than getting married, no matter how it is done. Taking a leap of faith, jumping off into the air, not sure if you're going to ever bounce back. I don't see myself doing it."

"Bungee jumping or getting married?" she asked.

"Either. They both require an enormous amount of courage," he said lightly.

"You don't strike me as being fainthearted," she said.

"Thank you," he said, though he wasn't sure she'd meant it as a compliment. "What I am trying to say is that I don't picture myself standing up in front of the whole world promising to love, honor and obey."

"Obey really isn't used much anymore," Carolyn said, looking at him over her coffee cup, her eyes slightly narrowed. "Not for many years. When my parents married, my mother promised to obey. He never let her forget it. Cherish is a word I prefer."

"So obey is out of style. Like Niagara Falls. Cherish is fine, but it's entirely different," he said. "Tell me what's wrong with obey." He set his cup down and leaned forward.

"Everything," she said firmly. "Obedience shouldn't be

a part of marriage. That implies that one person is the boss.''

"Of course. The man," he said.

She frowned. "I prefer to think of marriage as a partnership.''

"Do you? Perhaps that is why you aren't married.'' He almost said *Perhaps that's why you are still a virgin.* But he stopped just in time. He hoped to make this a pleasant, impersonal dinner with no arguments, no hard feelings. It had been a long time since he'd sat across a white linen tablecloth having dinner with an attractive woman by candlelight. It might be even longer before it happened again. He would try not to spoil the occasion.

"I'm not married because I don't want to be married," she said. "Not to a bully, that's for sure. Maybe your view of marriage as a union in which the wife obeys her husband is the reason *you're* not married.''

"I would never marry a woman who refused to obey me," he said. "Call me a traditionalist, but that's how I am.''

"I would call you a chauvinist." Her eyes shot angry sparks at him.

"A chauvinist?" He almost laughed. Was that the best she could do? It didn't bother him. He'd been called worse. "You sound like a feminist," he said.

"I'll take that as a compliment," she said. "I'm proud of being a feminist.''

"As I am of being a chauvinist," he countered.

"Now that we understand each other, I'll be leaving. I'm glad we've had this talk," she said, reaching for her jacket on the back of her chair. "It was an excellent dinner. Thank you.''

"Don't thank me," he said standing to help her with her jacket. "Thank the manager."

He too was glad they'd had that talk. As lovely as she was to look at, as soft and sweet on the outside, he'd found out how headstrong and stubborn she was on the inside. Not the type he intended to marry if he ever did marry. She was about as far from his ideal as possible. She was the kind his father warned him about. And with good reason. As they waited for the valet to bring his car to the front of the hotel, he could still hear his father's words in his ear.

"Marrying a woman from a different background is a sure way to disaster and a lifetime of misery. Choose a modest woman who puts duty and family first. A woman who understands her place in the world. Duty is a concept foreign to American women. They are too independent. They're unpredictable and emotional also, undesirable traits in a wife. Find someone who has as much to gain from the union as you do. Whose family is compatible with ours. Who shares common interests and who will benefit from the marriage as much as you will."

He hadn't listened to his father the first time his father gave him that advice. And he lived to regret it. For the past ten years he had buried his emotions and devoted himself to the family business. He learned once and for all not to allow his heart to become involved. The next time he chose a woman for his wife, he would not stray from traditional virtues. Modesty, humility, deference and yes—obedience, too. Nothing wrong with that.

Straying was what got him in trouble the last time. So far this woman, this Carolyn, had not shown her emotional side, but it was no doubt lurking just below the surface and she was certainly too independent. Perhaps even too independent for an ordinary American man, which was why she wasn't married. It didn't matter. It didn't matter to him if she never married. If she remained a virgin forever. What mattered was that she was planning his sister's wedding, but so far it looked like he was doing as much planning as she was.

Of course she'd ordered the invitations and she was planning the honeymoon, but he'd have to supply the guest list at least. And he'd found the church and the reception site. Maybe he didn't need her after all. On the other hand there were still the flowers, the photographer and oh, yes, the dress. He definitely couldn't choose a dress without her. He'd just have to put up with her for one month.

When he dropped her off at her shop it was dark, and he insisted on walking her to her car. She looked annoyed.

"Most women would be grateful to have protection on a dark city street," he remarked acerbically when they reached her car.

"I'm not most women," she said, shoving the key in the lock of her car.

"How true," he muttered to himself. "Wait," he said as she got into the car and closed the door. He rapped on the side window. She lowered it a crack. He braced his hands on the frame. "I have some other issues to discuss with you."

"Not tonight. I…I'm tired. I've had a full day."

"Tomorrow morning at my house then?"

"I'm busy tomorrow," she said.

"Busy? Doing what?"

"Working on another wedding," she said. "I'll get back to you next Monday. I should have some information for you then."

"What about the weekend? Don't you work on weekends?" he asked.

"Not this weekend. I'm taking my mother to the cat show at the Cow Palace."

He frowned. "A palace…a palace for cows?"

She almost smiled. But she caught herself just in time and pressed her lips together. Just as she tried to catch herself from relaxing and having a good time at dinner. She was trying too hard to be a businesswoman, and he could tell it was a struggle. She had all the right feminine, womanly instincts, but she wouldn't give in to them. It was a shame. But none of his business. In fact, the more businesslike she was, the more likely it was he would pull off this wedding.

"The Cow Palace is not really a palace, not the kind you're used to," she said. "And there are no cows there, at least not at the moment"

"Then why…"

"It's a long story concerning cows and cowboys and rodeos. All I can say for now is that this Saturday there will be a cat show at the Cow Palace, which is really a very large arena where they have events like rodeos and such and I promised my mother I'd take her."

"She likes cats?"

"She's always wanted a cat but my father never allowed us to have a pet. Now that she's divorced…"

"Ah, the joys of being divorced," he said not even trying to hide his sarcasm.

"I never said divorce was an occasion for joy. Relief is probably more accurate, at least in her case. It was something I urged her to do and if you knew her you'd see how happy she is. Happier than she's ever been. She's out from under the thumb of a tyrant." She took a deep breath. "And now if you'll excuse me…"

Before he could react she was gone. Before he could tell

her he was perfectly willing to agree that divorce was a reasonable solution for certain situations. Yet another evening he was left standing in the street behind her shop watching her drive away without having completed the conversation. He had more to say to her. Much more.

He was not used to being dismissed this way. He had many things to talk to her about besides divorce American-style. There were the ongoing wedding preparations. He hadn't brought up the wedding at dinner because he almost forgot it was a business dinner, and he got distracted. He thought they'd have time later. Now it turned out there was to be no later. Not until next week.

Back home in the huge house above the sea, it was quiet. Too quiet. Even the ocean was quiet tonight. Even with the windows open he could scarcely hear the waves crashing on the rocks below. He wandered from room to room. Meera was either out or she had gone to bed. He went to his office and studied the papers his lawyers had prepared for the merger. But his mind wandered. He kept thinking of Carolyn.

He said her name out loud in the silence of the empty house. Rolled the syllables around his tongue. The next time he saw her he would ask if he could call her by her first name. After all, they would be working together for the next month. How long could they keep up this formality? They were in America, weren't they? The land of nicknames and first names and strangers telling each other to have a nice day. He wondered if she'd enjoyed the dinner as much as he had. He remembered how the candlelight was reflected in her eyes and had softened her features. The curve of her cheek, the tilt of her chin. Perhaps she, too, had forgotten it was an all-business dinner until they got to the coffee. It was all downhill after that.

Not that it mattered. The only thing that mattered was that she plan this wedding for him. But if she insisted on going to a cow palace to see cats when she should be working for him, how in the name of Allah could she make the necessary arrangements in time? Speaking of the wedding, it was time to check up on his little sister. He checked to see what time it was in Switzerland, then picked up the telephone and put in a call to the boarding school in Lausanne.

"Tarik," his sister said. "I'm glad you called. I'm out of spending money. I'm going to Paris this weekend with a friend and I want to do some shopping. Can you wire me a bank transfer?"

Tarik frowned. "Paris? I thought you were studying for finals." Carolyn's words came back to him. *Perhaps she could buy a dress in Switzerland* and his reply that she was too busy studying for finals.

"I am studying, but I've been studying so hard I need a break."

"Who's the friend?" he asked.

"No one you know."

Her evasive answer bothered him. It was his duty as her legal guardian and her brother to know who she was friends with, who she was traveling with. But this was not the time to argue over that when he had more important matters on his mind. "I've sent your plane ticket," he said. "The wedding is in less than a month, you know."

"Look, Tarik," she said. "I've told you before I can't marry a man I don't love. I don't even know him."

Tarik picked up a pencil and tapped it forcefully against the edge of his desk. What was it with these women and their romantic ideas? "Of course you know him. You met him and his family during your winter holiday. I explained it to you then and you agreed.''

"You explained it to me, yes. And I agreed that it was important for the companies to merge. I never agreed to marry a stranger. If you want the families to merge, then you get married.''

"If the Bransons had a daughter I would be more than happy to marry her.''

"Even if you didn't love her?'' Yasmine asked incredulously.

"There's no such thing as love,'' he said.

"I knew you were going to say that,'' she said.

He exhaled loudly. "You know of course why Father married Mother?''

"Don't change the subject,'' she said. "Theirs was an arranged marriage in another country and at another time. It has no relevance to me and my life. Or to yours. I advise you to stop meddling in my life and worry about your own.''

Tarik shook his head in exasperation. "It is my job to take care of you.'' He carefully ignored the word meddle. "Since our parents are both dead, I'm your legal guardian, and I will be until you are twenty-one. I've explained to you over and over the reason for this marriage, how important it is to our family and to the family business. It is what our parents would have wanted. You are young, Yasmine, and you don't know what you're saying. When I was your age I felt as you do. But now that I'm older…''

"Older? You're not that old. You're not old enough to give up on love. Just because one woman…''

"Just what do you think you know about love?'' he demanded, unwilling to discuss his own past. There was a long ominous silence. "Who do you think you are in love with?'' he asked, suddenly more worried than he'd been since the merger was proposed.

"No one," she said lightly. "I'm speaking hypothetically only."

"Good," he said, only slightly relieved. She didn't yet understand how important duty and loyalty really were. But she would. And she would thank him in time for what he was doing. He didn't know she knew anything about his previous involvement with the American woman. It was the last thing he wanted to discuss with his little sister.

He let the pencil slide through his fingers and leaned back in his desk chair. "I called to tell you that the wedding plans are going very well. I have the cathedral reserved as you know, and now I've hired a wedding consultant to take care of the other arrangements such as flowers and the dress and the photographer and…"

"Yes, yes, that's fine, Tarik. I have to go to class now. Goodbye."

After she hung up so abruptly, Tarik looked at the clock. It was possible she had a class at seven in the morning in Lausanne, but it wasn't very likely. He retrieved the pencil and snapped it in half, venting his frustration only a little. What happened to the little girl who'd followed him everywhere around the compound, while he taught her to shoot with a bow and arrow and to swim in their pool.

Somewhere in the years between then and now he'd lost her respect. At least she hadn't out-and-out refused to marry Jeffrey. When she returned to San Francisco, she wouldn't have time to think. She'd simply get married and live happily ever after in a house he'd buy for them. Some day she'd thank him for what he'd done. Not that he wanted or needed her thanks. The merger and her happiness were all he wanted.

His satisfaction would come when the two families and the two companies merged and became as one to their mutual benefit. His sister would come to understand how lucky she was that he'd found her a suitable husband. Then and only then would he feel he had done the job he'd inherited from his father. He would make his father proud of him by completing the job he'd started years ago. The family and his country would benefit, just as his father had intended.

The noise in the Cow Palace was deafening. Nervous cats were meowing, and nervous owners were trying to calm them. "Mother, are you sure you really want to get a cat?" Carolyn asked.

"Why not?" Mavis Evans answered, peering into a cage that contained a small Angora. "I always wanted one. Your father didn't. So we never had one."

"I know, but is this the right time of your life to take on the responsibility of a cat? They need a lot of care. Feeding, brushing, cleaning up after…"

"Hmmm…" her mother said. "Sounds a lot like your father, except for one important point—cats are glad to see you when you come home."

"Do you mean that men aren't?" Carolyn said, absently petting a small friendly Manx.

"Some men, but don't marry a man to tame him, Carolyn," her mother said. "That's all I have to say."

"Don't worry, I'm not getting married any time soon."

"You're not meeting anyone, are you? You're in the wrong business. Have you thought of moving to getting into a different line of work or moving to Alaska? They say the odds are good there," Mavis said.

"The odds may be good but they also say the goods are odd. I meet enough odd men in my profession. Oh, no."

Across the vast arena of the Cow Palace, past acres of Siamese and Abyssinians and Persians, a tall man with a regal air was standing and scanning the crowd. Sheik Tarik Oman. Though he was wearing a casual sweater and slacks, he still stood out in the crowd, looking around imperiously as if all these cats were his subjects. She'd like to see him try to control them the way he tried to control everyone else in his life. What on earth was he doing there?

"What is it?" her mother asked.

"Speaking of odd men…" she murmured.

"Who? Where?" her mother asked, turning her head in his direction.

"Don't look now, but across the room is one of my clients. The tall one next to the podium."

"How nice. Shall we walk over and say hello?"

"No, definitely not. Come over here. Pretend we're interested in these Calicos." Carolyn crouched down to peek into their cage, but her mother continued to stand and stare across the room.

"What a handsome man," her mother said. "He doesn't look odd to me at all. Too bad he's getting married."

"He's not getting married, his sister is. Trust me, Mother, the whole situation is very odd and so is he. He doesn't see me, does he? He doesn't know I'm here, I hope."

"I don't think so. It wouldn't hurt to be polite, would it? I mean, how odd can a man who loves cats be?"

"But he doesn't. He's only here because…" Why was he here? Had he come looking for her because of some emergency regarding the wedding? Whatever it was it could wait until Monday. She refused to let business interfere with her days off. She needed a break from the intensity of his royal highness. "Or if he loves cats, they're only second to himself. He's a sheik."

"A sheik, a real sheik? That explains the air of confidence then," her mother said. "And the dark eyes and hair. He looks like he just got off the royal steed."

"Mother, your imagination is running away with you," Carolyn said "Tell me when he leaves." She shifted awkwardly on the hardwood floor. "My knees hurt and I'm seeing spots in front of my eyes."

"That could have something to do with the Calicos," her mother suggested.

"I feel like I'm getting a tension headache," she muttered. "Damn the man."

A few minutes later when she thought she couldn't possibly stay there on the floor, face-to-face with a bunch of Calico cats, for another second, she heard his voice.

"You must be Mrs. Evans, Carolyn's mother. Though you look young enough to be her sister, I see the family resemblance. How do you do, I am Sheik Tarik Oman."

Carolyn moaned softly. *Young enough to be her sister.* Where did he learn these things? Or did they come naturally to all sheiks? How did he even know she was there and how had he sneaked up on them? Why hadn't her mother warned her? And more importantly how was she going to rise gracefully when she had a cramp in her leg?

"How nice to meet you. My daughter has told me very little about you," Mavis said pointedly, nudging Carolyn with her toe. "Do you like cats?"

"Very much," he said. "But I didn't come to see the cats today. I came to see your daughter." He reached down and gallantly extended his hand. So he knew she was there all along. What could she do but take his hand and allow him to pull her to her feet.

Flushed and irritated that she couldn't take a day off without the sheik tracking her down and annoyed with herself for telling him where she'd be today, she crossed her arms over her waist and glared at him. If only she could forget how warm and strong his hand felt against hers.

"Yes?" she said.

"Forgive me for intruding on your day off," he said smoothly, his dark gaze including her mother, too, in his apology. "But I received a call from the cathedral this morning saying they had an opening this morning between weddings when the organist is available along with the deacon who will be performing the ceremony. It seemed a good opportunity to do a brief run-through of the ceremony with the music. Since they are usually booked solid on Saturdays, I agreed. It would be most helpful if you could come, too. If, that is, you could spare an hour or so of your time. After you've finished looking at cats of course."

"Go ahead, Carolyn," her mother said. "I can tell you've seen enough felines for one day. And I'm looking forward to the judging at three o'clock. You see," she said to Tarik, "I'm trying to decide what kind of cat to buy."

"Are you looking for a purebred or simply an ordinary tabby?" he asked. "A small cat or a large one, long or short-haired?"

"Well..."

"Mother hasn't decided, have you?" Carolyn asked.

"I have some suggestions," Tarik continued as if Carolyn hadn't spoken.

I'll just bet you do, she thought. She wouldn't be surprised to find he had suggestions and opinions on every imaginable subject. He proceeded to give her mother a rundown on the virtues and drawbacks of several breeds. While Carolyn watched and listened in amazement, her mother appeared to hang on his every word as if he were the world's expert. Did he really know what he was talking about, or was he trying to impress her and her mother? And if so, why?

"That's fascinating," her mother said, clearly in awe of both his looks and his encyclopedic knowledge of the subject. "How do you know so much about cats?"

"My father was fond of cats," he said. "Some lived outdoors, some in the house. I'm afraid he spoiled them all quite abominably."

"What happened to the cats when your father died?" Carolyn asked in spite of herself. In spite of the fact that she didn't want to engage in this conversation at all.

"The cats are well cared for," Tarik answered with a smile. "You can be sure of that. Father made the necessary arrangements before he died as he did with everything else."

"He must have been quite a thoughtful man," her mother said.

"It is my goal to live up to his legacy," Tarik said simply.

Her mother nodded and Carolyn could tell by the look in her eye that he'd won over yet another female. If only her mother could hear him giving orders, insisting on having his own way, making decisions for everyone including her who he'd hired to make decisions for him. But that didn't happen, at least not today.

"All right," Carolyn said impatiently. "But just an hour."

"Will you follow me in your car?" Tarik asked.

"My mother drove, so I'll have to ride with you." Now she'd be stuck with him and he with her, though the prospect didn't seem to bother him as much as it did her, if his benign expression was any indication. And he'd have to take her home afterward. She didn't like the idea of his knowing where she lived. If today was an indication, he'd think nothing of dropping in whenever he needed her.

They drove up Taylor Street to the top of Nob Hill, which in the last half of the nineteenth century was home to the men who had made their fortunes in gold mining and railroading. Now Nob Hill was covered with elegant apartment houses and hotels, like the ones they'd visited the other evening in their search for a reception site, as well as the impressive huge Gothic church where the wedding would take place.

Tarik parked in the church lot and they walked to the front of the church to admire the beautifully carved bronze doors of Paradise. Carolyn ran her hand over the smooth surface, admiring the quality of the work. Of course she'd been to the church before, but hadn't taken time to fully admire the many details of this San Francisco landmark and one of the nation's oldest cathedrals.

"Excellent reproduction," Tarik said. "Have you seen the original doors of Paradise on the Baptistery in Florence?"

"No, I've never been to Europe," she said.

"Never been to Europe?" he repeated. "But you must go. If only to acquire ideas for weddings. The lace in Belgium, the glass in Venice, the pastry in Vienna..."

"I suppose you've been there many times," Carolyn said.

"I go often enough on business to warrant keeping an apartment in Paris. It makes more sense than staying in a hotel each time."

"How nice," she said. "I understand how valuable such a trip would be for me, it's just..." How to explain to a man with limitless funds that she couldn't possibly find the time or the money to travel to Europe, no matter how beneficial to her career. No need to wonder how well he knew Europe, probably like the back of his hand.

"It's just that you are too busy at present," he finished for her. "Perhaps on your honeymoon. Oh, no, I remember, you are going to a deserted island where you can throw caution and your clothing to the winds and cavort in limpid blue water."

The way he looked at her, as if he could see her without her clothes, as if he knew how she'd look floating naked in aquamarine water made her feel breathless, as if she'd run up the steps to the cathedral. Carolyn bit her lip and turned away. She studied the doors once again, concentrating as hard as if she was planning to duplicate them in clay when she got home, but it was only to escape that all-knowing look in Tarik's dark eyes.

"I'm sorry," he said. "I've embarrassed you, Carolyn. I may call you Carolyn, I hope. Since we'll be working together. And you must call me Tarik."

She wanted to protest. It was so much safer being Ms. Evans. She'd never known what to call him. Tarik was easier than calling him Sheik or Your Royal Highness, so perhaps he had solved that problem for her anyway. Besides she felt foolish insisting on being called by her last name. So she didn't say yes and she didn't say no. But she knew he interpreted her silence as a yes.

They walked inside the cathedral and stood in silence, in awe of the classic architecture, the arched ceiling, the vast nave and the chapel. Strains of organ music floated through the air. Rehearsal for tomorrow's service, or perhaps for the next wedding.

"Do you have an appointment with someone?" Carolyn whispered, not wanting to interrupt anyone's private worship.

"With Reverend McClane," he whispered back. "Ah, there he is now."

A tall, portly man in a white robe approached them, introduced himself and instructed them in the details of the ceremony. He asked about music and Carolyn suggested several pieces for the organist to play while the guests assembled. Tarik had no objections to her choices, as well as the traditional wedding march and the recessional, and that much was quickly settled. Then the cleric suggested they do a run-through right there and then, taking advantage of the brief time between weddings.

"But we're not..." Carolyn began, afraid the good man thought they were the couple who were getting married.

But the man brushed off her protest and told Tarik to go to the altar and wait for her to come down the aisle. He told them the deacon was there and would run through the ceremony. Then he waved to the organist at the rear of the church to prepare to play the wedding march.

"Timing is very important," the minister said. "Of course we must take into account the wedding dress and the long train. That will add a few minutes."

Carolyn wanted to say that the dress hadn't been chosen so no one knew if it had a long train or not. "I really don't think..." she said, feeling distinctly uneasy at the idea of walking down the aisle of a church like the bride she wasn't with the sheik waiting at the altar. But before she could verbalize this thought, Tarik strode forward, and she was left behind. She gave a rueful glance at her khaki slacks and white sweater. She was dressed for a cat show not a wedding rehearsal.

When Tarik reached the altar, he turned and looked at her. If he ever did get married she knew he'd have that same solemn expression on his face. And how would his wife-to-be look? Pale, beautiful, wide-eyed? How would she feel? Nervous, jittery, with a fluttery feeling in her chest, just like Carolyn felt right now? The aisle looked as long as an endless highway. She'd never make it to the altar if her legs didn't stop trembling.

She told herself it was just a run-through. Not even a rehearsal. Not even *her* rehearsal. If it was her wedding, who would walk her down the aisle? Who would steady her nerves and tell her everything would be all right? She might have stood there forever woolgathering, if the organist hadn't started the music and the kindly minister hadn't come up behind her to nudge her gently and tell her it was time. Like a robot, she put one foot ahead of the other, her eyes riveted on Tarik's face.

So this is what it felt like to be a bride. All she needed now was the father, the flowers, the dress and the groom. The flowers and the dress were no problem. She knew where to get them. She'd supplied them for many brides, but the groom, that was another matter. She reminded herself that she was not a bride and wouldn't be any time soon and Tarik was not a groom and was not exactly on his way to the altar either. But she kept walking and approaching the altar and Tarik.

The way Tarik was looking at her made her heart pound. This was not real, she told herself. This was make-believe. This was a job. Then why did she feel as if time stood still and the whole world had stopped turning on its axis? That this is what it would be like if…if…

But it wasn't. This was make-believe. Instead of a wedding gown she was wearing khakis. Instead of a groom, it was Tarik at the altar, staring at her, his face a study in concentration.

"Four minutes," he said, looking down at his watch as she approached. "Can't you walk any faster?"

The mood was shattered just as surely as if he'd thrown a glass at a brick wall. But he didn't notice.

Carolyn clenched her jaw and joined him at the altar. "I'm sorry," she said under her breath so no one could hear but him, "but this is a once-in-a-lifetime walk down the aisle. It should not be rushed."

A man who was most certainly the deacon from the way he was dressed in a black robe and red mantle came down from the pulpit and joined them. He smiled benevolently at them as if they were the most wonderfully, ideally suited couple he'd ever married. Then he went through the traditional ceremony briefly, skipping the vows and the exchange of rings, but ending with "I now pronounce you man and wife."

For a long moment she and Tarik stood facing each other at the altar. The look in his eyes was unfathomable. She tried to drag her gaze away, but there was nowhere else to look.

Finally the deacon broke the spell. "You may kiss the bride," he said. Carolyn thought she'd collapse on the spot. This was going too far. Way too far. Though she thought he was informed as to the situation, the man must be under the wrong impression. They were not going to be married. They were stand-ins. She opened her mouth to explain this to him, but no words came out. All she had to say was let's go. All she had to do was grab Tarik's arm, turn and march back down the aisle. But she didn't. She couldn't move.

Why didn't Tarik say something? Why didn't he take her hand, tuck it under his arm and start walking? Surely he had no more desire to kiss her than she did to kiss him. Instead he leaned forward and angled his head so his lips were only a breath away from hers. He hesitated for a long moment. And she knew. She knew then he was going to kiss her. She knew she wanted him to kiss her. She also knew it was wrong. That if she had any sense she'd turn her head away and then his lips would land on her cheek. That wouldn't be so bad. That would be nothing to fear.

If he was going to kiss her, why didn't he just get it over with? The longer he stood there, the more intensely she felt the heat from his body in the cool air of the church. The chords from the organ still vibrated in the hushed silence. The sun shone through the stained-glass windows. The tension built until Carolyn couldn't stand it another minute. Just as she was about to bolt back down the aisle with or without him, Tarik finally closed the distance between them and kissed her. At first a brush of his lips across hers, clinging for a long, long moment, cutting off the light from those magnificent windows. Cutting off all rational thought also. Then a long deep kiss, but not long enough. Only long enough to tease, to tantalize her. To make her want more. So much more.

She took a deep breath and willed her voice to be steady. "Four minutes," she said lightly. "Can't you kiss any faster?"

"This is a once-in-a-lifetime kiss," he breathed without missing a beat. "It should not be rushed."

Touché, she thought.

Her knees trembled. If he hadn't taken her hand and tucked it under his elbow for the recessional at that moment, she might have.

"Go ahead," the deacon advised. "Now the pace can be quite brisk."

Tarik nodded and they marched back down the aisle toward the rear of the church.

She glanced at him, wondering if the kiss had really meant anything to him at all. *Once-in-a-lifetime kiss* was just a joke. She wondered if he'd felt anything at all. Probably not, if that grim expression on his face was any indication. Even if he did feel anything, he'd never admit it. After all, if he admitted to an increased heart rate or any other symptom, he'd have to head for the emergency room.

"I believe a smile is required," she said mildly with a glance at him. "The bride and groom are supposed to be deliriously happy. Is there any reason…"

"Why I can't smile? Of course not." He forced his mouth to turn up at the corners and gave what, on any ordinary man, would have been called a smirk. On him it looked ridiculous. So ridiculous, Carolyn's lips curled upward in spite of herself.

"Was that funny? Did I amuse you?" he asked, tightening his grip on her hand.

She nodded. "I hope your sister and her husband will be smiling more naturally."

"So you object that my smile is not natural. I'll try again. How's this?"

This time a beguiling slow smile creased his face. Natural or forced, the smile transformed his face. His jet-black eyes gleamed, his lips curved and he looked years younger and incredibly sexy. She reminded herself sternly this was playacting. On both their parts. But if the butterflies in the pit of her stomach were acting, they were doing a very good job of it.

They suddenly found themselves out on the front steps of the cathedral in the fresh air. Tarik turned to Carolyn, his smile suddenly gone.

"About the kiss," he said, his eyes narrowed. "I know

you thought it went on too long, but other than that, how was it?''

''It was fine, but…I don't really think it was necessary,'' she said, feeling the color rush to her face.

''Not necessary,'' he said. ''But enjoyable nonetheless.''

Enjoyable? she thought. That was not the word she would have chosen. Thrilling, exciting, dazzling, earth-shaking. That was more like it. Too long? Hardly. But she had to cover her feelings somehow. Being flippant was one way. She just didn't know if it had worked.

At that moment, the minister came through the bronze doors. He told them the rehearsal had gone very well. He said the deacon was pleased and would see them the day of the wedding. He made some suggestions and asked a few questions, all of which were answered by Tarik. Which was a good thing, because for some reason, Carolyn had nothing sensible to say. She simply couldn't concentrate on what the man was saying. The touch of Tarik's lips on hers lingered. She was still in a daze, but evidently the kiss hadn't made a lasting impression on him.

''What next?'' he asked.

''I have to go home,'' she said. The sooner the better. She needed a break from this man, as much time as possible away from him. ''You must have work to do, or don't you work on the weekends?''

''Yes, of course, but…'' Tarik glanced out toward the bay from the top of Nob Hill, taking in the sailboats bobbing in the water, the dark green islands of Alcatraz and Angel Island. Of course he had work to do. He always had work to do. And normally on the weekends that was exactly what he'd be doing. But with the wedding coming up he was distracted. Or was it the wedding consultant who had him even more distracted?

"Of course I have work to do and so do you. I've taken up too much of your weekend already," he said. "I apologize."

She looked startled. "I didn't think sheiks had to apologize for anything."

"How many sheiks have you known?" he asked.

She smiled. She had a lovely smile. He'd seen it twice today and he wished he could capture it on film or canvas. It was like watching the sunset over the Golden Gate. He had the feeling that no matter how many times he saw her smile, it would always have that effect on him.

"Just one," she said.

"So it is my fault that you have some kind of wrong impression of us," he said. "Perhaps I've been a bit overbearing at times. But it is only that I have many things on my mind." Those many things included her, unfortunately. It was her fault he was losing his focus. While he should be at his office, studying the terms of the merger, he was lingering at the entrance to the church, trying to think of ways he could prolong the encounter. Thinking of what excuse he could give for not taking her home yet. She appeared anxious to go home, but he didn't. He didn't want to go to his house, nor to his office. Neither seemed as appealing as spending time with Carolyn Evans. He wished she felt the same.

Kissing her had been a mistake. Perhaps he'd offended her. Kissed her too long? She could have pulled away, couldn't she? He hadn't forced her. For him the kiss wasn't half long enough. In all fairness, he'd given her time to turn away. She hadn't. Her lips were soft and warm and had only made him want to kiss her again. Longer and slower and deeper this time. To give her time to respond.

But would she? He could think of no more excuses to keep her with him. So he drove her home.

She lived in the part of the city called Cow Hollow. She explained that at one time in the eighteen-hundreds, there were dairy farms where charming Victorian houses like the one she lived in, stood today.

"So in America, cows not only have palaces, they have hollows also," he said as he drove down Greenwich Street toward her house.

"What about in your country?"

"No cows. Cows require grass and hay, which are in short supply in the desert. We do have camels though, but they are not allowed inside the palace. They are remarkable beasts of burden, able to withstand heat and sand and go for long stretches without water, and best of all, we can ride them across the sands where no other animal or vehicle can go. Your cows give milk, but I dare say they cannot be saddled."

"That's true, but cows are gentle and I understand camels are ill-tempered."

"They've been known to display some bad behavior, yes. But after a hard day, trekking across the Sahara under a blazing sun with a heavy pack on their back, perhaps they can be forgiven an occasional show of temper."

Before she could respond, he pulled up in front of her house and they both noticed her mother standing in front of her house with a cat in her arms.

"What on earth?" Carolyn said as she got out of the car. "What is she doing here?"

He, too, got out of the car to pay his respects, but before he could, Carolyn's mother rushed up to her daughter.

"Carolyn, I'm so glad you're home," her mother said, her voice tremulous, her forehead creased in a frown. "I got the cat, but the worst thing has happened. They won't let me keep him at my place.''

''But why didn't you ask before...'' Carolyn said.

''I never thought.... Other people in the building have pets,'' her mother said. Mavis Evans's lower lip trembled and the cat shivered pitifully as if he understood he might be homeless. ''But as soon as the landlady saw me with Max she came running out and said they weren't allowed. Only those who had their pets when they moved in, and when those pets die, they aren't allowed to replace them. I thought maybe you...''

''No, Mother, no pets allowed here. I'm sorry. He looks like a nice cat.'' She reached out to pet the striped tabby with the grey body and black stripes. ''And you've already named him.''

''Yes, I looked and looked and asked a lot of questions just as you said, Mr....''

''Tarik. Please call me Tarik, Mrs. Evans.''

''Tarik,'' she repeated with a wan smile. He could tell she was worried. Who wouldn't be with a brand-new cat and no place to leave him? He looked like a nice cat, too. Tarik felt all eyes were on him. Not just mother and daughter, but the cat too. They all seemed to be saying, what are we going to do now?

Chapter Five

"I'll move, that's what I'll do," her mother said.

"You can't move today, Mother."

"Well, I know, but…"

"In the meantime, I'll take him," Tarik heard himself say. He was almost as surprised as the other two by his offer. He certainly hadn't planned on offering to take the cat. The words came out of their own accord. Of course he was accustomed to living with cats in his father's house, but keeping a cat in the city would require some effort. But he said he'd do it, and once he'd given his word, he couldn't back down. He was rewarded for his spontaneous offer by the grateful look on Mavis Evans's face. Then Carolyn spoke up.

"You can't do that. You live in a mansion. He might soil your carpets and scratch your furniture. Where would you put him? Who would take care of him?"

"I'll take care of him. Let me worry about the details," he said. The woman just wouldn't leave well enough alone.

Here she was peppering him with questions he had no answers for. The truth was he had no idea where he'd put the cat. He could just imagine the reaction from Meera who already thought she was overworked. Nonetheless he was accustomed to succeeding in whatever project he undertook. There was no reason he couldn't care for a cat for a few days. Compared to a dog, they were self sufficient.

"I'll get a little cat house for him so he'll never have to come into your mansion," her mother said to him. "It would only be for a few days. I'll look for a new place to live tomorrow. Are you sure you don't mind?"

"Of course he minds, Mother. He's too polite to say so."

"Polite? That sounds like a compliment. Do you know that's the nicest thing your daughter has said to me," Tarik said.

Mavis looked from Tarik to Carolyn with a puzzled expression on her face. "I don't understand. That's not the way I brought her up."

"I'm sure it isn't," Tarik said. "You mustn't blame yourself. She must have gone astray after she left home."

"I'm standing right here," Carolyn said, glaring at Tarik. "There's no need to talk about me as if I wasn't here. I would prefer that you wouldn't talk about me at all, or at least until I've left. Which I intend to do as soon as possible. Mother, could I speak to you for a moment?"

"Of course."

"I mean alone."

Tarik noted that Carolyn's cheeks were pink and her voice had risen. He didn't know her very well, but he knew that she was upset with him. Because he'd offered to take her mother's cat? He thought she'd be grateful. He would never understand women. He watched them walk a few paces away from him and spoke in hushed tones while the cat snuggled into her mother's arms.

"You can't leave the cat with the sheik, Mother, he's my client," Carolyn said. "It puts me in a very awkward position."

"I'm sorry," her mother said. "It wasn't my idea. I'm just as surprised as you are. I mean I don't even know him. He must be trying to impress you."

"Don't you see?" Carolyn said softly with a glance over her shoulder at the sheik. "He's not trying to impress me, he's a control freak, just like Father."

"I don't see that at all," her mother said. "He seems like a kind, thoughtful person. Not at all like your father."

"That's because you don't know him," Carolyn muttered.

"Do you?" her mother asked.

"Well yes, I think I do. I know his type, anyway."

"How could you? You've never met a sheik before, have you?" Mavis asked.

"His being a sheik is beside the point. He has to have his own way. He has to be in control," Carolyn insisted.

"I need a place for my cat," her mother said. "I don't see that his offering to take the cat has anything to do with his being in control. What do you suggest I do?"

Carolyn shook her head, her arguments deflated. "I don't know. You have a problem, and I agree, you can't turn down an offer like that. I'm warning you though that with this man, one thing leads to another. I told him I was busy this weekend and here he is. He never gives up."

"That can be a virtue, in some cases," her mother said mildly.

"In this case it isn't, believe me." Carolyn looked from the cat to her mother to Tarik who was still standing on the pavement, looking remarkably patient. Finally she gave in. What choice did she have? She really didn't understand why he'd offered, and she really didn't want to know. Her desire to escape into her house, to be alone for the rest of the day, was stronger than ever, but impossible. She couldn't just leave her mother, the cat, and the sheik together to sort this out.

So after a brief discussion, it seemed logical that Tarik was to go home to prepare his housekeeper. Carolyn and her mother went to buy a cat house if there was such a thing, cat food and a litter box. The plan was for them to take the cat and his equipment to Tarik's house as soon as they had purchased the equipment.

Her mother strolled down the block carrying her cat and Carolyn leaned down to speak to Tarik through the side window of his luxury car. She braced her hands against the window frame, wishing he weren't so close. Wishing she weren't so aware of the fathomless depths of his dark eyes, so deep she could drown in them. Aware, too, of the small scar at the edge of his eyebrow. Wishing he wouldn't look at her the way he did, as if he knew something she didn't.

"Are you sure you want to go through with this?" she asked.

"Of course," he said. "The cat will be in the yard. Your mother can come by and see it and feed it, but otherwise he can take care of himself. It isn't going to be forever, after all," Tarik said.

"No, but I don't know how long it will be. Finding an apartment that will take a pet isn't going to be easy. Mother is a bit naive, I'm afraid. You see for years my father did everything. Made all the decisions, handled the money, took care of everything."

"As a husband should," he said.

"You see? You don't understand. Marriage should be a partnership. If it had been she would have had her cat years ago. But it wasn't. He wasn't just the boss in our house. He was king. The rest of us were just his servants."

"No, I don't understand," Tarik said with a frown. "But the past is the past. We must deal with the situation as it is in the present. We will find a way because we must. She wants to keep the cat and she shall."

We? Did he say *we* must deal with the situation? *We* will find a way? How did he get involved with them anyway? She blamed herself. Knowing that if only she hadn't told him she was going to the cat show none of this would have happened.

"Oh, she certainly does want to keep it," Carolyn said. "But that doesn't mean you have to take it in."

He shrugged. "Then who will?"

He had her there. Who indeed?

"It's settled," he said. "I have the space, and I'm taking the cat."

Yes, she thought. He had the space, he had the money, he had the servant, he had the power to do whatever he wanted. It was impressive, it was also a little overwhelming. Carolyn did not want to be overwhelmed. Why couldn't her mother see the resemblance between him and her father? Truthfully she was having a problem seeing it herself at that moment. All she could see was the look on his face. Not proud, not arrogant, he looked like an ordinary man for once. An ordinary man with more money than he knew what to do with, an ordinary man who was movie-star handsome and was going out of his way to be kind to her mother. Why?

"It pleases me to be of service," he said as if he'd heard her question. "I was brought up that way."

"Noblesse oblige," she murmured.

"Exactly," he said. He covered her hands with his. The warmth from his broad fingers spread and went straight to her heart. She tried to pull away but he held her hands where they were. But more than his hands, it was his gaze that held her. The silence stretched between them. She tried to think of something to say. If she pulled hard enough he'd have to let her go, but she couldn't. She couldn't tear her eyes away either. She wanted to stay that way forever. The memory of his kiss in the church came back to haunt her. Did he remember it, too? Did it haunt him, too? She'd never know.

Finally he took his hands away, broke eye contact and started the engine. "I'll be waiting for you," he said.

She stood on the curb with her arms wrapped around her, hugging herself to keep warm in the fading daylight as his car disappeared down the street.

"Fancy car," her mother said as she came up behind Carolyn. "How much money *does* he have?"

Carolyn shrugged. "I don't know and I don't care as long as he pays his bills. He's just a…"

"I know," Mavis said. "He's just a client."

Carolyn knew her mother would be impressed with the mansion. She was even more impressed when the huge iron gate at the entrance swung open as if on command, upon their approach in her mother's car. Carolyn remembered that she'd driven through the gate and parked in the driveway. Was that only two days ago?

"This is his house?" her mother asked in hushed tones.

"One of them," Carolyn answered.

Tarik was waiting for them. Instead of calling a servant, which Carolyn imagined a sheik would do, he untied the so-called cat house himself from the top of the car, lifted it off and carried it to the corner of the yard where it seemed most naturally to fit.

"But Tarik," her mother said, after he'd instructed her to call him that and not *sheik* or *Mr. Oman,* "this is a garden. What if the cat eats your flowers and chases birds?"

"What can you expect?" he asked. "Cats will be cats."

Carolyn had to admit the cat seemed deliriously happy in the sheik's garden. And who wouldn't be? It was full of blooming rhododendron plants with dense oleander bushes around the periphery. There was a small pond with lily pads and a brick patio. The air was fragrant with the scent of flowers mingled with the salt spray from the ocean far below. Carolyn couldn't help but think what a lovely spot it would be for a wedding. It was nothing personal—it was just how she viewed the world—from the eyes of a wedding consultant. She wondered if it had occurred to Tarik to have his sister's reception at home.

"This is far too good for a cat," Carolyn said to Tarik as her mother filled the cat's dish with the high-performance cat food she'd purchased.

"I'll be the judge of that," Tarik said. "It's time the yard got used. I never come out here. Now I'll have an excuse."

"Won't it take you away from your work?" Carolyn asked.

"Sometimes I need a break," he said. "Sometimes I get too immersed in things like the wedding and the merger. There are so many details."

"I thought that was why you hired me, to take care of the details, at least those of the wedding."

"I thought so, too, but the closer it gets, the more I get

involved. I must confess I'm enjoying participating in certain details more than I thought." The look in his eyes told her just what details he was referring to. She bit her lower lip thinking of the kiss. The endless kiss that was over too soon. In spite of the cool ocean air sweeping up from the sea below, Carolyn felt the heat from his gaze, the heat from his body. And yet she shivered.

"You're cold." He took his hand-knit sweater off and wrapped it around her shoulders. He tied it loosely over her chest, his hands brushing lightly across her breasts. She took a deep breath to steady her nerves and wiped her damp palms against her khaki pants. How many times had he touched her today? How close had she come to making a fool of herself by blushing and falling apart at the seams? The wool sweater was warm and soft and smelled of leather and fresh sea-washed air and something that was uniquely Tarik. She wanted to bury her face in it and close her eyes. "Come in for a drink of something warm, won't you?" he asked.

"Oh, no. I must get home," she said taking a deep breath of cool air. She told herself not to weaken. Not to go back into that beautiful house. Not to let her mother even see it. She knew just what she'd think and what she'd say. Something in the order of *it's just as easy to fall in love with a rich man as a poor man.*

"We've taken up entirely too much of your weekend as it is," Carolyn added. And he'd taken up too much of hers, she thought. Pretty soon she'd have no life left except for the sheik's wedding and when it was over—all the hoopla and the excitement of hotel dinners and run-through rehearsals at Grace Cathedral—she'd be back to her old life. Which wasn't that bad, she told herself. Making people happy. Making their dreams come true. She squashed that little voice inside her that asked what about her, what about her dreams. Those dreams were not relevant. Those dreams didn't pay the bills.

She hustled her reluctant mother away from her new cat while her mother was promising to find a new apartment as soon as possible, in between telling Tarik how grateful she was, how much in his debt she was...until Carolyn thought they'd never get through the huge iron gate and back onto the road.

"Did we really have to leave so soon?" her mother asked plaintively as she drove away from the house on the seacliff.

"We really did," Carolyn said. "I know you'd like to spend more time with your cat, but you can come back tomorrow. Tarik gave you the combination to the gate, didn't he?"

"Yes, he did." Her mother gave her a long look then turned her gaze back to the road. "He's quite something, your sheik."

"Mother, he's not my sheik. He's not anybody's sheik. He's his own man. I told you..."

"I know what you told me, but I know what I saw. I saw the way he looked at you. He's interested in you. I don't know why you're not more interested in him. He's handsome, he's rich and he's unbelievably kind. I can't believe you were hiding from him at the cat show. Unless you're afraid of your own feelings. There comes a time in life when you have to let go of your fears, take a leap into the unknown and take a chance."

"Is that what you did when you married Dad?" Carolyn asked.

Her mother's face fell.

"I'm sorry. I didn't mean that."

Her mother took one hand off the wheel and patted her daughter's knee. "Never mind. I asked for that. Yes, I took a chance and let go, and I'm the first to admit I made a terrible mistake. But do you know what? I learned a lot from being married to your father. I learned what to look for in a man. And what not to look for. Call me a hopeless romantic, but if the right man came along today I'd get married again. But, back to you and your sheik, Carolyn, you have to admit you've never met anyone quite like him."

Carolyn shook her head. What good did it do to remind her mother again that he wasn't her sheik. Her mother said it all—she was a hopeless romantic when it came to men. Never met anyone like him? Oh, yes, she had. But this was not the time to remind her mother of the similarity between her father and the sheik. Her mother just couldn't or wouldn't see it. It was clear to Carolyn the sheik was a dictator. A benevolent dictator, but a dictator nonetheless. "You're right about that, Mother. I've never met anyone like him."

Her mother smiled and pulled up in front of the Victorian house where Carolyn rented the top floor. She kissed her mother on the cheek and congratulated her on getting a cat and got out of the car.

"Remember what I said," her mother called before she pulled away. Carolyn nodded, but she didn't know what she was referring to. There had been so much advice. All of it in regard to you-know-who.

She'd been in her apartment for at least five minutes before Carolyn realized she still had the sheik's sweater tied around her shoulders. And her mother never said a thing. Neither did the sheik. They both let her walk out with it. She untied it and flopped down on her soft, nubby oatmeal-colored couch and gave in to fatigue and pent-up frustration. She covered her face with the soft wool and let herself be immersed in the scent of the man. A warm rush of desire flooded her body, leaving her trembling. Good thing she was lying down or she would have fallen.

She groaned. What did the sheik want from her? What did she want from him? The answer to the first question was simple. He wanted her to plan his sister's wedding. The answer to the second question? She wanted to plan his sister's wedding. Period. If she wanted anything else, anything more, she was an idiot and a fool. The man didn't believe in love, for heaven's sake. She'd forgotten to tell her mother about that. That would have stopped her suggestions cold.

Don't marry a man to tame him. Her mother had said that.

Carolyn tossed the sheik's sweater across the room and headed for the bathroom where she ran a bath in the old-fashioned, claw-footed porcelain tub. Immersed in the hot water, she felt the tension slowly leave her body. She was finally able to relax. Until her cell phone rang.

She shouldn't answer it. It was bound to be something that would spoil her mood. That would jolt her out of her repose. But she did. She reached across to the vanity and picked up the phone. It was Tarik.

"I forgot to tell you something in the excitement of the cat's arrival," he said.

What was it about the sound of the man's voice that had made her heart pound like a jackhammer? She rested her head against the end of the tub, slid deeper into the water and told herself to calm down. "How is he?" she asked.

"Fine, just fine. He's sitting at my feet right now, looking extremely content."

"At your feet? Are you outside in the yard?"

He chuckled. She'd never heard him chuckle before. Didn't know he could laugh. The sound sent waves of heat through her body that had nothing to do with the temperature of the water.

"I'm in the library," he said. "The fog came in and I couldn't leave the cat outside."

"But he's a cat. He has a fur coat. He has a house…" She stopped. The little house couldn't really compare to Tarik's mansion. Even the cat knew that.

"He's very well-behaved," Tarik said. "He hasn't laid a claw on the furniture or peed on the carpet."

"I'm glad to hear it, but…"

"I thought I shouldn't have a cat in the city, but I see it's no trouble at all."

"Is my mother in danger of losing her pet?" she asked.

Again that deep-throated, husky chuckle. "Not at all. One of these days I'll get one of my own. What I'm calling about… Am I interrupting something?" he asked.

She sat up straight in the tub. Maybe she hadn't given him enough credit. He had manners, she'd have to admit that. It was just that he only used them when he wanted to. "No, not at all."

"I thought I heard a splash."

"Yes, I'm… I'm…in the bathtub." As soon as she said the words, she knew she shouldn't have. Why hadn't she said she was washing the dishes? Or her car? There was a long silence. Her whole body turned pink. Of course it could have been the hot water. But it wasn't. It was his voice. It was the picture she had of him sitting in his library, his legs stretched out, a fire in the fireplace, a cat at his feet. So normal, so virile, so masculine, so…so…endearing. She didn't want to be endeared. She wanted to keep her original impression of him fresh in her mind.

"I see," he said, his voice turning rough around the edges. She had the feeling that he *could* see, all the way across town, all the way into her bathtub. But that was impossible.

"The reason I'm calling," he said slowly and deliberately, "is that I have the guest list for you. I'll drop it by tomorrow morning."

"But tomorrow's Sunday. I'm not working tomorrow," she protested. "The invitations haven't been delivered yet. So I wouldn't be able to address them anyway." Even as she said the words she felt guilty. If she didn't address invitations, there were other things to do. With the wedding only a month away, she should be working on it every single day. While she hesitated, she knew he'd be within his rights if he reminded her that she owed him big-time for keeping her mother's cat. Maybe he was too polite to do that, but he really didn't have to say a word. She knew she was in his debt. The debt weighed heavily on her shoulders.

"All right," she said. "I'll meet you at my office tomorrow."

"Why don't I come to your house?" he asked. "If you're not going in, it would save you a trip."

Her house. He would come to her house. Was there no place to hide from the sheik? No day to rest up from his presence, to shore up her resistance, to get a break from his relentless dark gaze, his mesmerizing voice and his imperial manner?

She sighed. It meant cleaning the house from top to bottom. And what else? How else to return the hospitality of a sheik? Would she have to prepare tea and cakes? No.

This was America. She would make coffee. Period. Hopefully he'd have something else to do afterward. He'd hand over the list and leave. But meetings with the sheik seldom turned out the way they were planned. They seemed to go on and on. The best way to prevent that was to plan something of her own. But what?

They agreed he'd come by at eleven o'clock the next morning and she hung up. By morning she had it all planned. She'd meet him at the door dressed in spandex shorts and a T-shirt for a run on the Marina Green. Sheiks might ride camels across the desert, they might swim in their own pool every morning, but she felt fairly certain they didn't run for pleasure. She didn't either. Still, she knew it was good for her so she'd bought the right clothes and had all the right intentions, but had never actually gone running on the green. She knew she should go. Not only was it good exercise, it was a great stress reliever. So they said.

The minute he arrived at the door, she knew she'd made a mistake. His gaze raked her up and down, lingering on the tight shorts and the snug T-shirt. But what choice did she have? Appear in a full-length Hawaiian muumuu?

"I…I'm going running," she stammered, unnerved by the look in his eyes.

"You run?" he asked, rocking back on his heels.

"Yes, oh yes. That is, whenever I get a chance." It wasn't an out-and-out lie, it was just that she hadn't ever got a chance. That was the reason she hadn't been running. "I mean it's such a beautiful day so I thought…"

"Then I'll join you," he said.

"You run?" she said, so surprised she almost fell over.

"I ran cross-country in college at Berkeley. I had always been somewhat fleet-footed, but I didn't know it was an organized sport over here. As a foreign student, joining the team was a good way to make friends. It was either that or soccer.''

"Of course." She should have known. There was no escaping him. The only thing that could save her was that he wasn't dressed to run. She didn't say anything, but she glanced pointedly at his tailored slacks and polo shirt with some sort of emblem on the pocket. The royal crest, no doubt.

"I always keep my duffel bag in the car with my Nike running sneakers and shorts," he said. "I never know where and when I'll need them. This is most fortunate. We can talk as we run."

Talk as they ran? Carolyn would barely have enough strength to run, let alone enough breath to run and talk at the same time. Besides, what exactly would they talk about? She shouldn't worry. The sheik always seemed to have something to say. What worried her was that he'd see how slowly she ran.

Reluctantly she invited him in. She might as well. He expected it and she'd spent the morning vacuuming and dusting. He gave her the guest list and accepted her offer of coffee, then proceeded to look around her living room.

"It must seem small to you," she said, setting his cup on the end table. It seemed smaller than ever to her with this broad-shouldered man taking up so much space.

"Small but charming," he said. "Like its owner."

Out of anyone else's mouth it would have sounded phony. But somehow the sheik could get away with it. It might have been the way he looked at her, his gaze so steady, so unwavering. It might have been the serious tone of his voice that said he meant every word. Or did she just want to believe him. In any case, the way he scrutinized her made her cheeks flame.

She looked away hoping he wouldn't notice the effect he had on her, but the sheik noticed everything. Her mind raced, thinking of a way to change the subject. There were so many problems yet to be solved regarding the wedding, but at the moment she couldn't think of a single one. Oh, yes, the gift registry. So she asked him if the couple was registered. He didn't understand the concept until she explained.

"A good idea," he said. "Friends have asked me what to get them for a wedding present. Tell me how to do it, and I'll register them."

"But do you know the couple's taste well enough to choose their china, their glassware and so forth?"

"With your help."

"But I don't know them at all. I've been hoping to meet Mr. Branson, your sister's fiancé. At least..."

"Yes, yes, in good time. For the moment he's out of town on business. In the meantime here's my sister's picture you asked me for. For the newspapers."

"Oh, my, she's beautiful," Carolyn said, looking at a heart-shaped face with huge dark eyes.

"Yes, I believe she is," he said seriously. "Especially her smile. You remind me of her sometimes, your smile and your joie de vivre. She, too, is a romantic, which is why I am so confident the wedding will go off without a hitch with you planning it. She'll be so happy with the arrangements. And the gift selections. Tomorrow would be convenient for me to visit the stores with you and establish these registries you mentioned."

"I thought you were busy working on the merger."

"There is nothing more important than the wedding. Without the wedding there is no merger."

"Doesn't that put a lot of pressure on your sister?" she asked.

"Why should it?" Tarik asked. But when he thought of his last conversation with his sister he had to admit he was concerned. He stood and paced the small room while he spoke. "Royal families are accustomed to pressure. Or they should be. Pressure to succeed. Pressure to do the right thing. We are brought up to accept responsibility and whatever comes with it. Yasmine knows what is expected of her."

But did she? She'd always been headstrong and willful. Now more than ever. Perhaps she did feel the pressure of the impending marriage, and she was reacting in her own way. But when the time came he was sure she would come through and do the right thing. She had to.

"Enough wedding talk," he said. "If I may intrude on your hospitality, I will change into my running clothes in your house."

She was gracious enough to let him use her white-and-black-tiled bathroom to change in. He glanced at the old-fashioned bathtub and imagined Carolyn in it as she was last night when he called. The image of her floating naked in hot water, her breasts breaking the surface caused a flood of red-hot desire to slam into him like a renegade oil derrick. He clenched his jaw in an effort to stop the overwhelming desire for a woman he shouldn't desire at all.

He looked into the mirror and gave himself a stern talking to. Not out loud or she'd hear him. He told himself it was all right to admire her looks. It was only normal. She was beautiful in a wholesome American way. But it was not all right to kiss her no matter how good it felt. The minute he saw her this morning he'd had an overwhelming desire to kiss her again. It was wrong because kissing Carolyn was addictive, and he couldn't afford an addiction of any sort. On the other hand it was all right to admire her talent for wedding planning. To be grateful to her for helping him get through this difficult period. It was all right to spend time with her if the activities were work-related. But where had the line between work and play become blurred?

It had been a long time since Tarik had played at all. That was the problem. Since the death of his father, he'd been immersed in the family business. There had been no time to enjoy life. Now suddenly he seemed to have taken leave of his senses. He'd taken in a cat, temporarily of course, but quite unnecessarily. He'd enjoyed a leisurely restaurant dinner with Carolyn, also unnecessary. Now he was going running on a Sunday when he should be at home working. What happened to his willpower, usually made of iron? How had it failed him?

They walked from her house to the Marina Green. Then after the obligatory stretching, they ran on the paved walkway, with acres of green grass on one side, the sea wall on the other. There was a cool breeze off the bay, and a spectacular view of the Golden Gate Bridge. But the view that captivated him the most was the view of Carolyn running next to him, her hair tossed by the wind, her cheeks pink from exertion and her trim, firm body. He forced himself to look at the Bay and the bridge, but his gaze kept returning to the woman running alongside of him. He slowed his pace so they were side by side.

"Do you come here often?" he asked.

"Yes, whenever I get a chance," Carolyn said, panting. She'd come to sit on the grass and watch the boats on the bay. But not to run. He must realize that by the way she was huffing and puffing. "But not often enough. As you can see, I'm having trouble keeping up with you," she said pressing her hand against her chest. "I should run more often, it's such good exercise, but I get busy at work and I let the job come between me and a fitness routine. Obviously I'm out of shape," she said breathlessly.

"Nonsense, you're in excellent shape," he said, keeping his tone neutral, his eyes straight ahead. Good shape was putting it mildly. Her shape was beyond compare. Just because she was a slow runner didn't mean she wasn't in good condition.

"You are, too," she said politely. He noticed she didn't look at him. She hadn't looked at him since he came out of the bathroom in his shorts and T-shirt when she'd blinked and looked away.

"We must do this more often." There he went again. Inventing more ways to see her. As if they didn't have enough to do. And even after the stern talking-to he'd given himself.

"After I recover. I don't usually run this fast. I had no idea you ran. I'm afraid I'm slowing you down. Of course after the wedding, you'll have time to run more often."

After the wedding. He would have no excuse to see her again. Ever. Which was just as well. She said *I'll* have more time for everything. Not *we*. She knew as well as he that they'd never see each other again. She must be relieved. But he wasn't. He was afraid he'd miss her. Miss sparring with her, miss watching her blush, miss her company.

Maybe he'd come running by himself after the wedding was over. Why not? It was exhilarating, refreshing and good for him. Maybe he'd run into her, quite by accident. But would she be glad to see him? He was afraid not. Afraid he'd demanded too much from her. Too much of her time and her energy. They slowed down, and after another stretch, they headed back to her apartment. One way to get there was to take Union Street where her shop was located. She didn't appear to be in a hurry and he'd quite conveniently forgotten anything he was supposed to be doing.

Union Street was filled with Yuppies shopping at expensive boutiques. When they passed her shop, they stopped to look in the window.

"I almost didn't come in that evening," Tarik said, remembering the sight of all the wedding finery, the acres of sample flower displays, model wedding cakes and honeymoon destination posters. But most of all remembering the sight of Carolyn seated behind her desk, speaking earnestly with her clients, her hair a vibrant copper under the ceiling lights. And then she'd looked up and smiled at him.

"Are you glad you did?" she asked casually, studying the display in the window of her shop as if she'd never seen it before.

"Of course. I could never have done this wedding by myself. I know that now."

"But the city is full of wedding consultants. Why me?"

"You came highly recommended," he said. But it was more than that. It was the moment she looked up from the clients that night and met his gaze. There was something about the way she looked at him that prevented him from following his first inclination, which was to turn and walk away. From going to find another wedding consultant, the kind he was looking for, the one with twenty years of experience and thick ankles.

Once he'd seen Carolyn and she'd smiled at him, he knew he had to have her. As a wedding planner, of course. Nothing more.

"I'm afraid I behaved rather impulsively that evening," he said.

"That's putting it mildly," she said. "I haven't seen those clients since."

"But that's terrible," he said. "I must do something about that. Shall I call them and apologize?"

"No, never mind," she said. "I have too much work to do as it is."

"Then you must allow me to compensate you for the money you lost."

"It's all right," she said.

"No, it isn't. I insist."

"We can discuss it later," she said.

"Over dinner," he suggested. He didn't want the day to end. Didn't want to go back to his huge, lonely house which had never seemed lonely or huge before he'd met her.

She looked startled at the suggestion of dinner. "I can't," she said.

"Why not?" he asked. "Do you have another date?"

"No, no dates," she said and he breathed a sigh of relief. Why? It was none of his business.

"No boyfriend?" he asked. "Or fiancé?" He had to know. If she was attached he wanted to know now.

She shook her head.

He stifled the urge to ask why not. It was none of his business and she might be offended.

"Well, if you won't let me buy you dinner, let's at least stop for a drink. If only to replace the fluids we lost while running."

Before she could say no, he steered her into the next sidewalk-front café. They sat opposite each other across a small wrought-iron table. He ordered an iced coffee, she ordered an Italian soda. The sun warmed his back and turned her hair to flame. He leaned back in his chair, as if afraid he'd be burned, and studied her face. The urge to ask was overwhelming.

"May I ask why not?" he asked. "Why doesn't a woman like you have a boyfriend or a fiancé?"

Again the color tinted her cheeks. She obviously didn't receive enough compliments to become accustomed to them.

"It's the nature of my job," she said. "The only men I meet are already taken. My mother thinks I should find a different job where I'd meet more men."

"What would that be?" he asked.

"I suppose I could join the army, or become a telephone line repairman."

He smiled at the image of Carolyn in camouflage or a hard hat at the top of a telephone pole. "That sounds rather drastic."

"Not as drastic as moving to Alaska. That was her other idea."

"I thought Alaska was full of polar bears and ice caps," he said.

"Polar bears and ice caps and bachelors. The odds of men to women are twenty-five to one, I understand," she said.

The idea of Carolyn besieged by twenty-five men was a disturbing one. He hoped she wasn't taking her mother's suggestions seriously. "But you'd have to leave your charming shop. You obviously like what you do and everyone says you're good at it."

"I've always loved it," she said a bit wistfully. "It's a rewarding job, making people's dreams come true."

He leaned back in his chair and observed her thoughtfully. "What about *your* dreams?" he asked. "How will you make them come true?"

Chapter Six

"Come now," he said after a long silence. "Don't tell me you have no dreams. Everyone wants something they don't have."

"Do you?"

"The merger and the wedding. The wedding and the merger," he said.

"In a few weeks you'll have those things."

"If all goes well," he murmured.

"Why wouldn't it?"

He shrugged. He couldn't tell Carolyn about his sister. About the worries that kept him awake at night that she would back out of the wedding. Talking about it with her would solve nothing. He must try to think positively. "There are loose ends," he admitted. Loose ends—to say the least. "You didn't answer my question. What do you want? What about marriage and a family? Wouldn't you like to be planning your own wedding instead of those of others?"

"Yes, of course, some day. But as I explained, it's rather hard to find Mr. Right in my line of work. And I'm not going to change jobs or move to the frozen North to find him."

"Perhaps he'll find you."

She nodded but she didn't look convinced. Instead she pulled a flyer from her back pocket. "Here's something for you," she said, handing it to him. On the glossy pages were photos of thatched-roof cottages on a blue-green lagoon. Smiling local women in native costume offered tropical drinks to tourists in hammocks.

"Ah," he said. "The honeymoon. Yes, I can picture you there." He could picture her only too well. Her shapely body clad in only a bolt of flowered material knotted at the waist. The image made his heart feel like someone had kick-started it.

"Not me," she said. "Your sister and her husband. Is it suitable for their honeymoon? Do you think they'd like it there?"

"Would you?" he asked.

"Yes."

"Then make the reservations."

"All right. Now I really must be getting back," she said. This time they walked briskly and said goodbye at the door.

From her third floor window, Carolyn watched Tarik pull away in his car. She was glad she was alone at last. Every muscle in her body ached, though she wouldn't have admitted it to him for the world. She would admit that running and talking at the same time with Tarik had been invigorating and not as hard as she'd imagined. She'd been keyed up, adrenaline flowing, enjoying the fresh air, the beautiful views across the bay and yes, watching Tarik run so smoothly, so effortlessly. But that was then, this was now. She glanced across the room and saw his forgotten sweater. She groaned. How could she have neglected to give it to him?

She could have avoided this whole encounter if only she hadn't made up the story about going out for a run. By doing so she'd found out more about Tarik—more than she'd wanted to know. She had to admit he was an amazing person. When she heard him say he'd run cross-country at college she couldn't believe it. It was too late to say she was off to play basketball instead. Knowing him, he'd probably played basketball in his former life as well. No wonder the man had such a well-developed body. He was an athlete. Along with being a businessman. It served her right for trying to put one over on him. It never worked.

Her stomach growled. Reminding her she could have been dining with Tarik instead of facing an empty stomach and an empty refrigerator. But having another dinner with Tarik was not a good idea. She had the distinct feeling he wanted more than just the planning of the wedding. The looks he gave her. The questions he asked her. The remarks he made. Or were they just part of the sheik's repertoire? Just something all sheiks learn at the mother's knee? How would she know? She'd never met another sheik, and she'd never meet another one, that was for sure.

So she'd dine on peanut butter on crackers and soak her tired and aching body in a hot tub. And this time she would not answer the phone. And she would not feel sorry for herself. It was her decision to eat crackers instead of rare rack of lamb at some wonderful restaurant where the waiter hovered over the sheik because that's just what people did around him. That's what made him so insufferable, he was used to servants fawning over him.

That wasn't fair. She knew it. He was not really insufferable as she'd first thought. She was just trying to talk herself out of this infatuation with the sheik. She was seeing too much of him. To be fair, she had to admit his housekeeper Meera didn't appear to fawn over him. Just the opposite. And though he was oozing with self-confidence, he wasn't above hauling equipment into his garden and allowing a stranger's pet into his home.

Why shouldn't he be self-confident? she asked herself as she dragged her body into the kitchen to rummage through the refrigerator for a can of diet cola. She munched on a stale cracker as she toted up his accomplishments. He ran, he swam, he ran a huge company and what else? She didn't want to know. She just didn't want to succumb to his charms.

At first she thought he had no charms. But that wasn't quite true. At least according to her partner Lily and her mother. But what did they know? They weren't spending the major portion of their days and evenings with the sheik as she was. She was glad to have the evening off. Glad to be alone in her apartment with nothing to eat. Of course she was. She'd see the sheik tomorrow when they went to sign up his sister at a gift registry. She knew she must have other things to do tomorrow for the other upcoming weddings on her schedule, but for the life of her all she could think of was Tarik and his sister's wedding. This was not good.

Before she stepped into the bathtub she carefully turned off all her phones. But as she lay soaking in the hot water, she wondered if he was trying to call her, and if not, why not? Uh-oh. She was losing it.

She went into the office early the next day to get organized and to try to pull herself together. She made calls, but no one was in. She made lists of things to do and realized she was dreadfully far behind on everything, including some major items on Tarik's sister's wedding. She thought of calling him to ask about the rehearsal dinner, the band, the dress and the bridesmaids, but she didn't. He'd probably be in his pool right now. She closed her eyes to try to forget how he looked in his swimsuit, but the image wouldn't go away.

Fortunately Lily came in. Carolyn was grateful for the distraction, but unfortunately Lily only wanted to talk about the sheik.

"What's new with the sheik's wedding?" she asked.

"The sheik's *sister's* wedding," Carolyn reminded her. "I'm worried. This is the strangest wedding I've ever planned."

"Stranger than the circus clowns who got married under the big top, stranger than the bride who carried her tiny Lhasa apso down the aisle instead of a bouquet?"

Carolyn sighed. "Those were pretty strange, but at least the bride was around. I feel like I'm operating in the dark here."

"What about the sheik?" Lily asked. "Isn't he being helpful?"

"If you call taking up my weekends being helpful, I guess so," she admitted. "If you call providing room and board for my mother's new cat, I guess so. But as for the wedding…"

"Wait a minute," Lily said. "Back up. I'm lost."

Carolyn had to recap the weekend for Lily. Lily's eyes widened and she shook her head in amazement. "The whole weekend," Lily said. "You spent the whole weekend with this man, and it doesn't sound like it was all business." She gave her partner a knowing look that Carolyn tried to ignore. "What's going on here with you two?" she asked.

"Nothing," Carolyn said. "So don't look at me that way. The only thing that's going on is I'm planning a wedding for a bride and groom I've never met. Which has created certain special problems," Carolyn said, standing and walking back and forth between the display of model wedding cakes and stacks of fashion books. "Instead of helping me out, the sheik is a distraction. I'm way behind on this wedding. What was I thinking?" She raked her hand through her curls. "I never should have agreed to do a wedding in a month. Do you know I don't even have the invitations out yet."

Before Lily could answer, the phone rang. Carolyn let Lily answer though she knew, somehow she just knew, who it would be. Lily held the phone out.

"It's for you," she said.

Carolyn's heart started beating way too fast because of a simple phone call. She took a deep breath and told herself to calm down.

"I thought we should get an early start," Tarik said after he wished her good morning.

"I have a list of things to do," she said, going back to her desk.

"So do I," he said, "have things for us to do. That will last all day. The first is breakfast."

"I've already eaten," she lied. There was no way she was going to start off the day, start off the week with breakfast with the sheik. Dinner had been bad enough. The way he'd looked at her across the table. Making her feel special, like she was his date. As if he'd be dating a bridal consultant. As if he'd be dating anyone at all. But breakfast would be worse. There was something more intimate about break-

fast. Something you don't do with a business client. Breakfast should be shared with someone you cared about. Someone you had feelings for.

Maybe the sheik was lonely. Maybe that's why he'd offered to take the cat. That's why he was inventing reasons
to see her. But she wasn't lonely. She had her mother. She
had her friends. And she had her job. A job she loved, she
reminded herself. A job that required her full attention.
Now.

She had to avoid any more meals with the sheik, as well
as unnecessary meetings. There were enough things they
had to do together without adding more. She ended up
agreeing he'd pick her up at ten, and they'd see how much
of a dent they could put in their respective lists starting
with the wedding invitations and moving on to the department stores.

When she hung up, Carolyn stared out the window, reminding herself this was a man who put business first, who
didn't believe in love and if he ever did get married, he'd
marry someone who had connections or would help him in
his business or someone chosen by his family. Though, in
his family, it seemed as if he was the one doing the choosing.

"Carolyn, Carolyn..." Lily said. "No need to ask who
that was. I swear, the man has cast a spell over you. I can
see why. He's gorgeous, rich and he's coming on to you
like gangbusters."

Carolyn snapped out of her reverie. "No, he isn't.
You've got it all wrong."

"Don't tell me it's all business. I don't believe you. I've
seen you handle the most difficult weddings without losing
your cool. This is something different."

"You think I've lost my cool?" Carolyn asked incredulously.

"Some of it. And I think you're in danger of losing it all. Completely."

Fortunately there was another call, this time for Lily, that cut off any further conversation. Because this was an argument Carolyn knew she couldn't win. What Lily didn't know was that just the sound of Tarik's voice had the power to make Carolyn lose her cool. Of course she always got it back. In time. At least so far.

The next call was from her mother asking if she'd come for dinner that night. She said yes immediately. She'd have the perfect excuse if Tarik suggested dinner. Not that it was likely. After a day of running errands with her, he'd most likely be tired of her by tonight. But would she be tired of him? That was the question.

Their first stop was to pick up the invitations, the second was to bring them to Tarik's office on the top floor of the Wells Building where his secretary would address them. Carolyn knew he was rich. She knew he was important, but she still wasn't prepared for Tarik's office with its spectacular wraparound views of the city. His desk was almost as large as her kitchen. His staff as large as a battle regiment. She imagined he probably treated his employees like soldiers, too, giving orders the way he had the first night she met him.

As soon as he appeared he was deluged with messages and besieged by people waiting to see him. He left Carolyn with his smartly dressed, fifty-something, gray-haired secretary while he went to see someone.

"I won't be long," he said with a backward glance over his shoulder.

"It must be a great job being a wedding consultant," the secretary said as she set the invitations and the guest list on her desk. "Tarik says you're the best."

"You call him Tarik?" Carolyn asked, surprised.

"Oh, yes. I've been with him for years. And it's very casual around here. Especially since his father died." She glanced up at a portrait of the old sheik in ceremonial dress. Carolyn decided this picture was even more impressive than the one in Tarik's library at his house.

"The atmosphere changed," his secretary continued, "and Tarik has put his own stamp on the company. Even though he's a sheik, you'd never know it. He's a great boss. Very thoughtful. He never asks you to stay longer than he does, or to do anything he wouldn't do himself. So I can't complain."

You'd better not complain, Carolyn thought. *Not if you want to keep your job.* Still the woman's praise seemed genuine.

"When he got us together we all hoped it was his engagement he was announcing."

Carolyn bit her tongue to keep from telling her that Tarik would never marry unless it was financially advantageous. Unless he found a wife he could dominate completely. Surely this secretary who knew him so well knew that. Or had he fooled her? No, he would only marry if it helped the company, his country or his family. He didn't believe in love, he believed marriage was a duty. If she'd been with Tarik for such a long time, she must know that. If she didn't, it wasn't up to Carolyn to tell her.

"It's time for him to settle down," the secretary said. "If his father was here…"

"I suppose his father would arrange something for him," Carolyn said.

''I think his father stopped arranging things for Tarik after he interfered the first time. But he'd certainly encourage him to find someone suitable. To look a little harder. But he's not the type to drop everything and pursue some woman, especially after what happened.''

Carolyn waited, hoping she'd go on and say what had happened, but Tarik came back and they left. There were still messages piled on his desk, his voice mail was overflowing and a line of people were waiting to see him. But Tarik said the wedding came first. Carolyn couldn't argue with that.

An hour later, the two of them stood in the middle of the fine china and glassware department of Gumps, the elegant store just off Union Square with a helpful clerk, clipboard in hand, by their side. The shapes and patterns, the dazzling array of beautiful place settings on tables were just a blur to Tarik. Fortunately Carolyn seemed to know what questions to ask. Unfortunately he didn't know the answers.

What were his sister's favorite colors?

How many place settings did she want?

Everyday dishes?

What pattern of silver?

He preferred looking at Carolyn instead of silverware. He could tell she was concentrating on the many choices by the way she drew her eyebrows together and bit her lower lip.

''Which one?'' she asked, holding up a tray of teaspoons.

He forced himself to look. ''That one.''

She nodded. ''I like that one, too.''

They proceeded on to candlesticks, goblets and juice glasses, then dinner plates and stainless steel flatware. Fortunately, they agreed on every one.

The clerk beamed at them. "I've never met a couple who had the exact same taste before," she said.

Carolyn opened her mouth to explain they weren't a couple, but the facts were so strange and unusual she decided not to.

"You have no idea," the clerk continued, "how many couples argue over every little thing. I sometimes wonder how they're ever going to make it through life. Now you two seem perfectly suited. I wish you every happiness."

"You've been very helpful," Carolyn said quickly. It was either that or tell her *they* weren't getting married, it wasn't *their* wedding and these weren't *their* gifts. As far as every happiness…that was another matter.

Out on the street, Tarik put his hand on her elbow protectively. Instead of protesting, she gave in and let him guide her across the street. He must know by now she was not a fragile flower who couldn't take care of herself. So why remind him? She decided to relax and let him play the gallant role he was so good at.

"It is remarkable," he said as they crossed the street to the parking garage, "how similar our tastes are."

"I guess it is," she said, "considering we're complete opposites. I just hope we've chosen the right things."

"Don't worry," he said. But she did. She worried about his sister's reaction to the reception, the honeymoon, the gifts and the dress—to the whole darn wedding that had been planned without her.

"Have you heard from your sister lately?" she asked.

He frowned. "No. It's hard to get in touch with her because of the time difference. Either she's asleep or in class or…" He didn't finish his sentence. Carolyn had the feeling he was holding back information about his sister. Something she might want to know. "She has her plane ticket.

She'll be here on time," he said. But there was a look in his eyes that belied his confident words. Carolyn stifled the urge to ask, *but what if she isn't?*

They got a lot done that day, but not enough. There was still so much more. It had been a good day. A busy day. They'd had lunch on the run, hot dogs from a stand on a street corner.

"These are delicious," Tarik pronounced with surprise.

"You've never had a hot dog?" she asked. "You went to college here, didn't you?"

"Yes, but I lived with friends from my country. We had a cook."

"I should have known," she murmured. "What about pizza, tacos, donuts?"

"Of course. I've tried them all. I haven't been living in a cave, you know." He cocked his head and studied her face. "Hold still," he said and reached over to run his thumb over her lower lip.

She felt as though he'd touched a live wire somewhere inside her. Every nerve ending went on alert. It was just his thumb. It was just her lip. But her body told her it was more than that.

"Just a trace of mustard," he explained matter-of-factly. But there was nothing matter-of-fact about the look in his eyes. Lunchtime crowds swirled around them on the corner of Sutter and Stockton Streets. She didn't see or hear them. All she saw was Tarik. When he took his hand away she gave a soft sigh of regret.

But that was five hours ago. They'd been busy every minute since. She looked at her watch and told Tarik she had to go. He said he did, too. She was relieved he didn't ask her to dinner. Relieved, but also a little disappointed.

Had he given up on her? Did he have a date? He didn't say.

She changed into comfortable drawstring Capri pants and an oversized white cotton shirt and drove to her mother's. Before she left she put Tarik's sweater on the table next to the door. She'd forgotten to return it today. She resolved to give it back to him the next time she saw him, which would be the day after next when they went to the bridal salon to look for the dress. Until then it would stay there, reminding her of how he'd wrapped it around her shoulders to keep her warm. Reminding her to return it.

There were delicious odors coming from her mother's kitchen. Mavis was a great cook due to years in the kitchen experimenting with recipes that would please her demanding husband. It smelled like *boeuf bourguignon* tonight. Her mother's eyes were sparkling. Her face was flushed with the heat from the stove.

"Have a good day?" her mother asked.

"Fine. I spent the whole day on Tarik's sister's wedding. But we got a lot done. The china is chosen, the invitations..." Out of the corner of her eye, Carolyn saw the small dining table was decorated with candles and flowers and set for three. "Who's coming to dinner?" she asked, truly puzzled.

"Didn't he tell you?" Mavis asked.

Carolyn took a deep breath. "You don't mean..." Her mother wouldn't invite him, would she?

The doorbell rang. A minute later Tarik appeared in the doorway, wearing immaculately pressed slacks, a polo shirt with another hand-knit Irish wool sweater over his shoulders. He smiled and handed her mother a bouquet of flowers. Her heart banged against her ribs. If only someone had told her she could have prepared. Somehow.

"Mother," Carolyn said under her breath. "You didn't."

Chapter Seven

"Why didn't you tell me you were coming here to dinner?" Carolyn asked Tarik after her mother had poured two glasses of sparkling apple juice for them, then excused herself to return to the kitchen.

"I thought you knew," he said blandly.

"No, I didn't."

"This is a nice place," he said looking around at the homey furnishings accumulated over a lifetime. "Your mother has excellent taste. As do you."

"You say that because as the saleswoman said today, we have the same taste."

"There is that," he conceded with a wry smile.

"Why are you here?" Carolyn asked.

"Because your mother invited me," he said, sipping his juice slowly. "I'm grateful for the opportunity to have a home-cooked meal."

"What about Meera?"

"She doesn't like to cook so she calls herself a housekeeper."

"Oh," she said. Who would have imagined the sheik would want a home-cooked meal when he could afford to dine anywhere he wanted every night. It made her feel guilty for not inviting him herself. As well as turning his invitation down to dine with him last night.

"Well," she said, uneasy with the sight of the sheik so at home in her mother's armchair, "I'll just go see if my mother needs any help."

She closed the kitchen door behind her. "How could you?" she asked her mother.

"How could I not?" her mother asked, giving the French stew a stir with a ladle. "The man has taken in my cat. I've tried to pay him, but he won't hear of it. I mentioned dinner and Carolyn dear, he positively jumped at the chance. Of course that may have had nothing to do with my cooking and everything to do with your coming to-night."

"This is so embarrassing," Carolyn said, running her fingers through her hair. If she'd known, she would have dressed more carefully. Painted her nails… No. He'd seen her windblown and frazzled. There was no point trying to fool him. Or impress him. "What if he thinks I put you up to it? That I told you to invite both of us to dinner?"

"I'm sure he doesn't think anything of the sort." Her mother looked shocked at the very idea. "Especially after seeing the look on your face when he walked in the door. Now, could you take the rolls out of the oven while I toss the salad?"

The dinner went more smoothly than Carolyn could have imagined. They talked about everything from her mother's cat, who was doing fine, to customs and food in his country, which were fascinating, to his and her favorite vacations. One of hers was on the Russian River where as a child she'd paddled a canoe under low-hanging branches and swam in fresh, cold river water. Which prompted Mavis to clear the table and get her photo album from the bedroom.

"Mother, I'm sure Tarik doesn't want to see a lot of pictures of our family," Carolyn said, shooting her mother a desperate look. There was nothing more boring than being subjected to someone's family pictures.

"But I do," he said.

"They aren't that interesting," she said, fidgeting with her napkin in her lap. She'd gotten through the evening so far without embarrassment, but this was going too far. They sat in silence until her mother returned, put the album on the table and retreated to the kitchen to make coffee. Tarik moved his chair next to hers. His arm brushed against hers. She should have moved away, even an inch or two would have done the trick, but she didn't want to. The warmth of his body, the smell of the natural wool of his sweater and the soothing aftereffect of a delicious dinner made her feel warm and contented and on edge at the same time.

On edge because she didn't know what he was going to do next. Probably he'd just look at the pictures. He'd make polite comments because he had to and then he'd go home. But what if she leaned against him and put her head on his shoulder? The thought was tempting. His shoulder was so close, so big and so strong. If she did, would he put his arm around her and hold her tight? Would she bury her face in his sweater? Would he even kiss her again? No, of course not. The first time was only because they were play-acting in the church. A kiss was required.

She flipped the pages of the album, but he forced her to slow down, asking reams of questions about the house they lived in, the friends and relatives. He paused at a picture of her in a formal dress taken at a dance.

"You look lovely," he said, staring transfixed at the picture.

She covered her embarrassment by getting up to refill his glass. When she returned he was staring at a picture of a young Carolyn wearing braces. She tried to turn the page, but he put his hand over hers and held it there. Then he turned to look at her straight teeth. Or was he looking at her mouth?

She wondered if he thought about kissing her again the way she thought about it every few minutes. But apparently he really was only interested in observing her teeth. "Those wires on your teeth worked," he said. "You have perfect teeth. And a beautiful smile."

She took her hand from his. "Thank you," she said.

On the next page there was a picture of her father.

"He doesn't look so bad," Tarik said.

"You don't know him," Carolyn said.

"Does your mother keep in touch with him?"

"Oh, yes. She says he's much better now. He appreciates all the things she did for him. Like giving up the best years of her life to wait on him hand and foot." She realized a bitter tone had crept into her voice. "They didn't get a divorce until I went to college. She should have done it years earlier."

"It sounds like she's forgiven him," Tarik remarked.

"She has, but I haven't," she said flatly.

She felt Tarik's eyes on her, his unspoken questions hanging in the air.

If your mother has, why can't you forgive and forget?

Why keep him out of your life?

What did he do that was so terrible?

She didn't want to talk about it, so she was glad he didn't ask the questions out loud. She closed the album. Her

mother came in with the coffee and an inquisitive look on
her face. If she thought this was a good idea throwing her
daughter at a wealthy sheik, she was mistaken. Carolyn had
half a mind to tell her Tarik's views on love and marriage
as soon as he left. But she didn't get a chance. Her mother
told Tarik she was on the trail of a new apartment and
thanked him again for keeping her cat. Then she brushed
off Carolyn's offer to help clean up and Carolyn left at the
same time Tarik did.

"Do you know how rare that was?" he asked as he
walked her to her car. She'd given up protesting his over-
protectiveness. She decided against telling him it was a safe
neighborhood and she was unlikely to be attacked in front
of her mother's building. It wouldn't change his ways. And
just possibly there was something about his attitude that
made her feel safe and secure. Maybe she was starting to
enjoy being looked after. Which was a scary idea. What
would happen when he wasn't around? Would she be nervous alone on the street at night? Heaven help her!

"What was rare?" she asked, realizing he was waiting
for an answer to his question.

"Sharing dinner with a family. I've never been invited
to an American home before."

"Really? Maybe people think that you dine on pheasant
under glass every night, and they don't dare invite you to
their humble abode to share an ordinary dinner."

"There was nothing humble about your mother's abode
or ordinary about that dinner. Did your mother teach you
to cook as well?"

She wondered if that was a hint. If he wanted to be
invited to her place next. Better let him know that was not
likely.

"Actually I don't really cook much. I get something to

eat on Union Street then I usually go back to work in the evening,'' she said. ''Why don't you hire a cook?''

He shrugged. ''It seems a waste to cook for one person.''

''Exactly,'' she said. ''Good night, Tarik.''

He put his hands on her shoulders and before she could duck or turn her head he kissed her, cutting off the light from the streetlight and cutting off all rational thought. She thought she'd be prepared for his next kiss, she thought she could handle it. But she couldn't. She felt her knees buckle. He caught her and held her tight against her body.

He slid his tongue between her lips, and she moaned in the back of her throat. She supposed the whole neighborhood could hear her but she didn't care. All she cared about was Tarik. All she wanted was for him to continue his barrage against her senses.

When he finally pulled away she was dazed and aching for more. She wrapped her arms around her waist.

''I've been wanting to do that all day,'' he said in a rough voice. ''I couldn't let you go until I had.'' He took the keys from her icy fingers and opened her car door. ''Drive safely,'' he said as she slid into the driver's seat.

She nodded, unable to speak. As she glanced up at her mother's window she thought she saw the curtain move. How was she going to explain this? How many people had seen her kiss a sheik on the sidewalk? Just one was enough. Especially if that one person was her mother.

When she got home she had a message from her mother waiting on her machine. She just knew what she was going to say. She could imagine her glee at having thrown her daughter to a bonafide sheik then watching while they kissed in front of her building. But her message had nothing to do with the kiss. It had to do with a missing photo from her album.

"It's the one of you at your first prom. Did you take it?" her mother asked.

"No, of course not. It probably fell out of the book, and it's on the floor somewhere," Carolyn said.

"Probably," her mother said.

But Carolyn knew what had happened and so did her mother. Why didn't he ask if he wanted the photo? "I don't know, maybe Tarik took it for some reason. I told you that was what he was like. He's used to getting what he wants. So it's just possible that he took it," she said.

She was annoyed. She was flattered. Why did he take the picture? It was old. She was young in it. She didn't really look like that anymore. And what was she going to say about it? Nothing. It was best to say nothing. Pretend it never happened. Maybe it hadn't. Maybe the photo really had fallen on the floor.

"Never mind," Carolyn said. "It doesn't matter."

The next day Tarik called to say there was an emergency at one of their oil fields. They'd had to shut down because of a breakdown of some equipment and he was flying back home. She gripped the phone so tightly her knuckles turned white. She didn't say anything, but the questions swirled around in her head.

How long will you be gone?

What about the wedding?

How will you fix the problem?

What if you don't come back?

"I don't know how long I'll be gone," he said, as if he'd read her thoughts. "But I know you'll carry on with the preparations without me."

"Of course. No problem," she said. A wedding consultant is always prepared for emergencies. A wedding consultant must remain calm while all around her are losing their heads. But there was a problem. There was more than one problem. There were dozens. Of course she could make the selection of a dress and a band and flowers and the rings by herself, but she didn't want that much responsibility. It was bad enough doing it without the bride and groom. But doing it without the brother of the bride was daunting. But what could she say? Don't go. Stay here. Let the oil wells take care of themselves? Obviously not.

He asked her to tell her mother that Meera would feed the cat, and then he said goodbye. Carolyn stared at the phone for a long moment before she called him back and offered to take him to the airport. Of course he'd probably say he'd call a taxi. But he didn't. He accepted immediately and seemed genuinely touched by her offer.

"That was very thoughtful of you," he said, when she pulled up in front of his house. He lifted his small valise into the trunk of her compact car. "I could have called a cab."

Thoughtful? If she'd been thinking she would have let him go in the taxi. She needed a break from him. The longer the better. Especially after that kiss last night. Now her heart was pounding and her hands were frigid. Nerves. He made her nervous. Besides, she had work to do.

"Sometimes the taxis aren't reliable," she explained. More to herself than to him.

"This is more efficient," he said. "And more pleasant. I never know what to say to taxi drivers. Whereas I always have something to say to you." He smiled, and she felt as if the sun had broken through a cloud.

She was going to miss him. Despite what she told her mother, despite the fact that this relationship was going nowhere, she felt the attraction and so did he. She told herself that opposites attract. But if they were opposites, what about their having the same taste? She told herself he was getting to be a habit. Because of the rush job they were doing, they'd been together almost constantly since he'd first walked into her shop.

"I must apologize for kissing you last night," he said.

She swerved to avoid a cyclist who came out of nowhere. She told herself to concentrate on the road and not on the passenger.

"The street is not the proper place to kiss," he added.

"I don't think anyone objected," she said.

"Not even you?" he asked.

"I found it enjoyable," she said primly, purposely repeating his comment after the kiss in the church.

"Is that all?" he asked.

She didn't know what to say to that. She could hardly tell him it was thrilling, exciting and memorable. Surely he knew that by the way she'd reacted. If she told him, it would go right to his head.

"I can't afford to get involved with a man like you," she said, fixing her eyes on the road ahead. "We come from two different worlds." She didn't say that his world seemed exotic and fascinating to her. That it made her world seem ordinary and humdrum.

"What kind of man are you looking for?" he asked.

"I'm looking for someone who respects me, who considers me his equal, who shares my values and my goals."

"Who will love, honor and obey you, I know," he said.

"I'm sorry, I mean cherish."

"That's right."

"You don't have to tell me what you're looking for," she said. "Someone to obey you but not love you because you don't believe in love." She glanced at his profile, at his stubborn jaw, proud nose and high cheekbones. She wondered if he'd deny it. He didn't.

"I'm much too busy to look for a wife," he said. "Perhaps I should have allowed my father to find me one as he offered. One with a similar background and one who shares my values and goals. I didn't do a very good job of finding my own."

She remembered his secretary saying *after what happened...* She wondered if she'd ever find out what did happen.

"Did you try?" she asked.

A long silence. Finally he spoke. He spoke slowly, choosing his words carefully and deliberately. "There was a young woman at my university. Very beautiful, very intelligent, very American. I thought I was in love with her. Now I know it wasn't love at all. It was only infatuation. My father saw it. He knew it. He warned me that a marriage of the heart would never work for someone like me. A sheik must marry out of duty, not love. I didn't listen. I thought I knew everything. The arrogance of youth. It turns out my father was right. I gave up everything for her and then she turned around and broke off our engagement. I never spoke of it and my father never said a word, but he knew. Of course he knew." Tarik's voice dropped to where she could barely hear him.

"I'm sorry," she said. She had the feeling the girl broke off more than their engagement. She'd broken his heart too. Carolyn wanted to reach over to touch him, but she didn't dare.

At the airport she let him out at the curb. Before he got out he leaned over and kissed her. A brief brush of the lips. Nothing to get excited about. It meant nothing. Only goodbye. But all the way back to her office, she felt his lips on hers. All the way back she thought she could hear him say what he'd never admit, that his former fiancée had broken his heart. He never said that it still hurt. But she knew it did. It was there in his voice.

When she got back to the office, her mother called. She didn't tell her she'd taken Tarik to the airport. That would give her mother the wrong idea. As it was, her mother was far too excited about him. She called to say that Tarik had sent her a bouquet of flowers with a thank-you note for the dinner.

"What manners," her mother said. "He's too good to be true. He'd be quite a catch for some lucky girl. Aren't you glad you didn't go to Alaska to find a man? There probably aren't any sheiks up there."

Carolyn groaned. "Maybe I should have. I'm not looking for a sheik, you know. Just an average, all-American Joe. If and when I do get married, it will be to someone who's sweet and kind and who's looking for a partner instead of a servant."

"Maybe I'm wrong," her mother said, "but if a sheik is looking for a servant, I'm pretty sure he'd hire one. I don't know what your sheik is looking for, I only know what I saw."

Did that remark refer to the embrace on the street in front of her apartment? Carolyn didn't want to ask. Didn't want to hear the glee in her mother's voice. Didn't want to hear her say I told you so. She said goodbye and went back to work. Tried to go back to work. But she'd been working on Yasmine's wedding so intensively she forgot what else she had to do. She could continue to work on the wedding, but it wouldn't be easy and maybe Tarik would be back in a few days. She could only hope. For the sake of the wedding plans of course.

But after a week spent trying to focus on other jobs, she kept thinking about him. Remembering how his kiss had caused her to forget where she was, forget that he was the last man she wanted to get involved with, manners or no manners. Remembering the things he'd said, the picture of his house on the sea and the way he looked in his running shorts.

Even Lily noticed Carolyn was distracted.

"You've been staring at that picture of wedding dresses for a half-hour," Lily noted one morning.

"What? Yes, I know," Carolyn said, closing the most recent issue of *Bride Magazine*. "I don't know what to do. How would you like to pick out a dress for a bride you don't know, never even seen?"

Lily shook her head. "Impossible, I'd say."

"Impossible, but necessary. Tarik claims his sister has no time to choose her own dress. Does that sound right to you?"

"Never heard of a bride that busy. But there's a first for everything. First time you've ever met a sheik, right?"

"And the last I hope." One sheik was enough in anyone's life.

Lily nodded as if she agreed, but Carolyn was afraid she didn't realize the effect the sheik had had on her.

"Seems kind of quiet around here without him popping in or calling. Don't you miss him?" Lily asked.

Miss him? Carolyn didn't want to admit how long the days seemed, how boring life was without him and how often she thought about him. "A little," she said. "But that's normal considering how much time I was spending with him. Only because of the wedding, of course."

"Of course."

Carolyn got up from her desk and grabbed her jacket.

"I'm going to the florist. At least I can pick out the flowers by myself. I don't think he'll mind. I just hope he likes hydrangeas, roses and amaryllis as much as I do. It's the strangest thing, the sheik and I have pretty much the same taste. So far anyway."

"Hmmm, that is strange considering how different you are. Although I think you exaggerate a wee bit," Lily said. "From your description I was expecting an ogre."

"Well? Didn't you see how he insisted he come along with me that day? He dragged me all over town on errands we could have done by phone. Then forced me to have dinner with him."

Lily bit back a smile. "Forced you to have dinner at the St. Francis Hotel? Oh, I feel for you. How mean can a sheik get?"

"That's not all," Carolyn said, ignoring her partner's remarks. "Then he insisted on taking in my mother's new cat."

"No wonder you're upset. No wonder you can't concentrate. No wonder he's driving you crazy."

Carolyn paused on her way out the door and surveyed her partner. "I'm no stranger to your sarcasm, Lily, and I know what you're trying to say. Okay, I admit I might be overreacting. But I'm telling you, I'm just glad it isn't the sheik who's getting married."

"Right," Lily said with a long look at Carolyn. "Not yet anyway. What if he meets someone while he's back in his country?"

Carolyn's heart lurched. What if he did? What if he met someone submissive and obedient, who wouldn't object to promising to obey him? Someone with similar values and goals. "Then I guess I'd be planning his wedding next," Carolyn said lightly. But she wouldn't. She couldn't.

Though she would wish him happiness, she would never be able to watch him marry someone else.

She waved goodbye to Lily and had just closed the door to the shop when she heard Lily frantically calling her name.

"Telephone," she yelled. "It's him."

Back in the office, Carolyn picked up the phone at her desk. Lily's words rang in her ears. What if he meets someone while he's back in his country? What if that was why he was calling?

But it wasn't. He only wanted to tell her he was returning at the end of the week. She heaved a sigh of relief.

"I'm glad," she said. "Because there's so much I can't do without you—for the wedding I mean. I'll pick you up at the airport," she said before she thought about it. She only thought that he might be glad to see her, as glad as she was to see him. He might kiss her again. She was so restless she went out to buy a cup of coffee instead of going to the florist. But when she got back she couldn't sit still. She paced back and forth at the window.

What would Tarik say when she reported she'd accomplished practically nothing on his sister's wedding? That she'd accomplished practically nothing period. She didn't know what was wrong with her or how she'd ever get back to normal. All she knew was she was counting the minutes until his return.

Tarik hung up the phone and went back to the massive power plant his father had built a long time ago when they first began drilling for oil in the hot desert sun. He remembered his father taking him to the construction site as a child, sitting on his father's shoulders and wearing an adult-size hard hat. How proud he'd been that his father was in charge of this massive project. How he knew even then that he was expected to fill his father's shoes one day. To fulfill his father's dream of finding a way to refine and distribute the oil from this country. Now that dream was about to be realized.

He wondered who would take over for him some day? So far there was no heir apparent to ride on his shoulders, and it didn't look as if there would be unless he did something about it. But what? After a week here, he knew he could no longer marry a woman from his country. He'd been away too long. However prominent, rich and well-connected she was, he no longer had much in common with a woman like that. For years he'd straddled two cultures, one foot in the United States and one foot in the Middle East. But now he realized he was more American than anything else. It made sense to marry an American woman. To have children with her. To carry them on his shoulders. To instill a sense of responsibility in them. To raise them. To love them.

But where and how? He had a house in San Francisco and the U.S. headquarters of the family business was there. He couldn't imagine living and working anywhere else. Other relatives would run the company from here in the desert. They didn't have the experience yet to fix problems like the one he'd just repaired, but they would.

Now that he was finished, he could go home. When exactly had America become his home? In the past he'd always thought of this country, the country of his ancestors as his home. That was no longer true. The house on the cliff in the city by the bay seemed more like home, and he was looking forward to going there. Did it have something to do with the woman who would meet him at the airport?

He couldn't deny that he'd been thinking of her often.

What would happen if he became involved with her? Wasn't it too late to ask that question? Wasn't he already involved? He had no father to warn him this time. He had only the voice inside his head to tell him to forget her. That she was wrong for him. She was emotional and romantic. Anyone with her job would be. But that voice was strangely silent about that. His head was full of images of her.

He wasn't thinking clearly. It was the heat, the blazing sun shining on his head. When he got back and got Yasmine married off he'd turn his attention to his own problems. Find someone for himself. If he expected Yasmine to marry out of a sense of duty, to someone of wealth and power, to expand the family's fortune, he must expect the same from himself. That night he called Meera to tell her when he was returning.

"Any word from Yasmine?" he asked her. He'd left messages for her and told her to call him.

"Nothing," she said. "Shall I send a taxi to fetch you at the airport?"

"No, I have a ride. What else has happened there?"

"That cat has been scratching the patio furniture," she said dourly.

"He's only a cat," he said. "We'll have it refinished. Has Mavis come by to see the cat?"

"Oh yes, every day. I watch her from the window."

He wanted to ask if Carolyn ever came with her mother. But of course she didn't. She had other things to do.

"If Yasmine calls, tell her I must speak to her. It's urgent. We don't have much time left now."

"Are you sure she'll come?" Meera asked.

What a question. Of course she would come. But deep down inside he was riddled with doubts. And thoughts that began with What if…

What if she refused to marry Jeffrey?

What if she never got on the plane and she stayed in Switzerland?

What if the whole thing fell apart?

No, it couldn't happen. It was too important. It meant too much. However stubborn she was, she wouldn't ruin their father's plans for the company. She knew as well as he did how important it was to make his dreams come true. To finish what he had started.

"Don't worry," he said. "Of course she'll come."

Chapter Eight

He was much too happy to see Carolyn for his own good. He felt light-headed and slightly dizzy. Of course that could be due to the long flight. Even in first class it was a long time to be cooped up in a plane. He'd thought about her nonstop, but he wasn't prepared for the real thing. She looked more beautiful than he remembered. Her auburn hair tumbled over her shoulders. Her face glowed. He intended to shake her hand, but when they met, he dropped his briefcase and swept her into his arms. Lord, how he'd missed her. Missed having someone to talk to.

She drove and they talked on the way to his house. He told her about the problems he'd faced and what he'd done to solve them. She didn't understand the technicalities, but she listened, sympathized and asked questions. She told him what progress she'd made on the wedding. The most important thing on her agenda was the selection of the dress. And after that the band, the rings, the photographer…the list seemed endless.

"You're well-organized. You have everything under control," he said watching her maneuver her small car out of the airport.

"Well, not quite everything," she said modestly.

"No, there is Yasmine," he said soberly. "You can't control her." Neither could he. Neither could anyone. He had to rely on his sister's sense of obligation and her family loyalty.

Carolyn turned to look at him, raising her eyebrows inquisitively. "Have you heard something?"

He shook his head. "That's the problem. I've heard nothing. She doesn't return my calls."

"You said she was busy with exams."

"That's what I said, but..." He didn't finish the sentence. It didn't have an ending. Or rather it had too many possible endings. None of them bore thinking about.

"I once tried to tell you my philosophy of weddings," she said.

"And I refused to listen, didn't I? You must have thought me boorish and arrogant. Go ahead. I'm listening now. Tell me." He fixed his eyes on her profile, the outline of her chin, the curve of her cheek, the curls that brushed her shoulder and wished he could take back his behavior at their initial meeting. Yes, he'd been anxious about the wedding, but he finally realized that was no excuse to interrupt her consultation with the other couple.

"Weddings are only a reflection of life. Of the bride and the groom's lives. They're funny and sad and happy. Like life. They're full of promise and hope and even an occasional disappointment. They are about human beings. You won't believe this but they are also about emotion. And love. Which is why they can't be perfect. Things go wrong no matter what. It's best to be prepared for that. It's Murphy's Law. Do you know Murphy's Law?'' she asked.

"Anything that can go wrong, does go wrong,'' he said.

"Exactly.''

"Nothing can go wrong at this wedding,'' he said, his jaw clenched. "There's too much at stake.''

"Believe me, things go wrong at the most perfectly planned weddings. If perfection is what you're after, you're bound to be disappointed. A wedding is a celebration of love whether you believe in it or not, with all of its ups and downs and imperfections.''

"If that's your philosophy, we're miles apart,'' he said. "I see a wedding as the merging of two families. As a presentation to the world of two people as a couple,'' he said. "That's my philosophy.''

"I can accept that,'' she said. "I was just trying to prepare you. Your sister's wedding is full of possibilities for everything to go wrong. She's not here for one thing.''

"She will be,'' he said.

"All right,'' she said.

"Drop me off at my office,'' he said abruptly.

"You're going to work now?'' she asked.

He rubbed his forehead. "I must.''

"I made an appointment at the bridal salon for ten o'clock tomorrow,'' she said.

"I'll be there,'' he said curtly. His mind was spinning. His mood was black. He hadn't slept last night, and he was suffering from jet lag. On top of that Carolyn thought things would go wrong at the wedding. Just the kind of observation he didn't need to hear right now. Her philosophy was diametrically opposed to his. He should have known and stuck to safer subjects. He got out of the car with his suitcase and briefcase and leaned down to thank her. She nodded but didn't speak. In a moment she was gone, her car had disappeared in the traffic. He stood on the curb staring blankly at the cars and buses without seeing them.

Carolyn felt as though she'd just said goodbye to a stranger. Certainly not the same man she'd picked up at the airport a short time ago. Not the same man who'd hugged her to him. Whose face was bronzed from the desert sun. Whose eyes seemed to light up when he saw her. Who made her feel like jumping for joy just to see him. Until she told him her philosophy. It wasn't that radical. It wasn't that strange. But he didn't like it. Didn't want to hear it. Because it wasn't his philosophy.

He was worried, she could tell. He was used to being in control of every situation, making things happen. Solving problems. But this wedding might be one problem he couldn't solve. Because of the human factor. She'd tried to tell him that. He didn't listen. He wouldn't listen the first night he came into her shop. And he still didn't. She'd almost fooled herself into believing he'd changed. He'd fooled her mother into thinking he was not a control freak, he was just a rich, charming, lovable man who happened to be a sheik. How she wished he was. But she knew better.

She went back to the shop determined to focus on one of her other weddings. She'd spent entirely too much time on Tarik, but it was no use thinking she could put him out of her mind. Especially with Lily around.

"So he's back," Lily said. "How did things go?"

"Things went fine where he was. He fixed the problem. It's the wedding problem he can't fix. Because there is no fix. I told him to expect the unexpected. Especially for this wedding."

Lily tossed the society section of the newspaper onto

Carolyn's desk. "It's official anyway. According to the newspaper. The bride's picture and everything."

Carolyn eagerly turned the pages. "Good. Yes, they got it all right."

"She's gorgeous," Lily said, leaning over Carolyn's shoulder. "Just like her brother."

"I just hope she's got a more flexible outlook on life," Carolyn said. "He described her as being stubborn, headstrong and spoiled."

"Uh-oh. I'm getting worried."

"Don't you get worried, too. It will all be over in two weeks. The happy couple will be off on their honeymoon and life will be back to normal. No more sheik. No more…"

"No more sheik? You mean you're not going to see him again?" Lily asked.

"No reason to," Carolyn said lightly. But inside there was a pain in the middle of her ribs. She'd been so wrong about him at times. Other times she'd been dead right. Right in her first opinion.

"I thought maybe you two…" Lily said.

"Oh, no. Didn't I tell you he was not my type?"

"Yes, but when I saw him in person he was so charming, so…so…"

"So debonair, so cosmopolitan, so distinguished…. Is that what you were going to say?" Carolyn asked.

"How did you guess?" Lily asked with a grin. "Here you are. The travel agent dropped off the tickets for you."

Carolyn reached for the manila envelope and stared at the tickets to Fiji and the connecting hop to the resort. She could see it as clearly as if she were there. The bamboo huts, the pristine white sand beaches and the aquamarine water. If the couple wasn't in love before they got to the small island off the coast, they'd have to be in love when they left. If not with each other, with the place. Unless they had their hearts set on Paris or Niagara Falls.

"That's where you'd go, wouldn't you?" Lily asked, with a nod at the envelope.

Carolyn nodded sheepishly. "I know it's not right for wedding planners to impose their own taste on their clients, but in this case I've never even met my client. Tarik told me to use my own judgment. So I picked my dream honeymoon spot. I've suggested it to various clients in the past, but no one ever went for it before. I hope it's not a mistake."

"Absolutely not. It's a wonderful idea. I can't imagine anyone not being happy there. I'm sure they'll thank you some day. So don't feel guilty about imposing your taste on them."

"I won't." She sighed. "I won't feel guilty, but I might feel a little envious."

"One of these days it will be your turn, Carolyn."

"Sure it will," she said glibly. "But it's time to stop fantasizing and get back to work. First I have a question for you. Where did you go on your honeymoon, Lily?" Carolyn asked.

"Camping at Lake Tahoe," Lily said with a dreamy smile. "It was wonderful. We hiked all day, made a campfire at night, then zipped our sleeping bags together. Oh, it was so romantic. Twenty years ago, but I'll never forget it."

"That's the way it should be. A honeymoon that sets the tone for your whole life. Did anything go wrong?"

"No, it was perfect except for the bear who broke into our rations and ate all our food on the second day out."

"See what I mean? Life is full of the unexpected. Exactly what I was trying to tell Tarik. He's determined that this wedding go off without a hitch. You and I know it's impossible.''

"We also know that love conquers all," Lily said. "It can withstand a disastrous wedding and a problematic honeymoon. So we do our job, then sit back and wish Tarik's sister and her husband every happiness. As for you, my dear partner, I'm certain you'll find the man of your dreams, and you'll be planning your own wedding and honeymoon one of these days.''

"Will I?" Carolyn asked wistfully.

Lily nodded emphatically and Carolyn forced herself to put the plane tickets in her top drawer and stop daydreaming. Maybe it was time to move to Alaska or get a different job after all. Because of all the weddings she'd planned, this was the most difficult. Not because the bride wasn't here, not because of the short notice. It was because this wedding brought out all her secret longings and wishes. By throwing herself so intensely into the preparations, it was almost as if it was her wedding she was planning. But it wasn't. Envy was a terrible thing and for the first time in her career, she envied the bride. Indulging in fantasy was almost as bad. Fantasizing about marrying a man who didn't believe in love and was out of her reach anyway, didn't help her find that sweet, gentle, caring man she'd always dreamed about.

She promised herself that after this wedding, she'd do something about her own life and her own future. A new job or a new location. Right now she had to concentrate on the wedding at hand.

Carolyn felt apprehensive about meeting Tarik at the bridal shop the next day. What if he was still in the same black mood as the day before? What if they couldn't agree on a dress? What if they picked a dress that didn't fit and that his sister hated? How was she going to pick out a dress that she loved and have it worn by someone else without feeling a sense of loss and failure, and worse, jealousy?

The answer was obvious. It was because she was a professional. She was not here to get emotionally involved with the dress or the gifts or the wedding itself. And especially not with the bride's brother. She was here to plan the wedding and then step back and watch from the sidelines like the director of a play. If the actors flubbed their lines, if the scenery got knocked down or someone forgot a prop, that was life.

She would do her best, but when the organ started playing the wedding march she would be somewhere behind a pillar—out of sight, and out of mind. That's the way it always was and always would be for a wedding consultant. Unless it was her wedding. Then and only then would she take center stage and play the lead in her own life story. Until then she was only the stage manager.

Up until now that had been enough for her. Now she was having doubts about the job and about her life. If Tarik hadn't walked into her shop that evening, would she still feel this way? No, she'd be deep in the plans for the ceremony with the penguin rock-giving exchange, keeping an emotional distance from the job and otherwise content with her life.

Carolyn was going through the rack of dresses at the bridal shop when Tarik came up behind her. She could feel his presence before he spoke, before she turned around. It couldn't have been anyone else because he was unique. Was it because he was a sheik or was it because he was Tarik? She didn't know. She only knew he smelled of expensive European soap and rich leather. She took a deep breath and turned around. He looked better today, the lines in his forehead had faded and his smile made her feel warm inside. Warm all over. So warm she fanned her face with her hand. She returned his smile and willed her heart to stop thumping with excitement.

"I'm sorry to be late," he said. He had manners like his clothes, impeccable and tailored just for him. Impossible to imagine him without them.

"That's all right." She flipped through a few dresses just to have something to do besides stare at him. How silly to be nervous around him. To find herself with a case of pre-wedding jitters. He was not her groom and she was not getting married. "I...uh...I'm not sure exactly what type of dress we're looking for. Are you?" she asked Tarik.

The clerk pulled out a dress inspired by Princess Diana's with puffed sleeves and a matching tiara. "This is very romantic," she said to Tarik.

He shrugged. "What do you think?" he asked Carolyn.

"Perhaps a little too..."

"Yes, I think so, too," he said, catching her meaning.

The clerk showed them another dress of ivory lace trimmed with pearls. "Classic," she said.

Another shrug. They were getting nowhere fast.

The next was a *peau de soie* column with narrow straps and a long veil. After that a tulle gown with an embroidered bodice. Tarik looked dazed.

"I'll try them all on," she told the clerk. "Maybe that will make a difference."

Tarik nodded. "I'm sure they'll look better on you than on the hanger," he said.

"Thank you, I think," Carolyn said.

The clerk smiled benevolently at him.

"Quite a romantic, your man," she murmured as she hung the dresses in the dressing room. Instead of going to the trouble of denying he was hers, Carolyn just nodded. It was all too complicated.

"It's clear he adores you," she added.

Carolyn almost choked. She must say that to all the customers. Because it wasn't clear to her at all. He respected her, which was quite a lot considering how he'd felt about her a short time ago. And sometimes she thought there was more than that. There was an attraction between them that both were fighting off. There were those kisses and the electricity in the air. Surely she wasn't the only one who felt it.

The first dress she modeled was an A-line satin with a drop-waist. The skirt billowed to the floor, the train trailing behind as Carolyn walked out into the showroom. Tarik was seated in a leather chair watching her. She walked slowly, feeling his eyes on her, on her bare shoulders, her hips and lingering on her breasts. It was nothing personal, she told herself. He was looking at the dress, not at her. There was no need to feel like she was spiking a fever of one hundred and five.

"What do you think?" she asked. Maybe he'd like the first one. It wouldn't be her first choice, but there was nothing wrong with it. Then another task could be crossed off her list. They could wrap up the dress and leave without further ado. She could go back to work and stop participating in this charade. So could he.

She turned around so he could see the train. She couldn't see him, but she felt his gaze traveling over her body. Goose bumps popped out on her arms although it was warm in the shop. Very warm. She turned to face him. He shook his head. "Isn't it a little too ruffled, too..."

"Frilly?"

"Yes."

She went back in the dressing room. "Something sim-pler," she said to the clerk.

"He has a mind of his own," the clerk said unzipping the dress from the back.

"Oh, yes," Carolyn agreed. That he did. The clerk took a charmeuse slip dress in the style of Carolyn Bessette Kennedy's wedding dress off the hanger and lifted it over her head.

"Ooooh," the clerk said. "Simple, yet elegant. That's your style. Here, let me adjust those straps."

Carolyn went out to show Tarik. From the look on his face and the hushed silence she thought this might be the one. He cocked his head to one side and contemplated the dress until she thought she might faint from exhaustion. Finally he shook his head.

"Let's see some more," he said.

She sighed and went back to the dressing room.

Tarik listened to the murmur of the voices in the dressing room. He crossed one leg over the other and settled into the chair. What a way to spend a morning. While papers piled up on his desk, while lawyers waited to see him, he was watching a fashion show. But what a show. He'd liked every dress Carolyn had tried on. But it wasn't the dresses he liked. It was her. But he decided to play it cool. Or the show would be over after the first dress. And he didn't want that to happen.

How could he ever choose? Carolyn looked sensational in everything she wore. Even running shorts. She was going to make a beautiful bride one day. He hated to think of her marrying, but she would. Even though she said she didn't meet any eligible men. One of these days she would. He hoped he wouldn't be around then because just the thought filled him with an envy for the unknown groom. Envy was a trait unbecoming of a sheik.

She was back in yet another dress, the creamy white satin décolletage blending with her creamy white skin. He took a deep breath and told himself to be objective. Focus on the task of choosing the dress. At the same time as long as he was closeted in the small shop he could give his mind a rest from the anxiety over the wedding and the merger. Even though he'd always denied he was prone to any kind of emotional problems or detours into fantasy, he had to admit he'd changed.

It must be the upcoming wedding that changed him because right now he was feeling just as susceptible to these weaknesses as the next person. Watching Carolyn try on wedding dresses made him feel like he was about to take a giant step off the deep end of a long pier. His heart banged against his ribs at the thought of jumping into unknown waters. Taking a chance. Hopefully, when the wedding was over he'd revert to his normal sane and sensible self. But right now, for example, it would be so easy to fantasize that this wedding was his. Carolyn was his bride, and he was going to claim her for his own in a classic, high-ceilinged cathedral. He'd kiss the bride the way he had during the run-through, only this time they'd live happily ever after.

If she were getting married she'd be wearing one of these magnificent dresses and her veil would cover her face as she came down the aisle toward him. At the last minute she'd lift the veil and he'd see her smile up at him. See her eyes glow and hear her promise to love, honor and… That was the problem. He couldn't promise to love her, and she

would never promise to obey him. That was crucial to his
and any sheik's happiness. His father had warned him over
and over. His father was right.

No matter how much he liked these dresses, and every
one looked beautiful on her, he decided to find some flaw
with each of them or the fashion show would be over. Carolyn would change back into her slacks and blazer and go
back to work. They'd both be jarred into reality. A place
he didn't want to return to. Not yet.

The clerk came out of the dressing room. He was glad
to see she didn't appear to be getting impatient. She
shouldn't for the money he intended to spend on this dress.

"The next dress is an embroidered mother-of-pearl
sleeveless top and a tulle gown with a ballerina skirt," she
said. "Your fiancée looks lovely in it."

"I'm sure she does," he said, not bothering to tell her
Carolyn wasn't his fiancée. Then he'd have to launch into
a discussion about his sister and try to explain why she
wasn't there, when he was beginning to wonder himself.
The clerk knew he knew nothing about tulle or mother-of-
pearl. But he knew one thing—Carolyn would look stunning in it.

"She's going to be a beautiful bride," the woman said.

Tarik frowned. Of course she would. That went without
saying. It was just what he feared. She'd be a beautiful
bride. Some day. But not his bride. She did look gorgeous
in the ballerina skirt, but he shook his head. He hoped they
weren't running out of dresses. He wanted to see more.
More dresses. More of Carolyn.

The next time she came out it was in a hand-beaded
chiffon gown. The clerk described it as sexy and a trifle
naughty. Tarik drew in a quick breath when he saw Carolyn

in it. It clung to her body, to her breasts and hips until it flared out halfway to the floor.

"How do you like it?" Tarik asked Carolyn, his eyes glued to the narrow straps, wondering how they managed to hold the gown up and what would happen if they didn't.

"I feel like a siren," she said with a little smile that could only be described as sexy and as naughty as the dress itself. "Would Yasmine like it?" she asked.

He didn't know. Yasmine was the furthest thing from his mind. He couldn't tear his eyes off of Carolyn. He wanted to say it was not a dress for a virgin. But he didn't trust his voice, so he merely shrugged. She went back in the dressing room. He didn't know if she was disappointed at his reaction or not. He only knew he wanted to hold the picture of her smile in his head. Even if it wasn't for him.

It was a long time before she came out again. So long, Tarik rested his head on the back of the chair and stretched his legs out. Strange how he wasn't impatient. Totally unlike him. He felt he'd left the old Tarik back in the office and a different man was devoting a morning to looking at wedding dresses. Who was he kidding? He was not there to look at dresses. He was there to look at Carolyn.

When she finally came out she was wearing a white-faille taffeta with an embroidered ruffle. Her hair was pinned up on top of her head with rich auburn tendrils trailing down her neck. While he watched she slowly pulled on a pair of above-the-elbow white gloves. It was such a natural gesture, but the way she did it sent a bolt of pure desire shooting through him. He shifted his position. Tried to tear his eyes away from her, but he couldn't. Their eyes met and held for an eternity. The clerk was rattling on about the well-known designer but Tarik wasn't listening.

He finally broke the spell, tore his gaze away and sat up

straight. He tuned out the clerk's voice so he could concentrate on the way the ruffle lined the top of the bodice,
gazing at the outline of Carolyn's breasts. Yes, this was the
dress for her. He could imagine her getting married in this
dress. In those gloves. She held her head high, her shoulders straight, as if she too could imagine it. He knew she
felt good in the dress. As good as she looked, which was
spectacular.

"We'll take it," he said.

"What?" Carolyn looked startled. As if she'd been in a
daze.

"You like it, don't you?" he asked.

"Yes, but…"

"Then we'll take it."

"You didn't ask how much it was," she said.

"It doesn't matter."

"What about your sister, will she like it?"

"Of course. Just as she'll like the silverware, the dishes,
the church, and the hotel reception. She's very easy to
please." He hoped God would forgive him for that white
lie. Yasmine was not easy to please. Unless she'd changed.
He could only hope.

"Just one question," the clerk said, turning to Tarik.
"How formally will you be dressed? Just so we have some
idea."

"Me? Not that it matters, but I'll wear the traditional
white headdress, which was my father's. In fact I have it
in the car to take it to the cleaner now."

"I've never seen one," the clerk said.

"I'll bring it in," he offered.

When he returned from the car and tried the formal attire
on, it made him feel different wearing the white cloth tied
with gold cord, older and more serious. Carolyn's eyes wid-

ened and she stared long and hard at him. He didn't know what she was thinking.

"Next is the ring," he said, when she'd changed back into her street clothes and he'd taken off his royal head-dress. He hadn't intended to go ring shopping, but he didn't want to go back to the office.

Her eyes widened in surprise.

"Didn't I tell you? We have to pick out the ring for the groom."

"I'm afraid I..."

"It shouldn't take that long," he said, steering her to his car with his hand on the small of her back. "Just a plain gold band is customary, right?"

She nodded and then he said they couldn't look at rings on an empty stomach. Though she protested, he insisted on driving through a drive-through at a fast-food restaurant, ordering a cheeseburger deluxe for both of them and eating it in the car on the way to the jewelers.

"I didn't ask," he said. "Was there somewhere else you'd rather go?"

"No, I just thought you'd be going straight back to work."

"I probably should," he said. "But my work is to see that this wedding comes off. If I'm not mistaken, that's your work, too. And we can't do our work if we're weak from hunger. Trying on dresses must be hard work. Which one did you like the best? Be honest."

"The one you bought. It was simple and elegant. I just hope your sister feels the same."

"She will. And if she doesn't, the wedding will be over before she realizes it."

"What will you do with the dress?"

"I don't know. Donate it to charity, perhaps," he said.

He drove and ate at the same time. She nibbled on a French fry. "Is this something else you've never had before?" she asked, looking amused at his obvious enjoyment as he reached into a bag for a soft drink.

"When I first came here to the university I ate many hamburgers until we got our apartment and our cook. I always enjoyed them immensely. But since then, it sounds funny, I know, but I haven't had time for your fast food. But I realized today it takes hardly any time at all which works out well for this afternoon. Most days I usually work right through lunch, or I have to host a business lunch at Jacks or some other restaurant where the waiters wear black ties and no one pays attention to the food because they're talking business.

"I appreciate your coming with me today," he continued. "One, because I hate to eat alone, and two, because it wouldn't hurt you to put on a few pounds. I noticed in the bridal shop that many of the gowns were a little large on you."

"Since I'm not getting married, it really doesn't matter," she said. "I don't think anyone has ever said I'm too thin, except maybe my mother."

"Next time I'll take you to a decent restaurant. I owe it to you."

"That's not necessary," she said.

"Not for you, but for me. I was brought up to reciprocate. And to pay my debts," he said.

"You may owe my mother, but you don't owe me," she said.

The argument ended when they reached the jewelry store. There was a security guard at the door and deep carpets inside with a few well-dressed, soft-spoken customers conversing with clerks.

Of course the clerk also thought they were the newly-weds-to-be. He brought out ring after ring until Tarik finally chose one.

"Excellent choice," the clerk enthused. "Why don't you put it on his finger?" he asked Carolyn. "Just as you'll do during the ceremony."

"No, I...all right," Carolyn said.

Tarik smiled at her to show he understood. Why bother to correct people when the truth was so complicated?

She grasped his hand and pushed the ring on. He looked into her eyes and the words ran through his mind as they must have run through hers.

With this ring I thee wed.

Tarik stared at the ring, at their two hands together, wondering if some day it would be his turn, his ring, his wedding, his bride....

Now that he had Tarik fitted, the clerk shifted his attention to Carolyn and did a double take when he noticed Carolyn wasn't wearing a ring at all. He almost rubbed his hands with glee.

"I have just the ring for you," he said, opening a glass case with a small key. He brought out a stunning diamond solitaire and slipped it on her finger before either one of them could stop him with the usual story about how it wasn't their wedding, they were just standing in for others. The story that never seemed to get past their lips.

Carolyn gasped as if the brilliance hurt her eyes.

"It's beautiful," Tarik said.

The clerk beamed and before Carolyn could take it off he'd found a platinum band studded with tiny diamonds to go with it. He handed it to Tarik and told him to put it on her.

"Now it's your turn," he said.

Tarik knew he should protest. He should set the man

straight immediately before he got any more ideas, but he
didn't. For some reason he just slipped the ring onto Carolyn's finger so that it nested there next to the solitaire.

"You see?" the clerk said. "It's perfect for her."

"Yes, it is," Tarik said, admiring her slim tapered fingers. She was meant to wear diamonds. He wished he could
buy them for her. Of course he could, but she probably
wouldn't accept them. She would barely accept a lunch
invitation, let alone precious jewelry. He turned back to the
clerk. "We're not in the market for..."

"A wedding ring lasts forever," the clerk said. "It's the
most important purchase you'll ever make."

"Yes, of course," Tarik said. Impulsively he took Carolyn's hand and held it up so he could admire the sparkle
of the diamonds. Her fingers were cool. Was it his imagination or did she smell like the roses she'd suggested for
the bridal bouquet? Was he getting too close to this wedding? Or just too close to the wedding consultant?

As if they'd rehearsed, both he and Carolyn took their
rings off at the same time, quickly as if they were burning
holes in their fingers, and laid them on the counter. Tarik
whipped out his credit card and bought the plain gold band
for his sister's groom. He told the clerk they weren't going
to buy the diamonds. The poor man looked as unhappy if
they'd told him they weren't getting married at all. At least
Tarik spared him the truth.

He put the ring into his pocket and drove her back to the
bridal shop.

"Dress. Ring," he said before she got out of the car.
"What is next?"

"Music. The band," she said. "I meant to tell you
there's a band you might like that is playing at a fund-
raiser on Saturday evening. We can drop by and see what

you think of them. I know they're available, but I don't know if you'll like them."

"Yes, a good idea. Only my cousins are arriving early for the wedding on Saturday to stay with me. They're twins, young swinging bachelors and I promised to take them out on the town. I'm afraid I'm out of touch with that lifestyle. I was hoping you could make some suggestions."

"You thought I would know where to take them?" she asked incredulously.

"You know everything," he said. "Or if you don't know, you know how to find out."

"I guess I can find out. I assume you mean the club scene. All I know is that the action is definitely in the Soma area, but I'll have to get the names of the places to go. I guess that means you'll be tied up on Saturday night."

"Both me and you. I assumed we could do both the fund-raiser and the clubs in one evening. The boys are presentable and will blend in with whatever crowd they run into, I assure you, so buy enough tickets for all of us and put it on my bill. The boys will certainly have an opinion on the band and the music, which might be helpful."

"Yes, sure, but…" She looked dubious. "When you say *we* do both the clubs and the party, who exactly do you mean?"

"You and I of course," he said. In two weeks, after the wedding, he'd never see her again. In the meantime he intended to see her as often as possible. Even if he had to invent excuses. Oh, the cousins were real, alright. But they hadn't asked to be taken to the clubs. They were club types, however, and he was sure they'd appreciate it.

He was infatuated with her. He admitted it. He loved the sound of her voice, the lilt of her smile, her lips, her eyes…everything about her. In two weeks she'd be out of his life forever. But until then…

Chapter Nine

Tarik had neglected to mention to Carolyn that his cousins were twins and full of the devil. They were almost as handsome as Tarik with their dark hair, and their sun-bronzed skin. Their youthful zest for life showed in their gleaming coal-black eyes.

"Where have you been keeping this beautiful lady?" Jared asked Tarik the minute he met Carolyn on Saturday evening.

Before Tarik had a chance to answer, his twin brother pressed his lips to Carolyn's hand and said he was enchanted to meet her.

Carolyn gulped in surprise then broke into a smile. She told Tarik later at the party at the San Francisco Yacht Club that they made her feel young again.

"You *are* young," he said, sitting next to her at a small candlelit table at the edge of the dance floor. He shot an appreciative glance in her direction. She was glad she'd worn a forest green dress and matching jacket that Lily said brought out the green in her eyes. Afterwards, if they did go to the clubs, she could take off the jacket and reveal thin straps and bare shoulders. Of course she could simply tell them where the clubs were and go home early. But in the festive atmosphere of a charity event that she hadn't planned and wasn't responsible for, she was able to relax and enjoy herself as she seldom did at these affairs. So much so she'd almost forgotten why they were there.

"What do you think of them?" Tarik asked leaning forward, his lips brushing her ear.

"What?" She shivered, his breath causing a shimmer to move up her spine. He looked so stunning tonight, in his dark suit and white shirt she couldn't keep her eyes off him. "Oh, they're adorable. Were you like them when you were young?"

"I meant the band," he said.

"So far so good. They seem to have a large repertoire."

"As for the boys, I was much more serious than they are. They're ladies' men, a different girl every day of the week. Maybe I should have been more like they are. Maybe I should have kicked up my heels a bit as they're doing. They'll have nothing to regret."

"Do you have something to regret?"

"Doesn't everyone?" he asked lightly. "Let's dance." He stood and extended his hand. "It's the only way to judge the band, isn't it, by dancing to their music?"

She had to agree, but she knew she should say no. She was having enough trouble resisting Tarik's charms without letting him put his arms around her and hold her close. Or she could wait for a fast dance in order to avoid any intimate physical contact. But she didn't. She let him lead her to the dance floor. She should have known he'd be a great dancer.

"Just part of a sheik's upbringing," he said when she complimented him. "Along with archery, falconry, etiquette, sailing, business. Oh, Carolyn…'' He pulled her close as his voice drifted off. This was no time to talk. This was time to move with the music. To give in and let her body mold itself to his, to feel the hard muscles of his chest, his thighs, to drink in the essence of the man. To let herself forget he could never love anyone.

She had to remind herself of this every other minute. Because otherwise she might be tempted to fall in love with him herself. She never thought she'd say it, but somewhere along the line, maybe it was in the church, or maybe at her mother's house when they were looking at photographs, or maybe it was in the jewelry store, she'd come to realize he wasn't what she'd first thought. She remembered telling her mother, or was it Lily, that no one would marry him.

Now she realized there'd be many women who would want to marry him. Why hadn't they? Because he wasn't looking. Like her, he didn't meet eligible, prospective spouses in his line of work. There weren't many women in the oil business. Or men in the bridal business.

If she had to write him a recommendation, she'd say the sheik was chivalrous in a way few other men were. Holding doors open, escorting her to her car, expressing concern for her safety. He was also exotic and fascinating as only a foreigner can be and yet familiar from having studied in this country. Kind and thoughtful—witness his treatment of her mother and her mother's cat. And most of all strong and virile. He was a take-charge man, no question about that. What woman wouldn't want such a man? What woman wouldn't fall in love with him?

A woman like her, of course, who was looking for a kind, gentle man who never gave orders, the complete opposite of her father. But other than her, if he let himself, he could have a line of women begging him to marry them. Just one drawback, she couldn't expect to be loved. Because Tarik didn't believe in love. So it would have to be someone content with respect, admiration and loyalty. Was that enough? Not for her.

She no longer believed he was a control freak like her father. Her mother was right about that. As head of the family, Tarik had many responsibilities both personal and financial. His father had left him in charge of a huge business and a family with many threads left untied. If he seemed demanding, it was because he had so many people depending on him. A whole country, in fact.

The music surrounded her, seeped into her pores. She could have danced all night with him. His arms around her. Swaying to the music, feeling his heartbeat through his tailored jacket. But the twins had other ideas. First it was Jared who tapped Tarik on the shoulder and cut in.

"Where have you been all my life?" he asked Carolyn, his dark eyes dancing with fun.

Carolyn shook her head in mock dismay. "Where did you learn such good English?" she asked.

"Boarding school in Boston," he said.

"Did they teach you to flirt, too?"

"They didn't need to. I was born to flirt. Why don't you dump that cousin of mine? We could have a great time together."

"I'm sure we could," she said agreeably, "but you've got the wrong idea. Your cousin and I are just, uh…doing business together. I thought he explained that."

"He didn't explain why he looks at you like he wants to eat you up. Why he's watching us dance with a fierce look on his face like he wants to bash my head in."

"Come on, Jared," she said. "You're exaggerating."

"Am I?" He twirled her around so she could face Tarik, and she had to admit he didn't look happy. He was staring at her with a frown on his face. "Why don't you get rid of him and fly away with me to my villa on the Riviera?"

"*Do* you have a villa on the Riviera?" she asked.

"The family does," he said with an offhand shrug. "You'll get to meet most of them this week. My parents and some more cousins. There will be a full house at Tarik's as we gather for the wedding. So what do you say? Dump Tarik and take up with me, his swinging cousin." He gave her a conspiratorial wink.

"I say I can't dump someone I don't have," she said sternly.

The song ended, some wild, fast music started and Rahman cut in on his brother. "We thought Tarik would never find anybody like you," he said as he threw himself into the dance, waving his arms and shaking his hips. "Wait till the rest of the family sees you," he said with a grin. "They'll be impressed, in fact they'll...how do you say...totally flip out. Good thing Uncle isn't here. Or the same thing would happen as happened last time."

"I don't know what you're talking about," she said breathlessly. "You and your brother have got it all wrong. I'm not involved with your cousin. I'm just..."

"Planning Yasmine's wedding, I know, but I saw you dancing together a few minutes ago. Were you planning her wedding then, or were you planning your own?"

Carolyn's face flamed. She blamed it on the dance. "Neither. I thought we explained. We're here to check out the band. What do you think of them by the way?" Carolyn asked, carefully changing the subject.

"Not bad," he said. "So you have no interest in my

cousin, is that what you're saying? Why not, what's wrong?''

''Nothing. I like him very much,'' she said.

''Then go for it,'' he said. ''From what I can see I'd say it's mutual. I'd say Tarik has got it bad. From the minute we got off the plane, he started talking about you. Carolyn said this and Carolyn did that. I said to my brother, 'we've got to see this lady.' Now that we've seen you, we're giving you a thumbs-up,'' he said, jerking his thumb in the air. ''Uh-oh, here he comes. I'd better watch out. He looks mad.''

Tarik did indeed look mad. He scowled at his cousin who was still holding his thumb in the air. ''What was that all about?'' he asked Carolyn with a glance over his shoulder at his departing cousin.

''Oh, you know, they're kicking up their heels, just as you said. Being boys on holiday, they're a little crazy.''

''They've been in and out of trouble all their lives. Nothing serious, but what one doesn't think of, the other does. I hope they haven't bothered you with their nonsense.''

''Not at all. They're very amusing.''

''Amusing,'' he repeated, but he didn't look amused. The music swelled and he didn't say anything. She sighed, so glad to be back in his arms. She wanted the music to go on forever. She settled into his arms as if she'd never left and never wanted to. When the dance was finally over, she was afraid she wouldn't be able to walk back to their table. Her knees were weak and her head felt like it was floating above her body.

''Okay?'' he murmured, his hands on her shoulders, his dark eyes locked onto her green eyes.

She nodded. ''We'd better go. I think we've heard enough to decide on the band. Did you like them?''

"I liked the dancing," he said. "I could stay here forever with you in my arms. I never want to let you go. But I must," he said dropping his arms to his sides. "You tempt me, Carolyn."

She swallowed hard, barely conscious that the band was taking a break and they were alone on the dance floor. "How? I don't mean to."

"By just being yourself. You make me want what I can't have."

She didn't say anything, but the words circled around in her brain. *But why? Why can't you have it?* Maybe some day she'd finally hear the whole story of Tarik's life. Of what had made him distrust his feelings and refuse to believe in love. Of what his father had done.

He shook his head slowly as if he'd heard her question. Maybe he'd seen the questions in her eyes. "It's a long story and not a very interesting one. I promised the boys we'd take them to the clubs. First I must speak to the band leader and give him a retainer fee."

She mentally checked off another item on the list. Another job done. The band was set. That's what they were here for and they'd accomplished it. No reason to feel let down because Tarik refused to confide in her. If that was why she'd come tonight, she was a fool. Because it wasn't going to happen. They drove the boys to the dance club and Tarik told them to take a taxi home.

"I hope you don't mind," he said to Carolyn after his cousins had piled out of the car headed for a very swinging club, judging by the noise coming from the open door. "I'm in no mood to be jostled by crowds of leather-jacketed, bleached-hair revelers where the music is so loud we can't talk."

"Are we going to talk?" she asked hopefully.

"I think I owe it to you," he said.

But he didn't talk at all until he reached her house. He parked on the street and looked up at the one window in her apartment with the light on.

"Would you like to come up?" she asked after a long silence.

He nodded and got out of the car so he could open the door for her.

Once inside the apartment, Carolyn made coffee and kicked off her shoes. She wished he'd do the same. How could anyone relax in dress shoes and a suit and tie? But Tarik wasn't just anyone. He looked as comfortable in dress clothes as he did in running shorts. At least he settled back in her overstuffed chair and put his feet on the leather ottoman.

Carolyn turned the lights low, curled up on the couch with her bare feet tucked under her and waited. She had so many questions on her mind, but she didn't dare ask, not until Tarik was ready to answer them. He looked so serious, sipping his coffee, she was afraid of what he was going to say. She thought she was prepared. But how can anyone prepare for someone else's story?

"I've spoken to you of my father," he began.

"Yes and I've seen his portrait. He looks like a remarkable man."

"He was. I grew up wanting to please him, to be like him in every way. He often took me with him to his office and to the oil fields. I always pictured myself following in his footsteps. That was always his plan. He instilled in me a sense of pride and responsibility, both to my family and to my country."

"Which you have," she said.

"In many ways, yes," he said. "With the merger I think

I can finally say he would be proud of me. In so many ways it's the most important thing I've ever done. Which is why your help has been so invaluable.''

"Any wedding consultant could have done what I've done,'' she said modestly, looking down into her coffee cup.

"I don't think so. I don't believe any other wedding consultant would have worked so hard, given up her weekends, evenings…no, I don't know what led me to your shop that evening, but I thank God for sending you to me.''

His voice was so rich and full of meaning Carolyn felt tears spring to her eyes. She was touched by his compliments because she knew he didn't hand them out indiscriminately. She tried to smile, but her lips trembled so much she gave up.

"Back to my father,'' he said. "I went to the university in this country as you know. It was the best place to study management. Naturally he was worried I would be corrupted by what he considered a certain moral laxity in this country, but I persuaded him by quoting his favorite proverb—The branch doesn't fall far from the tree.''

Carolyn nodded encouragingly and he continued.

"But in a way I did fall far from the tree. I fell in love. I know. I said I didn't believe in love, but I did then. She was a girl in my history class, bright and beautiful. When my father came to visit, he met her and seeing how infatuated I was with her, and how serious I was about her…which I was…he told me that marriages of the heart are not for men with vast wealth and power and responsibility. My parents' marriage was arranged by their families, and I must say it was very successful. She was a dutiful wife…I know you won't like that word dutiful…but that is the truth. More than that they had a mutual respect and affection for each other.''

''So you broke it off with your girlfriend?'' Carolyn asked. Did that explain why he had never fallen in love again or why he didn't believe in love?

''No, I didn't. I was young and headstrong and stubborn. And feeling very independent here in this country. I told my father it was my life and my decision. He didn't protest. But I'll never forget the look on his face. There was disappointment there and sadness. He nodded and said he hoped I knew what I was doing. Of course I didn't. I was young and full of myself. I was convinced this girl was the one for me. Even though looking back we didn't have much in common. She was not a serious student and I was. I knew I only had four years to soak in as much knowledge as I could, she looked at college as a way to experience as much fun as possible.''

''But you said this evening you should have kicked up your heels more,'' she reminded him.

''Perhaps I should. Knowing that so much responsibility was waiting for me in the future, that was my big chance, my only chance. But given my personality, perhaps I never could have, no matter how tempted I was.''

Carolyn wanted to throw her arms around him, to tell him it wasn't too late. To tell him there was still time to enjoy life, to live and love again. If only he would believe in love. She wanted to smooth his furrowed brow, to kiss away his regrets, to make him forget this girl...but she didn't. What made her think she could? She gripped the edge of the couch cushion and stayed where she was.

''What happened?'' she asked.

''She found someone else,'' he said briefly. ''She went to the Bahamas on spring break our senior year and met a boy there who she said was more fun than I was. I don't doubt it. I was writing my senior thesis on the disparity between oil prices and production in the developing countries, and I wasn't much fun at all. But I thought...we'd come to an agreement.... She said she loved me, she wore my ring..." He shrugged as if it didn't matter. But his expression was bleak. She knew that even if it didn't matter now, it mattered very much at the time. "In any case it all worked out for the best as you can see."

She couldn't see it at that moment. Not from the way he looked. So downcast. So lost.

"Is this the reason you don't believe in love?" she asked.

"That may have something to do with it," he said. "Would you?"

"I...I don't know."

"Give me some evidence that love exists," he said, meeting her gaze. He looked half hopeful that she could and half certain that she couldn't.

Her mind spun around in circles. How could she ever convince him when he didn't want to be convinced? "What about poetry? Could anyone who wasn't in love have written 'How do I love thee, let me count the ways...' or the classic love songs like 'Endless Love'?"

"Is that the best you can do?" he asked. "Come up with poetry and love songs? Those are cruel travesties, written to make money for the composers, to mislead innocent people into thinking they are in love."

"Don't you think you're being too pessimistic?" she asked.

"No. I think I'm being realistic."

"Then I'm sorry for you," she said sadly.

"And I'm sorry for you if you're waiting for someone to fall in love with you."

"No, I'm not," she hotly. "I'm waiting to fall in love with someone because I believe 'the love you make is equal to the love you take.'"

"Another song," he said with a half smile. "A nice one at that."

"But I haven't convinced you," she said.

"I want to tell you something," he said. "If I did fall in love, it would be with someone like you. Carolyn, you're everything I admire in a woman. Everything I want. Would you consider marrying someone who didn't love you?" His voice was low, there was no mistaking the meaning of the words.

"I...I don't know,' she stammered. But she did know. She knew after planning so many weddings that a marriage couldn't survive with only one partner in love.

"Never mind. I knew what you would say. But there are things I must tell you. Because I can't keep them to myself any longer," he said urgently. The words spilled out as if he couldn't hold them back. "You're beautiful, kind, thoughtful and sweet. That chemistry I talked about, those symptoms I made little of—the pulse speeding up, the heart pounding, all those reasons to head straight for the emergency room—I confess I'm a victim." He spread his palms out, face up, as if he was giving in to the symptoms, but Carolyn knew he wasn't. He felt them, but he dismissed them at the same time. "Tell me I'm not the only one who feels this way. Tell me you feel the same," he said, his eyes glowing like hot coals in the semi-darkened room.

"Yes of course I feel that way," she said, trying to sound matter-of-fact. "There's a certain attraction between us. Call it electricity if you want. At least we can agree it isn't love.'' The last thing she wanted to do was to confess her real feelings to Tarik. She crossed her fingers, keeping her hand out of sight in the depths of the couch. How could she say it wasn't love? If it wasn't, she didn't know what was. All she knew was that she wanted to make him happy. Help him achieve his goal, to fulfill his father's dream. And to achieve his own dreams. Was that love? If it wasn't, it would have to do until the real thing came along.

"Thank you for telling me this," she said. All of a sudden she was exhausted. Tired of listening, tired of talking, tired of working on a wedding that wasn't hers. Every muscle ached, every bone cried out for a respite. She was afraid she'd never even make it to her bedroom and would fall asleep on the couch.

"I'm sorry if I've bored you," he said, getting to his feet. He reached for her hands and pulled her up. She laced her hands behind his neck and clung to him.

"I'm not bored," she whispered. "I'm sorry. Sorry I can't convince you, sorry you had such a bad experience. Sorry…"

Sorry you can't fall in love with me. Sorry I can't tell you how I feel about you without sending you running for cover. But that's just the way it has to be.

He cut off her thoughts by kissing her. All her fatigue vanished in a moment. The energy flowed through her as if she'd had an injection of a powerful stimulant, instead of just a cup of coffee. She had. It was Tarik. It was his body pressed against hers. It was his voice in her ear whispering her name. His hands framed her face and she thought she'd drown in the depths of those black eyes. But instead of feeling lost, she felt like she'd been found. With one finger he traced the outline of her cheek, and she thought she'd faint. Gentleness and strength in that one movement.

The two qualities that were the sum of the man. The man she'd fallen in love with.

Slowly, carefully, he kissed her again. She kissed him back. She felt like she'd never get enough of him. That she could plumb the depths of his soul and never reach the bottom. She stumbled back against the couch, and he caught her just in time. She could smell the warmth of his skin, the coffee on his breath, the familiar smells of her own house surrounding her. He ran his hands down the sides of her arms. Every nerve ending went on alert. This is it, she thought. This is the man I've been saving myself for. The one man in the world I want more than anything, and he doesn't want me. Doesn't love me. Can't love me.

She tried to keep those thoughts in her mind, but his kisses blotted them out. Deeper and faster and more frantic they came. As if this was their last chance. Their only chance. Her whole body was on fire. No way to put it out. She didn't want to put it out. She wanted to burn until he caught fire, too, and they went up in flames together. She could have sworn that's what was happening.

They staggered forward and then backward like two drunken sailors. They were drunk on kisses, drunk on each other. Yet the strongest drink they'd had was coffee. She closed her eyes and gave in to the power of his kisses. She knew if he stopped she'd die. Right here in her own apartment.

When he finally let her go, she didn't die, but she felt like she'd lost a part of herself, like her heart or her soul or both. He ran his hand through his disheveled hair and moved backward toward the door of her apartment "If you change your mind..." he said. "You know where to find me."

She didn't answer. What else was there to say? All she

could do was to collapse on the couch and stare into space while his words echoed through the silent room.

Would you consider marrying someone who didn't love you?

Had she just rejected an offer of marriage from the richest, most generous, handsomest man she'd ever met? Had she just made the biggest mistake of her life? Or was that a hypothetical question he'd asked?

She went to bed but she couldn't sleep. Images flashed across her brain like a speeded-up, out-of-focus home movie. Tarik running with her in the park, Tarik in his study with her mother's cat, Tarik holding her in his arms on the dance floor and Tarik flooding her mind and her senses with his kisses. She told herself she'd waited this long, she could wait a little longer for a man to fall in love with her, to love her as much as she loved him.

She groaned and covered her head with a pillow. How long should she wait? It was possible he'd never come along and if he did, he wouldn't be Tarik. She sat up straight in bed. She'd do it. Tomorrow she'd tell him. She'd tell him she *would* consider marrying someone who didn't love her. She'd do more than consider it. She'd do it. Then if he was serious, if the question was real, he'd say she'd made him the happiest man in the world. And she'd be the happiest woman.

She'd finally be planning her own wedding. Because now she knew. Just as it was impossible to have the perfect wedding, it was impossible to find the perfect mate. But with Tarik she'd come as close as she possibly could. She smiled to herself. Those voices that kept saying what about love were finally silenced, and she fell into a deep sleep.

Chapter Ten

Carolyn woke early, pulled on sweatpants and a shirt and went out for a walk on the Marina Green before work. She tried to run, but her legs wouldn't cooperate. She'd made coffee when she woke up, but when she tried to pour herself a cup, her fingers shook too much so she stuffed her hands into her pockets and walked out the door. She needed fresh air to calm her nerves. The mist rose off the bay, a cool wind blew through the Golden Gate. She inhaled deeply but it didn't help. Her heart was pounding and her mind was going round and round in circles. What would she say? What would he say?

She put it off until afternoon. She had to give herself time to think. Besides she had work to do. Bills to pay. Last minute calls about the flowers, the church, the last fitting for the dress. That she would put off as long as possible. She jumped every time the phone rang. She thought he might call, but he didn't.

Instead, her mother called and wanted her to look at an

apartment with her after work. She was getting anxious to move and reclaim her cat.

"Have you talked to him today?" her mother asked when she picked her up in her car. No need to ask who "him" was. She knew.

Carolyn shook her head.

Her mother gave her a curious glance. "I noticed a lot of excitement going on at the house when I was there to see Max. People coming and going."

"His cousins are here for the wedding. Maybe some more relatives have arrived though the wedding is a little over a week away." That was why he hadn't called. He was busy with his relatives. Of course, that was it. She tried to pay attention to the new apartment, tried to make the appropriate responses as her mother asked her what she thought about the size of the closets, about the amount of the deposit, and the condition of the kitchen floor. But her mind was elsewhere and her mother knew it.

"Worried about the wedding?" she asked. "You shouldn't be. You've done many others, and they've all turned out fine."

"Yes, but this is special," Carolyn said.

"So is he," her mother said softly.

She smiled briefly and went home to pace around her apartment and stare out the window as if she expected a visitor. But no one came. It was her own fault. All she had to do was to call him or go see him. After all, she knew where to find him. But she couldn't or wouldn't. She was too scared. Scared he'd say yes, scared he'd say no.

After a sleepless night, she went to the office, shuffled papers on her desk and finally at ten o'clock, unable to stand the suspense another minute, she drove to his house. She didn't know what she'd say or how she'd say it, she just knew she had to go there. There were cars in the driveway, there was music coming from an upstairs window. She knocked on the front door but no one came. If they couldn't hear the sound of her fist, surely they'd hear the sound of her heart pounding. Finally Meera appeared, wearing a dark red sari and a deep frown, her hair pulled back from her face in a smooth knot, her face looking lined and tired.

"Yes? Oh, it's you," she said.

"Good morning," Carolyn said politely. She knew from experience that a wedding can frazzle even the steadiest nerves. Meera made no move to let her pass. "May I come in?"

Meera shrugged. "Might as well. Everyone else is here."

"Everyone?"

"Including Yasmine. They're in the library, but I wouldn't go there if I were you."

Carolyn teetered back and forth in the doorway, wracked with indecision. Yasmine, here, already? That was good, wasn't it? Maybe she should wait to hear from Tarik after all.

"Don't just stand there, come in," Meera said impatiently, turning on her heel, obviously expecting Carolyn to follow her. "Wait in there," she said pointing to the great room. Then she disappeared.

Carolyn stood on an antique Oriental rug in the middle of the room, listening to rock music coming from somewhere on the second story, admiring the way the light came through the skylight and illuminated the wall hangings. From the library came the murmur of voices, first soft, now louder. So loud she recognized Tarik's voice. But she couldn't make out the words.

She knew she shouldn't. She knew it was none of her

business, but her feet didn't get the message. She walked across the hall and stood next to the library door.

"You don't know what you're saying," Tarik said. His voice was tense, strained. "You're much too young to make a decision like that."

A young woman's voice answered with quiet conviction. "I'm nineteen years old and I know what I want." It was Yasmine. Carolyn raised her eyebrows and instinctively leaned against the door so she could hear better.

"If Father was here…" he said.

"But he isn't," she said. "You're here and I'm here and life goes on. This is my life we're talking about." Carolyn knew from the sound of Yasmine's voice she had much in common with her brother. Stubbornness and determination to begin with.

There was a long silence. Carolyn could picture Tarik pacing back and forth, his sister glaring at him from across the room.

"Your life, yes," he said. "But what you do with your life affects many other people."

"You, for example," she said angrily.

"Yes, me, of course. But the whole extended family is affected by what you do. Which is why, in some part, they are here to see you get married in less than two weeks."

"No."

Carolyn gasped. Maybe Tarik did, too. She couldn't tell.

"What?" he said, his voice ominously low.

"I said no. I came here to tell you I'm not going to marry someone I don't love to please my family. I don't even know the man."

"You'll get to know him."

"In one week?" she asked incredulously.

"You'll have the rest of your life. Mother and Father…"

"I know what they did. I know they never saw each other until their wedding day, and they lived happily ever after. But that was them, and this is me. I would never agree to anything like that, and I can't believe they would ask me. After all, you and I are of a different generation. We were raised differently. We were sent abroad to study. We've been exposed to other ways of life and to other people since we were small.

"The country has changed. The world has changed. I've changed. I don't expect a man to take care of me for the rest of my life. Not you and not my husband. I'm going to be independent. I want to work. Everyone has changed but you, Tarik. I'm sure even father would agree it's too late for arranged marriages."

"You're wrong. He wanted to arrange one for me."

"And…"

"And I was young and stubborn like you are. I refused," he said.

"Are you sorry you did?"

"That's beside the point," he said.

"It's exactly the point," she countered. "You wouldn't do what you're asking me to do."

"I've told you a dozen times that if the Bransons had a daughter I'd marry her in a minute and spare you whatever pain this seems to be causing you."

"And I've told you a dozen times I won't marry someone I don't love. To you marriage is only a contract. What would happen if you married, as you want me to do, for convenience. Then you met and fell in love with someone else. What would you do?"

"Nothing," he said. "Yes, marriage is a contract, but a sacred contract, to be kept at all costs."

"That's easy for you to say," she said, "because you

don't believe in love. Unless you've changed your mind.'' There was a long pause. "Have you?"

"Of course not," he said gruffly.

"I have no more to say to you, Tarik." Her voice dropped. She sounded more sad than angry. "You're my legal guardian, but you're also my brother. We're all that's left of the family. Just you and I. I thought I meant more to you than this. More than a chattel to be traded for favorable terms in a business merger. Since I'm underage you can stop me from marrying someone I love, but you can't force me to marry someone I don't love."

"You're tired, Yasmine. You've had a long trip. Go rest and we'll talk some more. Wait until you hear the plans for the wedding. You'll change your mind. We've found you a beautiful dress, and the church is magnificent."

"Return the dress and cancel the church. I never told you to go ahead with this. I told you I wouldn't be getting married and I'm not. Not to Jeffrey Branson," she said firmly.

"What about the condominium I bought you on Russian Hill to start your new life and your membership in the San Francisco Yacht Club. You're turning your back on all that?"

Carolyn pressed her forehead against the door. Her head was pounding. She felt like crying. It wasn't just a wedding he was planning for his sister, it was her whole life. She wanted to pound on the door, to call out, *let her live her own life*. This was much worse than Carolyn had imagined. Much worse than anything her father had ever done. How could she have been so misled into thinking he was just another rich, handsome, well-bred man with a strong will? When he was really a tyrant like no one she'd ever known.

"Just watch me," Yasmine shouted and the library door

flew open. Carolyn jumped out of the way just in the nick of time. If Carolyn had any doubts this young woman couldn't stand up for herself, she was instantly reassured. Dark eyes blazing, cheeks aflame, one-hundred-ten pounds of sheer willpower came storming out of the room with her brother close behind her. As Carolyn watched, Yasmine ran up the long stairway, her skirt swirling around her knees, while Tarik stood below glaring at her.

Carolyn knew she had to leave the house immediately. She knew if she left now he might not even know she was there at all. But she couldn't move. She felt as though she had turned to stone. Shock could do that to a person.

Slowly Tarik turned. He looked like the ceiling had collapsed on his head, when in reality it was much worse. For him it was his whole world that had collapsed. His eyes were hollow as if he hadn't slept all night. How long had this argument been going on? Despite everything he'd said, everything he'd done, Carolyn couldn't help the burst of sympathy that filled her heart. He was making a big mistake, of course he was. But it was plain he was suffering terribly. Before she felt too sorry for him, she reminded herself what she'd heard him say. How he'd planned to run his sister's whole life after choosing her husband.

"Carolyn," he said, rocking back on his heels. "I'm glad you're here. Don't go. I have to talk to you. About the wedding."

"I don't think there's going to be a wedding. Not after what I heard...."

"You heard?" he said, drawing his eyebrows together in a frown. "Then you know how stubborn she can be. But she'll get over it. Everything will go as planned." His mouth was set in a rigid straight line. The same mouth she'd kissed only last night. The mouth that had kissed her with passion and gentleness.

She shook her head. "I can't do the wedding. Not if she doesn't want to marry him."

"It doesn't matter what she wants," he said. "She *will* marry him."

Carolyn felt she was sinking into quicksand. Slowly but irrevocably down, down until she couldn't get out. Just as she used to feel when her father gave an order. She squared her shoulders and pulled herself up and out of the mire. "Not with my help," she said, proud of how steady and firm her voice was. "You'll have to find someone else."

He stepped across the floor and grasped her arm. "Someone else?" he asked. "We have a contract."

"The contract was made in good faith. You never told me Yasmine had refused to marry this man. But you've known all along, haven't you? This isn't a complete surprise, is it?"

"I thought she'd come to her senses," he said grimly. "I still believe she will."

"She has come to her senses. Don't you realize that? I apologize for listening to your conversation, but I'm not sorry I heard it. Your sister sounds like a remarkably mature young woman for nineteen. I know how much the merger means to you. But I would hope your sister means more. In any case, I can't be a part of a forced marriage. As she says, this is a different world, a different time. Women have rights, and she has the right to refuse to marry someone she doesn't love. Let me know if she changes her mind," she said. "Until then…"

She choked back a sob, turned and walked out the front door. She couldn't stand to look at his face another minute, couldn't stand to see the shock and disappointment. He'd wanted her support, he'd counted on her support, but she couldn't give it. If he'd wanted her love, he only had to ask. Because it was his and she couldn't take it back. But he didn't want it. All he wanted was for her to help him marry off his sister. That was all he'd ever wanted from her. She couldn't help him.

Tarik walked out the front door and watched Carolyn drive away. Every muscle in his body ached, every bone hurt as if he'd been beaten up by a chain-wielding gang of toughs. Instead he'd only been verbally assaulted by two strong women. He braced his arms against the door frame and exhaled loudly. What was wrong with everyone? Did no one but him see how important this wedding was? Was he the only one who cared about the family?

He heard voices coming from the inside of the house. To avoid anymore confrontations, he turned and circled the outside of the house and entered the garden. He sat on a wrought-iron bench, leaned his head back, and Carolyn's mother's cat ambled up to him and jumped into his lap.

"Thanks, boy," Tarik said, scratching the cat's ears. "I need a friend right now, and you're the only one who seems to understand me. What am I going to do, Max? If I cancel the wedding, the merger won't go through, and I'll let Father down. Not only Father but the whole family who think that money grows on trees." The cat purred softly as if he understood. "But Yasmine's right. I can't force her to marry if she refuses. I only hoped I could convince her." He shook his head sadly. "Women—with their romantic view of life. First Yasmine, then Carolyn, too, the one person I thought would understand. But she doesn't."

While he sat there, grateful for the cat's company, wishing he didn't have to return to the house, or see any one of his relatives, they came to see him. One by one, his cousins, Meera and his aunt all paid him a short visit to give his or her opinion. As if he didn't know what they were going to say.

Yasmine was right, and he was wrong.

He was being overbearing and difficult.

He should cancel the wedding immediately.

Love was the most important thing in the world. Love made the world go round, etc., etc., etc.

After getting his ears full of advice, he continued to sit there all afternoon thinking. What would his father do in this case? What had his father done when he'd refused to follow his advice about love and marriage? He'd simply walked away and let Tarik make his own mistake. Was that what he should do with Yasmine? What would happen if he canceled the wedding? What would his sister do? How could he save the business? When he finally got up from the bench, he realized the fog was rolling in off the ocean and the air was cool and damp. And he realized he had only one choice.

He went to his sister's room and knocked on her door. When she opened it he saw her face was pale and tear-stained. His heart contracted that he'd caused her so much pain. His little sister. The little girl who'd followed him around like a small puppy when she was small, begging him to play with her. She'd idolized him for most of their lives. She never would again, but perhaps they could be friends as peers and adults.

"I'm sorry," he told her. "I was wrong."

She flung her arms around him and hugged him tight. "Tarik, I'm sorry. Sorry I've been such a problem to you. Since you and I are all we have of our family, I wish I could make you happy. I wish I could love the man you want me to marry, but I don't. I love someone else.''

"What?''

"I know, I'm only nineteen and so is he. We're not going to rush into anything. I have three more years of school in Lausanne and so does he. By that time…I don't know. I'm serious about having a career, about being independent. The man I love understands this. I hope you will, too. Even more, I hope…I hope…that you'll find love, that you'll believe in its power.''

He couldn't speak. The words he wanted to say were clogged in his throat. Maybe he'd lost the merger, but he'd gotten his sister back. No matter what happened next he realized that was more important.

Dinner that night was noisy and joyous once he'd made the announcement they were all waiting to hear. Though they'd come for a wedding and now there was to be no wedding, his relatives decided to celebrate anyway. Meera outdid herself with a feast served in the baronial dining room, which he rarely used. Tarik looked around from his place at the head of the table, with a vast sense of relief. The look on his sister's face, the color that had returned to her cheeks was enough to assure him he'd done the right thing.

The only thing missing was someone to sit at the other end of the table. A woman who would share his triumphs and tragedies. Someone he respected and admired. Someone to bear his children, to fill this house with noise and laughter. Yasmine would return to Switzerland, the cousins to their high jinks and their school, his aunt to her country and Meera would once again run this house in her own fashion. As for him, he had work enough to fill every day and every evening. Life would go on as it had before he'd stepped into the wedding consultant's shop. Tomorrow he'd pay a visit to the Branson family's office and hope they'd understand. If they didn't…he'd work something out.

He excused himself from the table and called Carolyn. He only got her message machine. He left a brief message telling her to cancel the wedding and to call him. Of course he'd pick up any expenses incurred. Which would be considerable. At this point that was the least of his worries.

The strange thing was that the worst of his worries—the fear that the merger would fall through—failed to materialize. It was as if when he let go of his goal and concentrated on what really mattered—his sister's happiness and her right to plan her own life—everything fell into place. Call it fate, call it providence, call it luck.

First Jeffrey Branson had eloped with his girlfriend. Tarik stood in the Bransons' office when they made this announcement, unable to believe his ears. But it was true. It seemed that Jeffrey didn't want to marry Yasmine any more than she wanted to marry him. Tarik felt as if a huge burden had been taken off his shoulders. If he hadn't been so shocked and surprised, he might have laughed aloud. All his worries—for nothing. So much for interfering parents who all thought they were doing the best for their business and for their children.

The Bransons were very apologetic, so apologetic Tarik was spared the humiliation of telling them his sister had no intention of marrying their son. They had the papers on their desk ready to be signed, hopeful that the merger would go ahead as planned, which would benefit both companies equally. Tarik didn't have to think twice. He signed on the dotted line.

He walked back to his office from the Branson building.

The sun was shining brightly on the business district of San Francisco. The sidewalks were crowded with men in suits and ties and women in skirts and high heels. People were talking, laughing, arguing, holding hands, walking briskly or sauntering slowly, but he didn't see them. All he could see was Carolyn's face in front of him, her expression of disgust and disappointment when he emerged from the library after his argument with his sister. If only she knew. If only he could tell her. But she didn't return his calls. Didn't want to talk to him. He couldn't blame her.

When he arrived at his office, and he wasn't quite sure how he'd gotten there—he closed the door behind him, sank into his chair and looked up at the portrait of his father.

"Well, Father, we did it," he said softly. "Yes, *we*. I couldn't have done it without you. Every step of the way I felt your hand on my shoulder. The merger will go through. Yasmine and I have made up. We will carry on the family traditions, each in our own way. Some day I hope to leave the business to my son and if not..." He choked on the words and couldn't continue. How would he have a son if he didn't marry? The only person he wanted to marry wouldn't answer his calls and refused to see him. Just because he didn't love her.

Love. What was it? Did it really exist after all? How did it feel? Did it make you feel ecstatically happy? If so, he was not in love. He was miserable. He had everything he wanted and yet he felt terrible. He'd never felt lonely before and now he couldn't stand to be alone with only Meera in the big, empty house. He began to spend his days working until all hours of the morning, then usually falling asleep on the couch in his office and going home to change clothes as dawn broke over San Francisco Bay.

* * *

The wedding shop, I DO! I DO!, was busier than ever. Carolyn was glad she was overworked and overbooked. It took up the slack after Yasmine's wedding was canceled. She didn't want to think about it, but she couldn't get it out of her mind. Over and over she replayed the scene at his house in her mind like a discordant tune on a player piano. Each time she did the pain in her chest got worse. The realization that she'd been fooled by Tarik's charm and manners made her feel betrayed.

It wasn't his fault. He hadn't betrayed her on purpose. She had let herself believe what she wanted to believe until she couldn't believe it anymore. She didn't know if she should accept any credit or blame for the cancellation of the wedding. She only knew it never would have worked.

She hadn't returned Tarik's calls because she had nothing to say to him. She was hunched over her computer when the door opened and a breeze blew a stack of papers off her desk. She looked up to see a young woman with dark hair and black eyes and a confident manner that was partly due to her royal status and partly a family trait that Carolyn recognized immediately. It was Yasmine. Carolyn had only seen her once, under the most dire circumstances, and her appearance had changed drastically for the better, but Carolyn knew it was her.

"Are you Carolyn?" she asked.

"Yes and you are Yasmine."

She nodded, not at all surprised that Carolyn knew her. "May I sit down? I wanted to meet you before I returned to school. Tarik has told me so much about you, how helpful you were. The dress, the ring, even the honeymoon…"

"It was just a job," Carolyn said, hoping she sounded sincere. If it was just a job, then why did she feel so terrible that it was over? "And he compensated me handsomely, so there's no need to thank me. Did everything...is everything all right?"

"Everything is fine," Yasmine said with a smile. "Tarik and I have come to a new understanding. I understand how important the merger was and he..."

"But didn't it get canceled?" Carolyn asked. She'd been haunted by the specter of a failed business deal that she was partly responsible for.

"No," Yasmine said, beaming at Carolyn. "It didn't. It's a long story but it went through just as planned without the wedding. It turned out Jeffrey Branson didn't want to marry me anymore than I wanted to marry him. But that's not why Tarik canceled the wedding. He said he couldn't do it, couldn't force me to marry someone I didn't love. Love. I can't believe it, but I think he's coming around."

"Around?" Carolyn murmured.

"To believe in love. The first step to falling in love. If I didn't know him better, I'd say he's in love with you. Every time he talks about you, he gets this look on his face."

A flush crept up Carolyn's face. She tried to say something, to protest that he couldn't possibly be in love with her. She took a deep breath, licked her lips but her mouth was too dry to speak. All she could do was to look down at her desk.

"I came today to say hello and goodbye," Yasmine said. "I feel like I know you already. I also came to see if you feel anything for my brother. He was hurt badly once, and I don't want to see him hurt again."

"I would never do that," Carolyn said.

"Good," Yasmine said. She stood and kissed Carolyn on the cheek and left the office.

Carolyn sat at her desk staring out the window without seeing anything or anyone on the street. What an amazing girl. What an amazing family. What an amazing man. But Yasmine was wrong about Tarik. She wanted him to fall in love so she imagined it. Carolyn knew better.

But she had to see him. One more time. She'd been rude not to return his calls.

She went to his house the next day. Meera showed no surprise on her taciturn face when she opened the door. Just as she'd done the first time Carolyn had gone there, she showed her in and told her Tarik was in the pool.

Carolyn walked slowly to the glass-enclosed pool where Tarik was doing laps, faster and more energetically than before. Water splashed over the tiles as his muscular arms moved like windmills. She didn't know how long she'd be able to stand there and watch him. Didn't know if she should cough loudly to announce her presence or call his name. Or simply leave and forget the whole thing. She didn't know what she'd say when she got the chance anyway.

Just when she thought she'd give up and go, he pulled himself up and out by bracing his hands on the edge of the pool, his muscles bunching as he emerged from the water. He stood there for a long moment staring at her as if she was an apparition. Her heart banged against her ribs. The memory of that first day came flooding back to her. So much had happened in such a short time. Had she fallen in love with him that first day? She might have fallen in love with his looks, but it had taken longer to fall in love with the whole person.

"Carolyn," he said at last, his voice hoarse and rough. "You came." He stood there in his swimming suit while the water dripped off his broad shoulders.

"Yes, I came to see…I came to say…" What had she come to say? Had she come to ask if he believed in love?

"It doesn't matter. What matters is that you're here. You haven't forgotten me. You don't despise me though you have every reason to. I've been thinking about you, hoping…praying…you'd forgive me for being such a lout, a clod, a boor. I was so wrong, trying to control someone else's life. I thought I was doing what was best for Yasmine, but I was only thinking of business. I thought I knew what was best for her, what was best for myself and for everyone else, but I didn't."

"Then you've changed your mind. At least Yasmine said…"

"Ah, she told me she'd gone to see you. Yes, yes, I had to change my mind when I was confronted with the truth. Love does exist. It's real. And it's painful. Perhaps that's why I didn't want to accept it. But how else can I explain how I feel about you? How lost I've been without you." His eyes were brimming with emotion, with feelings she'd never seen there. Her heart fluttered in her breast. Could it be…could he really mean what he said?

"You…you've been lost without me?" she stammered, unable to believe his words. Was this the proud sheik she'd heard disclaim the existence of love only weeks ago?

"I thought I'd never see you again. I wouldn't blame you if you refused to speak to me ever again. I was afraid I'd never get the chance to tell you how sorry I am. Can you forgive me? Can you let me court you as a man courts the woman he loves? Maybe some day you'll learn to love me, because I've fallen in love, so deeply in love with you."

Carolyn felt the tears spring to her eyes. At the same time she wanted to laugh. She threw herself into his arms.

He pulled her tightly against his chest and she let the water seep through her blouse just as the happiness seeped into her body. Tarik, the man who didn't believe in love, had fallen in love with her.

"Is it true?" she asked, her voice filled with wonder.

"I only want the chance to convince you," he said and kissed her.

It didn't take long to convince her. Two weeks later after a whirlwind courtship of dinners, lunches, picnics, sailboat rides on the bay, Carolyn was planning her own wedding to the most wonderful man in the world. The richest, handsomest, most thoughtful and most of all, the most loving.

Epilogue

SAN FRANCISCO CHRONICLE

Sunday July 31

The Most Spectacular, Romantic Wedding of the Year

Wedding Planner Plans Own Wedding

Well-known wedding planner Carolyn Evans, who advises clients to allow at least six months to plan their weddings, had only one week to plan her own wedding to Sheik Tarik Oman, chairman and CEO of United Oil Company, in a ceremony at Grace Cathedral. The cathedral, usually booked for years ahead, had an opening due to a last-minute cancelation. That, along with the fortunate and coincidental visit of out-of-town relatives, prompted the bride to disregard her own advice and get married on the spur of the moment.

Ms. Evans wore a white faille taffeta gown with an embroidered ruffle and matching long white gloves. The groom was in the traditional wedding garb of his country. The bride's bouquet was hydrangeas and amaryllis and roses. Stephanotis blossoms tied to the end of each pew filled the church with their fragrance.

The bride's mother, who gave her away, wore a pink satin suit and hat. Out-of-town guests included the groom's sister, the groom's cousins, and aunts and uncles from the Arabian Gulf States. Following the wedding, the newlyweds will be honeymooning on a tropical island in the South Pacific.

After planning so many weddings for others and curing so many cases of prewedding jitters, how did Ms. Evans feel about her own wedding? We caught up with the glowing bride at the reception, which was held in the bucolic garden of the groom's home in the exclusive Sherwood Forest section of the city.

"It was completely different being the bride," she confessed. "Completely and totally wonderful, that is, after I stepped back from being the wedding planner and became the bride. For one day of my life, I was the star of the show, the princess with the glass slipper. Of course my husband makes me feel like a princess every day," she said with a blush.

"The thing to remember is that weddings are about life. About human beings. And emotion. I wanted six months to plan this wedding, to make it perfect, but I took my own advice and remembered that weddings are not about perfection. They're about life which is often imperfect."

"And love," her husband added, pressing his lips

to her hand with the stunning diamond solitaire and the matching wedding ring. "Don't forget about love."

* * * * *